THE NOWHERE GIRLS

By Carmel Harrington

The Nowhere Girls
The Stolen Child
The Lighthouse Secret
The Girl from Donegal
A Mother's Heart
The Moon Over Kilmore Quay
My Pear-Shaped Life
A Thousand Roads Home
Cold Feet: The Lost Years
The Woman at 72 Derry Lane
The Things I Should Have Told You
Every Time a Bell Rings
The Life You Left
Beyond Grace's Rainbow

Carmel Harrington

THE NOWHERE GIRLS

REVIEW

Copyright © 2026 Carmel Harrington

The right of Carmel Harrington to be identified as the Author of the Work has been asserted by her in accordance with the Copyright, Designs and Patents Act 1988.

First published in 2026 by Headline Review
An imprint of Headline Publishing Group Limited

1

Apart from any use permitted under UK copyright law, this publication may only be reproduced, stored, or transmitted, in any form, or by any means, with prior permission in writing of the publishers or, in the case of reprographic production, in accordance with the terms of licences issued by the Copyright Licensing Agency.

All characters in this publication are fictitious and any resemblance to real persons, living or dead, is purely coincidental.

Cataloguing in Publication Data is available from the British Library

Hardback ISBN 978 1 0354 3568 5
Trade Paperback ISBN 978 1 0354 2142 8

Typeset in 12/15pt Sabon LT Std by Six Red Marbles UK, Thetford, Norfolk

Printed and bound in Great Britain by Clays Ltd, Elcograf S.p.A.

Headline's policy is to use papers that are natural, renewable and recyclable products and made from wood grown in well-managed forests and other controlled sources. The logging and manufacturing processes are expected to conform to the environmental regulations of the country of origin.

HEADLINE PUBLISHING GROUP LIMITED
An Hachette UK Company
Carmelite House
50 Victoria Embankment
London EC4Y 0DZ

The authorised representative in the EEA is Hachette Ireland,
8 Castlecourt Centre, Dublin 15, D15 XTP3, Ireland (email: info@hbgi.ie)

www.headline.co.uk
www.hachette.co.uk

For my daughter Amelia Rose,
always my 'somewhere' girl.

Prologue

1 December 1995

The stationmaster took a moment to readjust his tie before stepping back onto the bustling platform. He was late returning from his lunch break for the first time in his forty-year career at Pearse railway station. However, today was a special occasion. President Bill Clinton and his wife, Hillary, had addressed eighty thousand people at College Green. The stationmaster hadn't planned to attend the event, but as the commuters arrived early in the morning, waving Irish and American flags, he became swept up in their excitement.

It had proved to be one of the best decisions of his life. Thanks to his last-minute dash to join the well-wishers at College Green, he had shaken the President's hand.

Humming 'The Star-Spangled Banner', the stationmaster placed his arms behind his back and commenced a regular patrol up and down the platform, his eyes darting from side to side to ensure all was well. His forehead creased when he noticed something amiss.

Two little girls sat holding hands on a bench near the public toilets, a battered brown suitcase at their feet.

Their matching lilac floral smocked dresses with starched white collars, reminiscent of a bygone era, caught his eye. You didn't often see children wearing dresses like these any more. The smaller of the two was sucking her thumb. Her hair was so blonde it was almost white. The poor mite seemed no older than a toddler. The elder girl, with dark brown hair, regarded him warily. Her eyes glistened with unshed tears as she draped a protective arm around her little companion. He observed their long braids, tied with lilac ribbons. These girls were well cared for, he decided. So why were they on their own?

He stepped closer and cleared his throat. 'Hello.' He gestured towards his uniform and added, 'I'm the stationmaster here. Where are your mammy and daddy?'

They watched him silently, their eyes wide with distrust. The younger of the two buried her face in the elder girl's chest.

He maintained a gentle voice and crouched low. 'It's going to be all right. Don't worry. I'm here to help.'

The younger child began to cry and burrowed deeper into the embrace of the elder girl, who bravely responded, 'Our mother told us to stay here. So we have.' Her jaw tightened as she glared defiantly at the stationmaster, prepared to stand her ground should he insist that they move.

He nodded approvingly. 'You're right to follow your mammy's instructions. How old are you?'

'I'm four, and my sister is just three,' the dark-haired girl replied, her eyes darting around the platform as she searched for her mother.

So, they were sisters, the stationmaster thought, despite their different colouring. It was clear he needed to gain the trust of the elder girl. 'I bet you're a brilliant big sister, looking after the little one. I want to help you find your mammy. How about I make an announcement and ask her to come to my office? We'll have you back with her in no time.'

The girl didn't respond, shrinking back from the question. So he set that aside for a moment and asked instead, 'Can you tell me what your mammy is called?'

She examined him from head to toe, weighing up whether to trust him. Finally, with a sigh, she replied, 'She's called Star.'

'That's a lovely name. And what's her surname?'

The girl shrugged, biting her lip.

'That's all right. Do you know where you live?'

'We live in the woods. Mammy says it's in the middle of nowhere.'

As she spoke, the strangest sensation washed over the stationmaster. He felt a shiver of unease run down his spine and shuddered inexplicably.

Whatever was happening with these girls, his gut instinct warned him that they were in a whole world of trouble.

PART ONE

As long as one keeps searching, the answers come.

Joan Baez

1

Vega waited until she heard Luka's breathing slow. His body quietened as he drifted into a deep sleep. The weight of his arm resting across her chest felt comforting rather than unpleasant. She lazily traced a finger over the tattoo adorning his forearm. A wolf gazed at her against a backdrop of mountains, forest and moon, all etched in black ink. When she had asked him about it, he'd explained that his father hailed from Poland while his mother was Irish. His full name was Lukasz Wilczek, the surname meaning 'little wolf' in Polish. He'd told her that adjusting his name slightly during his first year at primary school had made his life easier. However, while he was now known as Luka, the tattoo reminded him of his true identity and his roots, of which he was proud.

Vega's thoughts drifted back to her own childhood, recalling a day when a social worker suggested that she change her unusual name to something a bit more 'normal'. She had immediately dismissed the idea. She appreciated the fact that Luka, like her, held onto his past, refusing to let circumstances force him to forget.

She looked away from the wolf tattoo, feeling a shiver of unease as its eyes followed her. It felt as though it was judging her for what she was about to do. Shaking off her guilt, she gently moved Luka's arm and placed it on the bed. He stirred, murmuring in his sleep.

'Luka?' she whispered, stiffening as she waited for him to respond.

But there was only silence as he relaxed back into his dreams once more.

Vega slid out of bed, her naked body shivering in the cold night air. Spotting one of Luka's T-shirts draped over a chair, she grabbed it and slipped it over her head as she left the bedroom. She walked gingerly along the dark hallway until she reached the open-plan living area of Luka's flat on Monck Street in Wexford, then switched on the light and made her way to the kitchenette to pour a glass of water.

She gulped half the glass in one thirsty motion, sensing a tightening in her temples. They had shared a bottle of wine earlier with dinner, and its effects were now taking their toll. As she surveyed the living area, she smiled as she spotted her dress and Luka's jeans in a tangled embrace on the hardwood floor. Somehow they consistently ended up there. Their mutual attraction was as strong today as it had been the first time they met.

Luka's laptop lay on the wooden coffee table. She flicked it open, frowning as the screen prompted her for a password. She glanced behind her, towards the dark hallway, and sighed. She was on the verge of crossing a line – something she had done before to secure a story. But never with someone she... She frowned as she paused to determine what label to assign to their relationship.

She and Luka had been seeing each other regularly since New Year's Eve, which had also been his thirty-third birthday – he was a year younger than her. They had both been vying for the barman's attention at Wexford's Crown Bar. Vega won. On a whim, she bought a consolatory drink for Luka, who pretended to protest. An hour of outrageous flirtatious banter ensued, and as the countdown to midnight was announced, he leaned in to kiss her.

Over the past few months, he had made it clear that he was keen to elevate their relationship from casual to official. However, Vega had been equally clear with him that she had no desire to be anyone's girlfriend. While her university friends dreamed of future proposals from their boyfriends, she envisioned a life free from complicated entanglements.

A peal of laughter floated into the room from the street below. It was late, and the pubs were closing, with revellers making their way happily home. She glanced towards the hallway once more, concerned that the sounds might disturb Luka. However, all remained quiet in the apartment.

She turned her attention back to the laptop and typed *Luka Wilczek* into the small box. Incorrect. She wasn't particularly surprised; Luka was not that obvious. Nonetheless, he did possess a sense of humour, which made her recall an article she had once written for an online newspaper outlining the most common passwords used globally. He might just find it funny to do exactly what all the experts said you mustn't. Considering it worth a shot, she entered the word *Password*, followed by *1234567890*, and then *Admin123*. Each entry was incorrect.

She drummed her fingers along the arm of the sofa as she surveyed the living room for a clue. Her eyes landed on a book lying upside-down on a chair – *Klopp: The Liverpool FC Celebration*. Luka was a diehard LFC fan. She typed in *Liverpool FC* and nearly whooped with joy when she gained access to the laptop.

'What are you doing?' Luka asked from behind her, causing Vega to jump in her seat. She closed the lid of the laptop and turned to face him.

'What am I doing?' She paused, scrambling for a legitimate answer. 'I couldn't sleep, so I thought I'd do some mindless scrolling.'

Luka frowned, and then nodded towards her mobile, which lay on the coffee table where she had left it earlier. 'Isn't that what phones are for?'

'I'm almost out of charge,' she said, smiling as she stood up and walked towards him. She moved into his embrace, but his arms were stiff around her.

'That's a work computer, Vega. There are confidential items on it.' He extricated himself, retrieved the laptop and slid it into its case. The sound of the zipper closing sliced through the tension in the air.

'I'm sorry. I didn't think.' A flush stained Vega's face, and she was certain her blatant lie was obvious to him. She switched tactics and jokingly added, 'Who knew social workers had so many secrets?'

Luka's expression relaxed, and he grinned as he spoke in his best spy voice. 'If I revealed my secrets, I'd have to kill you.'

Vega moved closer to him and effortlessly slipped off the T-shirt in one smooth motion, saying seductively, 'Oh, but I have ways of making you talk . . .'

He scooped her up in his arms and carried her back towards the bedroom. As they left the living room, she cast one last glance at the laptop.

It could wait, because she was one step further than she had been.

She knew Luka's password now.

2

Vega walked into the plush entrance lobby of HLD Media, located on Haddington Road in Dublin. Five years ago, she had joined their team as a journalist for the weekly national newspaper *Ireland Today*. She had a couple of regular features each week: a quick-fire round of questions with Irish celebrities and well-known personalities published in every Friday edition, and a weekly in-depth interview with a person of interest, where she gave her take on a current cultural issue. Earlier today, she'd had a two-hour interview with Padraig Nolan, a clean-cut children's TV presenter whose affair with a colleague had been exposed, ruining not only his marriage but also his career. She itched to write that piece, because Padraig had opened a vein in the interview, sharing a vulnerability that Vega knew would make great copy.

Overall, she did not regret her decision to join HLD Media. The regular salary compensated for the loss of the freedom that her freelance work had afforded her up to that point. And she had saved diligently, so that three years ago she'd been able to purchase her first home – a small cottage in the Ballagh, a rural village between Wexford and Enniscorthy.

Having her own home was a significant milestone for Vega. It provided her with an anchor and a sense of belonging. She had felt outside of life for as long as she could remember. However, when she kicked off her trainers and closed the front door of her cottage, she experienced the peace that often eluded her.

She hadn't invited Luka to her home yet, and she wasn't sure if she ever would. He'd hinted multiple times about coming to visit her, and there had been occasions when she wished he were there with her. Like last week, when there had been a full moon that was so large and round it seemed she could reach up and pluck it from the sky like a ripe apple. The dark sky was dotted with stars, shining brighter in her rural haven than they ever had when she lived in the bustling city. She'd known that Luka was alone in his small apartment and regretted that he couldn't experience the majesty of the sky with her. More than that, she realised it wasn't just him missing out on the starry sky that irked her; she missed *him*.

At moments like that, she wished she didn't have so many rules for her relationships.

She frowned as she recalled him kissing her farewell the previous morning.

'Have breakfast with me,' he had urged.

'Can't. Deadline looming! I have a meeting with my editor in Dublin tomorrow, and Kieran wants an update on the piece I'm writing. I need to get to my desk.'

This wasn't a lie, but she could have lingered longer. Years ago, she'd established a firm rule against sharing breakfast with any of her romantic flings. There was something excessively intimate about that first meal of the day, with echoes of the previous night still resonating. It could weaken your resolve, and before you knew it, you'd gone from casual to all-in.

Tomás, the HLD Media security guard, called from behind his desk, 'Morning, Vega,' bringing her back from her reverie. 'The sun is shining, thank God.'

'It surely is, Tomás. And aren't we all pleased to see it?' she replied with a bright smile. Tomás spoke exclusively about the weather whenever she arrived at the office, but there was something comforting about that. You always knew where you stood with him.

Balancing a cardboard tray holding two takeaway coffees, she held her work ID up to the security barrier until the red laser detected the barcode, then made her way to the eighth floor in the lift.

The open-plan office buzzed with activity today. Vega never knew what to expect, as, like her, most of the staff worked from home these days and only came into the office for meetings. But at least a dozen of her colleagues were seated at desks, some on their phones while others bent low over their laptops. She called out a greeting to them and made her way to the editor's office.

Kieran Spain's door was closed. She tapped on it to signal her arrival, then pushed it open. Noticing he was on the phone, she mouthed, 'Shall I wait outside?' Kieran waved her in, and she sat opposite him as he finished his call.

She noticed that he looked tired, with dark circles under his eyes. His beard, which was typically neatly trimmed, appeared unruly and somewhat wild. Vega wasn't entirely sure how old her boss was; she'd estimate him to be in his late fifties. But it seemed he had aged a decade since their last meeting. She tutted softly as he stirred two sugars into his coffee. He disregarded her reproach. His doctor's warnings regarding diet and exercise were still being brushed aside.

Vega had never had a father figure, and she was self-aware enough to recognise that Kieran had taken on that role for her over the past couple of years. From the moment he'd interviewed her to join the staff, she had been drawn to his no-nonsense approach to life. He spoke plainly, a trait that she valued. They were close, but their friendship remained defined by their roles as colleagues. She could only hope that his wife and teenage children nagged him about his lifestyle at home and had better luck keeping him on track.

He took a deep gulp of his coffee. 'Thanks. I needed this.'

'All okay?'

'Just had a mouthful from Senan Delaney. Rising paper and printing costs are killing our industry, blah, blah, blah. None of which I can control. But Delaney believes I'm somehow responsible for the global paper shortage, making life impossible for the publishing industry!' He muttered an expletive under his breath as his face flushed with annoyance.

'But you've made significant changes over the past few years, transitioning *Ireland Today* to a digital platform as well. Surely he recognises that?'

'According to Delaney, it's a rapidly evolving era. I'm not sure. Perhaps he's right, and I'm too old for this game now.'

Vega's jaw tightened as she leaned forward, outraged on Kieran's behalf. 'What on earth does Senan Delaney know? I mean, you're sixty at the most, right? That's not old. Not these days.'

Kieran rolled his eyes and groaned dramatically, 'Ouch, that hurt. I'm fifty-five.'

'See, you've got years ahead of you. Experience trumps age, regardless of what Delaney says.'

Kieran made a face. 'From the whispers I've been hearing, the Delaneys are having a bad week, so he's likely just taking out his mood on me.' When Vega raised an eyebrow in question, he added, 'Something and nothing, just gossip. Ignore me.'

Vega knew better than to push her boss, so let it go. 'This place would collapse without you, Kieran. And if you went, I'd leave too. The only reason I stick around is because you make it tolerable.'

Kieran smiled appreciatively. 'Thanks, Vega. That means a great deal. And don't worry, there'll be no Jerry Maguire antics from me yet.'

'That's fortunate, because I don't own a fishbowl,' Vega replied, joining in good-naturedly. Kieran loved to reference iconic moments from his favourite films. Vega tried to play along, and she recognised this one, as she particularly enjoyed a good romcom.

She handed him her finished feature, and they shared their coffee in comfortable silence as Kieran read. Vega's body stiffened as she awaited his verdict. If he didn't like it, he would tell her, regardless of how well they got on. She had worked hard on this piece, about a newborn baby girl found at a fire station in Wicklow Town the previous month. The Gardaí had launched a nationwide appeal for her mother to come forward, and less than forty-eight hours later, a twenty-five-year-old woman named Annette had contacted them and admitted the baby was hers. Along with every national broadsheet, *Ireland Today* had sought an exclusive interview with the young mother, and once they succeeded, Vega was given the story.

While the media had been fair in their coverage, Annette had been put on trial on social media and found guilty on all counts. This did not sit well with Vega, who was determined to bring some nuance and balance to the discussion surrounding a parent abandoning their child. She had spent days talking to the young single mother, who had been reunited with her baby and was now under the care and supervision of a social worker. Annette had been out of work and homeless for several months, lacking family support, and felt that her baby was better off without her. Vega's heart ached for the woman and the impossible situation she found herself in.

'It's one of the best pieces you've written,' Kieran said, flicking through the pages in search of a particular paragraph. He cleared his throat and read aloud, ' "I know many people have expressed their shock that a mother could abandon her newborn child. I, too, have asked myself how Annette could do this. But let's discuss something more important – how brave she has been. First to walk away from her daughter, who she carried in her womb, her love growing deeper with every kick and turn, because she believed it was in Lucy's best interest. Driven by desperation and fear, knowing she was leaving herself open to judgement and abuse from us all. And second to come forward and admit she made a mistake and could not live without her child. I've spent hours in Annette's company, and as I watched her rock her little girl in her arms, her eyes never leaving her baby and hungrily taking in every detail of her perfect features, I saw only devotion. I trembled with the realisation that if she had not found her courage that second time, Lucy would never have felt her mother's love. Wouldn't that be the greater travesty?" '

He dropped the pages onto his desk and shook his head, his eyes glistening. 'Feck, Vega. You've got me. Unlike some other journalists, you have a real knack for getting to the heart of an issue. Truly brilliant work.'

To her surprise, Vega felt herself flush at the praise, and a lump formed in her throat. She wasn't one to cry. The last time she'd shed a tear was when she somehow managed to stab her pinky finger with a fork in a dishwasher-loading accident. Now that was painful.

'Thanks.' Her voice was strained and somewhat gruff. She picked up her lukewarm coffee and finished it off while she regained control of her emotions.

'When you care about what you write, your work transforms from good to great. Did you know that?' Kieran asked, waving a finger in her direction.

Vega shrugged. She was aware of that, but she was disconcerted that Kieran knew her so well.

'Find stories that you believe in,' he commanded. 'Then there will be no stopping you. I have a photographer going to Annette's later today, and we'll run the feature in Saturday's edition. It's gonna be a four-pager. Well done, kiddo.'

Vega took a deep breath to steady her emotions. Saturday had the most extensive readership; she'd hoped the story would be featured in that edition. It wasn't always a given. 'That means a lot to me, Kieran. I value your opinion more than anyone else's. As it happens, there's another story I want to run by you. It's one I've been considering for a couple of months and it ties in with this.'

'Go on,' Kieran said, watching her with interest.

'I want to write a story about children who were abandoned but never reclaimed. How did that impact their choices, and what became of their adult lives?'

Kieran took out his A4 jotter pad and started making notes. 'Have you anybody in particular in mind?'

Vega swallowed. 'Do you remember those children found at Pearse station the day the Clintons came to town?'

'As it happens, I *do* recall that story, as I was at College Green covering the presidential visit. I had a press pass and could get close to both of them. Hillary was a beauty; I never understood why Bill ever strayed.'

'A mystery,' Vega replied, rolling her eyes. 'But before we tumble down that rabbit hole, can we return to my story?'

Kieran grinned and nodded.

'I'd like to find out what happened to those girls. Discover where they are now.'

'What do you know so far?' Kieran asked.

'They were never claimed, despite a nationwide appeal. Not a single relative came forward. Isn't that strange? After all, they weren't newborns like little Lucy – two girls aged four and three. Someone must have known them. The younger one was adopted, while the elder grew up in foster care, and their names have never been released. There's a story there if I can find them or their family. I can feel it.' She thumped her chest lightly to emphasise her words.

Kieran glanced out of his office window for a moment. Vega remained silent, understanding there was no point in rushing her boss as he contemplated her pitch. 'When those girls mentioned that they lived in the woods in the middle of nowhere, Charlie Keane from the *Herald* labelled them the Nowhere Girls. Clever. And since we couldn't use their names or photographs when we covered the story, just general descriptions, that moniker stuck.' He frowned. 'That's where I believe you'll encounter a problem, Vega. Without their names, you don't have a story. You'll need first-hand testimonials for this to make it work.'

'I interviewed the social worker who was assigned to the girls. But she wouldn't share their details with me.'

Kieran gave her an I-told-you-so look.

'Look, you can take it that I'm working on obtaining their names,' Vega insisted. 'In fact, I've found a source to assist me in cutting through the red tape and discovering where the girls are now.'

While this wasn't strictly true, she permitted herself the little white lie. After all, if Luka had slept through the previous night, who knows what she might have uncovered on his laptop.

Kieran glanced down at his notes for a moment. 'Okay, I tend to agree with you. You've got something here. I'll give you two weeks to locate the girls or the family for an interview. But you need to find a few more cases to pursue. Enhance the story a bit more. Plus, I need the Padraig Nolan piece this week.'

'Two weeks!' Vega exclaimed. 'I'm going to need a month! You know I've got a week's holiday booked for the week after next. I'm heading to the States.'

'Well for some. Look, Vega, you were the one who said you have a source. Utilise it. You've got two weeks.'

'Ah, Kieran. Be fair.'

'Ah, Vega,' he mimicked. Then his expression softened. 'I'll tell you what: because you've managed to make this old cynic tear up today, something I rarely do, I'll give you a month. But that's all. Now off you go; I've work to do.'

'Living legend, that's what you are,' Vega said, a grin lighting up her face. 'Same time next week for a catch-up?'

Kieran grinned. 'Highlight of my week, kiddo.'

3

Extract from an interview with Susan Bailey

Vega: I'm recording our interview for my notes, Susan. Can you please confirm your name and profession for me?
Susan: I'm Susan Bailey, a retired social worker, with forty-nine years of service.
Vega: That's an impressive career, Susan. A true vocation.
Susan: My childhood best friend was in care and had a dreadful time, being moved from pillar to post. I resolved to become a social worker to try and make a difference.
Vega: That's admirable. As I explained earlier, I'd like to chat about the Nowhere Girls case from 1995.
Susan: An unforgettable one. It was the only case of its kind that I handled. Over the years I've dealt with hundreds of challenging and emotionally taxing cases, but that one has remained in my mind.
Vega: What can you tell me about the girls when you first met them?
Susan: They were scared. The younger one didn't speak for weeks, but she was barely three. The elder was like a lioness protecting her cub. It wasn't right. She was only just four herself.
Vega: From what I understand, the girls knew very little about where they had been living or any details that might help identify them.
Susan: It was odd. Yes, they were young, but most little ones are taught basic identifying details: their full name, where they live, and their parents' names.

Vega: And developmentally?

Susan: Both could count to ten and knew their alphabet. I remember showing them picture books, and the elder girl could read. Of course, neither of them had been to school yet.

Vega: How did you determine their ages?

Susan: The elder girl informed us. She didn't know the exact dates of their birthdays but she had recently celebrated her own. And she knew she was a year older than her sister.

Vega: Is it fair to say that they were well looked after?

Susan: Very fair. They'd obviously been taken care of and were beautifully dressed, albeit in a slightly old-fashioned way. They mentioned that their mother made their dresses and brushed their hair every night before bed. I remember thinking that it shone so much it resembled glass. I said as much to my husband.

Vega: So in your opinion, they were loved by their mother?

Susan: No doubt. They spoke fondly of her. She taught them to read. She sang to them and danced with them.

Vega: And did they talk about their father?

Susan: Very little. They confirmed they had a dad who lived with them, and if I remember correctly, they mentioned that there were other adults there too but couldn't provide any details about them other than their first names.

Vega: I've read the newspaper articles about the girls. It's so strange that no one came forward.

Susan: It was pretty bizarre. They were abandoned and left to fend for themselves. Anyone could have taken them. They could have fallen onto the tracks. I shudder when I think of that.

Vega: Can you tell me where they were placed?

Susan: You know perfectly well that I can't share that with you. However, I can confirm that the younger girl was adopted a few months later, while the elder one remained in foster care. She was assigned to another social worker, so I lost track of what happened to her. I hope she was eventually adopted too. But I wouldn't put money on it.

Vega: Why is that?

Susan: She didn't want to be adopted and made it abundantly clear to all that she felt this way. She was convinced her mother would return and wished to be available when she did. One of the most heartbreaking aspects of this case was witnessing that young girl becoming lost.

Vega: In the system?

Susan: Partly. But also lost within herself. She believed she was worthless and undeserving of love. And no child should ever feel that way.

4

Vega's phone pinged with a message from Luka as she parked in McCauley's car park in Wexford Town.

Don't come to the apartment. I'm in T. Morris.

She frowned as her stomach growled to punctuate her thoughts about hunger. She longed for a stack of pancakes from The Pantry. Luka's suggestion to meet at the pub surprised her slightly; neither of them was the type to enjoy a pint at lunchtime.

I need food, she replied.

You'll be fed. Promise.

The clouds parted, and the sun's rays glinted off the puddles on the ground from the earlier rain shower. She smiled as she walked purposefully towards the pub. She wondered if she would have a chance to see Luka's laptop today. She could suggest having coffee at his flat after lunch, then find a way to send him on an errand to the shops.

Her stomach muscles tensed, and she paused for a moment. She recognised the uncomfortable sensation for what it was: guilt. She knew she would cross a line if she opened Luka's laptop. He had made it clear to her that it was off-limits.

But then she thought of the two girls at the train station, vulnerable and frightened, alone, and her resolve was further cemented. She would do whatever was necessary to uncover why they had been abandoned.

She opened the door to T. Morris and stepped inside. The dark mahogany interior had always appealed to her, with its moody lighting and wooden parquet flooring – a nod to a simpler time. Waving at James behind the bar, she glanced to her right, expecting to see Luka perched on a stool by the window, people-watching as he waited for her. However, the place was empty save for a grey-haired man sipping a pint of creamy Guinness while perusing his newspaper.

'He's out the back,' James said, nodding towards the door of the Station, the bar's outdoor space.

Vega thanked him and made her way to the beer garden and courtyard, pausing upon entry. Luka stood by one of the tables with a goofy grin. At its centre was a large wicker picnic basket alongside an ice bucket holding a bottle of champagne.

'What's all this about?' Vega stammered, rooted to the spot.

'It's a celebration,' Luka replied as he removed the champagne and effortlessly popped the cork, the sound echoing through the leafy courtyard.

'Of what?' she asked cautiously.

'Your article in Saturday's *Ireland Today*.'

Vega felt a surge of emotion at Luka's unexpected gesture. Her heart racing, she stepped closer to him and accepted a glass of champagne. 'You didn't need to do this,' she said.

'Ah, but I did,' he countered. 'You know, since we met, I've read all your interviews and enjoyed them. However, that piece . . . it resonated with me. I'm not surprised it's gone viral.'

Kieran had called Vega excitedly a few hours after the article was published, both in print and online, saying, 'You're the most-read piece on our site. Well done, kiddo.'

Since then, the views had increased daily, with thousands reading every hour and sharing on social media platforms. This was a first for Vega, and she felt slightly overwhelmed by the article's success – and, if she was honest, a little proud of herself, too.

'Have you seen X?' Luka enquired.

Vega shook her head. 'Kieran has banned me from that platform. It's safer that way.' She pulled a face. 'I battled the trolls a few years ago, which isn't a good look for the paper.'

Luka grinned. 'I'd have liked to see that. I bet they didn't stand a chance against you.'

'I held my own,' she replied with a shrug.

'Well, there's nothing for you to worry about online. People are viewing Annette's situation with a fresh perspective. It was the main topic of discussion at work yesterday, and is again today.'

Vega took a sip of champagne. 'That's lovely to hear. I invested a lot of effort into that piece. But to be honest, Luka, this wasn't necessary. It's not that big a deal.'

'I disagree. Celebrating the wins is important, no matter how small they may be. Life is difficult enough.'

She stood on her tiptoes and gently kissed him, touched by his thoughtfulness. No one had ever done anything like this for her before. But there again, she had never been close enough to anyone to share her successes with them.

Luka began pulling items from the basket: pâté, cheeses, salads, crackers, crusty rolls and cooked meats. 'I bought half of the deli counter at Pettitt's,' he grinned. Then, like a magician, he revealed the last item with a satisfied 'Ta-da!' It was a tray of fresh cakes – a selection of jam and cream doughnuts and cream, coffee and custard slices.

'You are a good man,' Vega remarked, her stomach rumbling in gratitude.

'I know how sweet your tooth is!' Luka replied, holding a chair out for her.

She scooped hummus onto a cracker and held her hand over her glass as he picked up the bottle again. 'No more champagne for me. I need to drive!'

'Do you, though?' He raised an eyebrow suggestively. 'I've taken a half-day.'

Vega looked at him in surprise. 'That's not like you.'

Luka smiled. 'I've had a breakthrough in a case I've been working on. I managed to get an interim care order for a thirteen-year-old girl. She's been through the mill.'

Vega's stomach twisted. 'Is she all right?'

'In time, I hope so.' Luka's jaw tightened before he smiled.

'We're not discussing work today – at least not my work. But I reckon you should take the afternoon off too. We can play truant together.'

'I can't keep taking time off! I've got to write my Padraig Nolan piece before I head to Vermont next week.'

'I've always wanted to explore New England. I hear it's the best time of year to visit, too,' Luka said, raising an eyebrow suggestively. This was not the first time he'd dropped a loaded hint that he wanted to accompany Vega on her upcoming trip, sharing how many unused holiday days he had, declaring that they would all go to waste if he didn't use them before the year's end.

Vega pretended not to hear him. She intended to fly solo – literally – once again.

But Luka wasn't done cajoling. 'Come on, Vega . . . imagine you, me and a bottle of wine snuggled up on my sofa as we watch a film. You could stay over.'

And since Vega couldn't think of a single reason to say no, she extended her glass for a refill.

5

'Back in twenty minutes,' Luka called out as he left his flat to collect their takeaway from Vine Thai restaurant.

Their earlier picnic now seemed like a distant memory, and hunger pangs struck them once they had finished the second film of their movie marathon. Vega stretched her legs off the sofa, pressing mute on the remote control. She couldn't recall the last time she had spent an afternoon doing nothing but watching TV. Curling up in Luka's arms felt right.

He had been so happy to introduce her to the Star Wars universe, insisting they watch the films chronologically rather than in the sequence of their release. Another first for her. She had never been a fan of sci-fi or fantasy, but she was hooked by the end of *The Phantom Menace*.

She picked up her phone and checked her emails and WhatsApp, ensuring nothing urgent required her attention. Her gaze then drifted to Luka's laptop case in the corner of the room.

He wouldn't be gone for long, so she had no time to lose if she decided to do this.

She sat forward on the couch, perched ready to move as she grappled with her conflicting thoughts.

If she opened that laptop and Luka stumbled upon it, it would spell their doom. When trust vanished from a relationship, it was simply a matter of time before it fractured irreparably.

There was another option, she argued with herself.

She could ask him to obtain the information she needed. That way, there would be no need for fraud or deceit. She dismissed this immediately, knowing he would have questions she wasn't ready to answer.

Her eyes shifted to the hollow in the sofa beside her where he had lain moments earlier, his arms wrapped around her. She wasn't prepared to lose that. She would need to find another way. She stood and walked to the kitchen, grabbing plates, cutlery and two beers from the fridge.

Luka returned triumphant, holding up a large brown bag. In an exaggerated caveman accent he declared, 'Me man get food for woman.'

Vega grabbed the bag from him. 'Woman serve food. But woman not wash up.'

They both laughed, pleased with themselves for being so hilarious. Vega heaped jasmine rice, massaman chicken curry and pad Thai onto each plate.

'I overeat when I'm with you,' she said, twirling noodles onto her fork. She groaned as she took her first mouthful. 'But this is good.'

'Worth every calorie,' Luka replied, then added with a wink, 'I can think of a way to work it off later.'

Returning to the couch, they settled down with their meal. When Vega picked up the remote to restore the sound, Luka said, 'Leave it off. Let's have a chat.'

'All right. What do you want to talk about?'

'You never speak about yourself,' he remarked casually.

'Yes I do!' she protested.

'Nope. You always manage to steer the conversation away from personal stuff.'

'It's probably because there isn't much to say.' When Luka rolled his eyes, she added impulsively, 'How about this? I'll give you three questions. You can ask me anything you like.'

He put his plate down and rubbed his hands together gleefully. 'Oh, the pressure of choosing the right questions! You have to be honest, though.' He waited for Vega to nod before continuing. 'I'll make the first one easy. Why did you move to Wexford?'

Vega pushed a piece of chicken around on her plate, pausing before she replied. 'Wexford wasn't even on my radar. I had planned to buy a flat in Dublin, close to the office, but I couldn't find anything in my price range that appealed to me. Then Kieran mentioned that his friend had a cottage for sale in Wexford and persuaded me to go and see it. As soon as I saw it, I don't know, it just felt right. It felt like home and has everything I need. It's been one of my better decisions.'

'I'd love to see it sometime,' Luka said softly.

Vega quickly ate another mouthful of curry and made what she hoped was a non-committal sound. She had no genuine reason to deny him a visit. She'd spent the night here often enough that it was becoming rude not to return the favour.

'Having someone over to visit doesn't mean you have to marry them,' Luka joked.

But Vega could hear the vulnerability in his voice. 'I've never invited anyone over. Ever. It's nothing personal, I assure you.'

'Why haven't you?' He raised his hands quickly. 'That's not my second question, by the way.'

Vega smiled. 'Ah, that was a close shave for you. But I'll answer. I suppose there hasn't been anyone I've wanted to invite. I told you from the beginning that I'm not a relationship type of gal.'

'You did,' Luka agreed. 'All right, don't fret, your cottage is secure. I shan't come knocking on your door, I promise.'

Vega's stomach flipped and then sank at his easy acquiescence. She realised how contradictory she was, wanting him to fight for an invitation that she was scared to give.

Luka took a long swig from his bottle of beer. 'It's time for my second question. I've known you for nine months now. And during that time, I've never heard you mention any friends. So I want to know who your ride-or-die friends are.'

Vega glanced down at her plate, evading Luka's probing gaze. She had been foolish to instigate this game. 'I have plenty of friends. In Dublin.' She felt irritated as she noticed that her voice had risen an octave, indicating that she was on the defensive.

'Tell me about them,' Luka said.

'Well, Kieran, for a start.'

'He's your boss. That doesn't count.'

'He's also a friend. We meet for coffee every week, and I genuinely look forward to it. But if you're nit-picking and asserting that colleagues can't be friends . . .'

'I'll allow it,' Luka agreed with a grin. 'Because you also met quite a few of my work pals on St Patrick's Day at Maggie May's . . .'

'My liver still hasn't recovered from that night,' Vega grumbled. 'And to be fair, if you lived in Dublin, you might have already met my mates; we went out a few weeks ago.' Her mind grappled for something to say that illustrated how close she was to them. 'There's a social committee at HLD Media that organises cinema outings, hikes and pub quizzes, that sort of thing.'

'You're on the committee?' Luka asked, raising an eyebrow.

'Good Lord, no . . . but I receive an email about the activities each week.' She didn't mention that she regularly deleted the email without reading the details.

'You enjoy pub quizzes and walks?' Luka asked, sounding sceptical.

'Absolutely,' Vega lied. 'Who's *your* ride-or-die, then?' She studiously avoided Luka's knowing look; she'd proved him right by attempting to divert attention from herself once again.

'You've met Dec a few times. I know that if I call him in the middle of the night, he'll be there for me.'

'He's a nice guy,' Vega remarked. She had liked Dec whenever they'd met. It was clear that he and Luka had a shared history. They interacted with a comfort that only decades of friendship could bring.

'So back to you, Vega. Who is your Dec?'

'Who is my Dec?' She felt a pang as a flush crept across her cheeks. Who could she turn to in a crisis? There was no one. She felt judged and inadequate that she didn't have that one person there for her, no matter what. As Luka observed her, his expression softened, and she sensed sympathy in his eyes.

She leaped up and walked to the fridge, grabbing two more beers.

'I'm bored,' she said loftily as she returned to the sofa. She picked up the remote and pressed play, beginning their next movie *Revenge of the Sith.*

'Hey! I have one more question,' Luka said.

'And I've got work tomorrow. Let's finish the film.' She set her beer bottle down on the coffee table and began calculating how much she had consumed and how soon she could drive home. She had had two glasses of champagne at lunchtime and one beer this evening. Dammit. She would have to take a taxi home. To her horror, she felt tears welling in her eyes and a lump forming in her throat. If she had a bloody ride-or-die friend, she could call them right now and ask them to come and get her.

'I'm sorry,' Luka said, his forehead creased with concern as he took in her evident distress. 'I shouldn't have pushed you.'

'It's fine,' Vega replied, avoiding eye contact. 'Listen, I'm going to call a taxi and head home. I'll collect my car tomorrow.'

Luka looked taken aback. 'You don't have to do that. Honestly, I'm a right eejit for not leaving it alone. I could see you were uncomfortable. My only excuse is that I like you – a lot. I want to get to know you and understand you better.' His eyes pleaded with her to understand. 'We've grown close, but you have so many barriers that I thought I'd find a way to navigate them. Really. No more questions. Let's drink our beer and watch the film.'

Vega felt foolish for making such a fuss out of the standard questions any couple might ask one another. If she lost Luka, it would be entirely her own fault. His patience must be wearing incredibly thin at this point. She thought of the surprise picnic, his sincere support, and his enthusiastic encouragement of her achievements.

'Ask me your third question,' she whispered, disregarding caution.

He shifted closer to her on the sofa, gently cradling her chin in his hand as he placed a soft kiss on her lips. 'Today was meant to be a celebration of you, not to make you feel uncomfortable. So, no more questions.'

'That's precisely why I want you to ask me the third. I recognise that I'm guarded and prickly. I know I can be difficult. I don't want to be like that. Not with you. So go on, ask me.'

She steeled herself for a question about her family, which she logically felt had to be the next thing Luka would want to know about. She resolved to open up and share a little more about her background. She wanted him to truly understand her.

Yet even in her wildest dreams, she could never have anticipated his final question.

'What were you searching for on my laptop last week?'

6

Vega and Luka regarded each other silently, the air thick with tension. She had far too much respect for him to try to placate him with further nonsense, so she held back any claims of innocence. She had been naïve to believe he hadn't been suspicious of her last week when he caught her red-handed at his laptop.

'I'm sorry,' she said eventually, her face flushing with embarrassment.

Luka acknowledged this with a slight nod of his head. 'Why didn't you try again when I was fetching the takeaway? You had plenty of time.'

She glanced at the laptop case, which lay flat on its side with a book resting atop it. She realised that Luka had intentionally left it that way so he would know if she had touched it – clever.

She picked up her beer again and took a long swig. 'I thought that if I did, it would have meant the end of us.'

'And you didn't want it to be the end of us.' This was a statement, not a question.

She shook her head. 'No, I suppose I didn't.'

A ghost of a smile passed between them.

'If you knew I was up to no good with your laptop, why didn't you confront me?' Vega asked.

'I didn't realise at first. I was distracted . . .' He paused. 'By you. By us. Yet the following morning, it struck me that you'd been dishonest. You have a tell.'

'No I don't!' she protested, taken aback. 'What?'

'You repeat a question before responding. It's a tactic to buy time while you gather your thoughts.'

Vega nearly laughed. She had underestimated this man.

'I assume that whatever you were after is significant. Was it something to do with Annette and Lucy?'

She shook her head. 'No. Not that.' She bit her lip, her mind racing as she determined how much to tell him.

He sighed. 'It must be exhausting to live with so many walls up all the time.'

Vega couldn't deny this. Every part of her felt weary from her continual need to protect herself, refusing to allow anyone in.

'You can trust me, you know,' he said.

At that moment, she believed him. 'I've started working on another story but hit a brick wall. I need information I thought I could access through the Tusla case management system.'

Luka whistled slowly. 'The TCM? As in, the statutory body for child protection and fostering? What on earth are you searching for?'

'I'm trying to find out what happened to two girls who were in the system in the mid nineties.' She glanced at him through her lashes, attempting to gauge his reaction. His expression was hard to decipher, yet he leaned in and urged her to continue. 'In 1995, two sisters were discovered abandoned at Pearse station. Their mother had left them there, promising to return for them, but she never did. The younger of the two was adopted, while the elder was placed in foster care. I'm trying to trace them.'

'The Nowhere Girls. We discussed this case during my time at university,' Luka said. 'It was such a mystery as to where they had come from.'

Vega nodded. 'Precisely. Where had they been before that day? After their mother left them on the platform, she disappeared. Where did she go?'

'Not to mention that no family member or neighbour stepped forward, which is absurd. I mean, someone must have wondered where they had got to.'

Vega paused before responding. 'I think there's more to this story, and I'd like to discover what it is.' She started to peel the label from her beer bottle. 'I located the stationmaster who found the girls and alerted the Gardaí. He's in his nineties now, but remains quite clear about that day. He mentioned that the only details the girls could share about themselves were their first names and that they lived in the woods. He wouldn't say much about them, still insisting that he had to protect their anonymity. But he did share that he said he felt chills when they spoke, although he couldn't explain why. He just had a bad feeling.' She shivered herself and wrapped her arms around her body.

'Wow. That's strange. I mean, most children can give their surname and address by the time they're four years old. In my role with Tusla, I've dealt with some sad cases over the years, but I don't believe I've ever encountered anything like that.'

'If I just had their details . . . who their adoptive or foster families were . . .'

Luka's jaw clenched, and he replied firmly, 'I can't give you that information, Vega. It would be unethical of me. And a breach of those girls' trust. Not to mention that it would also put my career and reputation on the line.'

They both took another swig of beer, eyeing each other up warily.

'I'm sorry,' Vega said, lowering her gaze first. 'I would never wish to compromise you. I didn't consider that when I asked, which is rather irresponsible. Honestly, Luka, I really am sorry.' Her shoulders slumped and she picked up her phone.

'Who are you calling?'

'A taxi.'

'Why? I don't want you to go,' Luka said.

'But after what I nearly did . . .'

'Will you do it again?'

'No,' Vega replied, and to her surprise, she realised that she meant it.

'Then it's forgotten. Let's leave it.' Luka reached over and clasped her hand. 'You know, I might still have my college notes containing details of some of the other cases of lost children we studied. If you can't find the station girls, you could interview some of those. I think it's a wonderful idea for a story.'

'Thanks,' Vega said, smiling weakly.

'What about that baby discovered in Fairview Park seven or eight years ago? A homeless chap found him – an ex-doctor. Fascinating case. Do you remember?' Luka asked with enthusiasm.

'I remember. But I want my story to centre on where the children find themselves now, as adults. To explore how their abandonment has impacted them.'

'Hmm,' said Luka. 'Well, what about the fire station baby from Offaly? We discussed her case at uni. I'm certain she's gone public.'

'She has. Maeve Carroll. She's now in her late thirties. Married with children. I plan to talk to her, but her story has already been covered, and on its own, it isn't compelling enough. I need to find the Nowhere Girls,' Vega said firmly. She could see them in her mind's eye. Vulnerable. Scared. Alone. Confused. And she felt angry on their behalf.

'You'll find a way to locate them,' Luka said confidently. 'When you set your mind to something, you make it happen. I've learned that first-hand this year. I'll help you however I can, just not through the TCM.'

And at that moment, as Vega took in his face, which was so earnest and open, she felt something shift within her. A rush of emotion washed over her.

'Why do you tolerate me, Luka? I'm a handful. I'm aware of that.'

'Because the things worth fighting for are never easy. Nothing truly worth loving comes without a struggle.' His eyes sparkled and he spoke with such tenderness it made Vega shiver again.

She wanted to respond. She wanted to tell him she was falling for him despite her efforts to keep him at arm's length. Yet the words wouldn't come. Fear rendered her silent.

Her body slumped as a wave of exhaustion washed over her. A yawn slipped out, and she could hardly keep her eyes open.

'Let's go to bed,' Luka said, standing up and pulling her to her feet. 'But first, I want you to know something. You have a ride-or-die. If you're in trouble, you call me, all right?' He caressed her cheek gently.

Vega felt her body flood with tenderness and gratitude for this kind man. 'Come to Vermont with me,' she said impulsively, the words tumbling out before she had a chance to reconsider them.

Luka's eyes widened in astonishment. 'You can't be serious.'

She nodded. 'I want you to come.'

'I'll have to think about it,' he replied. Then, before Vega could respond, he added, 'Jeez, I thought you'd never ask! Of course I'll come!'

7

Vega eased the rental car to a gentle stop before Woodstock's iconic Middle Bridge.

'I feel as though we're on the set of that show *Gilmore Girls*,' she whispered, her eyes wide as she took in the 139-foot covered structure. The early-afternoon sun flickered through the latticed trusses. She glanced at the passenger seat and smiled at her travel companion.

Luka admired the view before them. 'If the bridge is this impressive, what must the inn be like?'

He picked up the visitor's guide to Vermont that he had been reading since they boarded their flight the previous day. Vega had left him to his holiday planning, putting her eye mask on so she could sleep while he contentedly marked pages with Post-it notes whenever he discovered something useful.

'That's the Otta . . . uque . . . chee river,' he informed her, struggling with the lengthy word.

'The say what now?' Vega asked with a laugh.

He ignored her teasing. 'And for your information, *Condé Nast Traveler* has named Woodstock one of the most beautiful towns in America.' He whistled in appreciation. 'I can see why. After your choice of hotel last night at the airport, I was concerned about what you had in store for us. I should have known you had something up your sleeve.'

'Ye of little faith,' Vega replied, although she had never paid much attention to hotels. She felt satisfied as long as she had a bed, shower and television. 'I found it difficult to secure a reservation anywhere here, as it turns out. So we're in the most expensive place in town. It looks cool on the website.'

'What made you pick Woodstock?'

Vega's eyes absorbed the tall trees adorned with resplendent autumnal ochre, russet and green hues, shimmering along either side of the winding river. 'I read an article about it.' This was true. 'I thought it sounded rather nice.' Also true. Kind of. She had scarcely glanced at the photographs. 'And you never know, it might spark an idea for a story. I always find inspiration when visiting new places. There are a few spots I'd like to explore while I'm here.' Again, partly true.

'Consider me a happy sidekick. Whatever you've planned, I'm ready to go along with it. But have you thought about Quechee State Park? The Quechee Gorge is one hundred and sixty-five feet deep and was formed thirteen thousand years ago. Imagine that! It's said to have incredible views.' Luka had his nose buried in his travel guide again.

'I'm glad you're here,' Vega said suddenly, finding his slightly nerdy self-appointed travel-guide persona rather endearing.

'Same here. And where else would I be?' Luka replied with a cheeky grin. 'Also, you need someone to share random facts while driving. For instance, that must be Mount Tom over there.'

It had been a momentous leap of faith for Vega when she'd asked Luka to accompany her on this trip. She had never been on holiday with a man before. While she had enjoyed holiday flings, she had always been relieved to say goodbye when the sun set on the final day. However, Luka appeared to induce many firsts for her.

An SUV pulled up behind them, prompting her to restart the engine and drive across the bridge. They continued into the village square. The small town exuded typical New England charm, with tree-lined streets, quaint shops, and restaurants inviting them to drop in. Bright orange pumpkins were scattered across driveways and pavements, catching her eye as she drove, ready for Halloween celebrations the following week. The car's GPS directed them to the Woodstock Inn within minutes.

'It's like a miniature White House,' Luka said, gazing out the window at a grand white building with black shutters and sweeping stairs leading to the large entrance overlooking a meticulously manicured garden. White loungers were scattered across the lawn beneath tall trees whose leaves murmured in the gentle breeze.

'I don't think I've ever stayed anywhere this posh before,' Vega said, biting her bottom lip. She glanced down at her battered black biker jacket, rarely off her back. Vintage and made of soft leather that felt like butter, it had almost become part of her. She was wearing it with joggers and a cropped T-shirt, and was worried she ought to have put a little more thought into her outfit.

Once she'd parked the car, they headed for the front entrance. A golden eagle sat atop the porch as if on watch. A carpet of leaves crunched beneath their feet, and the air was crisp and cool. They were greeted by a concierge in a tweed suit and beret, who smiled warmly as he opened the door and ushered them inside. At the centre of the spacious reception and lobby was an open fire nestled against a stone-clad wall. The oversized mahogany mantel displayed twinkling candles while the fire crackled and danced for the guests seated on comfortable sofas and chairs surrounding it. It was bustling, Vega observed, and not ideal if she needed a quiet spot.

'You were fortunate to secure this reservation,' the receptionist remarked as she checked them in. 'We're typically fully booked a year in advance during peak foliage months.' She gestured with her manicured hand towards the front door and the autumnal beauty outside.

'I can see why. It's stunning,' Vega replied.

After listening to the receptionist elaborate on the hotel's many wonders, Vega and Luka made their way to their room. It did not disappoint. Its sage-green wallpaper and mahogany furniture was complemented by blue-checked curtains that framed the view of the gardens. Vega had to admit it was a considerable upgrade from the functional yet soulless airport hotel they'd stayed in the previous night. Leaving Luka to unpack, she took a shower, closing her eyes while she held her face under the warm water, a welcome relief after all the travelling of the past twenty-four hours. Suitably revived, she quickly towel-dried herself and her short pixie-cut hair, then swapped places with Luka.

Twenty minutes later, they were strolling around Woodstock, picking up some souvenirs at a general store called F. H. Gillingham & Sons, which appeared unchanged since its establishment in 1866 – a date proudly stated on its signage. Luka spent an hour browsing in the Yankee Bookshop, allowing Vega time to concentrate on the Nowhere Girls story and her next steps in investigating.

'I'm hungry,' Luka declared, interrupting her thoughts. Vega's stomach responded with a loud growl.

'The concierge at the inn recommended we try a restaurant called Mangalitsa for dinner,' Vega said. 'We don't have a reservation, but let's give it a shot.'

Luck was on their side, and they got a walk-in table. Their host, Matt, welcomed them warmly, went through the menu dish by dish and explained the ethos behind the farm-to-table cuisine. He insisted they try the Brussels sprouts as an appetiser, topped with sriracha, maple syrup and crispy quinoa.

'I never thought I'd say this, but this is one of the best things I've ever eaten. A long way from the boiled-to-mush sprouts we had to endure as kids every Christmas!' Vega said.

'You should try my mother's red borscht with dumplings. I think you'd like it.' Luka said. 'And she'd love you,' he added softly.

This was entirely new territory for Vega. Meeting the parents was not on her bingo card. 'I'm not certain I'm any mother's ideal choice for their son.'

Luka frowned. 'You're wrong. My mother is one of the strongest women I know. She'd love you because you're strong too. But . . .' he raised his glass, 'that's for another conversation. Let's ensure I don't drive you to distraction on this trip first.'

They both laughed, and equilibrium was restored. Their main courses arrived: steaks accompanied by warm maple bacon biscuits. They tucked into the food in companionable silence, groans of pleasure the only sounds as they ate.

'Best meal I've ever had,' Luka said, adding with a cheeky grin, 'Don't tell my mam that when you meet her.'

Vega couldn't help smiling. He was so sure of them. Of their relationship. He was steady, no matter how hard she pushed back, planning a future for them. 'Your secrets are safe with me.' She watched him practically licking his plate clean. 'You're enjoying that!' she said.

'I never really had maple syrup before. I didn't give it much thought. But now I can't get enough of it,' Luka replied.

'You're reading my mind. Fancy going to a maple farm tomorrow?' Vega asked.

'That sounds like fun. Let's ask Matt for a recommendation. I noted a few mentioned in my travel guide, as it happens.'

'No!' Vega interjected. 'There's no need. I've read about a family-run farm that isn't too far from us. But I tell you what, it's not a bad idea to check with Matt if he knows of it.'

She caught Matt's eye, and he returned to the table to refill their wine glasses. 'Are you enjoying everything?'

'I think you can tell from our empty plates.' Vega said. 'Delicious flavours. Speaking of which, we wondered if you know where Red Maple Farm is. We wanted to visit it tomorrow.'

'Excellent choice! I consistently recommend that visitors experience this one. It's a mile up the road, and they offer some stunning products in their range. We incorporate one of their grade-A syrups in our biscuits.'

'I read that it's a family business.' Vega said. 'Do you know the family?'

'Yep. The Kensingtons. The farm has been in their family for generations. Mama Lulu, the matriarch, is adored by all of us in Woodstock. Everyone calls her that. She insists! With luck, you'll meet her if you join the tour. She's usually in the shop at the end, managing the tastings. Oh, and try their maple creemee – it's soft-serve ice cream. But be warned, it's addictive!'

'We'll make sure to do that,' Vega replied, her heart racing. 'Sounds like a lot of work for one woman! Do any other members of the family work there?'

'They've got plenty of staff. Some have been there for over thirty years. Mama Lulu's daughter, Felicity, took over the reins at least twenty years ago. Now, can I tempt you with dessert?'

Vega only half listened as Matt listed sweet-treat options. Her mind was filled with thoughts of what it might be like to belong to a family rooted in a farm that had been theirs for generations.

8

Red Maple Farm lay less than a mile from the main road to Woodstock. A long, winding, leaf-lined driveway was flanked by hundreds of tall maple trees on either side.

'Is this Woodstock the same one the festival was in?' Vega wondered out loud, trying to remember her popular culture trivia. She didn't need to worry, because Luka had the answer.

'It's not! That was the first thing I looked up when you said we were coming here. The festival in 1969 was on a dairy farm in Bethel, New York, about sixty miles from a different Woodstock.'

'If I ever get roped into a table quiz with work, you are so going on my team. Is there anything you don't know?' Vega asked with a grin. She reduced the car's speed as they neared a sign indicating a left turn, which directed visitors to a car park where large red barns with white tin roofs were situated at the foot of the green mountains. She opted to disregard the sign and turned right.

'I don't think we're supposed to go this way,' Luka said, frowning.

Vega ignored him. He ought to know her well enough by now to realise that she rarely followed directions. She continued driving, passing a man in a red flannel shirt stacking chopped firewood outside a barn. He waved cheerfully at them as she drove past. She waved back, wondering if he was part of the Kensington family.

The family home was a two-storey white wooden house, featuring an open porch at the front.

'I think this must be their private residence.' Luka said. 'You planning on getting out to say hello?'

Vega shrugged as she parked in front of the house. She hadn't considered anything beyond the instinct to see what the place looked like.

'I'd like to live somewhere like this one day,' Luka mused.

'Me too,' Vega agreed. She spotted a black tractor tyre tied to a rope hanging from a tall tree that must have stood for hundreds of years. She pondered how many members of this family had wrapped their limbs around that hand-made swing during that time.

Luka nudged her as the front door opened. Two women came out, both wearing blue jeans and bright sweaters. At first glance, they looked like sisters, with the same friendly oval face. One was slender and tall, with caramel-blonde hair piled into a soft bun. The other was diminutive, her shoulder-length ash-blonde hair peppered with grey. At second glance, Vega decided they were more likely mother and daughter.

'Bet that's the famous Mama Lulu,' Luka said as the older woman walked towards their car.

'Can we help you?' she called.

Vega pushed her oversized sunglasses firmly onto the bridge of her nose, then opened her window. A thousand questions raced through her mind. But she found herself dumbstruck.

'Sorry. Took a wrong turn. We're looking for the maple tour,' Luka replied, leaning over Vega.

'Easy mistake,' the woman replied with a wide smile. 'You should have taken the left, not the right, at the fork. I'll see you over there; it's where I'm heading.'

'Thank you,' Vega replied, regaining her voice. She'd liked Mama Lulu instantly. There was something undeniably amiable about her. She radiated warmth and quiet strength. With a quick wave, Vega turned the car around and returned to the visitor parking lot.

'What are you up to?' Luka asked.

'Nothing,' she replied, feigning innocence. 'I just fancied seeing what their house looked like.'

Luka made an I-don't-believe-you sound.

'If you must know, I've decided to explore writing a story about generational farming. I thought it would be interesting to compare a maple farm here with, for example, a dairy farm back home in Ireland.'

'That does sound interesting. Although I never knew you had such an interest in farming.' Luka flashed a dubious glance in her direction.

There's much you don't know about me, Vega thought.

She parked the rental car and they followed the signs to the reception inside a large red barn. On the way, they noticed another man dressed in red flannel, whittling wood while sitting on an upside-down steel bucket.

Luka and Vega exchanged an is-this-for-real glance and made their way inside.

The barn was home to a large gift shop. Tall shelves carved from trees were laden with dozens of types of maple syrup, mustards, preserves, chutneys, biscuits, crackers and nuts. A large fridge had pies for sale. There was also a decent clothing area with flannel shirts, hats, scarves and T-shirts.

'Look, there's the creemee,' Luka said, pointing to the ice cream Matt had insisted they try. He stepped up to the counter and bought two scoops for each of them from a friendly-faced young woman.

'The shop assistant mentioned there's an informational video in that room,' he told Vega, gesturing towards the far side of the barn. 'We can enjoy our ice creams while we watch.'

Vega followed Luka to the room. He pressed a button on the wall, and they sat on a long wooden bench that looked like it had been carved in one long piece from a tree. Had Mama Lulu's husband or maybe her father made it?

The video began with external shots of the farm and folksy background music. The camera shifted from the trees to the house and the barn they were in. Next, a woman's face filled the screen; it was the younger of the two women they had seen earlier at the house.

'Hello, I'm Felicity Kensington, but most people call me Flick. And you are very welcome to Red Maple Farm, which has been in our family for five generations. My great-great-grandfather learned how to tap the trees from Native Americans.'

Photographs and video reels showcasing the Kensington family over the years appeared on the screen. The house transformed from a quaint wooden structure built in 1854 to the expansive farmhouse it was today. Vega's heart raced when a more recent shot revealed a group of children playing on the tyre swing she had noticed earlier.

She swallowed a lump in her throat. The family's roots in Woodstock were as deep as those of the maple trees they now harvested.

The screen changed to show Felicity walking up a muddy path towards the maple trees. 'We have over four hundred acres of trees.'

'That's a lot of trees,' Luka said, licking his creemee.

Felicity continued, 'You might be surprised to learn that it takes forty gallons of maple sap to make one gallon of pure maple syrup. In winter, the sap settles at the tree's base and freezes. But as it thaws, it rises upwards. That's when we drill holes in the trees, as soon as the weather begins to warm, typically from late January to early February. Last year we collected over two hundred thousand gallons of sap, half sold commercially while the other half was used to create various maple gifts.'

The camera shifted to a close-up of her face as she concluded, 'Our family began the farm with a bucket hung on a tree. It's a far cry from the intricate tubing that connects every tree back to the sugaring room.' She surveyed the trees, adorned with vivid red, orange and yellow leaves.

The video then transitioned to a sterile room featuring large stainless-steel tanks. Felicity entered the frame. 'Each of these tanks can hold six thousand gallons; once they are full, the sap is boiled. After that, it is filtered and we begin bottling.' She held up a bottle to the camera. 'And if you would like to see the majestic maples for yourself, you can take a short stroll to the woods through the door on your right. Keep your eyes peeled for the first tree my great-great-grandfather tapped, which still holds a bucket to this day.'

Then Mama Lulu's face lit up the camera. 'Once you've worked up an appetite, come by the tasting bar in the gift shop, y'all hear?'

The video ended just as they finished their creemees.

'I reckon that's our cue to look at some trees,' Luka said, and they made their way out of the barn, following the signs for the walking tour.

He led the way towards the woodland on their right. The ground was wet and muddy, and a carpet of leaves lined the path.

'The yellow brick road to Mapleland,' Vega whispered, feeling like Dorothy in Oz.

As they entered the woodland, they saw the tubing that connected each tree to the next. They continued walking until they found the tall maple with a stainless-steel bucket affixed beneath a silver tap. Vega dashed towards it in excitement, placing her hand on the gnarled bark and closing her eyes, trying to envision the Kensington family ancestors standing in this spot, harvesting the golden sap.

'Where have you gone? You look miles away!' Luka said, touching her arm lightly and bringing her back to the woods.

'Sorry, I was thinking about the family,' Vega explained. 'It's astonishing to think that Indians taught them how to harvest all those years ago.' She dug out her phone and took several photographs.

The sound of wood snapping behind them made them startle and turn around. They both scanned the area but couldn't see anyone nearby.

'A bird or a squirrel,' Luka said, unconcerned. 'Come on, let's keep going.'

But Vega remained unconvinced. As they ventured deeper into the woods, she experienced an odd sensation, as if someone was watching them.

9

Vega continued to glance over her shoulder as she and Luka made their way back to the red barn. Throughout their ten-minute walk through the maple wood, she had felt like the trees were watching her. Luka hadn't noticed anything amiss, and she suspected that her overactive imagination was at play once again.

The gift shop was bustling, but Mama Lulu noticed them arrive and called them over. 'You've arrived just in time for a tasting. Did you enjoy the walk?'

'We did, and we found the bucket that your great-grandfather used,' Vega said, smiling warmly at the woman.

'He was a hard worker,' Mama Lulu replied. 'It was normal for him to work eighteen-hour days, especially during the harvest. At that time, he also ran a dairy farm to supplement the maple syrup sales.'

'Pretty impressive legacy he's left here,' Vega said.

'Absolutely.' Mama Lulu looked round at the group gathered in front of her. 'Now, let's start the tasting. Here at Red Maple Farm, we offer four different grades of syrup, ranging from light to dark. The colour and flavour are influenced by the season in which they're produced. We'll begin with the mildest and progress from there! But fair warning, ladies and gentlemen.' Her expression grew serious, and the group leaned closer. 'Once you've sampled our maple syrup, you'll never return to the generic corn-syrup-filled nonsense found in supermarkets!'

A ripple of laughter passed through the group as Mama Lulu popped the cork on a bottle of golden maple syrup. She poured shots into small paper cups, and everyone took one, tasting the syrup with expressions of delight.

'This one is delicate in taste. I like to pour it over my oats in the morning. My grandchildren like it over ice cream!'

She took a second bottle out and poured another round of shots, this time amber in colour.

'It looks like autumn in a glass,' Vega said as she picked up her cup.

'I always say that too,' Mama Lulu replied, nodding in approval. 'It has a much richer taste than the one before, with a hint of caramel flavour. It's the most commonly used grade of maple for pancakes.'

'I prefer this one to the first,' Luka said, licking his lips.

Vega leaned closer to the counter, catching Mama Lulu's eye. 'How many children and grandchildren do you have? How amazing to grow up with these sugary treats sprouting from the soil around you!'

Mama Lulu cackled. 'The syrup is a hundred per cent natural, so I've never felt guilty giving it to my family. Our products don't use harmful additives or preservatives. And they're fat- and cholesterol-free. I reckon that's why I'm so healthy!'

'You're certainly an advertisement for it,' Vega agreed. 'And your children, do they all work on the farm too?'

Vega could feel Luka's eyes on her, questioning again.

'My daughter does. The business is hers now. And I've got three grandchildren.'

Vega noticed a shadow pass over the older woman's face.

A little boy piped up. 'Is it time for some ice cream now?'

As everyone laughed, Mama Lulu prepared their third shot, which was dark brown and had a more pronounced malty flavour.

'I love this one! I think it will be hard to beat as my favourite,' Vega declared.

Mama Lulu nodded in approval. 'Our best seller. See what you make of this one, though. It's a bit strong for some, but it's popular with chefs because the robust maple flavour doesn't get lost in cooking or baking. All my pies use this grade.'

The syrup was the darkest, almost black, with a strong molasses flavour.

'We had this yesterday at Mangalitsa!' Vega said, recognising the flavour from the biscuits that had accompanied their steak.

As a woman in the group asked Mama Lulu about shipping gifts to Canada, Vega felt the weight of eyes upon her. She turned and saw Felicity Kensington watching from across the shop. She walked towards them, standing on the other side of her mother, her gaze taking in Vega from head to toe.

'Where are you from?' she asked.

'Ireland,' Luka answered. 'Wexford. It's in the south-east of the country. On the coast.'

Felicity breathed in deeply, closing her eyes for a beat. Then she asked, too brightly, 'And why did you decide to come to Vermont?'

'Vega read an article about Woodstock that made her want to visit,' Luka answered, his eyes moving from Felicity to Vega as the two women regarded each other. 'We're staying at The Woodstock Inn.'

'Must have been quite the article,' Felicity remarked wryly.

'It was,' Vega replied, feeling flustered beneath the woman's questioning gaze. She turned back to Mama Lulu. 'Thank you ever so much. It was lovely to meet you.' Then she grabbed Luka's arm and forcibly dragged him out of the gift shop.

'You okay?' he asked as they stepped outside.

'Just needed some air,' Vega replied, her heart racing. 'I'm grand.'

She glanced at the door, half expecting the watchful Felicity to follow her out.

'I'm going to buy some bottles of their dark syrup,' Luka said. 'Are you all right on your own for a minute?' He cast another worried glance at Vega. Her scathing look sent him scurrying back to the shop.

She turned her attention to the man in the flannel shirt, who hadn't moved from his spot, still whittling away at a piece of wood.

'Afternoon,' he said, nodding courteously to her as she approached him.

'What are you making?' Vega asked, peering over his shoulder.

'A queen for a chessboard. This is the last piece, then the board's ready for its first game.' His eyes never left the wood as he shaped it with slow, methodical movements.

'Impressive,' Vega replied. 'Have you worked at the farm long?'

'Next February will be my thirtieth harvesting here.' He paused and looked up at her. 'Irish?'

'Guilty. I'm Vega.' She thrust her hand out to shake his.

'Pleased to meet you. I'm Bill. We've had a few casual workers from Ireland here over the years. They're hard workers.'

'Farming is in the Irish blood. Maybe not maple trees, but we know about harvesting all the same.' She waved a hand around the surrounding woods. 'Looks like a nice place to work.'

'It is. A family-run business, where the staff have always been treated like family too.'

'That's nice to hear. Do you have children?'

'Four.' Bill's face brightened. 'Three boys and a girl. Fifteen grandchildren now.'

'I bet you spoil them.'

'I do, and I make no apologies for it. This chess set is a gift for my eldest grandson. He's in the club at school and is rather good too.'

Luka joined them, clutching a large brown bag full of goodies, and Vega quickly made the necessary introductions.

'Your grandson is a lucky boy,' she said warmly. 'I told Mama Lulu at the tasting that the farm must be a great place to grow up. There's a sense of history and family here.'

'You're not wrong. My children grew up alongside the Kensington girls; they all attended school together and got up to the usual mischief.'

'I can't imagine Felicity up to mischief,' Vega said, thinking of the woman inside.

Bill laughed. 'Oh, you'd be surprised.'

'You said Kensington *girls*. Does that mean that Felicity has siblings?'

He nodded. 'She does. But her sister left the farm a long time ago.'

'And she never came back?' Vega asked, her voice tight in her throat.

He shook his head, lowering his voice. 'Touchy subject. It's been difficult for the family not knowing where Cassie took off to.'

Cassie.

Vega's mind raced, and the air turned thick, making it difficult for her to breathe. 'It was nice chatting with you, Bill,' she managed to say before she turned and began walking towards the car.

Unlocking the door, she climbed in and leaned into the soft seat, fighting to catch her breath.

'What's happening?' Luka enquired, leaning in closer to her. Noticing her face reddening, he gently grasped her shoulders. 'Take a deep breath. Inhale. Now exhale. Once more, breathe in. And out.'

Vega focused on his voice, following his instructions until she could breathe freely again.

'Vega? Why are you so interested in the Kensington family? And don't feed me some ridiculous tale about writing a feature on farming.'

'My name is Vega,' she whispered.

Luka frowned. 'I know that.'

She turned to face him, her gaze reflecting the concern etched on his face. Was she finally ready to take another leap of faith and confide in him this hidden aspect of herself?

His hand was warm and comforting on her shoulder, and she realised she was.

'You don't understand, Luka. My name is Vega, and my sister's name is Nova. That's what I told the stationmaster in 1995.'

PART TWO

The answers are all out there, we just need to ask the right questions.

Oscar Wilde

10

Luka's eyes widened, his mouth opening to form a perfect 'O' of surprise. 'I don't understand...'

Vega placed a hand on her chest. 'There's a reason this story is so important to me. I'm one of the Nowhere Girls. And I believe Cassie Kensington is my mother.'

She watched as confusion turned to understanding, her words gradually sinking in. 'You're a Nowhere Girl... oh my God, of course you are...'

He reached for her, yet she recoiled, wrapping her arms around herself. Luka's eyes searched for hers, but she averted her gaze. Her hands trembled as regret at confiding in him pricked her.

'I've never told anyone that before,' she admitted.

'Thank you for trusting me.' He reached over and gently touched her hand for a moment. Then he pulled back as if he instinctively knew she needed her space. Vega wished she were the kind of girl who could fall into the arms of her knight in shining armour, but she wasn't and never would be.

She started the car engine. 'I know you have questions, and I want to tell you everything. But I need to get away from here. Seeing Mama Lulu and Felicity Kensington has taken a lot out of me.'

'Are you all right to drive? Why not allow me to take over?'

Vega wanted to concentrate solely on the road for a few moments until they reached their hotel – a chance to catch her breath. 'I'm fine. Thank you.'

Back in their room, Luka grabbed two small bottles of whisky from the minibar and poured them both a drink. 'I think we could do with this.'

They climbed onto the bed and leaned against the soft cushions and pillows. His eyes never left Vega, his concern evident.

'Bet you didn't expect this,' she said, every part of her feeling exposed.

He shook his head. 'No. I didn't. Just when I think I've got you figured out . . .'

'I never discuss it. Ever. It's too difficult.'

'I get that. Do you want to talk about it now? I don't want to push you.'

Vega shrugged. Then nodded.

'Do you remember much about it? You were so young.'

'It's all a bit blurry. Faded over time. But I remember the stationmaster, or at least the idea of him. I remember trying my best not to cry because Nova was so frightened and I knew I had to be strong for her. And I was scared when I couldn't answer any of the questions the Gardaí asked about the woods in which we lived. Apparently a social worker showed us photographs of hundreds of places, hoping it would help narrow down our origins. But none of them looked familiar.' She frowned. 'I spoke to the social worker last week. Susan Bailey. I didn't give her my real name, because I thought she might open up more if she was talking to someone removed from the situation.'

Luka looked at her questioningly. Vega shook her head. It hadn't made any difference. He stroked her hand with his thumb and the gesture comforted her.

'I don't know if it's a real memory or if it's simply what the newspaper clippings suggested at the time, but I believe I recall tall green trees. And a river. And the sound of the ocean.' Vega closed her eyes. 'But Nova's face has faded from my mind. Sometimes I wake up and think I must have been dreaming about her, because it lingers for a moment before vanishing again.'

'Oh, Vega, that must be incredibly difficult for you. Are there any photographs of Nova in your file with Tusla?'

'If there are any, I haven't been given them.' Vega's voice was flat.

'When was the last time you saw her?' Luka asked.

'We were with the same foster family for a couple of weeks, then they sent her away.' She shut her eyes and recalled the second-worst day of her life.

Nova sobbed, clinging to Vega as the social worker attempted to prise her away. Vega assured her little sister that she would find her, that they would be together again soon and that she loved her. But when Nova was gone, all that remained was a gaping hole that would never be filled.

Luka grabbed a soft caramel throw from the foot of the bed and draped it over Vega's shoulders. She wasn't cold, yet she couldn't stop shivering.

'After we were separated, Nova was adopted. But I remained in the foster system and moved around a bit.' She looked up at Luka with a rueful grin. 'You'll be shocked to hear that I was a troublesome child. An even worse teenager.'

He smiled back at her. 'What happened to you was monstrous. I don't believe any child could walk away from that unscathed.' He scrunched his nose as he mused, 'So where did your surname, Pearse, come from then?'

Vega raised an eyebrow until realisation dawned.

'The station where you were found. Of course.'

'When I was younger, I pretended I was related to Patrick Pearse.' Vega was referring to one of Ireland's renowned political activists, the man who read the Proclamation of the Irish Republic at the GPO on Dublin's O'Connell Street at Easter 1916, only to be executed nine days later. 'I thought that if I had to invent a backstory, I might as well make it a good one. I think that's why I wanted to be a journalist. Patrick Pearse was a poet and a writer, so I convinced myself I would follow in my imaginary ancestor's footsteps.'

'I had no idea,' Luka said, shaking his head again. 'No wonder you've been vague whenever I've asked about your personal life.'

Vega shrugged. 'When I told you I wasn't close to my family, that wasn't a lie.'

Luka's face was grim. 'And your time in foster care?'

She exhaled deeply. 'Up and down. It wasn't all bad. There were moments when I was happy. But I can see now that I was a difficult child to love. I wanted my mother. And I genuinely believed that she would come back for me. That's why I never wanted to change my name. I thought it was so uncommon that if anyone from my family ever looked for me, they'd find me quickly enough.'

'I can't envision you as anything other than Vega – the brightest star in the northern constellation of Lyra.' When Vega looked at him in surprise, he admitted, blushing slightly, 'After we met, I looked up your name. It captivated me.'

Vega spoke softly. 'That's cute. Thank you. But I wasn't the brightest star; that was my sister. You know, it's said that a nova occurs when a star flares up – a rare stellar explosion. However, its peak brightness only lasts for three days.' She sighed. 'For me, it lasted three years. That's how long I had Nova until her light vanished.'

'You'll find her again. I've never met a more determined person than you,' Luka said firmly.

Vega's stomach churned as doubt washed over her again. 'As Nova's records are sealed, I'm searching blind.' Vega closed her eyes for a moment and continued softly, 'I return to Pearse station every year on the first of December, at two o'clock.'

Luka regarded her with a puzzled expression.

'That day our mother left us at the station, she said she'd return by two,' she explained. 'I know it's a futile exercise, but I do it every year. Telling myself that perhaps this will be the year that Mum or Nova shows up . . .'

'Oh, Vega,' Luka said, moving closer to her. 'I'm so sorry.'

Vega shrugged and attempted to smile in reassurance that she was all right. 'Annette and Lucy's story stirred emotions I thought I'd long buried. And I promised myself I would keep looking until I get answers about where I come from.' She wrapped the throw tighter around herself. 'It's gnawing away at me, making a bigger hole every year. I need to uncover the missing pieces of my life before I lose myself. Does that make sense?' Luka nodded, his eyes glistening. 'Where was I born? Where did I live until I was four? Who are my parents? Why did they abandon me? And . . .' her voice faltered before she whispered the final and most crucial question, 'where is my sister?'

The prayer Vega had uttered several times every day since they'd parted rushed through her mind. *Please don't give up on me, Nova; I will find you.*

Luka moved closer and wrapped his arms around her. This time, she didn't pull away, allowing him to hold her tightly until her body melted into his.

'I'll help you in any way I can. Have you added your details to the CPR – the Contact Preference Register? It's the statutory register for sharing and seeking information regarding adoptions. You can leave an item, perhaps a letter, for someone there.'

Vega smiled ruefully. 'I submitted my request to the Adoption Authority when I was eighteen. I've maintained regular contact with my current social worker to see if there are any messages for me from my parents or Nova. But there's been nothing. I've left letters for all of them in case they ever reach out.'

'I should have known you'd be all over that,' Luka said approvingly. 'But why do you think your mother is one of the Kensingtons? Did you remember the name?'

'Nope. I did a DNA test. I'd thought about doing it for years, but I kept hoping that Nova would remember me, that she'd want to find me as much as I wanted to find her. So I waited and locked that part of myself away.' Vega took another sip of her whisky. 'But after I worked on Annette's story, it reopened the Nowhere Girls for me. I knew I had to do everything I could to find Nova. I hoped she might have uploaded her DNA for similar reasons, but no siblings were uncovered. However, I did find an aunt.'

She glanced at Luka, who mouthed, 'Felicity Kensington.'

Vega nodded. 'I emailed her and told her my name, saying that I'd like to chat further about our DNA connection. She wrote back, but she was vague and didn't reveal much. She had plenty of questions for me. I never replied.'

'I suppose you can see why she might be unsettled. How come you didn't answer her email?'

'I thought it would be better to come here in person.' She glanced away, feeling that Luka might judge her. Her situation was complicated, and it was hard for her to articulate how afraid she was to reveal her identity to the Kensingtons. What if they rejected her? 'And before you ask, I didn't tell her I was coming. I wanted to assess the family first. That's what today was about.'

'You have to tell them who you are,' Luka said. 'You can't hide this from them. I mean, they might know where your mother is!'

'I know,' Vega said. 'But that guy Bill who works for them didn't seem to think they do. He said Cassie left and never came back.'

'I bet they'll be overjoyed to meet you. You're Mama Lulu's granddaughter. She seems like such a family person.'

'Maybe.'

They sat in silence for a moment, and Vega sank deeper into Luka's embrace. She closed her eyes, her mind filled with the image of a tiny blonde girl holding her hand. Her little star, her little Nova.

She knew she had to be brave, as she had a promise to uphold.

Then Luka cleared his throat before posing a question that Vega had pondered countless times. 'Why do you think your mother didn't return for you?'

'I'm scared to think about that too long,' she admitted. 'Because when I do, there's never a nice answer.'

11

Overwhelmed by the emotional weight of encountering her probable aunt and grandmother, Vega eventually dozed off in Luka's arms. She awoke just as the afternoon sun was setting. Her mouth was dry, so she jumped up for a glass of water and downed it in one greedy gulp.

'Feel better?' Luka asked, emerging from the bathroom.

'Actually, yes. I'm not one for daytime naps, but I needed that.'

'We're still a bit jet-lagged too. Are you feeling hungry?'

'Again, yes!' To punctuate the thought, her stomach rumbled.

'I've ordered room service. It should arrive any minute now,' Luka said. The words had hardly left his mouth when a knock echoed on the door.

A smiling bellboy wheeled in a trolley, and Luka signed for it.

Vega inhaled appreciatively. 'Burgers?' she asked, lifting one of the silver cloches to unveil a colossal burger on a brioche bun accompanied by a side of chips.

'We'll have salad tomorrow,' Luka replied with a grin, setting the plates on the small table.

Vega switched on the TV and scrolled until she found an old *Fraiser* episode. They laughed together at the antics on screen as they ate their meal. Only after they had finished their last bite did they return to the Kensington family.

'I'm going to ring Felicity to ask if she'd like to meet up. Or do you think I should return to the farm?'

'Call first. Give her a chance to adjust to who you are,' Luka suggested, nodding towards the hotel phone. 'There's no time like the present.'

Vega searched for the farm online and noted down the phone number. Then, with her heart in her mouth, she dialled. Her heart sank when she was informed that Felicity had gone out earlier that afternoon. She replaced the handset.

'You didn't want to speak to Mama Lulu?' Luka questioned.

'She may not be aware of me. Felicity and I connected on an ancestry site. I don't want to be responsible for giving her an unpleasant shock if Felicity hasn't mentioned anything to her. For all I know, they might not appreciate a visit from an unexpected family member.'

'That makes sense. Ring back in an hour, and hopefully Felicity will have returned by then. In the meantime, you could email her again. Let her know you're here. Everyone has smartphones; she'll receive an email as quickly as a phone call.'

Before Vega had the chance to agree, the hotel phone rang. She picked it up.

'Hello, Ms Pearse? There's a Felicity Kensington here to see you. She's in the Billings Parlour, just off the lobby,' the receptionist said in a singsong voice.

Vega was astounded. Felicity had come to visit *her*. How on earth did the woman know who she was?

'I'll be down in fifteen minutes,' she said, looking at Luka with wide eyes. Once she had hung up, she said, 'She's downstairs. In the parlour! My aunt.'

Luka whistled slowly, looking as surprised as Vega felt. 'But you didn't introduce yourself at the farm.'

'Nope,' Vega stated. 'The ancestry site only shares basic information about who I am. My age, and that's not even accurate. The social workers gave me November the twenty-first, because I apparently told them that I vaguely remembered having a birthday when there was snow.'

'Does it share your location?' Luka asked.

'Hmm . . . yes, it indicates the country I live in. So it will say I'm Irish.' She leaped off the bed and dashed to the bathroom to freshen up.

Ever since she had connected with Felicity on the ancestry site, she'd been troubled by the faceless individual who DNA confirmed was her family. Her mind had worried and fretted about whether this new family would somehow find her wanting. At this thought, her stomach churned.

What should you wear to meet a long-lost aunt? she pondered, dismissing her joggers and Converse. She retrieved a burgundy silk midi skirt from her case and paired it with a simple black sweater and Doc Marten boots, then ran her fingers through her short hair and swiftly applied make-up.

'You look perfect,' Luka said as she tugged at her sweater, concerned that it clung too tightly to her curves. She had never been one to overthink her appearance; it was simply part of her identity. But suddenly, first impressions felt crucial.

'Put this on too,' Luka suggested, as he handed Vega her biker jacket. She felt better instantly – the jacket had always been her comfort blanket.

Luka nodded in approval. 'Now you're truly yourself. I'll be at the bar, waiting for you with a drink when you're finished. And if you need anything, send a text.'

A few minutes later, her heart racing with each step, Vega neared the Billings Parlour, pausing for a moment in front of the door. In that room lay answers to decades-long questions. With a trembling hand, she opened the door and stepped inside.

12

Standing at the window with her back to the room was a tall woman with caramel-blonde hair styled in a low chignon. Vega felt her breath quicken as Felicity turned to face her, taking her in properly for the first time. She noticed piercing grey eyes that until earlier today she had never seen before, yet that somehow felt as familiar to her as her own. Her stomach flipped as she wondered if her mother had those eyes. Felicity's skin was almost flawless, marked by faint wrinkles around her eyes and lips and enhanced by a rose-pink gloss. She had changed from her earlier outfit and wore high-waisted beige tweed trousers, a chocolate-brown sweater and kitten heels. She suited a parlour, Vega thought, glad that she'd changed into her skirt.

'Hello,' Vega managed to say. Her voice sounded strange, so she cleared her throat.

'Hello,' the woman echoed back. 'I'm Felicity Kensington, but you already know that.' She remained by the window, standing resolute and statuesque as she surveyed Vega.

They had reached an early stalemate, with neither party prepared to advance beyond a needless introduction.

'And I'm Vega Pearse. But you know that too.'

'Vega Pearse,' Felicity repeated. 'It's such a pretty and unusual name. When did you get to Woodstock?'

'Yesterday. The Woodstock Inn is beautiful, as is the town.'

'I may be biased, but I consider Woodstock the most charming of the Vermont towns. Is your room satisfactory?' Felicity asked. She spoke slowly, omitting the 't' from the end of 'Vermont'.

'Very comfortable, thank you. The shower has great water

pressure,' Vega replied, wishing she could take the words back as soon as she heard them aloud. She shuffled her feet, feeling awkward and shy.

'You've chosen a lovely time to visit. Woodstock is beautiful in all four seasons, but fall is my favourite. The Green Mountains are worth a trek if you're feeling energetic.' Felicity dropped the percussive 't' again so that 'mountain' sounded like 'mou-'in'. It was charming, and once more somehow felt familiar to Vega.

'We plan to explore some of the recommended walks and see more of the covered bridges.' Vega's mind fought against the surreal formalities of their exchange. However, she had no idea how to steer the conversation towards where they needed to go.

She decided that honesty was the only option. 'This is rather odd. I'm not certain what to say. However, I doubt I can manage any more small talk; it's never been my strong suit.' She took a deep breath. 'I'm a bit taken aback that you came here looking for me.'

Felicity's gaze met hers. 'I heard your boyfriend call you Vega. It's such an unusual name, I suspected you were the person I connected with on the ancestry website.' Vega looked at her in surprise and also admiration as Felicity continued, 'Of course, I wasn't certain to begin with. When you arrived at our house wearing those large sunglasses, I assumed you were another nosy tourist. However, your Irish accent made me halt. So I observed you. Don't ask me how, but somehow I *knew*.'

'You were watching us in the woods!' Vega exclaimed.

'I didn't mean to startle you. I suppose I needed to work out what it meant that you were here. Seeing you chat with Mama Lulu at the tasting was more than a little surreal.'

Vega grimaced. 'I'm sorry. That must have been difficult for you. I also want to apologise for not responding to your email. I suppose I was nervous. I had hoped to find a connection there, but when I did . . . well, it caught me off guard.'

Felicity laughed and nodded in agreement. 'It's all a bit bonkers.

I can hardly believe it's true, even though I've double-checked the accuracy of the DNA tests numerous times.'

'Ninety-nine-point-four per cent accurate,' they said in unison.

They both laughed this time, and inched a little closer to one another.

'I called you at the farm earlier to ask for a meeting,' Vega said.

'I've saved you a journey.' She paused, locking eyes with Vega. 'You've come a long way for a chat,'

'It felt far too significant not to meet you face to face.'

She acknowledged this with a nod. 'Mama Lulu isn't aware of you yet. I wrestled with telling her, but thought it best to wait for a response to my email before I said anything. I never anticipated you arriving on our doorstep, though! I hope you understand that I needed to meet you before introducing you to her.'

Vega grasped the reasoning behind that. She would have done the same thing.

Felicity's eyes searched her own. 'I have often wondered whether my sister had any children.'

Vega took a deep breath and clasped her trembling hands behind her back. She had prepared herself for rejection, so having her relationship acknowledged was monumental.

'But I'm struggling to grasp how you found yourself in Ireland,' Felicity continued.

'I'm afraid I can't answer that. I grew up in foster care. Much of my early years remains a mystery.' Vega smiled apologetically. 'That's why I wanted to meet you in person . . . There's quite a story to share.'

Felicity shrugged. 'When it comes to my sister, there's always a story.' She gestured towards the blue velvet sofa by the fireplace. 'Why don't we sit down and have some coffee or tea? Then you can share what you remember. And please, call me Flick; most people do.'

Vega took a few calming breaths before crossing the room.

'You don't look like her,' Flick said suddenly, which felt like a sucker punch to Vega. 'But you're like her all the same. It's the reason I knew that you were my niece.' She reached over to touch Vega's arm lightly. 'She had a leather jacket like that one for a while.'

Once more, in this emotional roller coaster, Vega sensed a connection that drew her nearer to her mother.

Vega sat down, but Flick remained standing. She shuffled her feet awkwardly, and when she spoke, her voice trembled slightly. 'I'm usually quite sure of myself, but this has me in a bit of a muddle. Please say no if this offends you, but I was wondering . . .'

'You can ask me anything,' Vega said hurriedly. 'I understand. That feeling of uncertainty? I feel it too.'

'Well, I wondered if I might hug my niece.' Flick's eyes sparkled as she awaited Vega's response.

Vega gulped, then leaped into her aunt's arms. She heard Flick softly weeping as her embrace tightened, and felt a wave of tenderness and affection.

'That's better,' Flick said as they broke apart.

They sat side by side as Flick poured coffee into delicate porcelain cups.

'I can't believe I've found you,' Vega said as she took her drink.

'Nor I. Mama Lulu will be delighted that we've discovered Cassie's daughter.'

'Cassie,' Vega repeated softly, rolling the name around in her mind, hoping it would resonate. But it still didn't strike any chords of recognition. 'Was that my mother's name?'

'Yes!' Flick replied. 'Sorry, I assumed you knew that.'

'I don't recall anyone ever calling her that.' And then Vega dared to ask the only question that mattered. 'Do you know where she is now?'

It felt as though time stalled as she awaited her aunt's response.

Flick shook her head sadly. 'She left home at seventeen, just after graduating from high school. And no one has seen her since. It broke my mother's heart back then. She lived in hope that Cassie would return one day. I always believed she would, too. I imagined her waltzing back in with her big smile, chiding us for missing her. Then she would delight us with tales of her adventures. That was Cassie's way.'

Vega's heart raced as she greedily absorbed this snippet about her mother. She bit her bottom lip. 'Do you have a photograph of her?'

Flick shook her head. 'I'm sorry. No, I don't. Not with me. And of course, you'd want one. I should have considered that. I'll get you one.'

Vega nodded, suppressing her disappointment. 'Have you searched for Cassie over the years?' she enquired. 'Checked social media and so on . . .'

'Now and again I search for her name in the usual places, but she's never turned up.' Flick sipped her tea. 'I've even checked the death records, just in case . . .' She paused, shaking her head as if to dispel that image. 'You mentioned there was a story . . . I'd like to hear it.'

Vega's heart began to race, as it always did when she was compelled to discuss her abandonment. 'It's a difficult topic for me,' she confessed, taking a steadying breath. 'When I was four, my mother left me at a train station in Dublin, instructing me not to move. She never returned.' She paused to allow those words to resonate. She witnessed shock, followed swiftly by sympathy flashing across her aunt's face.

Flick reached over and took Vega's hand in hers. 'That's horrific. Cassie abandoned her child.' She shook her head in disbelief. 'When you mentioned you were fostered, I assumed she had given you up as a baby. But this . . . to leave you after four years. Oh, Cassie, what a muddle you've found yourself in.'

Vega felt a pang of sympathy for her aunt. She steeled herself and continued. 'There's more. It wasn't just me. My mother left two of us. I have a little sister who is a year younger than me.'

Flick wrapped her arms around herself, her face taut and

drawn. 'Where is she . . . your sister?' she enquired, gazing at the door as though she half expected to see her walk through it.

Vega looked down. 'I don't know. We were separated shortly after being left at the station. She was adopted, but her records are sealed. I can't find her unless she wishes to be found.'

'What a mess,' Flick exclaimed. She stirred two heaped teaspoons of sugar into her coffee cup. 'Okay, so if you were four when Cassie left you, where were you before that?'

Vega shrugged. 'That's part of the mystery. It might have been a farm with animals and woods, perhaps near a beach, as I told the social worker that I remembered the ocean. However, I have no clue about where exactly that was. I don't have a birth certificate, so I suppose I could have been born anywhere.'

'What about your father?'

'I think I remember a man who might have been him, but I don't have any clear memories. My instinct tells me that we weren't close, and that he may not have been part of our lives before Mum left us. But I've no real evidence of that. Just a feeling.'

'What about other family . . . friends and neighbours? Surely someone must have missed you!'

'If they did, they didn't come forward. There was a campaign in the media to find our relatives, but no one claimed us,' Vega replied quietly, her trembling voice betraying her. 'I waited and waited, but no one came.'

'I'm so sorry, Vega,' Flick said, reaching over to pull her into her arms again. 'You don't have to wait any longer. I'm claiming you now, and I promise I won't let you go.'

13

'Are you ready for this?' Luka asked as Vega parked in front of the Kensington farmhouse the following morning.

Vega surveyed the expansive yard, feeling unexpectedly calm. 'I've gone from knowing nothing about my family history to this . . . I've never been more prepared for anything,' she said, her voice filled with wonder as she gazed around her. 'This is my family's farm. My mother lived here.'

'If Mama Lulu greets you as warmly as Flick did yesterday . . .' Luka said, smiling. Vega had brought Flick to the bar to meet him the previous evening, and the three of them had enjoyed a drink together, tentatively getting to know each other a little better.

As on the previous day, the car's sound drew Flick and Mama Lulu out to the front porch. However, this time Vega had hardly managed to climb out before her grandmother rushed towards her – a petite woman, slight but soft – and took her in her arms.

'I had no idea you existed, but what a blessing you found us. Thank you for reaching out. Thank you.'

'Erm . . . thank you as well . . .' Vega stuttered, wrapping her arms around her grandmother. 'It's a pleasure to meet you. This is . . .' She halted abruptly, glancing up at Luka, berating herself for not having thought of a label beforehand.

'Hello, Mrs Kensington. I'm Luka,' he added helpfully, casting Vega a knowing glance.

'You are both welcome. Everyone around here calls me Mama Lulu. Now come inside. I have food ready. Are you hungry?' She squeezed Luka's hand before directing them both inside.

'Flick warned me not to eat before we arrived,' Vega replied, smiling at her aunt and then quickening her pace to keep up with Mama Lulu, who appeared to be moving at double speed.

The farmhouse was precisely as she had envisaged it would be from the outside. Framed artwork on every wall, knick-knacks on shelves, large vases filled with flowers, and soft throws and cushions on well-worn, inviting sofas and chairs. It was a home, not just a house, which exuded the same warmth Mama Lulu was now extending to Vega.

'I hope you like pie,' she said as they followed her into a spacious kitchen and dining room. At its centre stood a long wooden table flanked by ten chairs. Mama Lulu seemed to enjoy entertaining. Vega breathed in a sweet and spicy scent that danced around them.

'If the pie tastes as good as it smells, then yes, I do like pie,' Luka replied good-naturedly.

'Mama Lulu sells her pies in our farm shop. People travel from miles around to buy them – both savoury and sweet.'

'And we've got both for you today – a chicken pot pie, followed by my apple and cheddar pie for dessert. I thought we might eat and chat. I always find that food is the best ice-breaker, don't you?'

Flick grasped Vega's arm and guided her towards a wall adorned with framed photographs. 'I have more to show you, but I thought you might appreciate this.'

Vega's gaze fell upon a young girl with shoulder-length straight dark brown hair, parted in the middle and framed by bangs. Her heart began to race so fast it made her breathless. She blinked, twice, hardly daring to believe her eyes. After decades of only seeing her mother in her imagination, she was there in front of her. Cassie's blue eyes looked up towards the camera, almost in question, as she beamed widely, displaying perfect white teeth and a petite nose.

'That was Cassie's senior photo. It's also featured in her yearbook,' Flick said. 'Are you okay? You've gone a little pale.'

'It feels surreal. I've dreamed about seeing her again for so long . . . I have her nose,' Vega said in wonder, reaching up to touch her own nose, which mirrored the one in Cassie's photograph.

'It's mine too,' Mama Lulu said, moving closer. 'Flick mentioned yesterday that you had a look of Cassie. Although you aren't her double, you resemble her quite a bit. I didn't understand what she meant then, but I do now. Your mannerisms, the way you glance sideways from beneath veiled eyes like just now, that's all Cassie.'

'Thank you,' Vega whispered, feeling the open wound inside her, ripped wide and raw thirty years earlier, begin to draw closed. 'It's lovely to hear that. I've always wondered if I resembled her. I have a memory . . . I'm not even sure if it's real or imagined . . . of Mum saying that I looked just like she did when she was a little girl.'

'Your hair is the same shade of brown. Natural copper highlights would pop out beautifully when the sun caught Cassie's head. She was fortunate. I used to tell her constantly that she should never change the colour. People pay a fortune to achieve that look in a salon.'

Vega took a deep breath to steady herself. Transitioning from nothing to anecdotal remarks about her mother's appearance was overwhelming.

Mama Lulu took her hand. Vega could sense the strength in her slender gnarled fingers, knotted by age.

'You being here is a blessing I needed. Now, come on, let's sit down and eat. We have a lifetime to catch up on, and food will help with that,' she stated firmly.

'Your mother was beautiful,' Luka remarked from behind Vega.

'Her face has been hazy in my mind for such a long time, but it's becoming clearer to me now. I think her hair might have been different when I was with her. Longer, maybe? I don't know . . .' Vega's eyes remained fixed on the photograph. She wished she could remember more.

Luka and Vega sat next to each other at the dining table. Flick and Mama Lulu brought out trays overflowing with food, and a golden-crusted pie was set in the centre of the table. Mama Lulu served them generous portions and urged them to help themselves to a large mixed salad.

'We don't stand on ceremony here,' she stated. 'Go on, eat up.'

Vega groaned after taking her first bite. 'That is delicious.'

'What's the dressing on the salad?' Luka asked, licking his lips.

'Maple and balsamic vinaigrette. We sell it in the shop,' Flick said with a smile. 'It's lovely, but I prefer our creamy maple dressing. You can try that one the next time you visit.'

Vega felt a warm flush rise from her chest to the top of her head, and a silly grin spread across her face. The statement suggested that she would visit many times. 'I shall look forward to that,' she replied warmly, smiling at her aunt and grandmother.

'Are the Kensingtons originally from Vermont?' Luka asked.

'I was born and raised in Woodstock, just like your grandfather, Mitchell.' Mama Lulu's eyes sparkled as she reminisced, 'We were high school sweethearts. He was an all-star quarterback, and I was a cheerleader – the only man I ever dated or loved.'

Vega nearly laughed out loud at this information. Her grandparents were truly as American as the apple pie promised for dessert.

'My parents had a perfect marriage; I can't recall a single instance of them arguing during my childhood,' Flick remarked.

'Oh, we did – many times. But we could never stay angry with each other for long. Besides, we were too busy. We took this place over from Mitchell's parents not long after we married. The farm has been in the family for five generations now.'

Flick said, 'And once my son finishes his economics degree at the University of Vermont, he'll come home to help run the farm.' She smiled warmly at her mother. 'Perhaps we could encourage Mama Lulu to take things a bit easier then. She seems to forget she's not twenty any more.'

Mama Lulu tutted. 'I have a few more years left. But it will be good when Brad joins us. He's full of ideas for modernisation, and we need that. Felicity made changes when she came on board, and we've flourished because of them. My grandchildren will ensure we keep going for another hundred years.'

Vega listened, enraptured, to her aunt and grandmother speaking. Their shared history electrified her mind, and she could have happily remained in that chair for hours.

'How many children do you have?' Luka enquired, turning to Flick.

'Three. All at the same university now. Ellie and Tiffany are twins, both in their first year. Their father, my ex-husband, lives in Burlington, near the university, so they all reside with him. I've been bracing for disaster since they returned under one roof, but so far, so good.' Flick sipped her lemonade and added, 'Ellie is a feeder, so he's enjoying home-cooked meals again. While he hasn't missed me since we split up, he has missed my cooking.'

They all smiled at her intended joke.

'What are Tiffany and Ellie studying?' Vega asked, her mind exploding once more as she realised she was talking about her cousins.

'Ellie is studying food systems and Tiffany is pursuing a degree in public communications. We hope that both will join the family business as well.'

Vega felt her stomach twist at the idea of another generation at the farm. She picked up her drink, perplexed by why this made her feel sad.

'And what about you, Vega? What do you do?' Mama Lulu asked, gazing at her intently.

'I'm a journalist at one of Ireland's national newspapers.'

'A renowned journalist,' Luka added. 'One of her latest features went viral.'

Vega felt a flush spread across her cheeks as Mama Lulu and Flick requested a link to the piece. Hundreds of thousands of people had already read it, which delighted her. Yet somehow having these two see her work made her feel vulnerable and exposed.

'Another way that you're like your mother. She was also good with words,' Mama Lulu said with approval.

'Did she write?' Vega asked, her heart racing once again.

'Yes, for the school newspaper in high school. She was also on the committee that put the yearbook together. I have a copy of it.' Before Vega could ask, she added, 'I'll show you everything, I promise. But for now, eat that pie.'

Vega took a sip of water and cleared her throat. There was one question she needed answered immediately. 'Did Mum have a second name or a nickname?'

Mama Lulu and Flick glanced at her with interest. 'No nickname, but her middle name was Louisa, after me,' Mama Lulu replied.

'Why?' Flick enquired, noticing a look of confusion cross Vega's face.

'It's just she wasn't called Cassie when I was with her; she was known as Star. When you said her name was Cassie, I assumed she'd started to use a nickname . . .'

Confusion gave way to a slight smile on Mama Lulu's face. 'If she were to change her name to anything, Star makes sense.' She reached across the table to take Vega's hand, turning it to reveal her wrist. 'Your mother had a birthmark right here.' Her fingers traced a shape on the skin. 'A café-au-lait mark, in light brown.'

'Nova – my sister – had one too!' Vega said excitedly. 'I've not thought about that in years. Hers was on the top of her arm!'

'They can be hereditary, as our family doctor told us,' Mama Lulu replied. 'Nothing sinister; in fact, it was quite pretty, in the shape of a star.' Her eyes grew misty as she remembered. 'One of the names on our list of possibilities for our new baby was Cassie. So when she came along with her birthmark, it felt as though it was . . .' she grinned ruefully, 'written in the stars.'

'Cassie is short for Cassiopeia, a constellation from Greek mythology!' Luka exclaimed.

Somehow Vega was not surprised by him knowing this.

'Yes, that's right,' responded Mama Lulu. 'Cassie was named after Queen Cassiopeia, the mother of Andromeda, who was wed to the King of Ethiopia.'

'And I got boring old Felicity!' Flick said, joining the conversation. 'Perhaps that's just as well. The myth states that Cassiopeia offended the sea nymphs by boasting that she was more beautiful than they were. She was punished for her vanity when Poseidon sent a sea monster to trouble the shores of her kingdom.'

Vega cast a sharp glance at her aunt. There was something in her tone that took her by surprise. Was it possible that Flick didn't like her sister all that much? Or, at the very least, disapproved of her.

Then Flick turned to Vega, her face sad, and her voice fell to a whisper. 'I've never given much thought to Cassie's name before. But now I find it sadly fitting.'

'Why?' Vega asked.

'Legend has it that Cassiopeia bound her daughter to a rock as a human sacrifice to placate Poseidon.'

The words raced through Vega's mind. Were she and Nova sacrificed too? And if so, for whom? For the first time in her life, she felt a new emotion seep through her as she thought about their mother: anger.

14

Extract from an interview with Julie Gainsborough

Vega: Thank you for agreeing to talk to me today, Julie. I met your father, Bill, at Red Maple Farm, and he told me how close you were with Cassie Kensington.

Julie: For a while. Yes.

Vega: Could you share a bit about your friendship?

Julie: All of my early memories include Cassie and Flick. Long before we began school, we played together on the farm. Mama Lulu always welcomed us warmly. She encouraged Dad to take us with him on weekends.

Vega: And I wager that Mama Lulu always had pie for you.

Julie: Yes! There were always treats at the Kensingtons', and we regarded their home as our own. It was the same for Cassie and Flick at my house; they were always welcome at our table.

Vega: What was Cassie like in those days?

Julie: Wild. Fun. Exciting. Life was always an adventure with her. She would come up with ideas for new games, but she could also get me into trouble. My mother used to say that if Cassie Kensington ran into a burning fire, I would run in after her.

Vega: So your mother disapproved of your friendship?

Julie: She was cautious about it. For instance, one day, we were spending time at the farm. Cassie got it into her head that she wanted to break a record set by the Gallagher brothers that week. They'd climbed a thirty-foot tree and boasted about it all around school. So we had to go one better. Cassie found a forty-foot maple and insisted we climb to the top. She grabbed Flick's Polaroid camera and planned to take a picture from the highest branch.

Vega: That sounds dangerous.

Julie: It was perilous; we could have broken our necks. But in any case, I proved my mother wrong about following Cassie into a fire.

Vega: How so?

Julie: I chickened out and didn't follow her up. But Cassie reached the top, her laughter ringing through the woods. I can still see her now, her hair whipping around her face, flushed with excitement at her accomplishment when she climbed down.

Vega: She was fearless.

Julie: Absolutely. As I mentioned, it was good fun to have her around. For a long time, we felt like sisters.

Vega: When did that change?

Julie: On our first day of high school, not long after that tree incident, she dumped me. My kids would call it ghosting now. When I went to sit beside her, she stated that I would be sitting next to a girl named Izzy. I was confused, because we had spent all of elementary school seated beside each other. But she insisted that she had orchestrated the change in seating for *my* benefit, not her own.

Vega: How so?

Julie: I was on friendly terms with Izzy because we were in the Girl Scouts together. Cassie said she knew we wanted to sit next to each other, but that I didn't want to hurt her feelings so I kept it to myself. This wasn't true. Izzy was a friend, but Cassie was my best friend. Anyhow, Cassie said she was willing to make the ultimate sacrifice. Before I knew it, she'd ushered me into my new seat, and I was thanking her for being such a good friend. Looking back now, I realise how bizarre it was.

Vega: Do you think her intentions were genuine, though?

Julie: Not at all. She wanted to sit next to the Gallagher brothers. She had started spending time with them and fancied them. She fabricated that story to get rid of me.
Vega: That seems rather manipulative.
Julie: It was. But do you know what? In the end, it turned out better. Izzy was my bridesmaid, and I'm godmother to all her boys. Cassie Kensington did me a favour.

15

After they'd finished eating, Mama Lulu stood up and beckoned to Vega to join her. 'I'd like some time with my granddaughter, if that's all right.'

'Sure. Luka can help me with the dishes while you chat,' Flick said, and together they began to clear the table.

'I love cooking, but I detest washing up,' Mama Lulu whispered conspiratorially. 'Shall we go upstairs?'

They ascended a wooden staircase featuring another gallery of photographs adorning the tall wall – dozens of snapshots capturing family life. Vega eagerly searched for any images that included her mother, her eyes carefully preserving the memories within her mind.

'Flick intends to get copies of family photographs for you,' Mama Lulu said. 'And you can take some photos on your phone later. But first of all, I thought you'd like to see Cassie's bedroom.'

She paused at the door to the right of the landing, grasped the black wrought-iron handle and opened it to reveal a dusky-pink room.

'I haven't altered much since Cassie left. This is her bed and her furniture. I took down the posters, which are all rolled up in the wardrobe.'

Vega glanced around at the pine dresser adorned with an oval mirror, the tallboy by the door, and the bedside lockers flanking a double bed draped in a pink bedspread featuring tiny white daisies.

'She liked pink,' she murmured, her eyes absorbing every detail.

'Yes, for a time. She selected the paint colour herself. I made the bedspread and curtains from fabric we purchased in Gillingham's store.'

Mama Lulu sat on the bed and patted it, indicating that Vega should join her. 'I find it difficult to understand how Cassie could have abandoned you.' Her voice was tight, as if the words struggled to escape. 'This was a happy home. She was loved here. And I hope she would agree that she had a good childhood. I would have taken you if she couldn't care for you and little Nova. All she had to do was ask.' A tear escaped Mama Lulu's watery eyes and trailed down her cheek.

Vega caught a sob in her throat, her gaze shifting to the bedroom window as she noticed the tall tree with the swing outside. 'I would have liked to live here.'

They sat silently for a moment, and Vega imagined a sliding-doors world where this bedroom had been hers and Nova's.

'She was never the same after Mitchell died,' Mama Lulu remarked. 'Cassie was a daddy's girl. From her first moments in this world, she only had eyes for him.'

'Did that upset you?'

'No! It was a pleasure watching them together. And I had Flick. She was a proper mama's girl, through and through.'

'So when Mitchell passed away, Mum took it quite hard?' Vega enquired.

Mama Lulu closed her eyes for a moment, immersed in her memories. 'Yes. It was a challenging time for the family. He left us too soon. We all found it difficult to come to terms with our loss.'

'I'm sorry you went through that.'

She patted Vega's hand. 'You've had your share of pain, too. I can see it in your face, especially when you talk about your mother. The way I see it, we carry our grief like pebbles, each weighing differently from day to day. Some days, the pebbles are so heavy that they drag us down.'

Vega swallowed hard as her throat constricted.

Mama Lulu took her hand and kissed it gently. 'I couldn't see it at the time, but your mother was drowning, and those pebbles prevented her from clawing her way back to the surface.' She sighed deeply. 'If I'd noticed, maybe she would never have left us.'

Vega brushed away a tear from her cheek as she asked tremulously, 'Is that why Mum left? Because she was grieving?'

Mama Lulu shrugged. 'Partly. She started skipping school and mingling with the wrong crowd. She'd take off for days on end, to goodness knows where. She got involved with Frankie Chalupka, with whom trouble always seemed to find its way.' She sighed deeply. 'It was a trying time.'

'What sort of trouble?'

'Do you know anything about the Vietnam War?'

Vega made a face, 'Only what we learned in school and what I've seen in films.'

'Cassie became obsessed with the war, passionately angry about the senseless loss of life. President Nixon had authorised the US to invade Cambodia to combat the Viet Cong, and protests naturally intensified against the expansion of the US war effort. Cassie, Frankie and many other students across America were outraged, and initiated a nationwide anti-war strike.'

'I read about that! Didn't the troops fire live rounds into the crowds?'

'Yes. It all came to a head in May 1970 when the National Guard shot and killed four students during a protest at Kent State University. Two of those students hadn't even participated in the demonstration. It was an incredibly shocking time for our country.' Mama Lulu shuddered as she recalled the tragedy.

'That's dreadful,' Vega said, shaking her head, trying to imagine her mother grappling with this as a young teen.

Mama Lulu nodded sadly. 'After the incident at Kent State, students intensified their actions. There was a generational divide in the country – some people sympathised with the students, but many others felt their protests attacked America and the brave men and women fighting for us. This divide was present in our house too; Cassie found me and Flick lacking somehow.'

'That sounds like a tricky time for you all.'

'I didn't sleep much back then. I was also trying to keep the farm running without Mitchell. It was a challenge to be accepted as the head of the business. I had to fight to earn people's respect. It's another regret of mine. I ought to have paid more attention to Cassie and the reasons behind her rants about the war.'

'There's a lot of clarity in hindsight,' Vega said sympathetically.

'Perhaps. A few days after the Kent State tragedy, Cassie told me she was going to Washington to protest. Over a hundred thousand people attended, and they were filled with anger. She returned a changed person. That trip was when I truly lost my daughter. Although she stayed in this house for several months, she was rarely present. She and Flick argued constantly. She displayed little regard for me. It was difficult.'

Vega shivered as Mama Lulu vividly portrayed her mother as angry and passionate. But she also felt pride that Cassie had principles and was willing to fight for them.

'I get the sense that my mother and Flick were not especially close,' she said tentatively.

Mama Lulu sighed. 'By the time Cassie left, that's true. But it wasn't always like that. Growing up, they were like two peas in a pod – always together, whispering, conspiring, laughing and playing. You couldn't find two closer sisters. However, they fell out about a year before Cassie left. I've never been privy to the details. I know it has cost Flick dearly that she didn't get to say goodbye to Cassie.'

Vega tried to determine the possible timeline for her mother leaving the farm. 'So she left home at some point in 1970?'

Mama Lulu nodded. 'She finished high school with barely enough credits to graduate. It felt like a waste, because she was a bright child – brains to burn. We argued often that summer about what she should do next. I wanted her to attend university and then come and work on the farm. However, she had no interest in pursuing further education and even less in living here.'

'And was her boyfriend, Frankie, still around?'

'Absolutely. When Cassie was here, so was he. A few weeks after her graduation, she announced that she was leaving. She said I suffocated her, that I represented the authoritarianism she refused to conform to. I pleaded with her to reconsider, but she declined.' Mama Lulu closed her eyes for a moment. 'August the twenty-first 1970. That was the last time I saw her.'

'Did she say where she was going?'

A shadow crossed Mama Lulu's face. 'No. She wouldn't provide me with an address. And there were neither mobile phones nor social media to keep track of people. She vanished.'

'And you haven't seen her since.'

'Other than in my dreams, no. She sent us several postcards over the years, and I still have them all. I'd be happy for you to have a look at them. They stopped in 1983.'

Vega did the mental maths. Eight years before she was born.

'What about Frankie? Do you think they might still be together?'

'I haven't a clue. I haven't seen him since he left Woodstock with Cassie in 1970. Flick and I called his family home several times to ask if they knew where he was. They either didn't care or didn't know, but they couldn't provide us with further information.'

Vega observed the lines deepening on Mama Lulu's face. She realised that she was not merely searching for her sister and mother; she was also seeking answers for her grandmother, who was desperate to find her daughter.

However, she now had a new question to ponder.

Was Frankie Chalupka her father?

She knew her next step would be to locate him and ask.

16

Vega followed Route 100 out of Woodstock, driving through the Mad River Valley towards Warren. Luka searched for the small dirt road Flick had described the day before, which would lead them to Frankie's family home.

'There!' he shouted, pointing at an abandoned rusty tractor that served as their marker.

Vega signalled left and gradually reduced speed as she navigated the narrow lane. The surface was coated with damp leaves, causing the car to struggle for traction. It jolted and trembled as it rolled over a hidden pothole masked by the fallen foliage.

'It's lovely out here, but we may need a four-wheel drive to continue on this road.' Luka said, his brow creased in a worried frown.

'We should park over there and walk the rest of the way,' Vega suggested, noticing a field gate on the right-hand side.

With Luka's nod of approval, she pulled the car over and unfastened her seatbelt. Reaching for her handbag on the seat behind her, she retrieved a small bundle of postcards secured with a sturdy brown elastic band. She snapped the band off and examined the cards Mama Lulu had given her the previous day.

'You really ought to know them by heart by now,' Luka said gently. Since their return to the hotel room the previous evening, Vega had read each one repeatedly.

'They must mean more than mere scribbles. There could be

clues within them that might help me find my mother. I need to decipher them.' She sighed in frustration. Each of the five cards contained no more than a few lines scrawled in the same distinctive cursive writing.

October 1970

Hello, Mama. I hope all is well with you and Flick. Frankie and I have found a beautiful place to live. It's on a farm, but very different from Red Maple Farm. I know you must be worried, but please don't be. I've never been happier. I'm in love, and it's the most wonderful feeling in the world. Here we can be the people we are supposed to be – free and peaceful, with like-minded friends who feel like family too.

Love, Cassie

December 1970

Hi, Mama. I'm thinking of you today and wondering if you have put the Christmas decorations up yet. Yesterday I made puddings, ready for Christmas Day! Life is idyllic here. I wake up each morning smiling, looking forward to a new day. It's a different way of life from ours at Red Maple Farm. Here we live as a cooperative, sharing our lives and ideas in a way I never could have if I had stayed home in Woodstock. I'm leading a life filled with love and understanding alongside Frankie and our many friends. I'm closest to Martha, who is teaching me how to knit and sew. I'm wearing a sweater I made myself. I hope you're pleased for me. Give Flick my love.

Love, Cassie

September 1972

Hello, Mama. I know it's been a while since I've been in touch. I'm sorry, I hope you've not been worried, but life is busy here. We have so much to do daily; time passes too quickly for me to think about letters. Frankie and I fall into bed every night exhausted! However, I often think of you and Flick selling pies and syrups in

the barn! Well guess what, together with Martha, I have a regular stall at a local market where we sell baked goods, candles and, of course, our maple syrup too. You taught me well! Please say hello to Flick for me.
   Love, Cassie

April 1975
   Hello, Mama. Well, there's been a lot of change since I last wrote. The owner of the farm decided to sell it, so we moved to a new commune. It's larger, with almost fifty of us in total. Last week, a former nun arrived who shares our philosophies: that we can live a life rooted in Christian principles without the suffocating constraints of the Church. Would you believe I haven't watched television or listened to the radio since I left Woodstock? It's so liberating to embrace a life unburdened by frivolity and the deceit propagated by our government. I choose peace. I choose love. I choose myself.
   Love, Cassie

December 1983
   Hello, Mama. The mountain is covered in snow, and the stove is lit twenty-four hours a day to keep the farmhouse warm. I hope you and Flick are well. I feel like one of the pioneers we learned about in school, in new settlements, making a better life for everyone. We have ten children on the farm now, the youngest of whom is only ten days old. Martha has two boys, and I adore them both! I haven't made you a grandmother yet, but I know it will happen one day. I am sure I will be a mother and long for that day. This will be my last letter, but you mustn't worry. I'm happy and loved. And I'm with my new family now, the one I've chosen and who have chosen me. I know it's hard to understand, but I've learned I must leave behind my family ties and all the boxes society tries to put us in. I am reborn. Know that I'm happy.
   Love, Cassie

'It's interesting, that last line. Her insistence that she's happy. Do you believe her?' Luka asked. Vega looked at him questioningly, and he continued, 'It's just she repeats that several times throughout the postcards, doesn't she?'

'Perhaps the lady doth protest too much,' Vega replied, shrugging her shoulders. 'There's a change in her tone from the beginning to the end, too.'

'Yep. And she was careful not to mention where this farm was, either,' Luka remarked, examining the postmark more closely. 'She also used pre-cancelled stamps. I wonder if it was clever or just chance. I looked them up last night; they're available through postage machines and don't require a postmark. So she could have been anywhere in America.'

'I'd wager it's deliberate, given that she never mentions her whereabouts in any of the postcards. Mama Lulu said that she never phoned her either. She didn't want to be found.' Vega bit her bottom lip and frowned. It was a bitter pill to swallow to discover that her mother had form when it came to disappearing without a trace. Perhaps there was no grand mystery about where she went in 1995. She simply chose to move on, as she had done when she was eighteen years old.

Luka watched her closely. 'I can only imagine where your mind is going. But what if your mother wasn't allowed to inform Mama Lulu of her whereabouts back then.'

'Do you reckon this Frankie could have pressured her to keep her distance?'

'Maybe,' Luka answered as Vega replaced the band around the postcards and returned them to her bag. She then took out another photograph that Mama Lulu had given her. This one was taken on the swing in the yard, with Cassie sitting on Frankie's lap, his arms wrapped around her. Both were smiling for the camera, a moment of joy captured.

'She looks so happy,' Vega said. 'They *were* in love at that time. You can see it shining through this photograph.'

Luka murmured his assent.

'It's mad to think that he could be my father,' she went on, scanning the photograph for similarities between Frankie's face and hers.

'You might have found two new families in two days,' Luka said, nodding towards the Chalupka homestead.

Vega felt somewhat light-headed just contemplating it. She reached over and squeezed his hand, then grabbed their jackets from the back seat. 'It's time to meet Frankie's father and see if he knows where his son is now. Mama Lulu said his mother has already passed.'

The ground was wet underfoot, and when they arrived at the Chalupka farm, Vega's boots and Luka's trainers were stained with mud. A dog barked, signalling their arrival in the small yard. It was cluttered with old machinery parts, rusty and forgotten, and two cars, one with the bonnet raised. Weeds filled every available nook and cranny on the ground and along the steps leading to the small wooden house.

Vega and Luka approached the front door warily, keeping an eye out for the dog, which kept barking. Vega rapped on the front door. No answer. She rapped harder, which only increased the dog's fury.

'Bloody dok,' an accented voice bellowed from inside. 'Shut up!' The animal complied, whimpering into silence, and then a man appeared at the door, dishevelled, wearing a dirty Van Halen T-shirt and joggers hanging low over his protruding belly. 'What do you want?' he asked, shooting daggers at them both from beneath heavy eyebrows.

'Mr Chalupka?' Vega asked.

'What's it to you?'

'I'm searching for your son, Frankie. I was wondering if you had a forwarding address for him.'

Anger flickered across the man's face. 'He's not here. And that's a good thing for him.'

Vega didn't need to use much imagination to speculate on the fate that might befall Frankie if his father were to find him.

'Do you know where he is? I'm hoping to locate one of his school friends and I think they might be together,' she continued.

'His mother died, and that good-for-nothing didn't even come to the funeral. I don't know and don't care where he is.' Mr Chalupka moved to close the door in their faces.

Vega looked at Luka in desperation, and he smiled reassuringly at her before calling out, '*Czy jesteś Polakiem?*'

Mr Chalupka stopped in surprise, regarding him with interest. '*Tak.*'

'*Jestem z Lubina,*' Luka answered with a smile. He reached over to offer a handshake to the man. 'Lukasz Wilczek.'

The anger disappeared from Mr Chalupka's face, and he relaxed slightly. 'I'm Franciszek.'

Vega's eyes widened as she listened to the two men converse rapidly in Polish. Mr Chalupka glanced at her several times during the conversation, then opened the door wide and invited them in.

The house was little more than a cabin, and the interior was as bare as the exterior. Frankie's father sat in a worn-out armchair held together with duct tape. He nodded towards the sofa across from him, and they settled in.

'So, you're Cassie Kensington's daughter,' he remarked, studying Vega intently.

Vega nodded. 'I'm trying to locate her and my younger sister, Nova. I was hoping your son might provide some insight into their whereabouts.'

Mr Chalupka growled and shook his head. 'I told you, I don't know where that boy is.'

Vega cleared her throat and decided this was not the time to be coy. 'I think there is a strong possibility that Frankie might be my father. I want to ask him if he is.'

The air in the room grew thick, and they sat in silence as the older man absorbed the news.

'I don't suppose you would want to be related to me.' He

frowned as he glanced around the room. Before Vega could respond, he continued, 'It didn't always look this way. When my wife was alive, it was spotless. But after she died . . .' He shrugged helplessly.

'I'm a bit messy at home as well,' Vega lied, sensing the man's embarrassment. However, he didn't appear to hear her.

'My parents came here from Lubina in 1948, after the Second World War. Their families all perished in German concentration camps. Yet somehow Mama and Tata survived. They believed life would be kinder here.' He made a tutting sound. 'My father was a farm labourer; my mother worked in a factory. Like my father, I toiled as well. For what? To provide our children with a better life.' Once more he tutted, then cursed under his breath. 'Two sons were lost in Vietnam. And the third is in prison. Or at least he was, the last I heard. He could be out by now, I suppose.'

'I'm sorry,' Luka said, his face etched with sympathy as Vega swallowed a lump in her throat, overwhelmed by another surge of emotion. 'Which prison is he in?'

'Monroe Correctional Complex, in Washington.'

Vega jotted a note in her small notebook. Her mind raced with possibilities as to what crime Frankie had committed. Gulping nervously, she asked, 'What did he do to end up there?'

'He was caught drink driving, nearly killing a child when he crashed into a family out for a walk.' Mr Chalupka's lips trembled, and it seemed he was on the verge of tears for a moment. But then he composed himself. 'If you locate him, tell him he's not welcome here. He broke his mother's heart. He broke my heart. Now please leave. I have things to attend to.' He stood up and moved towards the front door to see them out.

'*Będę. Dziękuję*,' Luka replied. 'We'll leave you in peace.'

As Vega passed him in the doorway, Mr Chalupka seized her arm. 'If my boy is your father, you keep away from him. Don't let him pull you down. He's nothing but trouble. Do you hear me?'

The hairs on the back of Vega's neck stood up. 'Thank you

for speaking with us today, Mr Chalupka. I hope you find some peace in life. I'm sorry for all you have endured.'

With one final nod, he closed the door behind them, leaving a shell-shocked Vega standing beside Luka.

'You okay?'

'I will be. But that was a lot to take in.'

'It is.' He reached for her hand, and she clasped it gratefully as they started walking back towards the car.

'How did you know he was Polish?' Vega asked.

'At first I thought he was Slovakian, considering that surname. However, once he began to speak, I realised he was from my mother's homeland. His accent is so similar to hers. I've tried – without success – to get her to stop calling dogs "doks". As soon as I heard that . . .'

'He wouldn't have spoken to me if you hadn't been there,' Vega acknowledged.

Luka smiled. 'Oh, you'd have found a way.'

'I felt sorry for him.' She glanced back towards the house. 'What a way to live.'

'His family has had it tough. To end up on your own . . . it's sad.'

They reached the car and got in, prepared to return to Woodstock.

'I just had a thought. If you *are* a Chalupka, you'll be half Polish, like me,' Luka said with a grin.

'That wasn't on my bingo card today, but I can think of worse things,' Vega replied, grinning back. She took out her phone and launched Apple Maps. 'Looks like the next stop is Washington. It's about fifty miles from Woodstock. Assuming I can obtain a visitor's pass from the prison, fancy a road trip tomorrow?' She felt a surge of adrenaline wash over her. 'We're getting closer. I can feel it.'

17

'Not sure how we managed to do anything before the internet,' Vega murmured as they approached the entrance of a dilapidated red-brick building – the Black Horse Tavern.

'Come to New England, she said. Visit charming and quaint new buildings, she said,' Luka teased as they both looked at the pub before them.

'I'm sure this isn't the sort of place you imagined enjoying for our holiday.' She nodded ruefully as the acrid reek of stale urine and cannabis smoke assaulted them. 'I'm sorry.'

'Finding Frankie is all that matters,' Luka said, dismissing her apologies.

Vega vowed to herself that she would make it up to him later, and she had plans in motion for that. Luka didn't know that she had made a reservation at the restaurant in their hotel in Woodstock for later that evening. She would do her best not to monopolise the conversation with her lost family, opting instead to talk to Luka about him, his work and his own family.

However, for the time being, they had a task to complete.

Vega had never considered herself lucky, but she had to admit that she had fortune on her side when locating Frankie. First she'd discovered a public online database detailing the status of prison inmates. Frankie's unusual surname coupled with confirmation that he had been convicted of a felony DUI convinced her that they had the right man. Since it was his fourth DUI, and given the severe injuries the child had sustained due to his impaired driving, he had been sentenced to five years.

Her second piece of luck was that he had been released six

months earlier. This meant she didn't have to organise a prison visit, which he might or might not have agreed to. After making several phone calls, Luka had uncovered details of an association that accommodated recently released inmates. They decided to start there, and visited it as soon as they arrived in Washington earlier this morning, where their lucky streak continued. A staff member confirmed that Frankie had been a resident but had left the facility once his electronic home detention ended.

The trail could have gone cold had it not been for a suggestion from a fellow inmate who had overheard Vega's questions. Luck was given a helping hand, and for the sum of fifty dollars, the Black Horse Tavern was revealed as the likely spot to find Frankie.

Vega zipped up her biker jacket and glanced at Luka. She realised that maybe the start of her lucky streak was when she had met him last New Year's Eve. 'Thanks, by the way.'

'You're welcome. But for what?'

'Being here. Helping me without question. Honestly, I don't think I would have got this far without your Polish skills. But more than that, it's really nice to have someone by my side.' She inhaled deeply. '*On* my side . . .'

'I keep telling you, I've got you.' His face darkened and his jaw clenched as he gripped her shoulders tightly. 'I've been to places like this, and finding trouble doesn't take much effort. If I give you the nod to leave, no arguments, we have to go.'

'I promise,' Vega said as she pulled open the double doors and they walked in.

A pinball machine echoed from a corner, and a large pool table stood in the centre of the room. Two women in low-cut tops played while a couple of men observed appreciatively. The room was dimly lit, with booths lining either side, past a long veneer bar.

They took a bar seat, and Vega ordered two beers from the stocky bartender. Condensation dripped down the sides of the glasses onto already sodden, misshapen beer mats. Her eyes darted around the room, but it was too dark to distinguish anyone who wasn't nearby.

'I'm searching for a friend of my mother's,' she said to the barman. 'A man from Vermont known as Frankie Chalupka. I've heard he hangs out here.'

The barman leaned in, looking her up and down. 'You the law?'

She held her hands up. 'Irish. Visiting and trying to look up old family friends. That's all.'

He wiped the counter with a grimy cloth, his eyes shifting to a booth in the corner. 'He's over there.'

'Thanks.' Vega flashed him a smile. She had hardly dared to believe that she would find Frankie here. It felt too easy. But maybe after a lifetime of difficult, the universe was throwing her a bone.

Her stomach flipped and churned as she strolled towards the booth with more confidence than she truly felt. She was grateful that Luka was close behind her. The man she was about to meet had known her mother, had once loved her, and perhaps held the key to the locked door that kept Cassie hidden.

Vega shuddered as a new memory overwhelmed her.

She was sitting between her mother's legs as Cassie combed her long, dark hair into two plaits, kissing her forehead as she declared her perfect.

She reached up and touched her forehead in wonder.

Perfect.

Whatever her childhood might have been, that memory had been a happy one at least. She'd remembered love. She was sure of it.

Luka touched her arm lightly, bringing her back to stark reality. She glanced to her right and saw a man lounging on a ripped leatherette seat valiantly held together with duct tape. His long, thinning grey hair and a face aged beyond its years made it difficult to recognise him as the young man who had left Vermont over fifty years earlier. But Vega had studied every detail of his features in the photograph, and while much had changed, the dark, brooding eyes remained the same. It was Frankie for sure.

She gazed at the duct tape holding the seat together and thought of Frankie's father back in Vermont, who sat in a chair in a similar state. Did she herself unknowingly reflect her mother's life at times as well? A lump rose in her throat, and she swallowed it down.

There wasn't time for emotion, not now.

Frankie glanced at them with little interest. He picked up a glass containing whiskey or bourbon from an oak table, its woodwork scratched with names and initials. Vega slid into the booth opposite him and Luka settled beside her. She discreetly pressed record on her mobile phone to ensure she didn't miss any vital information.

'You're Frankie Chalupka,' she stated.

'What's it to you?' His voice was cold but clear, and he seemed coherent.

'I'd just like to talk. About an old friend of yours.' She smiled, hoping to win him over. His dark eyes absorbed her presence, but he did not reciprocate the smile.

He downed his whiskey in one go, and then said with a sly grin, 'If you want to speak to me, you'll need to buy me a drink.'

'Happy to,' Vega replied, shuddering at the thought of her mother and this man ever being intimate. A stench of stale body odour and alcohol assaulted her nostrils, and she covered her nose with one hand.

'Send over a bottle of bourbon,' Frankie called to the barman. 'And this one's paying.'

They sat in silence until the bottle arrived. Vega passed the barman fifty dollars, while Luka poured Frankie a drink.

'Leave it open,' Frankie instructed as Luka reached to replace the cap on the bottle. He downed his drink in an eager gulp, then nodded at Luka to refill it for him. 'All right, now you have my attention. What do you want?'

'Your father mentioned that you were in Washington,' Vega explained.

'So my old man is still alive?' Frankie asked, raising an eyebrow.

'He's not in good health, but he's alive,' Luka replied evenly.

'Even hell won't take that old bastard.' Frankie's eyes flared with anger as he spoke. He took another long swig.

'You're not close to your father?' Vega asked, attempting to connect with him. She needed Frankie to share with her.

'Too close, some might say,' he replied archly. 'My old man used me as his punching bag until I grew big and wise enough to hit him back. Then I wised up even more and decided to get out of Dodge.'

Vega felt sadness wash over her, and her heart softened towards Frankie. He seemed to have endured a difficult life, and she, more than anyone, understood that.

'It sounds like you had a tough time at home. I wanted to discuss your departure from Woodstock. When you left, Cassie Kensington was with you.'

'Cassie?' A shadow crossed Frankie's face. Regret? Or could it be something else? He observed Vega intently, his eyes absorbing every detail of her. 'Yes, we left together. Cassie and I were happy. She was a good girl, always singing.' His grim scowl gave way to a rare smile, much like the one she'd seen in the photograph of him on the swing at Mama Lulu's. He'd loved Cassie then, and if she were to hazard a guess, he still loved her now.

Then her mind seized upon his last remark, and she mentally noted yet another of her mother's traits. Flick and Mama Lulu had never mentioned singing, but this detail felt right to her. And suddenly, volume was added to her earlier memory of her mother plaiting her hair. She could hear Cassie singing softly as her hands deftly wove Vega's heavy braid.

'She had a dreadful voice, mind you,' Frankie continued, erupting into laughter, followed by a loud belch. 'But that never fazed her. She was fearless, Cassie Kensington.'

Vega felt a wave of pride surge within her. She relaxed on the battered bench, now enjoying the conversation. 'Where did the two of you go after leaving Woodstock?'

'We'd met some people during a protest in Washington who lived in a commune. They mentioned that we were welcome to join them at any time. So that's where we decided to go.'

'Why did Cassie leave? You said you didn't see eye to eye with your father. What about Cassie? Did she find it difficult at home?' Vega dug her fingernails into her palms as she awaited a response. She needed Mama Lulu's hands to be clean amidst the mystery surrounding her mother. Until this week, she had been alone without any family. Now that she had met her grandmother and aunt, she fervently wanted to learn more about them.

Frankie sighed. 'Cassie was a free spirit. She felt caged in at home. Every day she would leave that farmhouse wearing a twinset, and by the time she reached school she'd replaced it with a tight tank top that made all of us boys half crazy. She knew that if she stayed at the farm, they'd try to change her, and she wasn't for changing.'

'So Mama Lulu was strict? Cassie rebelled against that?'

'Mama Lulu wanted her to conform. To do as all good little Americans were supposed to do: get a job, get married, buy a house with a white picket fence and have two point two children.'

'And what did Cassie want?' Vega asked softly.

'After her dad died, she wanted out.' His fingers drummed the table in front of him. 'I had to leave. My old man was going to kill me if I didn't get to him first. But it wasn't the same for Cassie. She sacrificed a lot to go. And I'm not that much of an ass that I didn't realise that. I told her before we left Woodstock that she had it good at home and was mad to leave it all behind.' His eyes crinkled at the corners as he chuckled to himself. 'She said she preferred spicy to sweet. God, that woman could make me laugh.'

Vega exhaled, relief making her shoulders sag. Cassie hadn't left because of any great trauma at home. It was normal teenage rebellion stuff. She felt Luka's gaze upon her and knew he understood. And a thought slammed her, that perhaps she wasn't as alone as she believed, regardless of her new family in Vermont.

'Where was the commune?' she asked, redirecting her attention to Frankie.

'A few miles outside Rochester. Fifteen others were already there when we arrived, sharing one large farmhouse. They were mostly students and graduates, long-haired hippies. All of them were as angry with Nixon and his bullshit Vietnam War as we were.'

'Was Cassie anti-war as well?' Luka asked.

'Passionately so,' Frankie said, taking another drink. 'That was how she rolled. All or nothing.' He reached up to touch his hair and sighed. 'We were a sight to behold back then, all of us with our long, flowing locks. That was our uniform. If you saw someone who'd given up going to the barber's, you could be fairly certain they shared the same beliefs as you.'

'So if long hair despised the government, what did short hair signify?' Luka asked.

'Conformity. Conservative beliefs.'

'That's why you never cut your hair to this day.'

'No. And I never will. It's my final act of defiance in good conscience.'

Vega couldn't help but grin at Frankie's words. And she felt a twinge of respect ripple through her for this man who refused to change who he was. 'Were you happy in that commune?'

Frankie's jaw clenched, and he angrily grabbed the bourbon bottle, splashing liquid onto the table as he topped up his glass.

'The happiest time of my life.' His expression shifted, and he frowned. 'But nothing good ever lasts. Not for me, at any rate.'

Vega exchanged a glance with Luka, and her heart rate quickened. It was evident that Frankie held more of the missing pieces that she needed to complete the puzzle, and the answers were tantalisingly close. 'I'm sorry to hear that. What changed?'

Frankie's finger traced the rim of the tumbler, and his eyes took on a glassy sheen. 'Cassie threw herself into life there. She became quite the little homemaker, learning to cook and sew. She also taught the students how to harvest maple. I worked the land, labouring as my ancestors had for generations. It felt good. We grew crops and kept chickens, along with a couple of cows. I had a best friend. Johnny Fallow. A Texas guy who wore a cowboy hat every day of his life. Voice like Dylan. Sang most nights around the fire pit. Never forgot that voice.' His face took on a dreamy, faraway look as he reminisced. 'We had nothing, yet we had everything. We lived in harmony. Everyone contributed willingly. No rules were necessary; when something was needed, it got done.'

'Sounds pretty cool,' Luka said.

'It was. I'd never experienced that kind of peace at home.' Frankie averted his gaze as he recalled his childhood. 'We were poor. We lived from one pay check to the next. Even though my parents weren't the type to express their love every day, I knew they cared. But everything changed when my brothers were killed in that godforsaken war.' Tears shimmered in his eyes, and his voice trembled. 'Killed in action. Both of them. Neither of them had even reached their twenty-first birthday.'

'That's horrific,' Vega said, feeling a twinge of understanding for the man before her, and his father, isolated in his cabin. 'I'm so sorry.'

He acknowledged her words with a curt nod. 'My mother never recovered. She locked herself away in her bedroom while my old man took his grief out on me. I had no choice but to leave. And living with Cassie on that farm, well, it was as close to heaven as I'll ever get. We had food on the table, great company, and love.' A tear rolled down his cheek, and he wiped it away roughly with his hand.

His eyes met Vega's, and he gazed at her so intensely that she had to summon all her willpower not to look away.

'So where is Cassie now?' he asked quietly.

Vega's eyes widened in surprise at the question, and her heart sank at what this implied. Frankie didn't know where her mother was either.

He raised his glass to her and spoke in a voice so soft it was nearly a whisper. 'I'd wager this drink that you're her daughter.'

All Vega could manage was a mute nod.

Frankie leaned in closer. 'You're just like her. You've got her eyes. Her nose. I didn't notice it at first when you sat down. But when you said you were sorry, you made this face. It was as if she were right in front of me. Because that's the last thing she ever said to me.' He paused for a moment, then mimicked Cassie's voice as he said, 'I'm sorry, Frankie.'

Vega's heart raced and she leaned across the table, grasping his arm. 'I don't know where my mother is, Frankie, but I came here hoping you could tell me where to find her.'

He shrugged her hand away. 'You've had a wasted journey. I can't help you with that.'

She closed her eyes for a moment and inhaled deeply. Her stomach flipped in disappointment, but also in dread-filled hope.

Because she had another question to pose to Frankie, one that terrified and excited her equally and that had been looping in her mind since she'd discovered his relationship with Cassie.

Taking a steadying breath, she said, 'Okay, you don't know where Mum is. But I'm also looking for my dad.' She leaned across the table again. 'Are you my father?'

18

The air felt heavy as Vega awaited Frankie's answer. His expression was inscrutable as he regarded her from beneath hooded eyes. Was he her kin? Did they share the same DNA coursing through their veins?

'The last time I saw Cassie was in 1975,' he replied with a sigh. 'So unless you have an elixir of youth, I'm not your father.'

Vega's stomach fluttered, leaving her confused. Was she disappointed? She realised that she was – at least a little. She glanced at Luka, who grimaced in sympathy.

'Be grateful I'm not your dad. As my old man no doubt informed you, I'm trouble.'

'I'm not convinced. You may have made poor choices, but that doesn't make you a bad person,' Vega replied calmly.

He looked up in surprise. 'I'm not certain many would agree, but thank you.'

'Is there anything else you can tell us that might help us find Cassie?'

'To begin with, the last time I saw her, she wasn't calling herself Cassie, so you'll need to alter who you're searching for.'

'What do you mean?' Vega asked, her eyes wide.

'She changed over the last couple of months. And I don't mean just her personality. By the time I left, she was going by the name Star.'

'That's what she was called when I was with her,' Vega replied. 'But I didn't know when she changed her name.'

Frankie sat in silence for over five minutes, steadily drinking his way through the bottle of bourbon. Vega worried that if he kept this up, he'd pass out before they obtained any further information.

'You want some food maybe?' she suggested hopefully.

He shrugged.

Luka grabbed the menu off the table and went to the bar to sort out some soakage.

Vega decided it was time to lay everything on the table between them. 'I haven't seen my mother since I was four, when she disappeared as if into thin air. I spent my entire childhood waiting for her to return. I just want to know where she is, what happened to her and why she left me.' She paused, aware that she was speaking in a rush. 'That's why this is so important to me. I need your help, Frankie. And if that means I have to buy you another bottle of bourbon, I'll gladly do so. But before you drink yourself into oblivion, I would be very grateful if you could tell me everything you know about her.'

Frankie looked up from his glass and shook his head slowly. 'Well, I take no pleasure in saying this to you, but my best guess is that Cassie is dead,' he replied, his words now slurring slightly. 'Because there's no way she would ever leave her kid. Not by choice, anyhow.'

Vega shivered as his words struck her. It felt as if someone had doused her with a bucket of icy water. Ever since she was a little girl, whenever sleep eluded her, she'd allowed her mind to escape to a place where her mother was no longer alive. But here in this dark and dingy bar, she could not permit herself to think that way, and every fibre of her being recoiled from Frankie's assertion. She had to hold on to the hope that her mother was out there, waiting for Vega to find her, to save her and to reunite their family.

'Why do you think she would never leave me of her own accord?' she asked, probing further.

'There were children at the commune, and everyone pitched in. Cassie and me included. It takes a village and all . . . She was a natural with the little ones.' He closed his eyes briefly. 'There was this one baby who would cry all day and all night unless Cassie held him in her arms. She had the touch. She was desperate to have children. We hoped she'd fall pregnant. But it never happened. Not with me, anyway.'

Luka returned and gave Vega a quick thumbs-up, which she interpreted as a signal that food was coming.

'When I think of Mum, I remember love,' she said. 'I don't believe she would have left my sister and me unless she had no choice. But I can't accept that she's dead. I can't . . .' she finished in a whisper.

The barman came over and placed a plate before Frankie. 'Today's special is fried chicken with fries. Enjoy.'

Frankie looked at the food with disinterest, then took another swig of his drink.

'I have a few postcards that Mum wrote to my grandmother. She passed them on to me this week,' Vega said.

Frankie whistled softly. 'Mama Lulu. I haven't thought about her for a long time. So she's still alive, then?'

'Alive and very well. In one of the postcards, Mum mentioned that she had become good friends with a woman with two children. Her name was Martha.'

'They were as close as sisters, those two. Martha Long – I haven't thought about her in a long time either. I didn't even know she'd had children. Martha was the one who invited Cassie and me to join the commune in the first place. She was at that protest we went to in Washington.'

'Do you have any contact details for her?' Vega asked hopefully. Frankie's derisive snort answered that.

'I often wonder what might have happened if we'd stayed in Woodstock or Rochester instead of moving on. Perhaps then we'd still be together.' He sighed and grimaced in pain before scooping up a handful of fries and stuffing them into his mouth.

'Mum mentioned you in the postcards as well. She said she loved you and you were happy together,' Vega said kindly.

A flush crept over Frankie's face, and his eyes blurred once more. 'I've never loved another woman like I loved Cassie. But I don't know if she ever really loved me.' The steel returned to his clenched jaw, and anger replaced sorrow.

'What happened between the two of you?' Luka asked.

'It all went wrong after we left the first commune.'

'That must have been around 1974, right?' Vega asked, thinking of the timeline in the postcards.

Frankie nodded. 'We found a new commune in Island Pond.'

'Where's that?' Luka asked.

'The Northeast Kingdom, in Vermont. The middle of nowhere.'

Vega felt a flutter in her stomach at the term that seemed to haunt her wherever she went. What was it with her mother and living off the grid?

Frankie continued. 'This farm was far larger than the first one. Over eighty acres. Owned by some poor little rich boy who'd left university after his parents died in a car accident. His loss, our gain, I suppose.'

Vega winced at his callous tone. She bit her lip to prevent herself from commenting. 'What was his name?'

'Look, I can't recall much from back then. But he wasn't in charge anyway.' He lifted his glass and took a hefty gulp of bourbon. 'A right pain in my ass held that honour – someone who went by the name Apollo.' He rolled his eyes.

'You remember *his* name,' Luka remarked.

Frankie laughed. 'Hard to forget that one for sure. The name alone should have had us all running for the hills. From the get-go, things were different on this farm than we were used to.'

'In what way?' Vega asked.

'We never had a leader in Rochester; it was a genuine cooperative. Everyone worked together and got the job done without any nonsense. But in this place, it was Apollo's way or the highway. He got a kick out of assigning roles to us all. Lording it over us like we were his minions.' He leaned in towards Vega. 'Funny thing, he never seemed to get his hands dirty.'

She was beginning to understand what this Apollo guy was like. She'd met people like him many times in her life.

Frankie refilled his glass, gazing mournfully at the bottle, which was now half empty. 'That dude had some weird ideas. He decided we should all leave our former lives behind, cutting ties to our families. That way, we could be reborn into this new family.'

'Sounds more like a cult than a commune,' Vega said, frowning.

'Yeah. I reckon it was heading that way.' Frankie waved a shaky hand in her direction. 'I tried to talk about it with Cassie, but she seemed to lap up every word he said. All of a sudden, it was Apollo says this, Apollo says that.'

'What about Martha? Did she feel the same way?'

'If she had a problem with him, she certainly wasn't expressing it to me. One evening, Apollo noticed the birthmark on Cassie's wrist and became excited, claiming that she had been sent to him from the gods. He reckoned they talked to him when he was high.'

'The star birthmark,' Vega whispered.

'That's right. Next thing I know, there's a group baptism organised in the creek at the back of the farmhouse. Cassie was to be renamed Star, and would formally renounce her family, promising never to contact them again.'

Vega shivered, even though it was warm in the bar. Frankie painted a vivid picture, and it was a chilling one.

'And she wasn't worried or upset about turning her back on her life in Woodstock?' Luka asked, frowning. 'I mean, that was a big statement to make.'

'She claimed she'd never been more certain of anything. Apollo had brainwashed her. So I confronted him about his bullshit. I couldn't just stand by and allow him to get away with it any longer.'

'How did he take that?' Vega asked.

Frankie smiled sadly. 'Well, he got rid of me. So if I had to guess, I'd say he wasn't best pleased.' He took another swig and leaned towards them. 'I've been called many things in my time: good-for-nothing, a deadbeat, a drunk, a bastard.' He waved his drink about, sloshing liquid onto the table. 'But I've never been called a goddam thief.'

'What did he do to you?' Luka asked, raising his eyebrows as he glanced at Vega.

'Stitched me up good and proper. There was a communal kitty in the office – the only room with a phone. Apollo didn't lock the door, but it was made clear that no one should enter except him. I never ventured near it; I had no reason to contact anyone back home. The only person I cared about was right there with me.' He shook his head. 'Apollo announced that he was going to conduct a search. Everyone had to watch him sift through their belongings.' He smiled again, though it lacked warmth. 'I should have realised what was coming my way. He smirked at me as he approached my bed, then he lifted the mattress and discovered the money hidden beneath it.'

He reached for the bourbon again but didn't bother pouring it into a glass; instead, he took a swig straight from the bottle. 'He was gleeful as he pointed his finger at me and told me to leave, and I could never prove my innocence, nor that he'd set me up.'

'Why did he do that to you, do you think?' Luka asked.

'To get his hands on Cassie, of course,' Frankie said.

'Surely Cassie knew you wouldn't have stolen the money?' Vega felt affronted on Frankie's behalf. She felt in her gut that he was no thief.

'Her silence, her judgement hurt more than anything else. She didn't have my back. I would have had hers. No matter what any shithead said about her.' Frankie shook his head sadly. 'When she became Star, that wasn't just the end of Cassie. It was the end of us, too. She said she could never forgive me for stealing from the group. From our friends.' He snorted. 'She watched me pack up my few pitiful possessions and walk out the door. She didn't give a shit about where I was going. The very last image I had of her was with that bastard Apollo, leading her back into the house with his arm around her shoulder.'

'That's rough,' Luka said.

Frankie slumped back onto the seat, his eyelids growing heavy, almost closing. 'I'm done talking.'

Vega reached over and touched his hand. 'Thank you for sharing this with me. It's been invaluable; you've given me clues about where to look next. I appreciate it so much.' Then, on a whim, she added, 'You know, your dad isn't happy. And I know nothing excuses the way he treated you back then, but it sounds like everyone was acting out of sorts, in grief. Just a thought, but maybe you could get in touch. He might like that.'

Frankie's face softened for a moment, and he nodded. Would he make the first move with his father? She had no idea, but she hoped with all her heart that he would. Her instinct was that they needed each other but didn't know it.

He grabbed her hand as she slid along the bench, squeezing it hard. 'Be careful. If you want to find Cassie, you have to find Apollo. And he's dangerous.'

'I'll be careful, I promise,' she said, a shiver running down her back.

'Oh, and do me a favour; when you do find them, you tell them I said I'll see them in hell.' Then he picked up his whiskey and drank.

19

Extract from an interview with Johnny Callow

Vega: You were a pretty difficult person to locate. I appreciate you taking the time to speak with me.//
Johnny: I move about a lot.//
Vega: Frankie Chalupka gave me your name. He mentioned that you lived with him and my mother in a commune in Rochester during the early 1970s.//
Johnny: Frankie! He was a good guy. Hard worker. He was always the first up, out on the land, and the last in for supper.//
Vega: And do you remember Cassie Kensington?//
Johnny: Of course. Those two were love's young dream. They were so into each other that they couldn't take their eyes or hands off one another. At least, that's how I remember them.//
Vega: They broke up not long after they arrived in Island Pond.//
Johnny: That's a shame. But from what I've seen, spending a lifetime with one person is rare. That's why I've never wanted to settle down. Now and then I meet a couple who make me long for what they possess. Back then, Cassie and Frankie were one of those couples.//
Vega: Frankie told me Cassie taught everyone how to harvest maple syrup.//
Johnny: Sure did. Cassie had talent! I learned a great deal from that girl. I can still picture her gently hammering a spout into the tree and suspending a bucket underneath from a hook. For the sap to start flowing, you need the right conditions. Did you know that?

Vega: Yes. I've learned that.

Johnny: We could produce about twenty-five gallons of sap from each tree in spring. We sold it at a farmers' market. It provided us with the funds to buy marijuana.

Vega: That's a new twist on the saying 'from the farm to the table'.

Johnny: Yeah! Right on.

Vega: Why didn't you go with them when they moved to Island Pond?

Johnny: No real reason. I'd spent a few years with that crew and wanted a change. So I went west to Oregon. Frankie wanted them to accompany me, but Cassie wanted to go with Martha. They were like sisters – always together. And what Cassie wanted, Cassie got.

Vega: She was in charge?

Johnny: Oh yes. She'd tell Frankie to jump, and he'd yell 'How high?' as he kicked his legs off the ground with a stupid grin on his face.

Vega: Did you think there was an imbalance of power, then?

Johnny: No, not on that level. They were just different. Seemed to work for them.

Vega: How so?

Johnny: Frankie was a man of simple needs. He was content with a cold beer, a bit of pot, and a full belly at the end of a hard day's work. There was an honesty about him. But Cassie was ambitious. When she arrived, the farm had little income. She recognised the potential in selling our harvest at the markets. Vegetables, fruit, hand-woven items, and of course, the syrup. She handled all the negotiations and managed the finances.

Vega: And was anyone upset by that?

Johnny: Nope. She was adept at managing everything. And we witnessed the tangible results of our efforts each week. I must admit, though, I always thought Cassie would ultimately return home. She told us about the farm she grew up on. Talked lovingly about her mama.

Vega: So you don't think she's still living in a commune? Off grid?

Johnny: It's possible, I suppose. But I suspect she would have become disenchanted and yearned for more – a big house with kids, a substantial bank balance, yada yada. If I had to guess, that's where I would say she ended up.

20

Vega sensed Luka's gaze upon her as she opened her eyes.

'You're staring again,' she said, smiling goofily.

'That makes me sound like a crazy stalker!' Luka replied. 'And I'm not a stalker, at least.' He leaned in and kissed her, gently at first; then, as she responded, moving her body closer to his, his tongue darted in, sending shivers sparking through every part of her. Last night, they had taken their time, exploring each other with tantalising patience. Now, they made love quickly and fiercely.

'You do something to me, Vega Pearse,' Luka said, collapsing back onto the pillow after they pulled apart.

'Right back at you,' Vega said, laying her head on his chest. 'I wish we could stay here all day.'

He swivelled his body to face her. 'Why can't we? Go on, what have you planned for us?'

'I'm almost afraid to tell you. I bet this wasn't the holiday you envisioned.' She bit her bottom lip. 'Me pulling you in every direction, chasing leads left, right and centre.'

'Nope. It's even better – exceeding every expectation I had.'

'But you're not getting to do all those things you'd marked off in your visitor's guide,' Vega teased.

'Are you kidding me? We've experienced far more in the past few days than I ever would have had we not embarked on this quest of yours! No complaints from me, honestly.'

'Well, that's a relief. You might need to buckle up – we're off to search for a commune today!' Vega declared.

Luka laughed aloud. 'If you'd given me a hundred guesses

when I left Ireland, I wouldn't have guessed commune! But I felt it was coming our way, even though you refused to discuss it last night over dinner.'

Vega felt shy as she admitted, 'I wanted last night to be just about us. That's why I insisted we leave all talk of the Nowhere Girls alone for a few hours.'

Luka leaned in and kissed her gently on the lips. 'That was sweet of you, and I appreciated it. But you should never feel like you can't share or discuss this with me. If it's important to you, then it's important to me. And I'm here for all of it. Promise.'

'Well, it might get a bit wild since we have no option but to go to Island Pond blind. I wish Frankie had been a bit less vague about the location of the commune.'

Luka sat up and stretched. 'I've been thinking about that, as it happens. I checked out the town online yesterday, and it's only a small place. So it's logical to assume that someone must know where the commune is. Let's just rock up and poke around.'

'Yep. Sounds like a plan. Can I ask you something?' Vega enquired, leaning over to gently touch his arm. When he nodded, she said, 'You talk a lot about your mother. And it was cool to hear about your extended family in Poland. But you dodged a question about your father, which I noticed because, let's face it, I'm an expert at dodging questions. Was that because you're not close to him?'

Luka's jaw clenched. 'You know that saying, "you can't choose your family"? Well, if I'd been able to choose another dad, I would have. He wasn't a good father and was an even worse husband.'

'I'm sorry. When did your parents split up?'

'I was about ten or eleven. He got involved with one of the neighbours. There was a confrontation in the front garden between her husband and my dad. Everything escalated quite quickly after that.'

'Did you see the fight?'

Luka shut his eyes for a moment. 'Unfortunately, yes. My father nearly beat that man to death. I had witnessed his temper before, but never to that extent. The red mist came down for him, I suppose. He ended up serving time for GBH, and by the time he got out, we had moved on.'

They sat in silence for a moment. Vega felt an ache for Luka, wishing she could take away the pain that memory had stirred up.

'Where is he now?'

'Last I heard, he was in Newry. But that might have changed. He's always lived on the edges, you know?'

Vega understood. 'How are you so together?'

'I haven't always been this way. As a teenager, I was in trouble, rebelling against my mother and anyone who attempted to tell me what to do. But I copped on.'

'Yes, you did!' Vega replied, reflecting on how frequently Luka checked in on his cases in Ireland, even during the holiday. 'And you're making a difference in the lives of so many children now. They're fortunate to have you.' She inched closer and pulled him into an embrace, wrapping her arms tightly around him.

They cuddled for quite some time, feeling comfortably secure in this space, until Luka remarked, 'That's the first time you've ever initiated a cuddle with me.'

Vega protested. 'I initiate sex all the time. I seem to remember last night...'

He grinned, 'I'm not talking about that. I'm talking about intimacy. So thank you. And before you start freaking out because I'm calling you out on your odd relationship rules, I'm going to jump in the shower. If you fancy ordering breakfast, I won't complain. Starving again!'

He sauntered to the bathroom, leaving Vega's jaw dropped. She felt seen and understood in Luka's company. Moreover, she wasn't judged. She listened to him singing off-key in the shower as she rang room service, then opened her iPad and continued her Google search for communes in Vermont. There were hundreds of online articles featuring interviews and reflections from the Vermont hippies. All interesting, but none provided any clue as to where Apollo's commune was.

'What about looking for Martha Long?' Luka suggested as he emerged from the bathroom, a towel wrapped around his waist.

'Good idea. I keep getting lost while watching archive videos, holding on to the vain hope that I might glimpse my mother in one of them. No such luck.'

'We'll find her. For all we know, someone in Island Pond knows where she is.' He pulled on a T-shirt. 'Have you ever considered that she might even be there now?'

Vega shook her head. She supposed it might be possible, but it didn't sit well with her. Would Cassie be so callous as to leave her daughters in Dublin, then return to America?

She opened a new tab and typed Martha's name into Google. Quickly she discarded the first half-dozen pages, which detailed an Irish author with the same name. She then refined her search by adding location parameters specific to Vermont.

'There's a retired teacher named Martha Wallace mentioned in an article in the *Island Pond Tribune*. She appears to be about the right age.'

'That could be her married name.' Luka looked over her shoulder. 'Is she listed?'

Vega pointed to another tab with Martha's phone number and address. 'Should I ring first?'

Luka pursed his lips. 'I honestly think we ought to drive there. Looking people in the eye when asking for information is always easier than doing it over the phone. If she's still there, someone will likely point us towards Martha or your mother. And with a name like Apollo, *he* ought to be easy to find.'

They were back on the road within an hour with a plan in place. The drive to Island Pond took two and a half hours along charming tree-lined roads.

'Isn't it mad that my mother lived this close to her family for years and never once went back to Mama Lulu's to visit?' Vega remarked.

'It's strange, to say the least,' Luka agreed. 'We've met your grandmother and aunt; they're either great actors or normal, decent people. It doesn't make sense that your mother would stay away.'

'And Frankie confirmed that they treated Mum well. Yet she still severed ties with them all. That's what she said in her last postcard to Mama Lulu. It was intentional. And her wording still worries me . . .'

'I know. Was she there of her own free will?' Luka asked, echoing Vega's thoughts.

As Vega drove, Luka continued his online search on his phone and called out snippets of information.

'Island Pond is named after a six-hundred-acre pond with a twenty-two-acre island in its centre. There have been UFO sightings, numerous Bigfoot sightings, not to mention sightings of ghosts. Everything about this town feels a little eerie.'

'Ghosts?' Vega shivered. Was she about to come face to face with the ghosts of her past?

He lost mobile coverage about twenty minutes before they reached the town, and warning signs along the winding road indicated that GPS directions were unreliable.

'That's not ominous at all,' Vega grumbled.

'The ghosts mustn't like visitors knowing where they're going,' Luka said jokingly. However, Vega could see frown lines creasing across his forehead.

As the road twisted around the shores of Island Pond, with tree-covered mountain slopes ahead, she tried to imagine her mother walking along these roads. Frankie had told them they had hitch-hiked here from Rochester in 1974. However, they'd had to walk for many miles. At that moment, Vega could almost see her mother trekking along with the road, her long dark hair swinging in thick braids down her back.

'Over there!' Luka said suddenly, gesturing to his right. 'DeBanville's. It's a general store and café. It could be a good place to enquire about Martha.'

'The satnav says we're about fifteen minutes from the village. We need fuel. Might as well stop here and see what they know,' Vega replied.

They entered the wooden building once she had filled the car with petrol. It displayed several flags, including those of the Americans and Canadians, and featured stands brimming with souvenirs, arranged alongside shelves stocked with groceries, housewares and alcohol.

'Fifty dollars of gas, please,' Vega said, walking to the counter.

'Can I get you anything else?' the cashier asked with a friendly smile.

'No. That's all. This place is great.' Vega glanced around the store. 'Has it been here long?'

'Open since 1917, honey.'

'Wow. If these walls could talk!' she responded, hoping to ease her way into a gossipy chat with the woman.

'For sure. This is a check-in station for hunters, who have to report when they've killed a deer or a bear. So we get a lot passing through our doors. We're always happy to shoot the breeze with them.' She peered more closely at the two of them, 'You're not from around here.'

Vega shook her head. 'We're heading to Island Pond. My mother lived here before I was born.'

'English?' the cashier asked.

'No, Irish, though my mother was from Woodstock. I'm hoping to locate a friend of hers – a woman named Martha Long, who lives in the area. Do you know her, by any chance?'

The cashier paused for a moment, then shrugged. 'Doesn't ring a bell. But I've only been here since 2013, so I'm still getting to know people.'

'There was a commune here in the 1970s and 1980s. Do you know where that might be?'

The woman's face pinched tight as she frowned. 'There were several communes around these parts, but as I said, that was before my time. Someone in Island Pond will remember. I recall some locals discussing a commune that used to sell things here: maple syrup, jewellery, some knitted gifts – that sort of thing.'

Vega felt another chill run through her, and once again it was as if she were walking in Cassie's footsteps. 'My mother made maple syrup. That might be the commune she belonged to.'

The cashier smiled. 'Well, if that's the case, she probably spent some time here. General stores have always been informal gathering places for folk in these parts.'

'She was called Cassie Kensington, sometimes known as Star. Name ring a bell?' Luka enquired.

A shake of the head. 'No. I'm pretty sure I'd remember if I encountered someone with a name like that. Quite unusual.'

Vega nodded.

'Make your way to the public library. They'll steer you in the right direction.' The cashier frowned once more. 'I hope she wasn't involved in that dreadful affair in '84.'

Vega's hand froze as she returned her bank card to her purse. 'What happened then?'

'A commune just south of the Canadian border was raided by state troopers.'

'Why?'

'A judge had issued a search warrant to authorise the round-up of the children. Social workers took away over a hundred kids from their parents.'

'That's awful. Were they in danger?' Luka asked.

'Depends who you ask,' the woman replied with a shrug. She turned away and started tidying a shelf behind her, indicating that the conversation was over.

Vega and Luka returned to the car with even more questions. 'We need to locate this Martha,' Vega declared as they continued to Island Pond.

21

When they arrived at Island Pond, it was a bright and sunny morning. The water was still, like a glass lake, reflecting the white steeple and rustic red trees. The village was a blend of Victorian and Italianate styles. The church on the hillside stood tall and proud, nestled among the autumn foliage.

'We know that Mum was here in 1983. Therefore it's quite likely that she was present at the time of the raid. I suppose the big question is, was she involved?'

'Maybe, but she didn't have any children then,' Luka said.

'Her 1983 postcard said she wanted kids. Who's to say I was her first? What if she had other children and left them too . . .' Vega shivered at the treacherous thought spoken out loud. 'The more I dig into her past, the more I realise how little I know about her, other than what we've found out from the Kensingtons and Frankie.'

'Let's not get ahead of ourselves,' Luka soothed, seeing that Vega needed reassurance.

The thought that her mother might have been guilty of neglecting her children cut Vega deeply. Her entire life had been focused on a loving mother, taken from her.

An image of her and Nova sitting in that busy train station pierced her. Because leaving them there, vulnerable and scared, well, that was neglect, too.

She banished the thoughts from her mind; they felt disloyal. 'The cashier mentioned several communes in the area, so it might not even have been her farm that was raided.' Her eyes were fixed on the public library. 'Shall we go in there to ask about the commune, or head straight to the address we have for this Martha Wallace?'

'Let's try the Wallace homestead first. It's just a mile outside the town, on North Shore Road,' Luka said. 'But can I have five minutes before we go? I need to call to check in on one of the cases I'm working on.'

'Your kids are lucky to have you in their corner,' Vega said, a rush of warmth for her kind-hearted boyfriend flooding her.

When Luka had exited the car, Vega picked up her phone and opened her emails, scrolling through the subscriptions she seemed to accumulate daily. Spying an email from Kieran, she opened it.

> Hey, kiddo!
> Congratulations are in order. Your story on Annette's baby has been shortlisted for an Irish Journalism Award in the People's Choice Feature of the Year category. The public vote opens tomorrow! So get ready to share the news when it goes out. And buy a frock! The black-tie gala awards night is in two weeks.
> I'm happy for you, kiddo. You deserve this.
> Hope you're enjoying your break. See you next week.
> Kieran

Vega felt a little dazed. This was her first award nomination. She closed her eyes, then slowly opened them again, looking back at the email to ensure she hadn't dreamed it. The door opened, and Luka got in.

'All good?' Vega asked.

'Nothing to report, which is good news,' he replied. 'Any craic for you?'

'Erm... I've been shortlisted for an award,' Vega replied, feeling a flush rise up her cheeks. She handed Luka her phone so he could read the email for himself.

'This is incredible news. And I'm not surprised one little bit!' he exclaimed.

'Wanna be my date?' Vega asked, imagining him in a black tuxedo.

'I'd be honoured. You'll win too. I'm sure of it. And I'll share with everyone I know. Make sure they vote.'

Vega laughed at his enthusiasm as she entered Martha's address into her maps and they continued their journey. The road narrowed as they neared their destination, with the trees bending towards one another, forming a canopy overhead. Sunlight filtered through the ochre and red leaves. The house was a three-storey late-century farmhouse on the edge of a lake, surrounded by green mountains that formed its backdrop. A paddock to the right held several horses, nibbling on grass and looking up expectantly when they heard the car's wheels on the gravel driveway.

'Looks like they have a private marina,' Luka said, pointing to the back of the property, where a boat was moored to the wooden jetty.

'So I see. With the mountains and the trees, this is quintessential New England.'

'Absolutely,' he agreed. 'All we need is a lobster roll and a chilled white, then we're in the New England of my mind's eye.'

'Look, I got you a cold beer in a spit-on-the-floor pub in Washington. What more could you ask for?' Vega joked as she parked in front of the house, with its impressive wooden porch.

Her heart began to race. Once more she was filled with hope and possibilities; she believed that answers might lie on the other side of that all-American entranceway.

They climbed out of the car, pausing when they heard a voice call, 'Hello there. You folks okay?' A tall, blocky man walked in their direction.

'Hi,' Vega said, turning on her megawatt smile. 'We're looking for Martha Wallace. Is she at home?'

'I'm her son, Bob. Who's asking?' He was smiling, but his eyes were guarded.

'I'm Vega, and this is Luka. My mother lived in this area until the early 1980s. I wanted to ask Martha about her. I believe they were friends.'

Bob's smile faded as the front door of the house swung open. A petite woman stepped out, and Vega recognised her as the retired teacher from the photograph she had discovered online.

'Are you Martha Long?' she called out, shifting her focus to the woman, realising she wouldn't make much progress with Bob.

Before Martha could respond, Bob spoke again. 'What do you want?'

'My mother was called Cassie Kensington, but also went by Star. She lived in this area for some time and had a friend called Martha Long. I'm hoping that's your mother. I want to ask her a few questions, that's all.'

'There's no Martha Long here. My mother is a Wallace. You've had a wasted journey,' Bob said firmly.

Vega turned to Martha expectantly, but the older woman shook her head with a hint of sorrow. 'As my son said, we can't help. I'm sorry.'

'Do you know where I might find Martha Long?' Vega asked, her heart sinking with disappointment.

'She'll be long gone by now,' Bob said. 'Over forty years ago . . .'

Vega and Luka had no option but to return to the car. Her stomach churned with disappointment. 'Back to the drawing board,' she said, sighing deeply.

Luka placed a reassuring hand on her shoulder. 'Let's head to the library. They might have some answers for us.'

In silence, they drove back to Island Pond, with Vega lost in her thoughts. She found a parking spot outside the library and left Luka to search for a coffee shop while she went inside to continue her enquiries.

However, it was yet another false start, and the young librarian could not assist them. Vega spent thirty minutes scouring newspaper archives online, but uncovered nothing beyond what she had already encountered in her Google searches.

'I hope you found a nice coffee shop. I'm ready for a caffeine fix,' she said, her face as dark as her mood, when she returned to the car. Luka was leaning against the bonnet.

'I found something even better,' he replied, nodding to his left.

Martha Wallace was standing a few feet away from the car.

'My son was rude. I'm sorry about that,' she said, offering a faint apologetic smile as she moved closer to Vega.

'Don't worry about it,' Vega replied cautiously.

'He's protective, that's all. Especially since his father passed away. But I've assured him I'm capable of looking after myself.'

Vega's heart started to race. 'Does this mean you *are* Martha Long?'

'I was, once upon a time. But it's been so many years, I've almost forgotten that person.' She shrugged. 'I heard you mention coffee. I know just the place if you fancy joining me for a chat.'

Then she turned and walked away, with Vega and Luka quickly following her.

22

They found a table, and Martha ordered three flat whites. The server greeted her warmly, and she appeared well liked in the community, judging by the numerous waves and greetings she'd received as they made their way to the café.

'You've got a lot of friends in Island Pond,' Vega remarked.

'I've been here for a long time. We're a close-knit community, always have been. Island Pond was established in the late eighteen hundreds, and not much has changed since those early days.'

Luka said, 'I read about it online before we arrived. The article mentioned that the area became popular when the mailroom was established in Brighton at the turn of the century.'

Martha smiled. 'Your research is correct!' She turned her attention to Vega. 'You said you're Cassie's daughter. I didn't know she'd had children. But I'm happy to hear she did.'

'She had two daughters. And I'm hoping you can help me find her.' Vega inhaled deeply and looked Martha squarely in the eye. 'Do you know where she is now?'

Martha gently patted her hand. 'I'm afraid I can't help you with that. I haven't seen your mother in a long time.'

Vega felt another wave of disappointment. She thought she ought to be accustomed to this feeling, yet its onset was once more stealthy and caught her by surprise.

Luka's eyes flickered to her, and he recognised she needed a moment. 'Frankie mentioned that you'd met at a protest.'

Martha raised an eyebrow in surprise. 'You found Frankie? You have been busy. Now that's a name I haven't thought about in decades. When I did think of him, I assumed he'd be dead by now, or in prison.'

Vega felt a surge of loyalty for the man she had briefly thought might be her father. 'Frankie is doing very well, as it happens,' she said. 'He lives in Washington.'

'Good for him.' Martha shrugged. 'As it happens, I met Cassie before the protest you mentioned. I could tell we were kindred spirits from the moment our paths crossed. I recognised myself in her, and she in me. We were close, your mother and I.'

Vega leaned in, eager not to miss a word. 'Why do you think you felt such a connection?'

'She was easy to chat with. We shared a great deal from the outset, exchanging life stories. It's fair to say that most of us in the commune felt different from our families, and that marked the start of our friendships.' Martha shrugged again. 'None of us quite fitted in with the communities we were raised in.'

Vega nodded, feeling a renewed bond with her mother. 'I understand what that feels like, to not quite belong.'

'The trick is to find your tribe. That led me to the Woodstock Music & Art Fair in upstate New York in 1969. You've heard of it, I assume?'

Vega and Luka nodded.

'Five hundred thousand souls all swaying together in generational solidarity to Janis Joplin, the Grateful Dead and Jimi Hendrix. On a dairy farm, of all places. Three days of peace and music. Tribes emerged over that weekend.'

'I can't begin to imagine what it must have been like to be there,' Luka mused.

Martha laughed softly. 'I went with a boyfriend. I didn't tell my parents; I just disappeared for five days without a word. When I think of what I put them through . . .' Her eyes glistened momentarily. 'You only realise how awful you were when you have children of your own.' She smiled nostalgically. 'We had to abandon the car four miles out and walk there with thousands of hippies. What a sight we were! The rainbow colours of our tie-dyed shirts clashed gloriously with those of our bell-bottoms. We carried our tents and sleeping bags. I fell into step with a girl who flashed the peace sign in our direction. That was the first time I saw your mother.'

Vega shook her head in disbelief. 'Whoa! My mother was there? She can't have been more than seventeen then!'

'She was so confident, I assumed she was my age.' Martha's face brightened as she recalled that day. 'It started to rain – just a drizzle. A man walking a few feet ahead began to play his guitar. Cassie stopped and started to dance, waving her arms above her head, lost in the music. I dropped my bags to the ground and joined in. We hadn't even reached the festival, but it felt like the best time of my life. Dancing on that muddy road was sensual, spiritual, and I experienced a freedom I'd never felt before.'

Another lost memory found Vega again, a fleeting moment when her mother had danced in a field, holding Vega and Nova's hands as she spun them around in a circle . . . She gasped, feeling dizzy with the thought.

'You okay?' Luka asked, his eyes clouded with worry.

She gave him a quick smile of reassurance, she'd tell him about it later. 'Did you get to spend time with Mum at the festival?'

'Yes. We pitched our tents next to each other and spent most of our time together. My boyfriend got on quite well with Cassie's date.'

'Frankie?' Vega asked.

'No. Not Frankie. Not then.' A shadow flickered across Martha's face. Just for a moment, then it vanished. But Luka noticed it too, glancing at Vega, who made a mental note to revisit this.

'Your mum had this great laugh. She thought it was hilarious that she was from a place with the same name as the festival. I remember her joking that the two Woodstocks were oil and vinegar, chalk and cheese.'

'I wish I remembered her laugh . . .' Vega whispered.

Martha flashed a sympathetic look in her direction. 'That festival was life-changing for your mother and me. It represented everything we believed in.'

'Can you tell me more about it?' Vega probed, desperate to understand this woman and, in turn, perhaps her mother too.

'There was plenty of downtime. The weather was so dreadful that the bands were delayed, so we smoked pot and chatted. Cassie was exceptionally eloquent. She had a certain way about her that could make people stop and listen.'

This was yet another version of her mother that Vega had not met before.

'We all wanted equal civil and social rights for everyone. I believe that was the crux of it. And somehow the music solidified those yearnings.' Martha began to sing softly, 'What would you think if I sang out of tune . . .' She paused, shaking her head a little self-consciously. 'We were spellbound when Joe Cocker sang "With a Little Help from My Friends". I'm not sure you'd recognise it from my terrible voice.'

'Didn't the Beatles sing that?' Luka said.

'Yes, that's the one. But Cocker's version was unlike any I had heard before. It felt like the music pulsated within him, bringing hundreds of thousands of us to church with him. Each lyric was his gospel. As he finished, the skies opened and an apocalyptic thunderstorm descended upon us. By then, we were at fever pitch, and I remember Cassie shouting with joy as she danced in the rain, believing it to be a message from God.'

'I didn't know she was religious,' Vega whispered, the hairs on her neck standing on end.

'She was spiritual. There's a difference. She proclaimed that we had to effect change ourselves. It was time to stand up for our beliefs. That we had to challenge the establishment, the materialistic society that our parents were attempting to force down our throats.' Martha's eyes widened as she looked at Vega. 'Your mother ignited a fire in us all.'

'I would have loved to have seen that,' Vega replied in awe.

'She was something else,' Martha said, her eyes glistening.

'What happened after the festival? Did you keep in touch?' Luka asked.

'Yes, we wrote to each other most weeks. The war in Vietnam was our main topic, along with boyfriends, to be honest. Then I heard about a commune in Rochester, a youth rebellion that offered an alternative to the world our parents had given us. I couldn't wait to leave home, so I needed little persuasion to embark on a new life there.'

'What did my mother think about that?' Vega asked.

'By this point, Cassie had begun dating Frankie. He had lost two brothers in 'Nam, and they were both passionate about finding a way to end the war. We arranged to meet at the protest Frankie told you about. I was shocked by the change in Cassie; she was furious about the senseless loss of life. She felt that her mother and sister didn't understand her perspective. She needed to escape from home, so I invited her to join me. She arrived with Frankie a few weeks later.'

Vega's mind reeled with all of this. To consider her mother at the forefront of a cultural shift she had learned about in university was surreal. 'Frankie said the Rochester commune was a joyful place. He spoke of it with fondness.'

Martha smiled and nodded her head in agreement. 'Sometimes I wonder if my memories are rose-tinted, but he's right. It was idyllic. There was always coffee on the stove, which was perpetually lit. Most nights we gathered around the fire pit, shared stories and sang songs. Mind you, we smoked quite a lot of pot back then . . .'

'My mother as well?'

'Yes. But she didn't go in for hallucinogenic drugs . . . well, she did once, but they weren't for her.'

'Did she ever mention her family?' Vega asked, crossing her fingers under the table. She needed her mother to have missed Mama Lulu and her sister, to have not turned her back on them without a thought. Because if she'd done that, then perhaps the obvious answer to why she'd left her little daughters at the station was that she didn't care.'

Martha shook her head. 'She didn't often speak about them. She insisted that she was where she wanted to be. And where she needed to be. She missed them, though. I'd sometimes see her gazing at a photograph of them all.'

'They were confused by her leaving and her prolonged absence. It's been difficult for my grandmother,' Vega said.

'I'm certain. As a mother myself, I've lost countless nights of sleep burdened by the guilt of the pain I caused my parents. You don't consider this when you're part of a free-spirited community. Now I realise that our motto of peace and love was somewhat flawed, for we didn't extend that same peace and love to those closest to us. I'm not sure if my parents ever truly forgave me for running away and then staying away, despite my efforts to make amends with them for decades.'

They all allowed that to linger between them momentarily as they sipped their coffees.

'And yet you left Rochester, despite being so happy there . . .' Luka said, breaking the silence.

'It wasn't by choice; the farmhouse was rented, and the owner decided to sell, so we had to move on.'

'To Island Pond.'

'Yes,' Martha replied.

'Before you tell us about that, can you remember who my mother was with at Woodstock?' Vega asked quickly. 'You said it wasn't Frankie.'

Martha frowned, biting her bottom lip. 'His name was David. I remember thinking they made an odd couple from the moment we bumped into them on the way to the festival. Cassie wore a maxi skirt that hugged her legs, a bright orange fitted vest, and beads adorning her neck and wrists. She was a striking woman. In contrast, David wore blue jeans with an ironed crease and a polo shirt. She was wild and free, but he appeared uncomfortable and anxious about leaving his car behind on the side of the road.'

'You're right; he doesn't sound like her type, from what I've heard about her,' Vega agreed.

'The thing was, he was utterly captivated by her. His gaze never strayed from her, and he found it impossible to keep his hands off her.'

Vega raised her eyebrows and pulled a face at Luka. Hearing about her mother's antics felt rather peculiar.

'They were passionate, but they clashed frequently. David disliked it when Cassie took centre stage. He attempted to calm her down, and it all came to a head on the Monday morning. The tension had been building since Sunday night. He wanted to leave after the last act, but we had found out that Hendrix was performing Monday morning, so we decided to stay. He grasped Cassie's arm a bit too forcefully for my liking. Cassie laughed it off, but I could tell he'd slightly rattled her.'

'Did he stay?' Luka said.

Martha nodded. 'There was an unusual atmosphere on Monday morning. Only a few thousand people remained in what had turned into quite a bedraggled field. I remember looking at David's face as Jimi Hendrix played "The Star Spangled Banner". He was scowling, his expression like the thunder we'd had over the weekend. The foolish man was so preoccupied with sulking about not getting his way that he almost missed the most memorable performance of the weekend.' She sighed. 'Cassie and I wept as Jimi sang. She told me afterwards that the performance was like a spiritual experience for her. And we weren't the only ones touched by it. A group of men beside us began tearing up their draft cards for Vietnam, and this infuriated David even more. He made it clear that he didn't share our anti-war sentiments.'

'Why on earth did he go in the first place?' Vega asked.

'Because of his infatuation with Cassie. However, he'd had enough by then and informed her that they were leaving immediately. She began to laugh, refusing to move and taunting him about how he wanted to return home to his girlfriend. That he was finished with her now that the weekend had ended.'

A whistle escaped from Luka.

Now it was Vega's turn to frown. 'So David wasn't Cassie's boyfriend?'

'Not Cassie's, no.'

She was half afraid to ask, but she knew she had to find out everything she could about her mother. 'That makes me think that you know whose boyfriend he was.'

'David didn't just have a girlfriend. He was engaged.' Martha took a deep breath. 'To Cassie's sister Felicity.'

23

Who the hell was my mother? Vega's mind reeled as she grappled again with this question that had plagued her for decades and that now had so many layers to it.

The revelation that her mother had attended the rock festival with her sister's boyfriend was astounding. Did Felicity know about their weekend away? Vega had sensed some negative energy from Flick towards her sister and wondered if it was merely her imagination. Now she was pretty sure there was more to their story.

'Mama Lulu said my aunt and mother were close once, but not so much towards the end . . .' she whispered. 'It has to be because of David.'

'So you've visited them recently?' Martha asked. 'Can't they help you with your search?'

Vega looked down sadly. 'I met them for the first time a couple of days ago, and they haven't seen my mother since she left home at the age of eighteen. Aunt Flick didn't mention a possible conflict with my mother. Do you know what happened when they got back home? Did Mum and David stay together after the festival, or did he return to my aunt?'

Martha shrugged her shoulders. 'I've no idea. Cassie never mentioned him again in any of her letters. You'll need to ask your aunt about that. But it wasn't long afterwards that Frankie appeared on the scene. So my guess is they didn't stay together.'

Vega parked this to one side – another question in her growing stack.

'You've explained why you had to leave Rochester. But how did you end up in Island Pond?'

'Word of mouth. One of our commune members had heard of it. And we'd been told it was a place where everyone was welcome, populated by like-minded individuals. A vast farm spanning hundreds of acres. So we made our way there.'

'And they accepted you all without question?'

'They did. You had to sign a book indicating your willingness to adhere to the community's rules. Beyond that, it was quite straightforward. There was no charge for moving in – only an expectation that all earnings went into a central fund.'

'Where did you all live?'

'Some were in caravans, others in tents; the barn had been converted to lodgings, too, with bunkbeds made from plywood. And of course there was the house. But not everyone lived in that.'

'Frankie said there was a leader there. Apollo. What was he like?'

Martha's expression darkened. 'Self-appointed leader. He had a Jesus complex. He had long brown hair and wore tunics over his jeans and beads on his wrists. He was remarkably good-looking. When he entered a room, he commanded attention.' She smiled, 'And his Irish lilt was utterly charming. When he spoke, all eyes were on him.'

'Apollo was Irish?' Vega exclaimed, her voice coming out in a high-pitched squeak.

'Yes. And you are, too, judging by your accent?'

Vega nodded, her mind spinning once again. Was this the connection between Mum leaving America and ending up in Ireland? It had to be.

'You didn't think much of him,' Luka interjected, picking up on Martha's disdain when discussing Apollo.

Martha shrugged. 'He never did anything to make me dislike him, strictly speaking. But I was aware of the considerable power he held over the group. At times, it felt unbalanced. While he could be charming and fun, I also witnessed his cruel side.'

'Like when he threw Frankie out?'

Her eyes widened in surprise. 'Frankie told you that, too? It was a shocking time. We learned after that episode that while we were free to move in, Apollo could kick us out without so much as a chance to defend ourselves. We saw it happen again several times. People who had spent years working hard, labouring with everyone else, were dismissed for breaking one of his rules.'

'Frankie swears he didn't take that money,' Vega said. 'And for what it's worth, I believe him.'

'I don't know,' Martha replied warily. 'It was found under his mattress. And he'd just had a big row with Apollo too.'

'He told us they butted horns,' Luka said.

'Like two rams. And I couldn't blame Frankie. Because Cassie and Apollo were like magnets, drawn to each other from the moment we arrived at the farm.' Martha reached for her clutch handbag and pulled out a photograph, which she placed in front of them. 'I thought you might like to see this.'

A man in a tunic stood at the edge of a lake. Cassie was beside him, wearing a low-hung maxi skirt in tomato red, a cropped fitted vest in orange that was so tight her nipples were visible, and beads around her wrists and neck.

'Apollo and my mother,' Vega said, her eyes round with awe. 'She looks so young.'

'A beautiful couple. They were together at this stage – a force to be reckoned with. Cassie moved into Apollo's bedroom almost immediately after Frankie was booted out.'

Vega peered more closely at the photograph. 'This is your farmhouse!'

Martha laughed. 'I wondered when you'd figure that out. Before it became my family home, it was our commune.'

Vega sank back into her seat, shaking her head in surprise. 'I have so many questions.'

'I'll answer as many as I can,' Martha replied warmly. She waved to the waitress. 'I think we might need another drink.'

'Is the farm still a commune?' Vega asked, thinking about Martha's son, Bob.

Martha scoffed good-humouredly. 'Goodness, no. It hasn't been a commune since 1984. The farm was owned by Ray, whom I went on to marry. After everyone left, we made it our family home. My son has always been slightly embarrassed about his parents' hippie past. He prefers to forget it happened; that's why he lied to you when you turned up today.'

Vega's mind reeled further. 1984. Earlier, the general store cashier mentioned there had been trouble at a commune that year. Could it be connected to this?

Before she could delve deeper, Luka took the photograph and tapped Apollo's image thoughtfully. 'Is it possible that Apollo set Frankie up so that he could have Cassie to himself?'

'That thought did cross my mind,' Martha replied. 'But then we got on with living. It wasn't all songs around the fire. It was a working farm, and we all had jobs. For a while, everything was calm, albeit not the same as it had been in Rochester. We harvested. We crafted. And we sold everything from beads to knitted ponchos, Indian psychedelic tunics and maple syrup. Although we didn't want to work for society or be part of it, we needed money. That's what Apollo took care of.' As she mentioned his name, she rolled her eyes.

'Did Mum marry Apollo?' Vega asked, her stomach tightening as she awaited Martha's reply.

'They had a commitment ceremony at the farm. Ray and I did the same. However, it wasn't a legal marriage. We only got married a few years ago; we'd never felt the need to do it legally until he fell ill. He wanted everything sorted; he was always looking out for me . . .' Her voice trailed off as a wave of loss washed over her.

They allowed her to sit silently to collect herself as Vega considered the real possibility that Apollo was her father.

'We heard about some trouble at a commune in 1984 when children were taken. Was that your farm?' Luka asked.

Martha's eyes glistened, and she sighed heavily. 'That was a difficult time for Island Pond. One hundred and twelve children were taken from a religious group called the Twelve Tribes by social workers. It wasn't our commune, yet it affected us all the same. The fact that state officials could carry out a dawn raid without warning or any specific allegations against individuals was unsettling. By then, Ray and I had two boys: Bob and his older brother, RJ. She shivered visibly before continuing. 'The thought that someone could come and take our children from us shook everyone in the community, but especially the parents in the group.'

Vega tried to envision what it must have been like for them back then, and her heart constricted in sympathy.

'Ray was the first to discuss disbanding the commune, and encouraged people to move on. We had both started questioning the authoritarian roles that Apollo and Cassie had assumed. They had effectively made themselves king and queen, which did not sit well with many of us living at the farm.'

'Did you tell Cassie this?' Luka asked.

'Not at first. But the knock-on effect of the raid at Twelve Tribes lasted for weeks. The thing was, we had all grown older. The artists, poets and writers who comprised our community had evolved just as we had. We came together because we all felt disconnected from what was considered normal. We matured. We fell in love and had children. And I suppose the essence of it was that children alter you. We smoked pot occasionally, but it wasn't enjoyable any more. Not like it was when we were young and carefree.'

'How many kids were there?' Luka asked, his eyes wide as he took in Martha's story.

She scrunched her nose for a moment. 'Let's see. I reckon around forty of us lived at the farm, including eight families and at least twenty children.'

'And my mother didn't have any children at that time?' Vega asked, seeking confirmation of this fact once more.

Martha shook her head sadly. 'She desperately wanted kids and was actively trying to conceive, but it never happened for her – at least not while she was with me.' She leaned over and patted Vega's hand. 'But that changed. I'm happy that she experienced motherhood first-hand. She was a great help to me with the boys.'

Vega felt a familiar regret at having to burst someone else's bubble. 'Not for long, I'm afraid. She left my sister and me at a railway station in Ireland when I was four, and I haven't seen her since.'

Martha exhaled loudly. 'When you mentioned you were searching for her, I never imagined it had been so long since you last saw her! You poor thing.'

Vega brushed her sympathy away, keen to keep the conversation on Island Pond. 'That's why I need your help. I'm trying to piece together my mother's footsteps, from when she left her home in Woodstock to ending up in Ireland. Can you remember the last time you saw her?'

Martha frowned. 'Let's see. Several families left after the Twelve Tribes raid. Ray, as I mentioned, started expressing his doubts. The more we discussed it, the more I agreed with him. We approached Apollo and Cassie with what we believed was a fair solution for everyone. Ray was prepared to offer those who wished to stay a field for pitching their tents and camper vans, for a nominal rental fee. However, the house was to be vacated and would become our family home.'

Luka whistled. 'How did Apollo take that?'

'We were both incredibly nervous. I was convinced Apollo would attempt to talk us down. Ray always claimed he could sell sand to the Arabs. However, it wasn't contentious at all. Apollo smiled and mentioned that he and Cassie had already made plans to leave the farm. They had decided to return to his home in Ireland. Once they departed, others followed suit, and before we knew it, it was just the four of us.' She smiled wistfully. 'I was concerned it might feel lonely, but it didn't. We integrated into the community when everyone else left, and made good friends.'

'Whereabouts in Ireland did they go?' Luka asked.

'All I know is what Cassie told me. Apollo's father died, and they moved to his childhood home. I have no idea where.'

'And they left in 1984?' When Martha nodded, he continued, 'At least we now know how she ended up in Ireland.'

'I need to find out what Apollo's real name is so I can start searching for him,' Vega said.

Martha beamed at her. 'Well, I can help you with that! After they left, we discovered a letter Apollo had left behind. It was from his father.'

'Do you still have it?' Vega exclaimed, her heart jumping in hope.

'No, I'm afraid I dumped it. But I'll never forget his name.' Martha grinned. 'Have you ever seen that movie, *Jaws*?'

Both Vega and Luka nodded.

'I've watched it countless times. My favourite character was the shark hunter, Quint. Do you remember him?' Vega nodded again, willing Martha to get to the point. 'He was portrayed by an actor named Robert Shaw. And that was Apollo's real name. I'm one hundred per cent certain. Does that help?'

Vega glanced at Luka, who was smiling at her, and then back at Martha. 'It helps immensely. Now I have a solid lead to pursue. If I can locate Robert Shaw, then maybe I can finally find my mother.'

24

Robert Shaw. A new name now etched into Vega's mind.

From the moment Martha mentioned it, it played on repeat. A quick Google search on her iPad yielded numerous results with a few potential leads, but Vega understood it would take time to find a match unless she could refine the parameters.

When they said goodbye to Martha, they swapped contact details, promising to stay in touch. To Vega's surprise, Martha called before they had even reached their hotel.

'Something has been niggling at me. You mentioned that your grandmother and aunt haven't seen Cassie since she left home. Is that right?'

'Yeah,' Vega replied, turning up the volume on her CarPlay system to ensure she heard every word.

'Well, that's not accurate. Your aunt visited Island Pond. I distinctly remember her being there. Because we rarely had family members stop by. It was frowned upon by Apollo.'

'Do you remember when?'

'Not exactly. But both my boys were born by then, so it must have been in the early eighties. Cassie and Apollo were a couple for sure. Frankie had long since left.'

This news baffled Vega. Why hadn't Flick told them about her visit? She could have spared them a lot of trouble had they known about Island Pond!

And Vega intended to find out. They were at Red Maple Farm today to bid farewell to her aunt and Mama Lulu. Vega and Luka gave them updates on everything they had discovered over the past few days.

'I'm going to check on Frankie's father tomorrow. I'll take him some food and see if he needs anything. It's hard to hear of him alone in his cabin,' Mama Lulu said.

Vega flashed her a grateful smile. 'That's kind of you. I liked him, and Frankie too. I think they've both had difficult lives and made mistakes, but both are desperately lonely. I encouraged Frankie to call his father. But I don't know if he will.'

'After losing those two boys in Vietnam, it doesn't surprise me that they have struggled ever since,' Mama Lulu said, shaking her head wearily.

Aunt Flick began to clear the empty plates, refusing all offers of assistance. They moved outside to the porch, where Vega and Luka sat on a swing that rocked gently back and forth. Mama Lulu occupied her favourite rocking chair. Vega had to pinch herself, because it felt so surreal. This all-American duo, as wholesome as the apple pie they'd just eaten, were her family. She sensed Mama Lulu's gaze upon her and turned her attention back to her grandmother.

'I'm proud of you,' Mama Lulu said suddenly.

Vega felt a flush of heat run through her body. 'Why?' she asked warily.

'You've become quite the remarkable young lady. Many would have faltered under the weight of the baggage you've inherited. But you are strong. Here and here.' Mama Lulu gestured to her head and then her heart.

The flush now blossomed, turning Vega's face beetroot red. She tried to respond and couldn't find the words.

'I'm in awe of her, too,' Luka added, smiling lovingly at Vega.

'Thank you,' she muttered to them both. She was unaccustomed to receiving words of affirmation on a personal level. She was beginning to adjust to having Luka as a cheerleader; adding her grandmother to the team felt overwhelming.

'If you find Cassie, will you call me?'

'Of course,' Vega replied.

'No, I mean, will you call me before you go to see her? I want to come to Ireland to be there when you do.'

Vega nodded, understanding that of course, as a mother, Mama Lulu would want to be there.

'I don't just want to see Cassie; I want to be there for *you*. After all this time, facing her will be difficult to handle,' her grandmother continued.

Vega wrapped her arms around herself, once again unable to speak. This was what it was to be part of a family, she guessed, and she liked it.

Flick joined them, pulling on her jacket. 'I'm going to check on everything down at the barn. I'll be back in twenty.'

'Can I come with you?' Vega asked, seizing the opportunity to have a private chat.

They fell into step as they set off.

'You doing okay?' Flick asked, linking arms with her niece. 'It's been a lot for you this past week – meeting all of us, and finding Frankie, then Martha.'

Vega's heart began to race. Flick was giving her the perfect chance to broach a complex subject. She had rehearsed several versions of how she would bring it up with her aunt. Delicately, with the hope of not hurting anyone's feelings. But in typical Vega fashion, when the moment came, she dived in head-first.

'Why didn't you tell me you saw my mother in Island Pond?'

Flick halted and took a deep breath before turning to face her. 'So, Martha told you. I was curious if she'd remember it.'

'I don't understand why you didn't tell me.'

Flick sighed, her fingers threading through her hair. 'Mama doesn't know. And, selfishly, I didn't want her to discover the truth. That I'd kept it to myself all these years.'

'I don't understand,' Vega said.

'I had a challenging relationship with Cassie. I don't wish to delve into it, as she's your mother and it wouldn't be right for me to tarnish her reputation in any way.'

Vega reached over and touched her aunt's arm. 'I know she attended the Woodstock festival with your boyfriend.'

Flick groaned and gestured towards a long tree stump fashioned into a bench. They sat down next to one another.

'She broke my heart, you know.' Flick's face was pinched tight, and her eyes glistened as she spoke. 'I'd confided in Cassie how much I loved David. We'd been dating for nearly two years, engaged for six months. Happy, as far as I was concerned. I was blindsided when they went to the festival together.'

Vega whistled softly. 'That must have hurt.'

'It broke me. I had no idea that David viewed Cassie as anything more than my irritating younger sister. We all used to hang out together when he spent weekends here. And I swear I didn't notice a thing. But that just goes to show what a fool I was.'

'When did you find out?' Vega asked, her heart constricting in sympathy for her aunt.

'From one of David's friends, the day they left. Mama had sent me out to look for Cassie, who hadn't returned from school. I called David for help, as he had a car. But he had vanished, too. I never imagined they were connected until I asked some of David's friends if they knew where he was, and they sniggered. It took me a minute to get them to confess what they were laughing about.'

Vega's heart constricted at the thought of how difficult that must have been for her aunt. 'What happened when they returned home?'

Flick's face hardened. 'Cassie didn't care. She told me she'd only asked David to take her because he had a car. She swore that they were just friends and nothing had happened between them. But David at least had the decency to confess.'

Vega's stomach fell. 'Mum wasn't sorry?'

'Not in the slightest. Cassie did what she always did – whatever she damn well liked!'

Vega felt an irrational need to defend her mother, even though she perhaps didn't deserve it. 'She was so young. She likely didn't even realise what she was doing.'

When Flick rolled her eyes, Vega couldn't blame her. She knew how lame her excuses were.

'So how did you end up going to Island Pond?' she asked.

'I heard Frankie was back. I hassled him until he told me where he'd last seen Cassie, then I went to see her.'

'To bring her home?'

Flick stood up and brushed her jeans down. 'No. Not that.' Vega's eyes widened as her aunt met her gaze defiantly. 'I told myself I would check on her to ensure she was all right. Even though I hated what she'd done to me, I loved her; she was my baby sister. We'd been close until that weekend when she betrayed me. But I was deceiving myself. The real reason for my visit was to tell her to stay away. You see, David and I had gotten back together, and we were engaged to be married again. I was terrified that if she returned home, she'd find a way to come between us.' Her head dropped. 'I needn't have been concerned. When I arrived, it was evident that Cassie had no intention of returning home any time soon.'

'She was with Apollo by then.'

'Yes, and they were utterly enamoured with each other. He never left her side, not even briefly. He was impossibly condescending.' Flick shuddered. ' "We have no secrets in our marriage" – that's what he told me. Then he said I should consider why David had attended the festival that weekend, and claimed it was my fault they'd hit it off. Certain weaknesses of mine were to blame. All the while, Cassie smiled benevolently at me as if she possessed the secrets of the universe.'

'In your opinion, was she there under duress?'

'Goodness, no. She was happy, glowing. Cassie had always been pretty, but that day, I recall thinking she had never looked more beautiful.'

'What did she say when you told her to stay away?'

Flick sighed. 'I didn't get the chance. She told me that she was never coming home, that Apollo was her family now. They asked me to tell Mama, but I refused and said she could do that herself. It wasn't long afterwards that she sent her last postcard.'

Vega scrunched her nose as she tried to remember the exact words on that postcard. 'She never mentioned in the postcard that you had visited.'

'No. She didn't. And I never told Mama Lulu that I had gone. It seemed kinder at the time to prevent her from being shunned like I'd been. Months turned into years, and my omission soon felt like a lie – shameful and too immense to own up to.'

Vega understood. 'I get it. But I wish you had mentioned it to me privately. I wouldn't have shared it with Mama Lulu, but it would have been useful and saved me trekking around looking for the Chalupkas!'

'I'm sorry, truly. I want to support you in your search. I genuinely do. I made an error of judgement and couldn't find my way out.'

'Oh, we are sooooo related,' Vega said with a rueful grin. 'I tend to mess things up a lot. And don't worry, I won't say anything to Mama Lulu. It's up to you if you want to tell her.' She linked arms with Flick again and they continued their walk towards the barn. 'But you can tell me more about this Apollo . . .'

When they returned to the farmhouse, they were in sync. As Vega embraced her aunt and grandmother goodbye, she sensed it would not be long before they reunited again.

25

Extract from an interview with David Lawton

David: I'm not comfortable with this interview, but Flick insisted. And I owe her at least this much.

Vega: I'm grateful for your time, and I'll try to make this brief. Can you tell me why you went to the Woodstock festival with Cassie?

David: Because she asked. And I was a fool.

Vega: Were you in a relationship with her as well as Flick then?

David: No. I loved Flick and had never looked at another woman until shortly before that weekend. I never noticed Cassie; to me, she was just Flick's slightly annoying younger sister.

Vega: What changed?

David: I know you'll think I'm just saying this. That it's always the man who is the predator. But I swear to you, on my children's lives, that Cassie actively pursued me. She found ways to lightly touch my arm or the small of my back as she passed. And I could see that my discomfort pleased her. She knew that she was attractive, sexy as hell. And she liked seeing my reaction.

Vega: At what age was this?

David: She was seventeen. Flick and I were eighteen.

Vega: Whose idea was it to go to Woodstock?

David: Cassie's. She told me it would be our opportunity to be together, away from prying eyes. I knew it was wrong; I realised I could lose Flick, yet I couldn't bring myself to say no.

Cassie had a certain charm about her; she was persuasive. And like I said, I was a fool.

Vega: So what happened between you there?

David: We were so different. She was a free spirit, and I was more conservative. It didn't seem to matter for the first day or two. I was so caught up in being with her. And quite bluntly, I wasn't thinking clearly. Not to mention the excitement of the festival.

Vega: What changed?

David: I realised that Cassie wasn't really interested in me. She began to make fun of me and my fuddy-duddy ways. Her words, not mine. She disappeared for hours on end, leaving me alone. It became apparent that I had made the biggest mistake of my life.

Vega: Did you argue with her?

David: Yes, quite a bit. My guilt and shame caught up with me and made me curt, which only intensified her fury. She was enraged with me and called me weak and dull. By Saturday evening, we were hardly speaking to each other. I wanted to cut and run, but there was no chance she would leave early. And while I was a complete arse for two-timing Flick with her sister, I wasn't such an arse that I would abandon Cassie. I felt a responsibility to ensure she got home safely.

Vega: Martha Long mentioned that you disagreed on Monday morning at the Hendrix set. Could you share what you remember about that?

David: The festival was at fever pitch. Men began tossing their draft cards into a huge bonfire. It was unpatriotic. I was deeply uncomfortable with it all.

Vega: Were you drafted?

David: No, I was granted a deferment because I had won a scholarship, something I struggled with at the time. But now, in hindsight, I realise that I was blessed to have received that scholarship.

Vega: So you and Cassie fought about the Vietnam War?

David: Partly. Look, I wasn't a fan of the war. However, I recognised that the situation was nuanced. For Cassie, there was no grey area. She picked flowers to wear in her hair on the first day, and that's my memory of her, frozen in time. Then on that Monday morning, she held the flowers up to the crowd and spoke about an incident at the Pentagon in 1967. You won't know about it; you're too young. But it was a pivotal moment in our history. A protester placed a flower in the barrel of a rifle aimed at his head by one of the military police. It marked the birth of flower power and a turning point in the anti-war movement.

Vega: She sounds so confident for someone as young as she was.

David: Cassie had no fear. As she captivated the crowd, I remember thinking that she would go on to achieve great things. She possessed a remarkable voice, and I always believed that if she used it wisely, the world would be her oyster.

Vega: What happened when you got home to Flick?

David: Cassie wanted to keep our relationship a secret. Pretend we went to the concert in a platonic way. She could spin a tale so convincingly that she might have fooled everyone. But I had to tell Flick the truth. I loved her, and she deserved that respect from me. She was devastated and ended things between us. Not long after, Cassie left with the Chalupka lad. I spent every day trying to convince Flick to forgive me. It took me years, but in the end, she did, and we got married.

Vega: It would be a hard thing for any person to forgive.

David: It was. And it ended us all the same. Cassie was always there, caught between us, invoked whenever we argued. Guilt and shame plagued both of us for different reasons. They were so corrosive and damaging that we ultimately decided to call it quits.

Vega: You've shared how guilty you felt. What about Cassie? Was she ashamed of her actions?

David: You'd need to ask her that. But from where I was sitting, the answer is no. She didn't care in the slightest about the mess she left behind. Cassie only cared for one person, and that was herself.

PART THREE

What we know matters, but who we are matters more.

Brené Brown

26

Vega sat across from Kieran, watching as he read the essay she had just given him. Her coffee remained untouched on his desk; her stomach was churning too much to enjoy it.

During the flight home to Dublin, she had thought of nothing but her next steps. She had spent her entire life hiding her identity and origin story. However, somewhere over the Atlantic Ocean, she realised that opening up and letting people in was not as frightening as she had imagined.

Luka continued to surprise her with his unwavering support. She recognised that it was unfair to Kieran to withhold this vital information about who the Nowhere Girls were. But she struggled with how to tell him. It was Luka who suggested that she use her superpower to inform her boss.

'Write to him. Share your story in a story,' he had urged.

She had opened a vein and poured herself into the piece. She'd doubted every word as she'd driven to the HLD offices that morning. Until fifteen minutes ago, she hadn't even been sure she would hand it over to him during their weekly catch-up. But somehow she found the courage.

Kieran paused, taking a moment to sip his coffee as he read. He kept his eyes on the pages, making no effort to convey his thoughts while he absorbed her truth.

It was the longest ten minutes of Vega's life. Perhaps she should have emailed him the piece and spared herself this torturous wait. But that wasn't their way. She had developed a habit of submitting her stories in person, accompanied by a cup of coffee, so Kieran could provide immediate feedback.

Finally he placed the A4 sheets on the table and looked across at her. 'Damn,' he croaked, his voice tight with emotion. Then he stood up and walked around the desk. 'Come here, kiddo,' he said, opening his arms to enfold her in his warm embrace.

To Vega's horror, she felt tears prick in her eyes. She wasn't one to cry; this wasn't her style. She was the girl who was as tough as nails.

'You've been through it, haven't you?' Kieran said, giving her a pat on the back before pulling away.

Vega replied with a muffled 'Yes,' and they both settled back into their seats. 'I bet you didn't see that coming.'

'No. Suffice it to say, you caught me by surprise. I'm not sure where to begin. First of all, are you all right?'

Vega smiled through her tears, because with that first question, Kieran had validated her decision to confide in him. 'I'm better than I probably ought to be. Meeting Mama Lulu and Flick was monumental for me. They're the only blood relatives I've known since we were found in 1995.'

'I can't imagine what that must have been like. They sound like absolute legends. Their characters leap off the page. I could almost smell the pie crust from your descriptions.'

'I've been craving it since I arrived home. It's pretty special,' Vega agreed.

'This changes everything, you know. This story has immense potential. We could turn it into a series. You could write a book, for heaven's sake.'

'I've never thought beyond using the story as a tool to find Mum and Nova. I need to know that they're all right, have survived this and are living a good life somewhere. Even if they don't want me as part of it, I need to know. I had planned to keep my identity to myself. But I don't know . . . somewhere in Vermont I realised that it wouldn't be the end of the world to tell people who I am.'

'Well, I'm glad you have told me. And Luka. This is too big to deal with on your own. And this Apollo fella is most likely your dad?' Kieran asked. 'How do you feel about that?'

'I've thought over the years about who my father might be, and it's the strangest thing. I don't remember him. He was always a blank silhouette. I was just four when Mum left us, so I don't have many memories to draw from. However, I do have occasional flashbacks to moments with her when I felt loved. I think it's odd that there's nothing with him. Perhaps he wasn't there. Or maybe . . .'

'Perhaps you've shut him out because your memories of him are not ones you wish to retain,' Kieran concluded for her.

Vega nodded sadly. 'If he's Apollo, as I now suspect he might be, then I also suspect he's rather unpleasant. There aren't many kind recollections about him from the few people we met who knew him. Either way, I believe he holds the key to all of this. If I can find him, he'll be able to answer my questions.'

'Let me help you with that. I'm invested in this story now. It's personal for you, so it's personal for me.'

'Thank you,' she said, her voice tight again as tears threatened to overcome her.

He waved away her thanks and began jotting down notes as he spoke rapidly. 'I'll enlist the newspaper's researcher to investigate records relating to when Robert Shaw returned to Ireland. We'll do the same for Cassie Kensington. Or perhaps she's Cassie Shaw if they did get married. Oh, and we'll need to look into the land registry for properties owned by the Shaws, though it may be challenging to narrow that down. First we should attempt to locate Robert Shaw's birth certificate. We have a rough age for him, which will help.'

'Wow, thank you, Kieran. That will speed up my search.'

'In the worst-case scenario, if we don't find him, we can run a story appealing for Cassie and Nova to come forward. If they read it, perhaps they'll get in touch. There aren't many children out there who were left on a bench at a train station. If Nova sees the story, she'll know it's about her.'

Vega's heart lurched, and she held her hand up. 'Don't run anything yet! I've been having second thoughts from the moment

I started typing it up. Somehow, putting it on paper has made it real. I'm not ready for the story to be published.'

'I understand. Don't worry, I won't pull any stunts.'

'Thank you. This was just a rough draft for you. I need to do some revisions before it goes public and Mum and Nova see it. It has to be perfect.'

Kieran's face softened as he assured her, 'I keep telling you, when you write from the heart, you're on to a winner. I wouldn't change a single word in this piece. But I promise you that all of this will be on your terms. I've got your back, kiddo. You can trust me.'

Vega swallowed another lump, whispering, 'I know that.'

27

Vega had been thinking about Mama Lulu and Flick all day, and yearned for one of her grandmother's savoury pies. So much so that she decided to try her hand at making one herself. After an afternoon of slicing, dicing and sautéing, she was finally ready to place her chicken pot pie in the oven.

But a wave of loneliness washed over her. Pie was meant to be enjoyed with family, gathered around a long wooden table carved from a maple tree in the woods beyond your white porch.

She picked up her phone and dialled Luka's number.

'Have you eaten?' she asked quickly, as soon as he picked up.

'No. It was gonna be a Pot Noodle night for me. You want to grab a bite somewhere?'

Vega inhaled deeply. 'I've made a pie. It's going in the oven and will be ready in forty minutes. I'll send you my address if you'd like a slice.'

She heard him take a sharp breath. If he turned this into a big deal, she'd take back the invitation. There was silence for an eternity before he finally cleared his throat and said, 'I can bring dessert if you fancy. Ice cream?'

'Vanilla or caramel would be nice. Come round the back when you get here. I'll be out in the garden.'

She ended the call and felt a wave of giggles wash over her. What was happening to her? She was breaking all her rules, but she didn't mind. She dashed around each room in the cottage, scanning it to ensure it looked its best. She plumped the cushions, wiped down the countertops and set the small table in preparation for the pie, which looked rather decent when she dared to glance at it. Satisfied that she was ready for her first date to visit her home, she poured a glass of wine and went outside.

Despite it being the end of October, it was a warm evening. She sat in one of the lounge chairs beside the flickering flames of her gas-fuelled fire pit, which she had lit an hour ago. When the Irish weather permitted, she sat outside under the stars. She had learned long ago that lighting a fire pit made stargazing a far more enjoyable experience.

She heard footsteps crunch on the gravel path, and moments later, Luka appeared around the gable end of the cottage.

'Hey, you,' he said softly.

She jumped up and kissed him as he pulled her in close.

'Cold!' she squealed as the bag he was clutching struck the small of her back. 'I'll get you a glass of wine and put the ice cream in the freezer. The food will be ready in ten minutes.'

He stood awkwardly as she took the ice cream from him and headed for the kitchen. 'Are you coming in?' she called, and a smile broke out on his face. 'What? You thought I was going to make you sit outside all night?' she teased.

'The thought had crossed my mind,' Luka replied, ducking as he stepped into the cottage.

'Any taller and you'd lose your head,' Vega said, handing him his wine.

'I tried to imagine what to expect. This is great.' Luka surveyed the kitchen and dining room. The walls were painted a soft caramel, providing a perfect backdrop for the dark beams overhead and the vibrant furnishings that made the space a home.

'I'll give you the full tour after dinner, but let's enjoy the outdoors for a few minutes before it gets too cold,' Vega said, and they went back outside to the warm fire pit.

'I don't think I've ever seen stars shining as brightly as they are tonight,' Luka said softly as he gazed upwards to the inky sky.

'I feel at peace when I see the stars. It reminds me of my place in the world and puts all my problems into perspective.'

'I get that. I can feel today's stress washing away from me just looking up.'

'Bad day?' Vega asked. 'What happened?'

'Had to relocate a family. Youngest only three months old. Parents both have an addiction.'

'I'm sorry.'

'Yeah. Me too. But let's not talk about that. Tell me about the stars. What am I looking at up there?'

'Right, just a warning, but if I were on *Mastermind*, stars would be my specialist subject.'

'Noted.'

'I'll try not to geek out too much. The constellations typically visible in Ireland include Orion, Taurus, the Big Dipper, the North Star and Cassiopeia. I always look for her first of all.' Vega set her glass down and took Luka's left hand in hers, guiding his finger to point upwards.

'Can you see that large W-shaped constellation?'

He shook his head, and she readjusted his hand until he said excitedly, 'I can see it!'

'Seeing Cassiopeia makes me feel closer to Mum and Nova. Silly really. But I tell myself that perhaps Mum is looking at the same sky right now and thinking about both of us too.'

'I'm certain she is,' replied Luka. 'I can't imagine how difficult this must be for you.'

'It's not easy, but it's better than it was. I've spent my life having only the stars in the sky for my family. Now I have Mama Lulu and Aunt Flick. And I'm learning about my mother. It might not all be good, but she sounds like a lot of fun. Hearing about her at Woodstock, dancing on the road and leading a revolution, makes me proud.'

'She was a force,' he agreed. 'And I think you're very much like her.'

Vega shrugged. 'I'm not sure. I'm headstrong. I recognise that about myself. However, I'm uncertain about what I've accomplished, especially compared to her.'

'You're far too hard on yourself. Your writing impacts. It leaves a lasting impression on people.'

'Perhaps. I often wonder what Nova might be up to. She was far too young when I knew her for me to understand her talents. I reckon she's successful at whatever her chosen path is.' She glanced at Luka. 'Nova is the brightest star in the sky. That's how I regard my little sister. Shining so brightly up there, I must surely be able to see her . . .'

They sat silently for a moment, and she was grateful to him for allowing them that grace and not trying to fill the silence with platitudes.

'This is incredible,' he said, his eyes wide in wonder. 'I'll never look at the sky in the same way again.'

Vega felt ridiculously pleased that he was enjoying this so much. 'We'll turn you into a star-gazer yet.'

The sound of her iPhone alarm going off interrupted their amateur astronomy. 'Come on, the pie is ready!'

Luka sat at the small dining room table and Vega self-consciously placed the golden-crusted pie in the centre, just as Mama Lulu had done a week earlier.

'That looks and smells delicious!' he said.

'I didn't make the pastry. I bought it from Tesco,' she admitted in a rush of honesty.

'But you made the pie! Honestly, this looks great.'

'I used some of the dark maple syrup we bought in the sauce. We'd better taste it and see if I've got it right.'

Holding her breath, she sliced large portions for Luka and herself, then passed him a bowl of green salad.

She didn't take a bite until Luka had sampled the pie, and she only released her breath when he made the appropriate noises of appreciation. Once she'd tasted her own, she felt a flush of pride. Perhaps not Mama Lulu quality, but not a bad effort.

After they'd finished their meal, she took him on the promised tour of the cottage.

'It's small, so this won't take long,' she told him as she led him down the narrow hallway. 'Watch your head!' she called out as they entered the cosy sitting room. The room was drenched in a rich navy, with bookshelves stretching from floor to ceiling on either side of the fireplace.

'This is so you.' Luka said, taking in the books that filled the shelves and spilled out onto the coffee table and one end of the navy velvet sofa.

'My haven. I know it's dark, some might say gloomy, but I love it. The fire, lamps and candles are the only light in the room. All I need, really.'

'It's perfect. I can picture myself happily reading the Sunday papers on that sofa with a nice coffee.'

'You hinting?' Vega teased.

'Maybe.'

'Come on, I'll show you upstairs.'

Luka followed her upwards and poked his head into a small box room that was now Vega's office, with a single bed against one wall. 'I haven't done anything with the upstairs other than put a lick of paint on it. It's next summer's project. But the shower in the bathroom is decent.'

'That's all you need,' he agreed.

Then she opened the door to her bedroom, and his eyes scanned the room, which boasted a chintzy wallpaper in shades of green and yellow. 'I inherited this,' she told him. 'So it's not my first choice of decor, but I've gotten used to it.'

'It's pretty. I like it,' he said.

Seeing him, tall and masculine, in her bedroom took Vega by surprise, and heat began to surge through her body. He felt the energy spark between them, too, and they simultaneously moved towards each other before falling onto her king-sized bed.

28

They went downstairs an hour later, Luka wearing one of Vega's dressing gowns. Vega stifled her giggles when he put on the fluffy bright pink robe, shaking his head when she kept a navy one for herself.

'I know your game, Pearse!' he said. 'But I'll forgive you. Because I'm the first person you've brought back, I know that must make me special.'

'If you keep going on about it, well . . .' She gestured ominously towards the back door.

'If you think I'm going anywhere in this get-up, you've got another think coming.' He tightened the belt around his waist. 'Mind you, aside from the colour, it's rather comfy.'

They both laughed as Vega fetched the ice cream from the freezer and began scooping it into two bowls. 'Would you like a glass of wine with this? Or will I make some tea?'

'I'm driving . . .' Luka raised an eyebrow.

'You can stay over if you like,' Vega said, burying her head in the freezer as she replaced the ice cream.

'In that case, I'll have a large glass!' he replied, a grin on his face.

They went into the sitting room to enjoy their dessert, and Vega noticed her phone flashing on the coffee table where she had left it. There were several missed calls from Kieran and a message from Martha Long.

She opened Martha's message first, and her mind raced as she read it. She turned to Luka and grabbed his arm as she relayed it to him. 'Martha has tracked down some of the people from the Rochester and Island Pond communes.'

'That's great,' he enthused.

'That's not the best part. One of them was in Ireland with Mum and Apollo. A guy called Mark Perry. She's reached out to him and asked if I could call him. He said yes.'

They locked eyes. 'You're getting closer to Cassie every day,' Luka said softly.

Vega nodded, feeling goosebumps running down her arms. She sipped her wine, the dry, sharp tannins calming her. 'I need to ring Kieran back. But then I'm going to call this Mark guy. Back in a sec.' She dialled Kieran's number as she walked into the kitchen.

'Bad news, kiddo,' he said as soon as he answered.

'What's up?'

'I had my weekly catch-up with Delaney. You came up, because of the award nomination, and he asked me what you were working on. I didn't tell him about your personal connection, but mentioned you were working on a story about the Nowhere Girls. He pulled the plug on it.'

Vega cursed in surprise. 'I don't understand. Why?'

'He said it's too similar to Annette's story. Not original enough. He's concerned about falling readership and feels we're moving in the wrong direction. He wants to chase more viral content.'

'That makes no sense.'

'I know, but he's adamant that you concentrate on a story about GLP drugs for weight loss.'

'You cannot be serious.'

'I'm afraid I am. But look, just because we're not going to publish the story in the paper doesn't mean you have to let it go. My friend works as an editor at one of the Big Six publishers. They'd leap at the opportunity to release this as a memoir. I can organise a meeting.'

Vega's heart raced at the thought. 'I'm not sure if I'm ready for that.'

'Okay, but either way you need to keep digging and writing.

We'll find a way to share your story when you're ready. And look, you'll be meeting Delaney at the Journalism Awards next week. When you see him, grab your chance and do what you do best: persuade him to change his mind.'

'Okay, that I can do. I need to sort out a dress. Tomorrow's job! Oh, by the way, I have a lead I'm about to follow up. Someone who was in Ireland with Mum and Apollo. Hopefully this guy can tell me where they ended up.'

'Keep me posted. Listen, something else for you to consider. Maybe it's time to report your mother as missing.'

Vega frowned. 'I wondered about that too. But I'm not sure she is missing yet. I need to find Robert Shaw first. See what he has to say.'

'That's probably wise. But if you do decide to report this, you could speak to my brother-in-law – Detective Tony Gilmartin. He's a nice guy. Top of his game. I'll have a word and make sure he takes good care of you.'

'Thank you, Kieran, that's appreciated.'

'Good luck, kiddo. Keep me posted.'

Once she'd hung up, Vega filled Luka in on the call.

'That's short-sighted of Delaney. I think he's wrong about what readers want. But is it a bad thing? You started this story as a means to find out more about your mother. You don't need the paper to continue your search.'

Vega nodded, deep in thought. 'I will keep writing it, because it's cathartic putting my thoughts on paper. But whether I ever share them is undecided.'

'One step at a time.'

'Yep.' She sighed deeply. 'It's complicated for me, Luka. I planned on writing the piece for the paper as a journalist, never divulging that I was one of the Nowhere Girls. But now it's become so personal, I can't keep myself out of it, and I'm not sure I'm ready for the world to know that about me.'

'I get it.' Luka reached over to stroke her hand. 'Do you want to call Mark Perry now? Or leave it till tomorrow?'

'Now. I won't sleep if I don't at least try.' She found the contact details Martha had sent and hit call, putting the phone on speaker so that Luka could listen in.

'Mark Perry,' a deep voice with an American twang said as soon as the call connected.

'Hi, Mark. My name is Vega Pearse. I'm—'

'I know who you are,' he interrupted. 'That was quick. I only spoke to Martha an hour ago.'

'This is important to me; I hope it's a convenient time to chat,' Vega said. 'I'm desperate to find my mother and sister.'

'Fair enough. What do you want to know?'

'Everything. How did you know Mum, and when was the last time you saw her?'

'Okay.' Mark cleared his throat. 'I met your mother in Island Pond. I'd been at the commune for two years before she arrived.'

'Were you friends?'

He hesitated. 'I don't think I'd call us friends. But I knew her. She was . . . let's say she was passionate. And whip-smart.'

'You didn't like her,' Vega acknowledged, hearing a change in his voice as he spoke about her. 'Can I ask why?'

'I didn't trust her, I suppose. She'd only been at the commune for a few short weeks and she began giving orders. Making changes to how we ran things.'

'What kind of orders?'

'How we sold our products, how we ran the farm . . . She had a lot to say for someone so young.'

Vega rolled her eyes. This man's tone suggested he wasn't a fan of strong women. But she bit back a retort, determined to get answers.

'And what about Apollo? What did you think of him?'

'He was a friend. For a time at least. A complicated man in many ways. We arrived at Island Pond within a few days of each other. I liked him then.'

Luka and Vega swapped a sceptical glance.

Vega cleared her throat. 'Martha Long and Frankie Chalupka

were not as complimentary about him. Did most of the group feel like them?'

Mark laughed. 'Look, Apollo could ruffle feathers. If he wanted something, he would get it, no matter who stood in his way. He and Frankie clashed, so I'm not surprised Frankie felt like that.'

'Over Mum?'

'Yeah. They were both in love with her. But it was no contest. Star was always going to choose Apollo. There was this energy when they were together. Fire.'

'Martha told me they left Island Pond and moved to Ireland. You visited them there?'

'Yeah. I went back and forth a few times throughout the eighties. I would stay for a few months, help on the farm, and then return home before my visa ran out. But it got weird, so I took a step back.'

'In what way was it weird?'

'Look, I've lived in several communes. While there might be natural leaders, they always felt like a collective, a group of like-minded people who shared the same goals and vision, working together. And they were welcoming. The door was always open. But that changed in Ireland.'

'How?' Vega asked, her voice little more than a whisper.

'Apollo became controlling. He didn't like outsiders. He wanted to keep everyone on the farm isolated from the wider community. If you ask me, he overdid the psychedelics. They altered his brain.' He paused. 'I'm sorry, but I've got to be somewhere. I'll have to split.'

'A couple more minutes. Please.'

Mark sighed, as if he were put upon, but didn't hang up.

'What about their relationship, the last time you saw them? Were they still in love?' Vega asked.

'As I said, it got weird during that last visit. Apollo accused me of having an affair with Star.'

'And were you?' she asked calmly, even though her heart was racing.

'Listen, I'd have been more likely to have an affair with Apollo than Star. It was preposterous. I knew it was time for me to leave. I never went back. Now I really must go.'

Vega knew that this was it. 'Before you go, do you remember the address of Apollo's farm?'

She held her breath as she waited for Mark's answer. Seconds felt like minutes, and she steeled herself for another dead end.

'I'd have to go digging around for the exact address. But I remember the general area. It was in Connemara.'

'Connemara?' Vega repeated, somehow shocked by this.

'That's right. Middle of nowhere.'

A shiver ran through her body at the phrase.

'Can you tell me anything more about the place, to help narrow it down?' She cursed herself for never having been to that part of Ireland. Or at least not to her recollection.

'Well, it was near a stunning fjord about seven or eight miles long between Galway and Mayo. The name is on the tip of my tongue. But it's been a while . . . Actually, I remember Apollo saying it was Ireland's only fjord. No idea if that's true or not.'

Luka picked up his phone and began searching, then turned the screen towards Vega.

'Was it Killary Harbour?' she asked.

'That's the one! Yes, I'm fairly sure that's it.'

Vega had so many questions she wanted to ask him regarding his visits to the farm, but restrained herself for the moment, aware that she needed to address the crux of the matter. 'Mark, can you tell me when you last saw them?'

'How old are you? Because the last time I visited them was when you were a couple of months old,' he replied.

Vega slumped back against the sofa, shaking her head in surprise. 'You've met me?'

'Sure have. I even rocked you to sleep once. I was there the night you arrived, kicking and screaming into the world. You had quite the set of lungs for such a small thing!'

A sob escaped her. 'I'm sorry . . . this has taken me by surprise. I've never met anyone who knew me before I was four.'

His voice softened. 'Martha mentioned that you were abandoned. That sucks. And for what it's worth, it makes no sense to me. Your parents were thrilled when you came along. You were loved. Now, I do have to go.'

'One more question. Please. Is Apollo my father?'

He answered within a split second, but it was the longest wait of Vega's life. 'Yes. Apollo is your father.'

29

Vega did what she knew best – she began a comprehensive investigation of all social media accounts on Facebook and Instagram mentioning Killary Harbour, but didn't find any mention of a commune online. She tried to focus on a new story for the paper on weight-loss drugs, but her mind kept shifting back to the man who could be her father.

Why was she such a blank when it came to Apollo? She had concluded that after Nova's birth, their mother must have left him, and that was why she had no recollections of him. But if that was the case, it only presented further questions.

She could only hope that Apollo still resided in Killary Harbour. She and Luka had made a plan to go there together that weekend. But once Luka had left for work that morning, Vega realised she couldn't put it off for another day. She packed an overnight bag without informing him of her changed plans, as she was sure he would try to dissuade her from going alone. He could not be expected to comprehend the depth of her need to finally return to where she was born – the last known address she had for her mother. She reasoned with herself that he had to go to court that afternoon to testify in an ongoing child protection case. His phone would be switched off most of the day, and he'd warned her that he'd be working late. It was better not to involve him until tomorrow, when she could update him on how she had got on.

It was a five-hour drive, and aside from stopping for fuel and a takeaway coffee, she didn't pause. With each mile, she replayed the conversations she'd had over the past few weeks with everyone who had known her parents. Then she remembered her promise to Mama Lulu to contact her if she found Cassie. After checking the time difference, she called her through CarPlay.

'This is a nice surprise!' Mama Lulu said warmly.

'Killary Harbour, Connemara!' Vega exclaimed hurriedly. 'That was where Apollo and Mum went when they came to Ireland.'

'Slow down!' Mama Lulu said. 'Begin at the start. How did you discover that?'

Vega recounted her conversation with Mark Perry, holding nothing back, including Mark's disdain for Cassie. Mama Lulu took it all in her stride, calmly asking, 'Is Luka with you?'

'No. He wanted to come with me at the weekend, but I couldn't wait until then. I've got to see for myself if Mum is there. And if Apollo is my father.'

'No, I don't suppose you could be expected to wait. You've been on hold for nearly your entire life looking for answers.' Mama Lulu sighed. 'But I don't like you doing this solo.' She paused, then admitted tremulously, 'The thought that Cassie could be there after all this time . . . it's making me feel a little dizzy. One moment, I'm going to take a seat.'

'Oh, Mama Lulu, are you okay?' Vega asked, worried that she'd caused her grandmother further stress. 'I should have waited to call until after I'd been there.'

'You've done the right thing calling me now. I was a little overcome momentarily, but I'm okay. I'm made of strong stuff, don't you worry.'

'Try not to get your hopes up,' Vega said. 'We have no real evidence to suggest she's still there. And the more I explore Mum's past, the more I realise that none of us truly know her. I've learned about so many different versions of her that I can't discern who she really was back then or what her next move was likely to be.'

'Me neither. From your descriptions, I don't recognise her as the little girl I raised.'

'If she's in Connemara . . .' Vega paused, her voice trembling, 'if she's been there all along, it's going to be difficult to forgive.'

'I know, love. I know,' Mama Lulu replied. 'My heart aches every time I think that my baby girl stayed away from me all these years. It's cruel. But as a mother, contemplating that she could walk away from her daughters . . . it's unthinkable.'

A heavy silence enveloped the small car as grandmother and granddaughter dealt with their painful thoughts.

'Promise me you'll be careful,' Mama Lulu said after a moment.

'I'm made of strong stuff too, promise,' Vega replied, though her voice betrayed her. She cleared her throat and said more forcefully, 'I truly am fine. Whether Mum is there or not, I'm getting closer to her; I can feel it.'

'That's all very well, but you should have someone to look after you when you meet this Apollo,' Mama Lulu insisted. 'You know you don't always have to do everything on your own. You've got Luka, you've got me and Flick.'

Vega bit back her immediate thought that she was accustomed to managing her affairs independently. She realised the words would hurt her grandmother, who was blameless in this situation, so she said, more gently, 'It's taken me a while to get used to having people around me who care. I'm very grateful to have you all now. But be honest, Mama Lulu, would you wait if it were you?'

'No. I don't suppose I would,' Mama Lulu agreed.

'I'm going to be fine. I'll speak to Apollo, if I can find him, ask if he knows where Mum is and then leave. And I'll ring you as soon as I do. All right?'

Mollified by Vega's reassurances, Mama Lulu said her goodbyes.

Vega slowed down as she drove along the N59, and when she spotted a viewpoint signposted, she pulled over. From here she could see the entire fjord, and even though it was a dull day, the grey skies appeared almost translucent as they skimmed over the glassy azure water. Half a dozen kayakers sped by, then suddenly something broke the surface, making a splash. She peered closer and could have sworn she saw a fin. Dolphins were known to be in the area, so perhaps she had struck lucky. She decided that was a good sign.

Her eyes wandered over the towering Mweelrea mountain, which loomed over the northern side of the bay. She felt a pang as thoughts of Luka surfaced. If he were here, he would have an array of fascinating facts to share with her.

She returned to her car and continued driving, passing a group of hikers who waved cheerfully in her direction. Behind the stone walls flanking the road, sheep grazed on lush grass.

As she approached Leenaun, the small village nestled in the heart of Killary Harbour, she decided that she first needed to eat. Hunger pangs and nervous anticipation made her stomach ache and churn. She needed to feel more settled before confronting Apollo.

Spotting a pub with vivid blue paintwork called Hamilton's Bar, she reckoned that was as good a place as any to refuel and enquire about Robert Shaw. She parked across the road and followed her nose inside, the delightful aroma of fish wafting through the air. She sat at the bar on a high stool beside an older gentleman wearing a peaked cap and a bright orange jumper.

'Howya,' he said, lifting his pint of Guinness in her direction.

'Hello,' Vega replied. 'Guinness good?'

'The best.'

'What about food? Any recommendations?'

'Go for the seafood chowder with a couple of slices of brown soda bread and butter; you won't get a finer meal.'

A barman wandered over, smiling. 'I see Jimmy is giving you the run-down on the place.'

'He is. And on his recommendation, I'll have the chowder and half a pint of Guinness.'

'No bother. Do you want it here, or would you like me to find you a table?'

'If Jimmy doesn't mind, I'll stay put.'

Jimmy's face broke into a broad smile. 'Best offer I've had in years. Stay right where you are.'

'I'm Vega.' She reached over to shake his hand.

'Vega, eh? Don't think I've met one of those before.'

'I like to think I'm one of a kind,' Vega responded with a shrug. 'Are you local, Jimmy?'

'Born and bred. Seventy-two years living in Leenaun. Or Leenane, as most call it now.'

'Which do you prefer?'

''Twas Leenaun when I was a young fella, so it will always be that to me.'

'Well that's what I'll call it as well,' Vega said, thanking the barman as he placed cutlery and water before her.

'You don't look like a tourist,' Jimmy said, lifting his Guinness to his mouth and sighing contentedly after taking a large sup.

'I'm not. I'm looking for someone.'

Jimmy opened his arms wide and smiled. 'You've found him!'

Vega cackled with laughter, instantly liking him. 'If I weren't already taken, you could easily win my heart,' she told him.

The barman set her glass of Guinness before her, its flawless creamy head resting atop its dark body. She lifted it, admiring its perfection. '*Sláinte*, Jimmy.'

'To your good health,' he replied, and they both took a drink.

Her chowder and brown bread arrived, and for the next few minutes she concentrated on one of the best meals she had ever had. Every creamy spoonful comforted her, easing her nerves and settling her stomach.

'Told you,' Jimmy said, nodding in approval when she cleared her bowl. 'Now that you've eaten, tell me why you're here.'

Vega had prepared several potential explanations for her presence in Leenaun, but she found herself telling Jimmy the truth. 'I'm searching for a man called Robert Shaw. He has a farm around here. He might go by the name Apollo; I've been told he uses that alias.'

Jimmy pulled a face.

'I'm guessing you know him, judging by that expression.'

'Aye. I know him all right. He's what you might call a colourful local character. He sells vegetables in the local market every week. What do you want with him?'

'I'm trying to find my mother and sister. I discovered yesterday that I was born on Robert Shaw's farm, and that he might be my father. So I have some questions for him.'

'Well, I'm sorry for your trouble, so.' Jimmy shook his head sorrowfully.

'He's that bad?' Vega asked, feeling unease nip its way down her back.

He shrugged. 'Look, I take people as I find them. But I find that fella to be a right eejit. Full of himself. He'd eat himself if he were a bar of chocolate.'

Despite the seriousness of the situation, Vega couldn't stop a bellow of laughter from escaping. She wasn't normally good at meeting new people, forming connections so quickly. But somehow, over the previous few weeks, she'd found herself changing. Opening up, letting others in. She leaned in to Jimmy and asked, 'Do you know a woman called Cassie, who might go by the name Star?'

'It's hard to keep track of who lives up there. Since returning from America in the eighties, he's had many people from all over. Some commune, or cult, depending on who you talk to. I don't know what goes on up there, and I don't want to know. Stay clear is my advice.'

'Cassie is my mother. And I know she lived there once. I need to talk to Apollo,' Vega said, her eyes shining fiercely. 'I can't stay away.'

'Fair enough. Well, there are a few women up on the farm for sure. Tommy Barnes leases land off them and has said he's met them. I think one of the women, around Apollo's age, has been there as long as he has. I don't know her name, though. She never comes down to the village. Keeps to herself.'

A shiver ran down Vega's spine as she imagined her mother

being held captive on the farm, not allowed to leave or contact her family all this time. She pushed her drink away and grabbed her purse; the need to get to Apollo's was overwhelming. 'Is the farm far from here?'

'You won't be walking it. Drive to Tullycross, between Leenaun and Kylemore. Follow all the trekkers doing the Killary Famine Walk; there are always dozens of them. You'll pass Lough Fee and Oscar Wilde's father's house, along with cottages in ruins. Then you need to watch out for Salrock Pass – you can't miss the gap in the hills. The Shaw farm is located on the right-hand side. It's called Cosmo Farm now.' Jimmy rolled his eyes.

Vega dug into her bag and jotted down the instructions in a notebook, then opened her phone to search for Salrock Pass, feeling delighted when it appeared on her Apple Maps. She glanced at her watch; it was nearly four o'clock.

'If you're going today, you'd want to get going before dark. Those roads have surprises around every corner. Watch out for the devil . . .'

'You mean Apollo?'

Jimmy grinned. 'Strange as that might sound, he might well be. No, I'm talking about the legend of Salrock Pass. The gap was formed when the devil found St Rock wearing a cross around his neck. So he dragged him over the hills with a chain and made the gap.'

'That's a cheery story,' Vega said, frowning as an image of Apollo with red horns filled her mind.

'You're not wearing any crosses, are you?' he asked.

She reached up and touched her bare neck, shivering again.

'Would you stop scaring the nice girl!' the barman said as he wiped the countertop.

Vega pulled forty euros from her wallet and beckoned the man over. 'For the food, and get a couple of pints for Jimmy.'

'You leaving me already?' Jimmy said when she stood up. 'The story of my life!'

Vega touched his arm gently and smiled. 'It's my loss, and I know it! I need a hotel for tonight. By the time I leave Apollo's farm, it will be too late to drive home. Any recommendations?'

'The Leenane Hotel on the Clifden Road. If you have any difficulty getting a room, come back here. I'll find somewhere for you. And thank you for the pints. That's decent of you.'

'My pleasure. Wish me luck, Jimmy.'

The smile disappeared from his face, and he frowned as he took her hand. 'Be careful up there. There have been rumours for as long as I can remember. Drugs and goodness knows what else. I wouldn't trust that fella as far as I could throw him. I'll be here if you want to come back for another drink afterwards. You might need it after spending a few minutes with that eejit.'

And with one final squeeze of her hand, he let her go.

30

Extract from an interview with Tommy Barnes

Vega: How long have you been leasing land from the Shaws?

Tommy: Let me think. Well, Dermot Shaw – a gentleman, I might add – died in 1984. He was Apollo's father. When Apollo came back from America, he initially managed the farm himself. I don't know, he had thirty-odd people living there – a commune. I've never seen the likes of it in my life.

Vega: Is your farm next door to the Shaws'?

Tommy: That's right. My father and Dermot Shaw were born the same year, went to school together and farmed side by side. Robert is a few years older than me and had gone to America before I came along. My dad took a while to settle down and have kids. When I heard he was back, I went up to the farm, delighted to say hello for the aul' fella's sake. He didn't like it when I called him Robert and insisted that he was Apollo now reborn or some such nonsense.

Vega: What did you make of that?

Tommy: Sure, it was clear he was off his rocker. His eyes were glassy, and he was as high as a kite. A party was going on, and they were laughing around the fire pit. The smell of weed nearly knocked me out. I didn't stick around.

Vega: Have you ever met a woman named Cassie, or Star?

Tommy: Couldn't tell you. I occasionally saw some women in the village selling vegetables at the farmers' market or picking up groceries. You'd recognise them a mile away because they wore the same drab grey dress. Plus, they kept to themselves, never engaged in conversation other than a polite hello or goodbye.

Vega: You never said when you began leasing land from Apollo.

Tommy: Sorry, I got sidetracked. That would be in 1996.

Vega: Why did he decide to lease the land then?

Tommy: I suspect it was because the numbers at the farm had dwindled. There were only a handful there when he approached me. He couldn't manage it all on his own. We made a deal: I took fifty acres and bought all but ten of his cattle. I graze my sheep and cattle there now. I got the feeling he needed the cash.

Vega: What about Apollo's wife? Was she involved in negotiating that deal?

Tommy: Not a bit of it. When I got there that day, she was in the kitchen, white as a ghost, with eyes red raw. She scurried away as soon as I walked into the house, apologising to Apollo for being there. Gave me the shivers. Not a normal relationship.

Vega: Have you ever spoken to her when you were up on the farm?

Tommy: Nope. Never had a single conversation.

Vega: Ever? That sounds strange.

Tommy: Well, it's a strange set-up, to be sure. There are two women there now, Apollo's wife and a younger woman, and a little boy. When they see me coming, they all disappear into the house. I'm only allowed to deal with Apollo. He likes cash payments for the lease. I call up there once a month.

Vega: He sounds controlling.

Tommy: He's the boss and wants everyone to know it. He believes women are there to serve and men to lead – his words, not mine.

31

Vega's car crept steadily along the narrow, winding road, its tyres crunching softly on the gravel as she turned onto the minor road to Tullycross. The air around her was crisp, infused with the earthy scent of damp leaves and wildflowers that lined the sides of the road. Following Jimmy's directions, she caught her first glimpse of the shimmering waters of Lough Fee, its surface reflecting the grey sky. As she continued her journey, she passed the house of Oscar Wilde's father, its once grand facade now a mere shadow of its former glory. She spotted the roofless ruins that Jimmy had told her about. They dotted the landscape like forgotten memories, and the whispers of their former owners floated around her, telling her she was getting close. Her eyes scanned the road on either side, and finally she saw the gap in the hills.

'Where are you, devil?' she called out softly, then indicated right to the small laneway that led to the Shaw farm.

Lush emerald-green fields stretched on either side of the narrow lane, cradling a flock of fluffy sheep that raised their curious heads to gaze at her as she passed. Towering trees, their trunks thick and sturdy, formed a dense copse on her right, their leaves whispering secrets in the gentle breeze.

She braked and her breath left her.

This was not quite the forest she'd remembered, yet she was absolutely sure of one thing.

She had been here before.

A wooden sign was nailed to a sycamore tree, with the words *Cosmo Farm* painted in black.

She shifted the car into first gear and proceeded up the lane towards a farmhouse standing proudly against the grey sky. It had ivy creeping up its weathered stones and windows with closed curtains, hiding its secrets from the world.

The sound of a tractor drew her attention to a muddy yard behind the house. Two men in overalls came into view, tearing hay bales into troughs for the animals. She stopped the car and stepped out onto a muddy driveway, where green algae shimmered on the cement base.

Her senses were heightened, and the sound of linen flapping in the wind drew her attention behind her. She swivelled around and observed a woman hanging white sheets on a long washing line. The woman was slender, with dark brown hair, and was wearing a faded grey midi dress. Vega's heart sank as she acknowledged that she was too young to be her mother.

A child's voice echoed towards her, quickly accompanied by the sight of a young boy sprinting through the neighbouring field, tugging a kite that soared through the clouds.

And a new memory pierced her, of two little girls chasing a kite on that same hilly field many years ago. 'Nova . . .' she called out softly, her body aching for her little sister, who she hadn't held in her arms for thirty years.

She pulled herself together because the woman by the washing line was moving towards her.

'Can I help you?' she asked, her voice and face filled with suspicion. Vega reckoned she was around her own age.

'I hope you can. I'm looking for Robert Shaw, or Apollo, as he's known. And his wife.' Vega was surprised that her voice sounded as assured as it did, because she was falling apart inside.

'Who are you? What do you want with them?'

'I'm . . . well, I'm related to them,' she ended lamely. She didn't feel comfortable enough to say who she was. Yet.

The woman's brow furrowed. 'Stay here. I'll check if they're free to talk.'

Vega stumbled and had to grasp the car door to steady herself. 'They're both here? Apollo and his wife?'

'Yes,' the woman replied. 'I'll be back in a minute.' She disappeared around the back of the farmhouse.

The minutes dragged on agonisingly, each second stretching as if it were an eternity, until at last the dark-haired woman reappeared. Her expression was unreadable.

'Come with me.'

Vega trailed behind her as they stepped into the expansive cobblestoned yard, where the air was filled with the earthy scent of the farm. To the right was a patio area, adorned with about a dozen eclectic plastic chairs, all clustered around a large, weathered fire pit. Beyond the fire pit was a swing set, once a vibrant red, but now dulled by the relentless passage of time and countless playful afternoons. Had Vega kicked her legs out on that swing as a child? Along the back wall of the house, a series of rustic barrels stood in a neat row, ready to collect rainwater. A stack of chopped firewood loomed nearly six feet high to the left of that.

Vega had been here before. She knew it with every part of her.

And then a figure moved towards her. It was a woman, slight, with wavy greying light brown hair worn loose over the shoulders of her grey dress, similar to the younger woman's. Round sunglasses covered half her face.

'Mum?' Vega tried to call out, but her voice abandoned her. Her legs buckled, and she reached out to steady herself against the back of one of the chairs. She closed her eyes and counted to ten, then opened them as the woman arrived at her side.

32

Vega and the woman locked eyes, and it felt like time stood still, the world around them faded into a blur as they regarded one another. Vega scrutinised what she could see of the woman's delicate features as she searched for any hint, any confirmation that this was indeed Cassie.

'What do you want?' the woman asked, her voice a melodic whisper, each word almost sung.

'I'm searching for my parents: Cassie and Robert, or Star and Apollo, as they may be referred to,' Vega replied, her heart racing fast, making her breathless.

The woman's complexion paled at this revelation. 'I see. And that must mean that you are Vega or Nova.' Her voice was tight and thin.

'Yes. That's right. I'm Vega.'

A heavy silence descended between them, an almost tangible pause, each lost in their thoughts.

'Are you . . . are you Cassie?' Vega finally managed to utter, her voice barely above a whisper, laced with hope.

'No, of course not! I'm Petra,' the woman replied, shaking her head at the question's absurdity.

Vega felt a wave of disappointment surge within her, surprising her with its intensity. Even though she'd had knockback after knockback in her search for her mother, hearing another *no* struck her harder than she'd expected.

'Is Cassie here?' she asked, her voice trembling with urgency.

'Here, there, everywhere,' Petra said, her hand rising gracefully, waving towards the expansive late-afternoon sky, painted in orange and pink hues as the sun descended.

A swell of annoyance replaced Vega's disappointment. This woman was beginning to get on her nerves. 'What does that mean?' she demanded, her eyes narrowing with frustration.

'Every living being is composed of the remnants of stars,' Petra explained, gesturing elegantly towards the boy flying his colourful kite, his laughter echoing through the air. 'He is made of stardust. Like him, you, Vega, are a star. We all are,' she concluded, her eyes sparkling with a profound wisdom that Vega struggled to grasp.

'I'll take your word for it. Can I talk to Apollo, please?' Vega had reached her limit with this woman, who was clearly unstable.

Petra frowned. 'Apollo is resting and does not like to be disturbed until the sun goes down.'

It took all of Vega's willpower not to roll her eyes. 'It's important that I speak to him. Can you tell him that I'm here, please? I think he might want to speak to me too.' Surely the man would have mild curiosity, at the very least.

Petra's brow furrowed deeply, lost in contemplation of Vega's words.

'Sit,' she instructed at last, her hand sweeping gracefully towards the bright plastic chairs on the patio. 'Estelle will bring you refreshments.' With that, she glided around the side of the house, disappearing through a door.

Moments later, the younger woman emerged, balancing a wooden tray adorned with delicate flowers. She presented Vega with a tall glass filled with a vibrant green mix that looked like half the garden had been immersed in it.

'Thank you, Estelle,' Vega said with a smile. She leaned in, inhaling the refreshing aroma. 'Mint?'

'Yes. You have a good nose. It's water infused with fresh mint, parsley and sweet cucumber,' Estelle explained, her voice warm and inviting.

Vega's mind drifted momentarily to Jimmy back at the bar, and the stark contrast of the chilled Guinness she'd enjoyed only an hour before. 'Thank you,' she responded, lifting the glass to her lips. She took a sip and bit back a wince before gingerly setting it beside her. It was earthy, and a taste that was acquired, she believed. She wondered if Estelle would be any more forthcoming. 'Is Petra your mother?'

Estelle nodded, her wide eyes scanning the patio.

'Can you sit down for a moment?' Vega asked.

Estelle nodded, then hovered lightly on the edge of a chair, her eyes darting about as if she expected danger to emerge any second.

'Is that your son over there having so much fun with his kite?' Vega enquired, gesturing towards the child, whose laughter and playful shouts echoed through the late-afternoon air.

A radiant smile spread across Estelle's face, lighting up her features. 'Yes. That's my son, Altair.'

'Is he named after a star as well?'

'Yes, Altair means the flying one. Which feels a little apt . . .'

Their gazes drifted towards the boy, who dashed about with such exuberance that it seemed he was nearly soaring through the air, a blur of joy and energy in the golden sunlight.

'You know,' Vega said, 'I always thought I had a strange name. I'd have fitted right in here with Vega, wouldn't I?'

The two women giggled together.

Vega leaned in closer, her gaze fixed on the fresh-faced Estelle. There was a beauty about her, almost ethereal, as she sat gracefully in her flowing dress, hair cascading around her shoulders.

Vega's heart quickened as it struck her that this woman might be related to her.

'Is Apollo your father?' she asked.

When Estelle shook her head, Vega exhaled deeply and leaned back in the plastic chair. 'I think he's *my* father.'

Estelle's expression shifted with surprise, her eyes widening in shock and a hand flying to her mouth as if to stifle an involuntary gasp.

'It's a lot, I know,' Vega said. 'I've been searching for my sister, Nova, and my mother for a long time.'

She stopped when she saw that Estelle looked close to tears. 'Are you okay?' Her voice softened, sensing the tension.

'I'm fine,' Estelle replied, though her voice betrayed her. She took a deep breath, then spoke in a stronger tone. 'Star is not here. I'm sorry. But Apollo sometimes speaks of you and Nova. His lost stars, he calls you.'

Vega felt every hair on her arms rise to attention as she continued probing. 'And has he mentioned where my mother is?'

'No. He's not spoken about her for a long time.' Estelle's eyes darted nervously from side to side. She clasped her hands tightly in her lap, twisting them anxiously.

Vega decided to leave that aside for a moment. 'Do you have any other family?' she asked, feeling a rush of curiosity combined with a tinge of excitement.

'No. My father used to live on the farm too, but he left us years ago and went back to England.' A shadow passed over Estelle's face as she spoke.

'I'm sorry to hear that. I know how hard it is to be left behind.' The two women shared a sad smile.

'So did Apollo give you all your star names?' Vega asked.

'Yes.' Estelle threw her a questioning look. 'How did you know that?'

'I heard he did the same for my mother. I've spoken to some people who lived here on the farm years ago, or with Apollo and Star when they were on a commune in America.' She looked around the farm and asked, 'So who else lives here besides your mum and your little boy?'

'Just us now. But the community is fluid. We have guests coming and going. Although not as often as we used to when I was a little girl. A local farmer rents land, and he and some of his staff come and go in the fields.'

Vega wondered where Estelle's partner or husband was, but parked that question for another time.

'He talks about you,' Estelle said. 'At night. When he takes his medicine.'

'What medicine?'

'A drink he has every night that is designed to help him find harmony with the vast universe,' Estelle replied, her voice slightly wistful. 'That's when he brings up you and Nova. He says you were lost amidst the stars, wandering in an endless expanse of cosmic mystery. But you're not lost, are you?'

Vega frowned, a cloud of uncertainty hanging over her. 'No, I'm not lost. But Nova and my mum seem adrift in a world I can't reach.'

'You really don't know where they are?' Estelle pressed, concern etched on her features.

'I'm afraid not. I've been searching for them for what feels like an eternity. I came here for answers and in the hope that Apollo might help me find my mum.'

A hint of sadness crept into Estelle's eyes and she bit her bottom lip. 'When you meet him, you need to be ca—'

Whatever she intended to say was interrupted by the sudden appearance of Petra, who appeared beside them.

'Apollo will see you,' she announced, her tone brisk and businesslike.

'Er . . . great . . . thank you,' Vega stammered, feeling a mix of anticipation and anxiety.

Petra nodded curtly and turned to her daughter. 'It's time to put Altair to bed. He needs his rest.'

A sense of disorientation washed over Vega as she realised she must have lost track of time. However, when she glanced at her watch, it was only half past five, the day just beginning to darken.

'Surely it's not bedtime already?' she asked, bewildered.

'Apollo doesn't like to be disturbed by children in the evenings,' Estelle explained. 'We normally retreat to our bedrooms when he rises. He likes to spend his time out here, where the stars can whisper secrets to him.'

This man, her father, was crazy, Vega thought.

'Do you have a mobile phone?' Petra asked.

Vega nodded, but instant regret washed over her as Petra added, 'Phones are not permitted here at Cosmo Farm.'

'I'll switch it off,' Vega replied, her heart racing as she reached into her pocket. A glance at the home screen revealed several messages from Luka and one from Mama Lulu, alongside a missed call from Flick. She sensed they held an unspoken urgency. But before she could look at them more closely, Petra cut in.

'Please switch it off now, and we will take it from you until you leave. It will be quite safe, don't worry.' When Vega hesitated, her eyes moving back to the screen, Petra pressed on. 'No phone, no visit with Apollo. Your choice.'

Vega noted that her melodic, sing-song voice had been replaced by a harsher, firmer tone that left no room for debate.

There was no real choice to be made. Vega had to see this man, who might well be not only her father, but someone who held the key to unravelling the mysteries surrounding her mother's past and her own identity. The prospect of that connection outweighed her reticence about losing her lifeline to the outside world.

She passed the phone to the older woman and followed her inside.

33

'You can leave your shoes in the basket,' Petra said, kicking off her own ballet pumps delicately.

Vega bent down and slipped off her trainers, placing them in the half-filled basket, then followed Petra through a spacious kitchen. Every surface was cluttered with jars and containers. A peculiar aroma wafted through the air – a blend of fried meat mingling with an earthy, muddy scent that she couldn't quite place.

'Lamb kebabs tonight,' Petra said, sniffing appreciatively. 'Perhaps you'll join us for supper.'

Vega smiled politely, but she had no intention of sticking around. She wanted to get the information she needed, then go. Perhaps have a drink with Jimmy in Hamilton's as he'd suggested.

They walked down a lengthy hallway adorned with tapestry artwork. Petra paused at the final door on the right and knocked softly.

A muffled voice replied, 'You may enter.'

They ventured inside, much like Dorothy and the Scarecrow in Oz. Vega half expected Petra to curtsey.

The room was dimly lit, with heavy curtains drawn across the windows. It took a moment for Vega's eyes to adjust. Wooden bookshelves lined every wall, stacked with volumes. More books lay in disordered piles around the room. Candles, their wax melting down the sides, bordered the wooden floor, casting shadows.

'I'll leave you, but ring for me if you need anything,' Petra sang out.

Vega's eyes searched for Apollo and found him sitting regally in a wingback leather chair with a rich burgundy hue and intricate detailing. The years had been kind to him. That was Vega's first thought as she intently examined every detail of his face. His thick white hair was a striking contrast to his deeply tanned face, which was adorned with a meticulously trimmed white beard that framed his strong jawline. He wore a fitted light blue denim shirt and dark denim jeans, both of which accentuated his blue eyes. As he stood to greet her, his bright smile radiated warmth, almost illuminating the room.

'I knew you'd come home to me,' he said, opening his arms wide to welcome her. 'My lost star, back at Cosmo Farm again.'

Vega stood rooted to the spot. Every part of her resisted him, and she was unsure why.

He looked at her quizzically, then clutched his chest in mock hurt. 'You don't have an embrace for your father?'

Vega felt her stomach flip at his words. She gulped, then asked tremulously, 'So you are my father then.'

His face softened, and his eyes glazed over. 'You don't remember me. Of course you don't. But not a day has passed when I haven't thought of you.'

Vega stepped closer to him. 'I remember my mother. I remember my sister. But I'm afraid I have no memories of you.'

He frowned and gestured towards a chair beside him as he settled back into his seat.

'You were so young when your mother took you both. It is perhaps understandable that your memories are buried deep within you. You will need time to get to know me again. And then you will see that I love you and have missed you all this time.'

Vega searched his face to determine if he was genuine, but it was impossible to tell. She only had her gut instinct to go on, and that was that this man should not be trusted. 'Do you know what happened to me and Nova?'

Apollo leaned in and shook his head. 'I presume your mother

took you back to America. You vanished as if off the face of the earth.'

Again she found it impossible to discern whether he was telling the truth. His face was open and earnest, and he gazed at her unflinchingly.

'We haven't been in America. Mum left us at a train station in Dublin in 1995 and never came back for us.'

'That's outrageous!' Apollo exclaimed, two spots of colour blossoming on his cheeks.

'You weren't aware of this?' Vega enquired.

'Of course not!' he replied. But his voice had changed; it was tighter and higher.

'There was a nationwide appeal to find our family. It's strange that you didn't know about it. Surely news of two abandoned girls the same age as your missing daughters would have prompted you to come for us.' To Vega's horror, she felt a wave of emotion surge within her, threatening to unravel her composure. She swallowed back a lump and pinched the palms of her hands with her nails until she regained control.

Apollo watched her closely and smiled sympathetically, as if he could see what was happening beneath the surface. He gave her a moment and then explained, 'I know it must seem strange that I did not know about two abandoned girls, but you must understand that we have no television here. We do not buy or read newspapers.'

'What about radio?'

'No, we don't need any form of indoctrination or propaganda. We have no use for it. The government has controlled all media for hundreds of years, dictating everything we are told. I made a choice years ago to boycott it.'

'Then how do you get your news?'

He pointed to his head. 'Everything I need to know, I already know. Everything I need to learn, I get from the stars.'

Vega shifted restlessly in her chair. He talked in riddles, like Petra. It was deeply unsettling. She wished Luka were with her and regretted her impulsiveness in coming alone. It was time to get answers and then get out. 'Do you know where my mother is?'

'No,' Apollo replied instantly and without hesitation.

'Do you know where Nova is?'

Again an immediate negative response.

'When did you last see either of them?'

'The same time I last saw you, Vega: the last day of November, in 1995. I said goodnight to the two of you and sat outside with Star. The next day, when I awoke, you were all gone.'

'And was this a normal occurence? Us not being there?'

'No. It was unusual, but even so, at first, I didn't worry. I presumed your mother had taken you into town for supplies. We're self-sufficient here but occasionally require items we can't produce ourselves. Once it grew dark, I went to Killary Harbour, but there was no sign of you.'

Vega digested this information for a moment. 'I'm guessing you never reported us missing.'

Apollo looked down and shook his head mournfully. 'I didn't go to the Gardaí. I have always rejected political and social orthodoxy. We favour peace, love and personal freedom in this house.'

'But surely you must agree that to have personal freedoms, peace and love, we need to be policed?'

He gave a derisive grunt. 'If we are to continue this conversation, we need some refreshments. Have you eaten?'

'Yes.'

'Okay. Surely you'll have a drink with your father. Do you prefer hot or cold drinks? Tea, coffee or a glass of our infused water?'

'I drink coffee. Black. Thank you.'

Apollo nodded solemnly, his gaze unwavering, before reaching for a small, ornate bell on the table. He rang it, the sound resonating through the tense atmosphere in the room. Petra appeared with such swiftness that it seemed she had been hovering just beyond the door, ready to respond. Casting a piercing sidelong glance at Vega, she moved gracefully to Apollo's side, leaning in conspiratorially. He whispered something into her ear in hushed tones, prompting her to turn and leave, though not before glancing at Vega once more.

Vega felt a shiver run down her back. There was something about Petra that gave her the creeps. Clearly she was not happy that the prodigal daughter had returned.

She turned to Apollo. 'Let's pretend I buy that you didn't report us missing, and that you didn't see a newspaper headline about abandoned children. And that you truly believed that Mum had taken us back to America. How come you never called my grandmother to ask to speak to us?'

He hung his head and sighed. 'You have every right to be angry with me. I *should* have called your grandmother and demanded to talk to Star. But the thing was, I knew that if your mother had chosen to keep you away from me, there was nothing I could do to alter her decision. And I would not want to keep anyone against their will.'

'You should have tried!' Vega cried out, feeling a rush of anger assault her. 'Do you even care that I was raised in foster care? That I grew up feeling abandoned, scared, hurt and alone? That every day since that poxy day at the train station, I've been looking for my little sister? Waiting for my parents to give a damn and find me?'

Apollo rose to his feet, stretching out his arms pleadingly. 'I do care! And I'll never find the words to express my sorrow that my inaction has caused you harm.' His voice was thick with regret.

'Words! Such hollow sounds to me!' Vega said, her voice climbing in intensity, the pain radiating from her like a palpable force. She clenched her fists tightly at her sides. 'You could have altered the course of my life. You could have saved me and Nova!' The anguish in her tone filled the air with unspoken bitterness. 'You should have come for us! You should have come for me!'

Hot tears now streamed from her eyes, each one like a molten drop of anguish, scalding as they cascaded down her face.

In an instant, Apollo sprang towards her, enveloping her in his arms.

'I'm so sorry,' he whispered fervently.

Vega pushed against him fiercely, her fists pounding his chest as if trying to beat the pain away. Yet he held firm until, wearied by her emotions, she finally succumbed.

For the first time in her memory, she melted into her father's embrace.

34

Vega remained in Apollo's arms until Petra returned to the room. She smiled when she saw them together, but the smile did not reach her eyes.

She was not happy that Vega was here – that much was clear. The why, though, was a mystery.

She poured coffee from a large silver pot into two mugs. 'I know you wanted it black, but I've put cream and sugar in yours. For the shock. You've had quite an emotional reunion,' she said as she handed the drink to Vega.

Vega sniffed the rich, nutty aroma of coffee beans appreciatively. 'Thank you.' She sipped it, but was too hot, so she placed it on a nearby side table to cool down.

'Our beans are imported ethically from Uganda. I have found a company that sources from a partner in a farming community, which insists on paying fair prices.' Apollo said, with a note of pride in his voice.

Vega was impressed. While there was a lot about Apollo she disliked, this was an ethos she could get behind.

'I knew you'd find me.' He smiled as he sipped his drink.

'So you said,' Vega replied. 'Why were you so sure?'

He pointed to his head again. 'I told myself.'

Vega frowned. 'I'm not sure I understand.'

'My inner self is my guide. We all have one. But most do not allow themselves to tap into this hidden oracle.'

She tried to keep her expression neutral. She had heard enough about Apollo to expect him to be eccentric at the very least, but even so, this was heading into territory that she was uncomfortable with.

'Some people need a little guidance to talk to their inner selves. Connect with their guides in the stars,' he said. 'I can help you with that.'

'How?'

'What do you know about MDMA, psilocybin and LSD?'

'You mean the drugs?' Vega asked.

'Exactly. Many people have dabbled in psychedelics re-creationally. I'm wondering if you have.'

'It's a little late for fatherly concern over my drug use,' Vega said jokingly.

'Humour me. Have you ever taken MDMA, Ecstasy or magic mushrooms? While in college, perhaps?'

'No. They've never interested me. I'm too much of a control freak. I like to be aware of everything I do. I enjoy a glass of wine, but that's about it.'

'Ah! You distrust drugs. Very telling. So fear is your cage.'

Vega rolled her eyes. 'I'm not in a cage.'

'If you say so. Humour me and tell me what image comes to your mind when you hear the word "LSD".'

Half-naked hippies dancing in a field with flowers in their hair was the image that immediately came to Vega's mind. But she tempered this by saying, 'I suppose I think of the Summer of Love in the sixties.'

'I thought as much,' Apollo said, then sighed deeply. 'There is so much misdirection – again from the government – about the safe usage of psychedelics. But there is hope. Scientists are optimistic that there will be a clear path to FDA approval for psychedelic drug use as an antidepressant medication. The studies are fascinating. I could direct you to several sources if you want to follow up.'

'I thought you didn't read newspapers or watch the news,' Vega said.

'I read books. I go to the library,' Apollo bit back, his smile darkening for a moment.

'Why are you telling me this?'

'You have missed so much growing up out there . . .' He waved towards the curtained window. 'And as your father, there is so much I want to share with you. I want to help you understand who I am, who your mother was and who you are. Let you escape from that self-induced cage you are in.'

Vega smiled encouragingly. She would tolerate his eccentricities if they helped her understand more about her parents. If he wanted to share, she was here to listen. 'Go on then.'

'Did you know that many geniuses have used psychedelics?' Apollo asked.

'I've read that LSD can boost creativity. But in small doses,' she replied.

'Of course. And without dropping acid, what heights would Dylan, Hendrix or the Beatles have risen to?' He shuddered. 'But I'm referring more to people who have changed the course of history. Einstein. Steve Jobs. Men who have shared how their drug usage has helped them achieve greatness.'

Vega noted that every example he gave was of men. She parked that for now. 'So what? Are you going to tell me that you've achieved greatness, too, through your drug use?' She could not hide the derision in her voice.

'I don't think. *I know*,' Apollo answered with a smile. 'Humanity's mental health would be dramatically improved if we could only remove that ridiculous adage that all drug usage is bad for you.'

'Careful, Apollo, schools will be queuing up to get you in to do talks for the kids,' Vega said drolly.

'I thought you were a clever girl, yet here you are repeating the same old propaganda the government has fed us for decades. Take Mike Tyson. Do you know who he is?'

'Of course. The former heavyweight champion boxer.'

'That's the one. Well, he has found a cure for his depression and suicidal thoughts through his use of psilocybin.'

When Vega raised an eyebrow in question, he explained, 'You might know them by their more commonly used moniker. Magic mushrooms.'

'Had he been taking them before he bit off Evander Holyfield's ear?' Vega asked, referring to the infamous incident in the boxing ring.

'You've just punctuated my point!' Apollo declared. 'If he had found psilocybin earlier, that nasty incident might never have happened.'

'I take it you are a regular user of psychedelics?'

'Yes. I have been since I was eighteen years old. Your mother was, too.'

This surprised her. 'When I spoke to her friend Martha, she said that Mum only smoked pot. No LSD.'

Apollo frowned. 'Martha was part of your mother's past. In America. She went through many rebirths after that time. LSD changed our perspective on the world.' He smiled beatifically. 'For me, it allows me to talk to a higher power.'

Vega leaned in, crossing her arms across her chest. She wished she had her phone to record this conversation and replay it to Luka later. 'You think you speak to God?'

'Not directly. I speak to an emissary of the higher power, who helps me understand my place in the world. And advises me. Warns me.' Apollo took a sip of his coffee. 'This is good. Don't let yours go cold.'

Vega picked up her mug and drank. 'Okay, I'll bite. What has this higher power told you?'

'Over the years, many things. I was told to look out for the woman called Star. That she would be my partner in this world. A few weeks later, your mother arrived at our commune in Island Pond. When I saw her wrist . . . the birthmark in the shape of a star . . . I knew it was predestined.'

'And Mum believed this too?'

'She did. When we took LSD together for the first time, it was the most beautiful experience as we became one entity, one being, one star . . . It was transcendent. '

An image came to Vega's mind of her parents tripping together and dancing around the fire pit outside. Was that a memory or something she'd imagined?

She glanced at the closed door. 'And what about your new wife? Was she predestined too by your emissary?'

'Yes! I was a broken man when Star left with you and Nova. But then I was told that a new star was waiting for me. Not long afterwards, Petra and I became a couple.'

'This emissary of yours should set up a matchmaking app,' Vega said sardonically, taking another drink of her coffee.

'You have a similar sense of humour to your mother. Very dry,' Apollo stated. But somehow Vega didn't think this was a compliment. His voice darkened. 'I was warned about your mother. That she was a dangerous woman who would destroy me if I let her. But I ignored that message at my peril.'

Vega's heart began to race as her mind filled with everything she'd discovered about her mother from Flick, Frankie and Martha. 'Dangerous. That's a strong word to use,' she countered. Feeling light-headed, she closed her eyes briefly and drank more coffee to steady herself. She had eaten very little today, other than her lunchtime soup at the pub. She'd leave soon, check into that hotel Jimmy had mentioned and have some dinner.

'I don't use the word lightly; I witnessed first-hand how ruthless Star could be.'

'You'll need to give me examples.'

'Really? Surely the fact that she abandoned you shows the cruelty she possessed. But no matter. I can provide further instances. Before we fell in love, Star was with another man: Frankie Chalupka.'

Vega almost spluttered out her coffee at the mention of Frankie's name.

'He was completely infatuated with her. Yet she desired me.' Apollo shrugged as though this were the most natural thing in the world. 'We had a heat, a fire between us that nothing could ever douse.'

'I've met Frankie,' Vega stated quickly, trying to move on from further references to her parents' passion. 'He had quite the story to share. One in which he claimed you set him up to get rid of him so that you could be with Mum.'

Apollo started to laugh. 'I can see him now, still complaining about his lot. I knew he blamed me. But it wasn't me who placed the money under his mattress. I could see that Star felt the same about me as I did about her. It was only a matter of time before she set Frankie free.'

'He swears he did not take that money,' Vega said, feeling a sense of loyalty to the man she'd met briefly in Washington.

'I know he didn't take it,' Apollo answered. 'Your mother orchestrated the whole thing.'

Vega gasped, unable to hide her shock at this news. 'She wouldn't . . .'

Apollo shrugged. 'Why would I lie? She wanted me. Frankie was in the way. So she got rid of him. When your mother wanted something, nobody could stop her.'

Vega picked up her coffee once more and took a deeper sip. A pounding echoed in her ears. Was her heart beating so fast that its rhythm reverberated around her head?

'I feel a little strange. I might need something to eat. Low sugar . . .' she said, her voice trembling.

'Have some more coffee,' Apollo said, standing up to refill her cup. He rang the bell again, and Petra appeared. 'Bring some cake for our guest. She's feeling a little light-headed.'

'Thank you,' Vega replied, leaning back in her chair. She glanced at her watch, but her eyes played tricks on her and the numbers spun around. She should leave now and return tomorrow to talk to her father again.

Suddenly Petra was beside her, passing her a small plate of

fairy cakes. Vega took the plate but placed it on the table beside her, not trusting herself to hold it steady.

'Star took you from me!' Apollo said, raising his voice now. 'She denied me my rights as a father and my opportunity to provide guidance and knowledge to you and your sister.' He watched Vega with sorrow. 'This troubles me deeply. However, this evening, I will address that imbalance. My gift is to open your mind, set you free so that you can converse with your inner self.'

Vega recoiled as understanding hit her. 'I don't . . . don't want drugs. I don't want—'

He raised both hands and smiled kindly at her. 'Don't worry, my little star. You are safe here with your father. I will protect you.'

She tried to stand, but her body felt like it was melting.

'Psychedelics amplify what already resides within you. Your memories of your time here at the farm, with your mother and me, remain in your mind. I am assisting you in unlocking them. Allow your mind to ignite with infinite love, light, truth and beauty.'

Vega's heart began to race as she struggled to comprehend what he was saying. 'I do not want drugs from you.' Yet even as the words escaped her lips, she felt the strangest sensation creep inside her, and her eyes fixed on the coffee. 'What did you give me?'

'You are about to enter a state of altered consciousness. Oh, how I envy you this first time . . .'

35

The room started to shift around her. She observed the candles rising, positioned upright, and parading around the space, left, right, left, right. She must be dreaming. It had to be a bad dream, and she desperately wanted to wake up.

'Open your mind to the hidden rooms of your consciousness,' Apollo said, suddenly appearing before her. His face distorted, then came into sharp focus, only to warp and blur again.

'What did you do?' Vega tried to say, but the words would not cooperate.

'I am helping you. You want to retrieve your memories. Question your inner self, for you were the last person to see your mother. Search for her in your mind, reflect on your time spent here on the farm, and you will find her. You will find Nova. You will find me . . .'

Vega needed to escape this room and distance herself from this deranged man. She attempted to stand, but her legs felt like jelly.

Suddenly she felt cold wind whipping her hair around her face. She blinked, confused, realising she was outside. How did she end up here? She moved around the side of the house, clinging to the wall as her eyes searched.

Then she heard a baby crying. It was a soft whimper at first, but growing more insistent by the minute. She forced her legs to move, and this time they obliged. She followed the sound of the cries until she saw her.

'Mum!' she called out.

Her mother cradled a newborn baby, singing softly to her.

Was that Nova? She rocked the bundle back and forth, and Vega felt tears spring. She longed to feel her mother's arms around her.

'Hello, darling. Look at your beautiful baby sister. You must take care of her. Promise me you will make sure no harm comes to her.'

'I promise,' Vega said, running to them, desperate to hold them both. But just as she reached them, they vanished into tiny stars, floating high in the sky. She ran around the yard, her hands reaching for the stars as they slipped away from her grasp.

'Vega, are you okay?' Estelle asked, appearing suddenly in front of her.

'They were here. And now they're gone!' Vega cried, grabbing Estelle's arms. 'Can you help me find them? I have to catch them.'

'I told you to be careful,' Estelle said, biting her lip. 'I knew he'd do this.'

Vega halted, feeling a chill run down her spine. She scanned the yard frantically, searching for the danger she instinctively sensed was lurking. 'I'm scared. I need to hide.'

'You need to come inside. It's not safe for you out here. Come with me,' Estelle said, taking Vega's hand in hers.

'You have soft hands,' Vega said. And then, to her amazement, Estelle's hands metamorphosed into two pink marshmallows. She prodded one with a finger. 'Can you eat them?'

Estelle ignored her and pulled Vega behind her into the kitchen.

Vega cried out jubilantly when she saw her mother at the table, chopping orange carrots with long green leafy tops into a large pot. 'Mum! You're not a star any more. Are you Cassie again?'

She ran to the table and sat down beside her mother. 'Have you been hiding? It must be a good spot, because I've been looking for you everywhere.'

'I've been here all along, you silly thing,' her mum replied. She reached out and cupped Vega's face in her hands. 'You need to be quiet, Vega. You know that you and Nova must use indoor voices when Apollo is talking to his inner self.'

'I think Dad is a little crazy,' Vega replied.

Her mother nodded earnestly. She thought so, too. 'You need to go, Vega. Now!'

Vega scanned her surroundings, looking for the threat she sensed was present.

Her father. Apollo. He could get so angry sometimes. She just needed to find Nova first. She had to protect her sister.

Run.

Hide.

She reached out in the dark. She was crouching behind a tall double bed with a brass frame. How had she gotten here? It felt familiar; she had been here before. This was their hiding spot, and they liked it here. It was cosy and safe. Then she felt a warmth nestle closer to her.

Nova!

Her sister was asleep on her lap, and Vega brushed her golden hair with her fingertips, just the way she liked it.

She was safe here.

'Why don't you get into bed?' Estelle asked, reappearing and extending a hand towards Vega. The marshmallows were gone. Vega was pleased about that. However, when she attempted to grasp Estelle's fingers, they elongated like jelly, and no matter how Vega tugged at them, they continued to extend.

'Your poor hand,' she said, feeling tears prick her eyes.

Then she was on the bed, and her mother was beside her, wrapping her arms around her as they lay back together. The soft mattress gave way, and Vega felt her body sink lower and lower until she disappeared into its centre.

Her mother whispered to her, 'Apollo is going to kill me. We have to run. We have to hide. We have to leave now . . .'

And then everything went dark.

36

Vega awoke to the sound of muffled raised voices. She stretched and opened her eyes, feeling disoriented as she looked around a strange bedroom.

Cosmo Farm.

She rubbed her eyes, and her head began to pound. Her mouth was so dry. She licked her lips and tried to remember the events of the evening.

Her last recollection was being in Apollo's room, discussing his crazy belief that he spoke to a higher authority.

She sat bolt upright, and her stomach churned at the sudden movement.

Apollo had drugged her. Anger and betrayal flooded her.

How dare he do that to her without her consent?

She'd confront him. Demand an explanation. Then get the hell out of this madhouse and never return.

She gingerly swung her legs over the side of the bed, looking down at her bare feet. She had no memory of getting into bed, never mind taking her socks off. She was still wearing her jeans and sweatshirt, which was reassuring.

She tried to open the door, but it wouldn't budge. She was locked in. Now fear joined her anger. A trickle of sweat ran down her back, and she began to shake.

Curling her hands into fists, she began banging on the door. 'Let me out, you bastard! Let me out of here!'

She heard the door click and instinctively took a step backwards as she came face to face with a sullen Petra.

'Stop screaming, you stupid girl,' Petra said shrilly.

'Let me out and I'll stop screaming,' Vega shouted, as loudly as she could.

'You are going nowhere. Your father has requested that you remain as our guest.'

Vega felt her blood run cold. 'You cannot keep me here against my will.'

'It's Apollo's will. You must obey him,' Petra stated bluntly. 'Or we will have to teach you to obey him.'

Vega rushed at the woman, knowing she had to escape and fast. But her legs felt heavy and she couldn't get the momentum needed to push past. Petra grabbed her with both hands and manhandled her back into the room with ease, pushing her onto the bed.

Then, with one last withering look, she walked out, locking the door behind her.

Vega pulled her knees up under her chin and began to cry. Why had she been so headstrong, insisting on coming here on her own? And she'd willingly given them her phone, even though she'd felt in her gut it was the wrong thing to do.

She had to escape.

But in order to do that, she would need to shake off what felt like the worst hangover of her life. She lay back down on the bed, watching the door fearfully. She knew that this used to be her bedroom when she was a little girl. At least, it felt familiar to her. She looked down at the space beneath the brass bed frame, and a memory pierced her with clarity: of her cradling Nova while both of them hid from Apollo. They'd been afraid of him. Their father. The master and the monster of the house. Her head pounded and she thought she might throw up. She closed her eyes, willing herself to feel better so that she could work out how to get out. But she was so very tired . . .

She was woken by a hand touching her brow. She startled, shrinking back, then groaned in relief when she saw it was Estelle.

'Do you feel nauseous?' Estelle asked, her face etched with concern.

'Like I've drunk three bottles of Cab Sauv,' Vega croaked back. 'Where are they? Apollo and Petra?'

'In Apollo's den. He's not up yet. But he likes to eat about now, so she's brought him his breakfast.'

'What time is it?'

'Midday.' Estelle leaned in, 'Somebody was here looking for you first thing. A man.'

Vega sat up. 'What did he look like? What did he say?'

'Tall, dark. Good-looking. He said he was your boyfriend.'

Luka! Vega felt her body sag with relief, knowing he was out there looking for her. But how could that be? She hadn't told him she was coming to Connemara, something she deeply regretted now.

'Where is he now?' she asked, terror suddenly filling her that he might be locked up in another part of the house.

'He left after Petra insisted that you'd not been here. She moved your car around the back last night.'

'That bitch!' Vega replied.

Estelle didn't disagree.

'You have to help me get out of here.'

She looked behind her to the closed door. 'I can't. I'm sorry. Apollo would be so angry with me if I did that.'

'To hell with Apollo. This is kidnap. And he drugged me. I'll see he gets arrested for this. Surely you don't want to be an accessory to that!'

Estelle bit her bottom lip. 'I've got to think of Altair. Protect him.'

'Where is he?'

'Outside. Apollo doesn't like to be disturbed during the day while he naps. We try to stay out of the house as much as possible.'

'He's a monster!' Vega said, her whole body shuddering.

'They both are,' Estelle answered. 'You look flushed. Do you want something to drink? Are you thirsty?'

Vega's throat felt dry and raspy, and she desperately needed water. But she said, 'If I were in a desert, I'd not accept another drink from this house.'

Estelle nodded sadly. 'I stayed up all night, watching over you. I made sure you were safe. Away from him.'

Vega could see the genuine concern on the woman's face, and felt a rush of warmth towards her. 'Thank you,' she replied. On impulse, she reached out and hugged her. 'You need to leave here with me.'

'I can't,' Estelle said, 'I have nowhere to go. No money.'

'There's always somewhere to go,' Vega said. 'And you must know that this is not a safe environment for you and Altair. I presume you've taken Apollo's special coffee before, too?'

Estelle's eyes brimmed with tears as she nodded. 'Not often. It costs too much money, so he keeps it for himself. But he's made me take it a few times. When his guide advised him I should.'

Vega felt a shiver run down her back and her stomach flipped queasily, 'What about your son? Has Apollo made him drink the coffee?'

'No!'

'Well take my advice, don't hang around long enough for him to want Altair to open his mind to his inner self, too. Listen, I'll help you. You have to find my keys. Then grab Altair and whatever you need and we'll leave.'

Estelle shook her head. 'Petra won't let me go.'

Vega frowned. 'You call her Petra, not Mum, that's odd.'

'There are no mothers or fathers here. Altair calls me Estelle.' The woman's face fell, as fresh tears filled her eyes. 'I wish . . .' She stopped and shrugged.

'Go on, what do you wish?'

'A few years ago, I was in Killary Harbour and I saw a woman and her toddler. About Altair's age at the time. And he called his mother Mama. The sweetest sound I've ever heard. I wished that one day I'd hear my son call me that too.'

'You can make it happen. You just need to leave.' When Estelle shook her head again, Vega reached into the back pocket of her jeans and pulled out a business card. 'My number's on this. If you won't come with me now but you change your mind in the future, call me and I'll help you. Okay?'

Estelle stood up, brushing creases from her grey dress. 'I will, I promise. Are you all right to drive?'

Vega still felt shaky, but nodded that she was okay all the same.

'You need to make a run for it now, before Petra comes back. I'll get your phone and trainers for you, and the keys.'

Vega stood up and moved to the door, but when she opened it, Petra was standing on the other side, her arms folded across her chest.

'Now where do you think you're going?'

37

Vega squared her shoulders, clenching her hands into fists, ready for battle. 'I'm leaving. And this time you won't stop me.'

'You can't keep her here, Petra. People will come looking for her again,' Estelle said, moving forward. 'You don't want the Gardaí knocking on the door, do you?'

Petra looked at her sharply. And hesitated. Then the sound of shouts from outside drifted into the house. Vega heard banging on the front door, and someone called her name.

'Vega! Vega!'

She almost sank to the ground when she recognised the voice. It was Luka. But then the shouts stopped for a moment and she doubted herself. Had she imagined his voice? Were the drugs still causing her to hallucinate?

Then he called her name again and she shouted back as loudly as she could, 'Luka! Luka, help! Luka!'

She turned sideways and pushed Petra with her shoulder as Estelle moved to the front door and opened it. Luka burst in, his face taut with worry.

'Did they hurt you?' He ran towards her as Estelle backed away from the door.

It was too much for Vega. Over the past twenty-four hours, she'd met her father for the first time in her memory, found that her mother was still elusive, and then been betrayed by Apollo in the worst way. She fell into her boyfriend's arms. 'He drugged me. They tried to keep me here, locked me in a room.'

'The bastard!' Luka cursed. He pulled back and searched her face, then looked at her arms. 'Did he inject you?'

'No. He put something in my coffee. He's not a sane man, Luka. He claims he doesn't know where Mum is, but I don't believe him.' She wiped her eyes and composed herself, taking several steadying breaths. 'How did you know where I was?'

'Mama Lulu called me last night. She was worried because you hadn't rung back. I cannot believe that you came here on your own, Vega. You should have let me know where you were going.'

Vega could only nod in response. Her single-mindedness had gotten her into trouble many times, but it left her shaken to the core now.

'You were here earlier too,' she said.

'Yes, at eight a.m. I left at dawn, because I couldn't sleep with worrying. I stopped at the petrol station in the village for fuel and to ask if anyone knew where Robert Shaw lived. They gave me directions, but that woman swore you had never been here.' He threw a disdainful look at Petra.

'Why did you come back?'

'I started looking for you at the hotel, then in the pubs in the village. I met an aul' fella. He said he'd spoken to you yesterday and had a drink with you at the bar.'

'Jimmy!' Vega said.

'Yeah, that's him. He'd been bothered all evening when you didn't return to the pub, so he insisted on driving up here with me. He's outside. I think you've got a fan there.'

'Oh, Luka.' She moved back into his arms and clung to him even tighter. 'I've made a mess of things. I should never have come here.'

'Not on your own, you shouldn't have. But it's okay. I've got you now.'

'My ride-or-die,' she whispered.

'Always. Let's get the hell out of here.'

Estelle handed Vega her trainers and phone. Luka put the trainers on her like a small child. And for once, the fiercely independent Vega did not protest.

'You can tell me everything once we've put some distance between us and this madhouse.' He turned to look at Petra and Estelle, and practically spat at them, 'You should be locked up.'

But there was something Vega had to do before she left. She walked over to Petra. 'Is Apollo in his room?'

'Yes. But he doesn't rise until the sun is about to set,' Petra sang back, the fixed smile back on her face.

Vega pushed past her and walked towards Apollo's room, Luka close on her heel. 'What are you doing?' he asked.

Vega couldn't stop, though. Anger had descended, and her whole body was on fire. She didn't bother to knock, but barged in, calling Apollo's name. He was in his seat again, wearing a long burgundy robe, unperturbed by her entrance.

'Ah, you're up!' Seeing Luka behind her, he added, 'And you've got a guest.'

'You. Drugged. Me! How dare you?' she hissed at him.

'I'm your father. I am within my rights. Take a seat and let's have a chat. Tell me everything you experienced. Who did you see? What did you learn?'

'We're not sitting down for a cosy catch-up with you!' Luka exploded, his face flushed with anger. 'You need to get a lawyer, mate, because I'll see you behind bars for this.'

He moved closer to Vega, his hands clenched into tight fists by his sides, ready to fight.

'Oh my. Such passion. I think this man loves you, Vega,' Apollo said, chuckling to himself. 'Are you sure you wouldn't like some refreshments? Estelle bakes delicious scones. With butter from the farm, they are a delightful breakfast.'

'Is he for real?' Luka asked Vega. He turned to Apollo. 'What did you give her?'

'It's perfectly safe. Psilocybin. The psychedelic compound found in mushrooms.' Apollo smiled at Vega. 'I didn't give you a full dose. Not for your first time. But we can build up to it.'

Vega couldn't believe her ears. He showed no remorse because he thought he'd done nothing wrong.

'Let's get out of here,' Luka said again.

'One minute,' Vega replied. She walked right up to Apollo. 'Where is my mother? And don't give me that crap about being everywhere, or with the stars, or that you don't know.'

'I don't like this version of you, Vega. I'm not sure your boyfriend has a positive impact on you.' When Vega cursed, he shrugged. 'I told you yesterday that I have no idea where Star is. She left here with you and Nova in 1995.'

'Why did she leave? Was she running away from you?'

Apollo shrugged. 'I wish I knew.'

'Bullshit!' Vega responded. 'She was afraid of you. My "inner self" told me that much last night. That I had to hide from you as a small child.'

The smile finally left Apollo's face. 'I have never hurt my children.'

'Well, excuse me for doubting that when you've just drugged me! What about Mum? Did you hurt her?'

'I loved her!'

'So what? O. J. Simpson loved Nicole. Look where that got her!' As the words left her mouth, Vega began to shake as she contemplated the sinister possible reason her mother had not returned to get her at the station. She repeated her question, her voice little more than a whisper. 'Did you hurt my mother?' When Apollo didn't answer, she dug deep inside herself and shouted, 'What did you do to her, you sick bastard!'

His lip curled, and his jaw clenched. 'I think you should go. I will not be spoken to like that by you.'

But Vega was so worked up she couldn't walk away. She was sick and tired of misdirection and dead ends as she searched for answers. 'I spoke to your friend Mark Perry.'

Shock registered on Apollo's face.

'He told me that the last time he was here, when I was a newborn baby, you accused him and Mum of having an affair.'

'That's not how I remember it.'

'Well, it's how *he* remembers it. It appears that your inner self was making up shit, because Mark had no interest in Mum or any other woman!'

'Why are you bringing all that up?' Apollo said, his face now fixed in a permanent sneer. 'That was years before your mother left, either way.'

'That may be the case, but it's quite illuminating. It shows me that your relationship wasn't as perfect as you'd like me to believe. Why did Mum need to run?'

Apollo stood up, pulling the cord of his robe tight. 'You disappoint me, Vega. I thought yesterday that you had potential – the ability to see more than what is right in front of you.'

'I disappoint you?' Vega asked, her voice dropping low. 'You have no idea how much you disappoint me, *Father*.' She closed her eyes for a moment, then tried one last time. 'If you have even an ounce of compassion, or if you love me as you claimed yesterday, you'll tell me where my mother is. That's the only thing I want from you. You can do that, can't you?'

Apollo began to pace the room, moving between piles of books, circling Vega and Luka. He paused at the window, still with the curtains closed tight, and lifted his hand to his brow, sighing deeply. Then he turned to Vega. 'The last time I saw Star, we fought. We had come to an impasse in our relationship. She'd lost faith in our path. She claimed I was irresponsible. That she needed to protect our children.'

Vega's eyes filled with tears as she imagined her mother fighting for the safety of her and Nova.

She squared her shoulders and walked up to her father to stand face-to-face with him. 'I will not rest until I find out where Mum is. And if I discover that you hurt her . . .' Fury made her heart race, and she took a deep breath before spitting out, 'If you hurt her, I will kill you myself!'

Apollo held her gaze as he said, 'Your mother loved you and Nova.'

He delivered this statement with such fervour that it was the first thing he'd uttered that Vega truly believed. Her body sagged with relief at his words; the doubt that had lingered for years about her mother's love for her was finally dissipating.

'But she had a cruel streak,' he went on. 'This quest for answers you've been on, you must have seen that for yourself.' He studied Vega's expression, and smiled knowingly. 'Yes. I thought as much. You have worked that out already.' He sighed dramatically, then added one final disclosure. 'You accuse me of hurting your mother. But you've never considered that it might have been the other way around. Because before Star left me, she had one last swipe. She told me she'd been in love with someone else for years.'

Vega glanced at Luka, then at Apollo again, her heart racing at this new information. Just as she thought she was getting closer to the truth, another curveball was sent her way. 'So you're telling me she left you for someone else?'

'That's exactly what I'm telling you. I was devastated by her admission. And yes, I was angry with her. But I never hurt her. To find your mother, you must find whoever that new love was.'

38

Once they'd returned safely to Wexford, Luka stayed with Vega in her cottage. He took care of her with such tenderness that it almost erased the horror of the twenty-four hours she'd spent in her father's house. And by the time the Journalism Awards arrived, she was finally feeling like herself again.

'You look beautiful,' Luka said for the third time, as they walked through the doors of the Convention Centre, the venue for the awards ceremony.

'You don't have to keep saying that,' Vega said, smiling, though she thought she could get used to hearing it. 'I think if anyone turns heads tonight, it's you in that tux.' She noticed several people giving her boyfriend an appreciative glance as they walked into the lobby. He wore a black suit well.

Throngs of people gathered in groups, and the noisy, happy chatter and laughter echoed around the room. Vega called out hello to several friends, and held hands with Luka as they made their way towards the bar to get a glass of bubbly.

'Over here!' Kieran called, spotting the two of them. He embraced Vega warmly, then turned to shake Luka's hand. 'Good to meet you, Luka. She's kept you quiet!'

'It's great to meet you too, Kieran. I've heard a lot about you. It's nice to put a face to the name.'

Kieran turned back to Vega, looking at her face closely, his brow furrowed. 'I swear I could kill that man. Drugging you. It's abhorrent. Are you okay?'

'I'm fine. Felt like I had a very long hangover, but I'm back to normal now. Took me a few days, mind you.' She shrugged, putting a brave face on it. 'At least I know he's an asshole and I haven't missed anything all these years.' She tried to joke, but it landed wrong.

'Did Tony get in touch? I told him he'd better take care of you, or he'll have me and the missus to answer to.'

Vega smiled, 'That explains Detective Gilmartin's overzealous attention! We met earlier today, and I've officially reported Mum as missing. It was a difficult conversation. But he listened and agreed that it's worth a visit to Apollo. He's going to handle it himself and plans to drive up over the next day or two.'

A waiter carrying a tray of champagne flutes stopped to offer them one.

'I think we need one of these. Mind you, I'm only allowed a couple of drinks. Orders from the wife,' Kieran lamented.

'Is she here?' Luka asked.

'No, her mother's recovering from an operation, so she's staying with her this week. I'm flying solo.'

'Have you seen where we're sitting?' Vega asked.

'Yeah. There are two tables for HLD Media. We aren't at Senan Delaney's table, though.' Kieran looked at her thoughtfully. 'Are you going to ask him about the Nowhere Girls feature?'

'I don't know,' she replied honestly. 'Part of me wants to fight for the story, but I'm unsure if that's because I'm being contrary about him pulling the plug or because I want it published. I might play it by ear.'

'Good plan. When you win tonight, you'll at least have his ear when you make your pitch.'

'I won't win,' Vega said, shaking her head. Lifting her champagne to her lips, she added, 'But it's nice to be here.' This event had been on her bucket list. It felt good to be acknowledged, mainly because it was an award voted on by the public.

Moments later, a bell rang to summon everyone to their seats. Senan Delaney approached their table to shake hands with each of them.

'Best of luck tonight, Vega. We're all rooting for you,' he said warmly.

'Thanks, Senan,' she replied.

'It was a wonderful piece. Very emotive,' he continued. He turned to Kieran. 'Keep the champagne coming for our star journalist.' Then he returned to his own table, chatting with a blonde who was sitting with her back to Vega.

'Is that his wife?' Vega asked.

'No, his daughter,' Kieran replied. 'His wife doesn't do work events. Don't think I've ever seen her at one of these.' He leaned in conspiratorially. 'Have heard she's a bit of a handful. Diva with a capital D.'

'Where do the Delaneys live?'

'He inherited his parents' estate after they died. It's in the Wicklow mountains. His father was a judge. More money than sense.'

Luka nudged her, nodding towards a tall, dark-haired man, greying at the temples. 'Isn't that your man from the TV show, *The Sunday Debate*?'

'Yes!' Vega replied. 'John O'Brien. He's up for an award. TV Journalist of the Year.'

'Wow,' Luka said, his eyes wide with delight. 'Wait until I tell Mum. She loves him.'

'I'll introduce you later on,' Vega replied with a smile. 'Oh look, here comes food!'

It was only when the first award was announced by their MC, Miriam O'Callaghan, that Vega began to feel nervous. She had been so engrossed in her search for her mother that she hadn't even thought about the ceremony. She clapped and cheered for her colleagues as they won their respective categories. Finally it was time for the People's Choice – the category in which she'd been nominated. She felt a prickle of sweat on her upper lip and quickly wiped it away when she saw her face appear on the large screen behind Miriam.

'Win or lose, you're my winner,' Luka said, squeezing her hand.

'You've got this, kiddo.' Kieran patted her hand on the other side.

When she heard her name called out, she looked in disbelief from Luka to Kieran as they ushered her towards the stage. She had won!

Miriam kissed her cheek, handed her the small glass trophy and congratulated her. Clutching it tightly, Vega stood at the podium and gazed out at the packed room, which was still clapping and cheering for her.

'I . . . I don't know what to say,' she began hesitantly. 'I'm genuinely surprised. I never thought for a moment that I would be chosen . . .' She took a steadying breath, closed her eyes for a second and then looked out at the audience. 'I'd like to thank my editor, Kieran Murphy, and Senan Delaney and the entire team at HLD Media, of course. But most of all, I'd like to thank Annette for her courage in coming forward and sharing her story. It can be difficult to understand why a mother might abandon her child, and how that heartbreaking decision changes a child's life for ever. How we respond to these stories reflects who we are as a society. I am overwhelmingly grateful that readers have shown compassion to Annette and, for a moment, put themselves in her uncomfortable shoes, understanding that her decision to leave Lucy during that torturous time was not made lightly or without cost to her. I hope her words will help ease the pain that other mothers in similar situations might carry.'

She thought of her own mother and hoped that, wherever she was, she knew that Vega did not judge her. Then her eyes rested on Luka, standing at their table, recording her speech on his phone, his face beaming with pride. 'Lastly, I'd like to thank all the dedicated social workers, one of whom is my boyfriend, Luka, who support the most vulnerable children in our society. The world is a better place with you in it.'

As the room erupted into further applause, Vega walked off the stage, her heart pounding in her ears.

She posed for a photograph and answered a few questions for the social media team covering the awards. Then she slipped away as Miriam announced the final nominees of the night, heading for the ladies', needing a moment before returning to her table.

The spacious marble bathroom was vacant. Vega approached the sink, delicately setting down the award as she ran cold water over her wrists. Suddenly the door burst open and a woman walked in, tears streaming down her cheeks. She was glamorous, clad in a black tuxedo – an oversized jacket with cigarette trousers – and outrageously high heels. She glanced at Vega before moving into a cubicle and closing the door behind her. Muffled sounds of sobbing came from within.

'Can I get you anything?' Vega called out, feeling sympathy for the woman's plight.

She heard loud nose-blowing, then the cubicle door opened and the woman emerged. 'I'm done crying over that jerk. Thanks. I'm good.'

Vega shrugged. Clearly she wasn't okay, but it was none of her business. She was about to leave when the woman pointed to her glass trophy.

'You won an award. Congratulations.'

'Thank you,' Vega replied. 'I can't believe it. Everyone always says they didn't expect to win—'

'But in reality, they've rewritten their acceptance speech dozens of times,' the woman interrupted, and they both giggled.

'Exactly that. But I'd no acceptance speech, I promise you!'

'What did you write about?' the woman asked, wiping mascara from under her eyes.

'A piece about a mother who abandoned her baby and later returned for her.'

She turned away from the mirror and smiled. 'I read that piece. It was beautiful. You made me cry!'

Vega couldn't help but smile back. 'Thank you. And sorry!'

'You must have been told that by hundreds of people. It went viral.'

She shrugged. 'I've been away in the States. I haven't seen any public reaction myself.'

'My dad will be pleased,' the woman said, nodding at the award.

And then Vega realised who she was. 'You're Senan Delaney's daughter!'

'Guilty as charged.' She reached over to shake Vega's hand. 'I'm Caoimhe.' She frowned and added, 'Please don't tell Dad I was crying, will you?'

'Of course not!' Vega replied quickly. 'That's none of my business.'

'I wasn't supposed to be here. He didn't want me to come, which is weird because I always come as his plus-one whenever Mum refuses to go.'

'Did you fight with him?' Vega asked, wondering if Senan was the jerk that Caoimhe had referred to.

'Oh God, no. Dad would never make me cry, even if he is a bit overprotective sometimes. I'm crying because I'm an idiot. These tears are entirely my own fault. Don't fall in love with a married man. That's my advice.'

'Oh dear,' Vega murmured sympathetically. 'I'll remember that.'

'I believed every cliché John bloody O'Brien uttered to me.'

Vega gasped and felt a trickle of glee, knowing that Luka would be delighted when she shared this titbit of gossip.

'He swore that his marriage was over. And that he was leaving his wife. Any day now.'

'And he's not?' Vega asked.

'Not according to his pregnant wife, who is his date tonight! Poor woman hasn't a clue who she's married to.' Caoimhe frowned and shook her head. 'I'm such a bitch. I never even thought about her and what this would be like for her. Not until I saw her waddling towards the table!'

'She doesn't know, I take it?' Vega asked, feeling Caoimhe's embarrassment.

'Not a clue. And his face when he saw me. He didn't know I was going to be here; it was supposed to be a surprise. And now

I know why my dad didn't want me to come along. He told me that he knew about my dalliance with John, which is even more mortifying. God, I need a drink!' Caoimhe opened her gold clutch bag and took out a small bottle of Mirabeau gin. She took a delicate swig, then passed it to Vega, who shook her head to decline. 'I'm mortified. I mean, I believed what he told me, and now I have to go back to that table to listen to his lovely wife talk about her birth plan!'

'You won't be the last to fall for a married man's lies,' Vega said softly. 'How you respond to it is how you move forward. Don't let the bastard think he's got you down. Put on some lippy and Beyoncé your way out of here.'

'Yes! You're right!' Caoimhe replied. 'Hey, you never told me your name. Sorry, I know I should know, as you're a famous journalist.'

'I'm Vega.'

Caoimhe smiled. 'That's such a pretty name. I'm sure I've heard it before.'

'Probably from the article,' Vega suggested.

'That makes sense. Will you walk back with me? Sisters in solidarity and all that!'

'Of course,' Vega replied. There was something so endearing about the woman, she warmed to her immediately.

'Time to show that bastard what he's just lost.' Caoimhe pulled off her jacket, revealing a minuscule camisole top in black lace. 'Too much?' she asked, noticing Vega's eyes widen as she looked at her exposed flesh.

But Vega couldn't respond; her heart was racing as her gaze locked onto the café-au-lait birthmark on Caoimhe's upper right arm – an unmistakable mark that sent a wave of memories crashing through her until she could barely speak.

'You've gone as white as a sheet!' Caoimhe said, her nose wrinkling in concern. 'Are you sure you don't want a drink?'

Vega shook her head, unable to trust her eyes. Finally she found her voice and whispered, 'Nova?'

PART FOUR

The trouble with life isn't that there is no answer,
it's that there are so many answers.

Ruth Benedict

39

Vega repeated her question, this time in a stronger voice. 'Nova?'

Caoimhe's eyes narrowed, and she looked at her in concern. 'I'm Caoimhe. I think I told you that a few minutes ago.'

Vega reached over to point at the birthmark. 'I know you're Caoimhe, but that birthmark . . . My sister, Nova, has one just like it. I've been searching for her for the longest time.'

Caoimhe tilted her head to one side and made an 'ah' sound. 'You poor thing. I'm sorry you've lost touch with your sister. That's tough. I've always wanted a sibling, since I'm an only child.'

Vega didn't reply. She could not take her eyes off the birthmark, convinced it resembled the one that Nova had had as a child.

'My sister had a birthmark in the same place,' she repeated.

'That's a coincidence. But you'd be surprised how often I've met someone who has one like it or knows someone who does. It's quite common! Come on, let's go back. I'm sure you want to celebrate that win, and I need a proper drink.' Caoimhe walked to the door, her jacket slung over one shoulder.

'Wait!' Vega called out. 'Are you adopted?'

Caoimhe turned around in surprise. 'No. I'm not. Why?'

'My sister was adopted when she was a little girl. I thought that perhaps . . .'

Caoimhe's face scrunched in sympathy, but she took a step back. 'I'm sorry. But as I've said, you've got the wrong person. Look, I'm going to head back. Thanks for listening to my love worries. You've been a star.'

Star.

The word sent shock waves through Vega's spine. She was sure it was a sign.

'Our mother was called Star,' she said, watching Caoimhe's face closely for a sign of recognition. But the other woman remained impassive as she exited the bathroom and held the door open for Vega for a moment. When Vega didn't come through immediately, she allowed it to swing closed behind her with a sharp click.

Vega felt her breath come in ragged gasps as her mind wandered back to her childhood, to that moment when she'd cradled her sister in her arms for the last time.

Could they have stumbled into each other after all these years?

She grabbed her award and left the bathroom, quickly returning to the table.

The ceremony had concluded, and people mingled in the room, congratulating the winners and celebrating the success of their media outlets.

When he spotted her arriving, Luka ran over to her, scooping her into his arms and twirling her around. 'I'm so proud of you! I knew you'd win. I just knew it. And when you thanked me, I nearly cried!'

'He did!' Kieran said, joining them both and pulling Vega into a hug. 'Proud of you, kiddo.'

But their congratulations were lost on Vega.

'I found her,' she said, eyes scanning the room for Caoimhe, who was standing a few feet away, whispering to her dad.

'Found who, kiddo?' Kieran asked, his gaze following Vega's.

But Luka sensed what she meant, and he searched her face with concern.

'Caoimhe Delaney is Nova,' Vega said.

Luka and Kieran shared a worried look.

'Start at the beginning,' Luka said.

Vega shared details about the chance encounter in the

bathroom and the discovery of the birthmark. 'Don't you see?' she begged them.

'I can see how it must have thrown you into a tailspin. But the girl said she's not adopted,' Kieran said sceptically. 'And I'll be honest with you, Vega, I don't remember any gossip about adoption. That's the kind of thing people talk about.'

'She might not remember,' Vega replied. 'She was only three; she's probably forgotten.'

'Okay,' Luka said. 'That's possible. It's also possible that it's a huge coincidence that she has a birthmark. Can you be sure it's in the same place as Nova's?'

Vega felt irritation nip at her at Luka's question. Doubt raced through her mind as she desperately tried to recall which side her sister's mark had been on.

'Delaney is heading over,' Kieran hissed.

Vega's heart started racing again as her boss neared her side.

'Vega. Congratulations,' he said, smiling expansively as he leaned in to kiss her cheek.

'Thank you,' Vega replied. She glanced over at Caoimhe, who was watching them from her table. She wondered if she had mentioned their conversation to him.

'I believe it should be me thanking you. Caoimhe mentioned she was a bit upset, and you helped her.'

'That's okay. I was happy that I was there,' Vega replied.

'She also mentioned that you got it into your head that she was your sister,' Delaney continued, his eyes now narrowing. 'She was concerned about you, that she had upset you somehow.'

Vega swallowed a lump. 'I didn't mean to worry her. It's just that my younger sister was adopted when she was three. And she had the same birthmark as Caoimhe.'

Delaney looked from Vega to Kieran and Luka, chuckling softly. 'You writers and your vivid imaginations! Just because of a little birthmark? I know she's already said this to you, but let me put an end to this nonsense: Caoimhe is not adopted.'

Vega couldn't shake the feeling that Delaney was protesting

too much. Then, a thought struck her. She moved in closer. 'Look, I'm sorry. I got so excited when I saw the birthmark that I jumped in. I should have considered that she might not realise she's adopted, or that she may have forgotten that fact. After all, she was so young back then. I apologise for my clumsy way of asking her. I should have spoken to you first.'

The smile vanished from Delaney's face. 'Yes, you should have. But it wouldn't have made any difference. I'm not sure how to express this other than by repeating what I've already said. And I dislike repeating myself. Kieran will tell you that. Caoimhe is my daughter. For goodness' sake, look at her. If I had a euro for every time I've been told she's my mini-me . . .' He rolled his eyes in irritation.

And Vega doubted herself again, because there was no doubt that Caoimhe resembled Delaney. They shared the same eyes, the same nose.

'Look, it's an easy mistake. I'm sure you must be feeling overwhelmed, what with winning the award and everything.' Delaney's face softened. 'Let's consider that the end of it. Okay?'

Kieran interjected before Vega could protest further, clapping Delaney's shoulder. 'Understandable conclusion for Vega to jump to. But as you said, that's the end of it. I think it's time I buy these two a proper drink. Will you join us?'

Delaney shook his head. 'Caoimhe wants to go home. She's had quite the evening, so we'll call it a night. But put the drinks on the company expenses, Kieran. It was a remarkable achievement winning that award, Vega – it has to be celebrated.' Then, without a backwards glance, he moved away.

Kieran whistled softly. 'That is a man who does not enjoy being questioned.'

'I don't care who or what he is; he's lying,' Vega stated.

Luka put his arm around her shoulder. 'I think Kieran's idea of a drink is a good one. I'd murder a Guinness. Let's get out of here and we can talk this through. Okay?'

It was clear that Kieran and Luka shared the same scepticism. However, despite this and Delaney's protests, something felt off to Vega.

Caoimhe was Nova.

She was sure of it.

40

Ever since the awards two nights previously, Vega felt as though she was losing her mind. On the one hand, she knew it was implausible for her lost sister to be her boss's daughter at HLD Media – it was simply too coincidental.

On the other hand, Caoimhe's birthmark was located in the same spot as Nova's.

Vega had tried to forget it by writing her copy for the newspaper. She could usually switch off everything while she wrote. But as soon as she finished her pieces, ready to submit them to Kieran, she was right back to Caoimhe again.

She wished she possessed a photograph of Nova as a little girl to verify that her memory hadn't failed her. All she had were her memories, though, and she was not so delusional as to deny that they might be flawed.

She decided to call her social worker again to double-check if any messages had come in from Nova or her mother. She tried to wait at least six months between calls, and it had only been a few weeks since her last check. But it was worth a shot. Her chat with Caoimhe might have sparked something.

Disappointingly, her social worker confirmed that there was nothing further to report, and reiterated that she would contact her immediately if that changed.

Her mobile buzzed. It was Luka calling again. She sent it to voicemail and returned her attention to the coffee table. Sitting cross-legged, she straightened the rows of Post-it notes lined up in front of her. She'd decided to try to make sense of the clues and facts she'd accumulated since she began her search for her mother.

The Nowhere Girls

There was a pink note for every person Cassie/Star had been in a relationship with: Flick's boyfriend David, Frankie, Apollo/Robert.

She reflected on her phone call with Mark Perry and quickly wrote down his name with a question mark. After all, she only had his word that he hadn't been interested in Cassie, which could have been a cover-up. She'd follow up with him and Martha Long in case either had insights into other love interests.

She focused on the blue Post-it notes that detailed where Cassie had lived: Woodstock, Rochester, Island Pond, Connemara.

Why was her mother in Dublin in 1995? Why did she leave Vega and Nova at Pearse station? Was it because it was far enough from Apollo that she felt safe, or for another reason?

Cassie's family and friends were on green Post-its, and Vega felt a swell of love fill her as she looked at their names: Vega, Nova, Mama Lulu, Flick, Martha.

She tapped the notes with her pen. What or who was she missing? Was there another friend in Cassie's life that she'd turned to in 1995, perhaps living in Dublin? Again, a question for Martha.

The final group of Post-it notes were yellow and contained unanswered questions. Where did Cassie go in 1995? Who adopted Nova? Why Pearse station? Was there another love interest in 1995? Her eyes rested on the question that had burned in her mind since the day before: *Is Caoimhe Delaney Nova?*

She'd exhausted every avenue online that referenced Senan Delaney, hoping that an adoption might be mentioned, but came up blank. At this point, she had to leave that question aside and keep focusing on her mother's whereabouts. She would find another way to prove or disprove her theory that Caoimhe was her sister.

Her phone rang again, distracting her from her thoughts, so she put it on silent. She would call Luka back before the end of the day, but for now, she had to make some calls. After confirming that the time difference was acceptable, she video-called Martha Long.

'I was just thinking about you! And then you call. How lovely!' Martha said warmly as she answered.

'How are you?' Vega asked, returning the smile. There was something genuinely likeable about Martha. Vega understood why her mother had bonded with her so strongly. She suspected Martha would have been a significant part of her life if her mother had stayed in Island Pond with Apollo. It was nice that they were in each other's lives now.

'I'm doing very well,' Martha replied. 'And I've been eager to hear if there are any updates on your search.'

'Actually, yes. I found Apollo – and he still goes by that name, by the way.'

Martha rolled her eyes. 'He hasn't changed at all. Why am I not surprised? Does he know where Cassie is?'

'No,' Vega replied, shrugging her shoulders. 'He claims that the last time he saw her was the day before she left Nova and me in Dublin.'

'Your expression suggests you don't fully believe him!' Martha replied.

'I'm sceptical of everything he claims, to be honest. He still talks to his inner self and a higher entity he describes as an emissary from the stars. Aided by drugs, of course!'

'His brain must be fried by now!' Martha exclaimed. 'I mean, I had my moments back in the day. We all did. But there comes a time when you have to move on.'

'He's unstable, Martha.' Vega took a deep breath before admitting what Apollo had done to her. 'He laced my coffee with a psychedelic when I visited him.'

Martha gasped out loud, holding her hand up to her mouth. 'That's outrageous.'

'I know. I wonder what might have happened if Luka hadn't followed me to the farm. I was locked in a bedroom there. Would Apollo have let me go? I don't know.'

'Stay away from that man! Under no circumstances are you to return there!' Martha commanded, her eyes blazing with intensity.

'I have no desire to go back.' Vega grimaced. 'I've waited my whole life to find my family, and now that I've located my father, I know I never want to see him again.'

'That's sad, honey. I'm so sorry,' Martha said gently.

'I remembered some things from my time at Apollo's farm. Or at least I believe I did. I feared him as a little girl, and my mum felt the same way. Do you think he could be violent?'

Martha sighed. 'I've thought about that a lot since you were here. I remember how your mother was with my boys. She loved children and was eager to start her own family. I cannot reconcile the Cassie I knew with the one who would abandon you and your sister.'

'Frankie said the same thing,' Vega replied.

'As a mother, I've asked myself what circumstances could lead me to abandon my children. I believe Cassie left you there to ensure your safety. She was trying to protect you and Nova by escaping from Apollo.'

'That makes the most sense to me, too,' Vega said.

'Apollo on and off drugs were two different beasts,' Martha continued. 'He could be charming, friendly and fun, both when he was high and when he was sober. But he had a darkness in him. He could be cruel. It was one of the reasons my husband and I wanted the commune at Island Pond to end; it felt like an unsafe environment for the kids.' Her jaw set and her voice hardened. 'He suggested that we microdose our kids.'

'Maybe he was threatening to do that to Nova and me,' Vega suggested. Then her stomach sank. 'He has a new partner up there: Petra, who seems as batshit crazy as he is. But her daughter, Estelle, and grandson are there too, and they seem sweet. I didn't like leaving them behind. I'm worried for them. What if he drugs Estelle's son? I told her to find me if she needed help, but I'm not sure she will ever leave.'

'What a mess. At least you tried. There's not much else you can do.'

Vega sighed. 'I'm at a standstill again in my search. I know

Mum left Connemara to go to Dublin on the day she left us at the station. But the trail ends there. Apollo claims there was another man involved. But I've no idea who that could be.'

'Somebody must know where she went!'

'Is there anyone else you can think of from Rochester or Island Pond who might help me retrace her steps?' Vega asked.

Martha shook her head. 'I've followed up with everyone I'm in touch with. And I'm afraid no one has heard from Cassie in decades. I have nothing further to help you. Mark Perry was the only one who spent time in Ireland with Apollo and Cassie.'

'Is Mark gay, by the way? Apollo accused him of being in love with Cassie.'

Martha laughed. 'Mark was in love with Apollo! We all saw that. He followed him around like a lovesick puppy dog. That's why he went to Ireland over and over again.'

'That makes sense. I don't think he cared for my mother very much, from how he spoke.'

'They didn't get along; both were competing for the same person, which always leads to disaster. I'm sorry I can't help further, but I'm here any time you want to discuss it.'

'Thank you, Martha. I truly appreciate it.'

They said their goodbyes, and Vega decided to call Mark Perry next. He rejected her video call but returned an audio call a few moments later.

'I don't do videos this early in the morning,' he said, an edge to his voice.

'Sorry! I hope I didn't wake you,' Vega apologised.

'You're not sorry,' Mark replied grumpily. 'I'm up now anyway. What do you want?'

There was no point going through pleasantries with this man, so she got straight to the point. 'I found the farm. Thank you. Honestly, you have no idea how helpful our chat was last week.'

His voice softened. 'Glad to be of service. So were they both still there?'

'Apollo is, but my mother hasn't been there since 1995.'

'So she left him after all. How is Apollo?' Mark asked quickly. Vega guessed he still had lingering feelings for her father.

'I found him mad and bad,' she replied truthfully. 'He spiked my coffee, and swore he hadn't seen Mum since she left in 1995 but claimed she was in love with someone else.'

'He had form for spiking coffee. I witnessed him doing that a few times on Island Pond. But it was a different time back then. You can't do that sort of thing now.'

'He's lucky I didn't report him,' Vega muttered. 'What about his claim that Mum had another fella?'

'Paranoia! He never used to be like that until he went to Ireland, and he got worse after you came along.'

'A baby made him paranoid?' Vega asked, her voice rising in indignation.

'Yep! As soon as Star found out she was pregnant, she became obsessed with living clean – no drugs, cigarettes or alcohol. Apollo didn't like that; he always wanted company when he took acid. She mentioned to me that he was jealous.'

This was a lot for Vega to take in, but it made sense, too. 'His assertion that Mum was cheating on him could all be in his head.'

'It could. But I suppose thinking about it now, it wouldn't surprise me either. The last time I saw Star, she was at the end of her rope with him. They fought constantly. In many ways, it's a miracle she lasted until you were four before leaving. I always thought she'd come back to the US. To her mother's house.'

'If only she had,' Vega said, sighing. 'For now, I want to assume that Apollo is telling the truth. Is there anyone you can think of who might know who Mum was seeing? Or, for that matter, any clue about who it might be?'

Mark paused. 'No. Nothing comes to mind. If you've been to Apollo's farm, you'll know it's in the middle of nowhere. We could go weeks without seeing another living soul unless we needed to head into town for some reason.'

'Who else was on the farm the last time you visited?'

'Four or five from England, about half a dozen Irish and a Dutch couple. I hadn't met any of them before. They were all new. And no, before you ask, I don't have any contact details for them. I can't even remember their names . . . Wait, one of the Dutch crew was Erik, a good-looking guy, but the others . . . No, they've long faded from my memory.'

Vega's heart sank. How could she find these people when she didn't even know their names?

'Did you notice if Mum was particularly close to any of them? Any details would be helpful.'

Mark tutted, clearly irritated by her questions. 'No. I told you. Nothing. I don't remember her being especially close to any of the men; she was with the women mostly. That's how Apollo liked it. Women in the kitchen, men outside. All the commune members had tents and camper vans in one of the fields; I was the only one who stayed in the farmhouse with Apollo and Star.' He cleared his throat. 'Look, I don't know what happened after I left, but I was glad to say goodbye. They used to be a united front. But when you came along, it changed their dynamic. Star was obsessed with you. Apollo . . . not so much.'

Even though Vega suspected that her father had never loved her, hearing it stated so starkly was difficult.

'I saw the same thing with my sisters,' Mark went on. 'They became mothers, and their attention shifted entirely to their children, neglecting their husbands. From where I was sitting, Apollo grew irritated with Star. Mind you, he seemed irritated with a lot back then. He was snappy with me. I became sick of being his whipping boy. It used to be fun, but it became a chore.'

'Was he ever violent towards Mum?' Vega's heart raced as she waited for the answer.

'Define violent. Shouting? Yes. Game-playing? Yes. But physically? Not that I ever witnessed. I wouldn't have stood for it if I had.'

'When I met him, I thought he seemed menacing. It was like

there was an undercurrent of violence simmering beneath his smiles and welcoming facade.'

'Maybe. Look, I don't believe Apollo would ever consciously have hurt someone. However, when he was out of his mind, high on drugs, well, that's a different matter. I saw him do some shit in my time that would turn your hair grey . . .'

'So it's possible he hurt Mum without even realising it.' Vega felt a shiver run down her back.

'Maybe,' Mark replied. At some point during the five-minute conversation, he had softened towards Vega, and now he appeared sincere, saying, 'Look, I'm sorry. This must be overwhelming for you. I wish I had more information to share.'

'You've been incredibly helpful, truly. Apart from Apollo, you're the last person I know who saw Mum. I need to find out what happened in 1995, but I'm not sure how to proceed. If you remember anyone else she was in contact with back then, please let me know.'

'Sure. Good luck with everything; I hope you get the answers you seek. And while I was never close to Star, I hope she's okay. I wouldn't wish any harm on her.'

As Vega said her goodbyes and hung up, she gulped down a lump in her throat.

Are you alive, Mum? If you are, please let me know. I'm not upset with you for leaving Nova and me. I'll understand; I promise. I just want you to be safe.

Had her calls with Martha and Mark helped? She supposed they confirmed that Apollo was a loose cannon. And deepened her suspicion that he was involved in her mother's disappearance.

Had Apollo followed Star to Dublin and harmed her? Had she escaped from him and was too scared to come back for her girls, choosing to hide all these years? Or had she dumped them and run away with a new man, not caring that she'd left them behind?

If that was the case, Vega didn't care any more. She just wanted to know her mother was unharmed.

Her head pounded from the questions that swirled relentlessly in her mind. She stood up and stretched her arms above her head, feeling sore from sitting cross-legged for so long.

She decided to have a coffee and call Luka back.

But then her phone rang again.

'I thought of something,' Mark said jubilantly.

'That was quick,' Vega replied with a smile.

'Ha! Probably nothing, but when I was there in 1991, there was a film crew in the village making a documentary about communes in Ireland. They stopped by the farm to request interviews with Apollo and Star. He wasn't keen, but she was. They were still discussing it when I left. As I said, it's probably nothing.'

Suddenly Vega felt the familiar tingle of excitement at breaking a potential new story. Could there be footage of her parents from 1991 in some dusty archive?

41

Vega was finally in territory she was familiar with. She began searching for possible media coverage of communes in the early 1990s, and found features online about a seventies hippy commune in north-west Donegal known as the Screamers. She discovered that a documentary had been made about them, but it was deemed too disturbing for Irish audiences and wasn't broadcast on television until several years later. She spent hours watching video footage on YouTube about other communes, hoping there might be a reference somewhere to Cosmo Farm.

But she failed to get any results, so she moved to the archives of the *Connacht Tribune* and *Galway City Tribune*, hoping that news of a film crew in Connemara had been worth mentioning.

She awoke the following day on the sofa, the laptop balanced precariously across her thighs. She hadn't pulled an all-nighter researching a story for years. Still, she felt jubilant, because at four a.m. she'd found an article referencing a promising-sounding documentary by a national broadcaster.

She stood up and stretched, regretting not having gone to bed. She spent twenty minutes in the shower, then brewed a pot of coffee, knowing that one cup would not suffice. Her mind raced through potential contacts who could provide access to archived programmes. By the time she'd finished her second cup, she had found the answer.

John O'Brien.

He'd previously worked for the broadcaster in question before moving to HLD Media, and Vega was confident he would still have contacts there.

Time to call in a favour.

'Vega Pearse, how's your head after the other night's celebrations?' John asked.

'Grand. I didn't stay out late.'

'Me neither. I had to get home with my wife. She's due any day now.'

'First baby?' Vega asked.

'Yes! We're very excited. This is a special time for us. What's up?'

'Well, I could do with your help. I'm searching for a documentary about communes in Ireland from the early 1990s, focusing on a commune on Cosmo Farm in Connemara. Your old broadcaster made it.'

'Ah, sorry I can't help you, but I'm out of there for years,' John said. 'Listen, I've got to spin. I'm due in the studio in an hour.'

'I'm hoping you might know someone you can pull a favour from.'

'I can't do that. Sorry.' He sounded impatient. 'Give them a call; one of the producers will help you.'

'I don't doubt they would. But it will take too long. Experience has taught me that I could be waiting weeks. I need details today,' Vega said firmly.

'You need a genie in a bottle, then,' John said.

Vega had not intended to play dirty, but she was desperate and willing to stoop low if necessary. She lowered her voice, 'I ran into a friend of yours at the awards.'

'Oh?' John replied.

'A good friend. A very pretty young friend. Caoimhe.'

He cursed. 'I don't know what she told you . . .' he spluttered. 'Wait, are you blackmailing me?'

'Think of it more like a gentle incentive for you to make that call for me. That's all. I'll owe you then.'

Silence fell between them, broken only by John's laboured breathing as he contemplated her words.

'Text me the details again,' he said before hanging up.

Vega swiftly drafted a message detailing the information she had about the documentary and sent it to him. She felt a flush of shame at using Caoimhe's confession. However, she reasoned that the woman wouldn't mind if she understood what was at stake. Then she opened Instagram and searched for Caoimhe's profile, clicking on her stories. The first three were meme shares, but the most recent one had been posted just a few minutes earlier.

A photo of a café was accompanied by the caption *Brunch time*.

'I know that place!' Vega exclaimed. She googled to confirm she was correct. Yes, it was the Fern House Café in Avoca, Kilmacanogue. She grabbed her car keys.

Traffic was in her favour, and she arrived just over an hour later. She rechecked Caoimhe's stories, but no additional posts had been made. She knew she might have missed her, but hoped luck was on her side. She walked to the café entrance and peeked inside, scanning the room.

There she was, sitting opposite an auburn-haired woman.

Vega stepped back, concealing herself from view. Should she go in for lunch and take a seat near Caoimhe? No, that might be too stalkerish. A flush spread over her body. Her actions today were undeniably in stalker mode.

I'm doing this for you, Nova.

She hovered near the café entrance in the retail section of Avoca. She picked up items and pretended to examine them, but her gaze was fixed on the café door.

After a while, Caoimhe walked into the bathroom just a few feet away. Vega waited outside, her stomach flipping with each passing second.

When the door opened and Caoimhe stepped out, she froze in shock. 'You . . .' she said, her mouth falling open.

'Oh . . . hi . . . this is a coincidence,' Vega said.

Caoimhe raised a perfectly groomed eyebrow. 'I didn't know you were from around here.'

'I'm not. I live in Wexford. However, I often stop by to pick up dinner when I'm passing. I enjoy the soups here.'

This was a wild guess; she knew there was a takeout section and assumed soup would be a safe bet.

'Mum likes their soup too.'

'Is that who you're with?' Vega asked.

'Yes, we try to do brunch once a week.' Caoimhe turned to leave, but paused and said, 'Look, thanks again for your support the other night. I appreciated it.'

'My pleasure.' Vega took a deep breath, aware that this was the best opportunity she would likely receive. 'And I apologise for catching you off guard with my theory that you were my sister.'

Caoimhe offered a soft smile and gave a delicate shrug. 'It's okay.' But it was obvious that it wasn't.

'I didn't mean to upset you,' Vega continued. 'It's just . . . You look like I imagined Nova would look now. And you resemble my mum a bit, too. Add the birthmark . . .'

Caoimhe frowned. 'You still think I'm this Nova!'

Vega nodded, her body trembling as she observed the other woman's reaction.

Caoimhe stepped closer and touched her arm, sending shock waves through her. 'It's awful that you're going through this, but I'm not your sister.'

'But what if you are?' Vega whispered, a tear prickling her eye, then drifting down her cheek. 'I'm sorry.' She wiped it away with the back of her hand.

'It's okay. You don't have to apologise,' Caoimhe said kindly. 'I'm sure this must be so upsetting for you. When was the last time you saw Nova?'

'When I was four and she was three. She was adopted, while I remained in foster care.'

Now Caoimhe's eyes glistened as well. 'It's sad they didn't keep you together.'

'I fought hard to be with her, but her new family didn't want two girls.'

'And you can't find the adoptive family's name through your social worker?'

And that was when it struck her. 'You need to call my social worker. Tell them your name, and they'll confirm if you're Nova or not!' Vega practically punched the air in triumph. But while she could see how simple this solution was, Caoimhe disagreed.

'I'm not calling any social worker.'

'Please!' Vega pleaded.

'Look, if you had even a hint of evidence or proof, I would consider it. But . . .' Caoimhe raised a hand to silence her, 'all you have is an ordinary birthmark. That's all. I'm sorry you're experiencing this. But I need to return to my mother.'

And she turned on her heel and walked away.

42

Vega called Luka, but his phone went straight to voicemail. Assuming he was in court again, she sent him a WhatsApp asking if she could call to see him. His response came back instantly.

I can't talk right now. I've left a key with James in T. Morris for emergencies. Let yourself in and I'll be there as soon as possible.

Vega didn't waste any time. She desperately wanted to see him and talk through her spiralling emotions. She didn't know which part was worse: believing her father was a murderer or suspecting she had found her sister but couldn't prove it. Luka was her anchor, her safe harbour in this storm. He would wrap his arms around her and tell her everything would be okay.

She drove to Wexford and retrieved the key from James. Then she let herself into Luka's apartment, calling out his name even though she knew he wasn't there.

She tossed her bag onto the sofa in the open-plan living area and quickly scanned the apartment's four rooms. He'd added a new framed photograph beside the one on the mantelpiece in the living room of him and his mother on his graduation day. Arms looped around each other, both smiling happily for the camera. Now, in a bougie gold frame, there was a photo of Vega sitting on Luka's lap on the swing outside Red Maple Farm. Aunt Flick had taken the shot, capturing them mid laugh, with Luka looking at Vega instead of the camera.

Vega's heart swelled with love for her boyfriend. She'd missed seeing him these past few days, hearing his voice.

Was she in love with him?

She had asked herself this question multiple times since their trip to America. She didn't trust herself to find an answer because she had never genuinely known love, at least not that she could remember.

She yawned, feeling tired and achy all over. Her night on the sofa had not been good for her back. She moved into the bedroom, thinking she'd rest on Luka's bed until he arrived.

Then she spotted it.

His laptop bag. Sitting at the foot of the bed.

Caoimhe had stated that she would only call Vega's social worker if she had some concrete evidence. Vega's heart raced as her eyes fixed on the laptop. Was it possible for her to find details linking Nova to the Delaneys there? Could Luka confirm her suspicions without breaching his code of ethics? Give her a nod of affirmation that she was on the right track?

She glanced at her watch. It was three o'clock. She reopened WhatsApp on her phone and checked Luka's messages. He had been vague about when he would be back. She wasn't even sure where he was. If he were in court, he could be home any time.

She sat on the edge of the bed, her mind racing.

The cast-iron evidence she needed could be sitting right in front of her. Before she could talk herself out of it, she unzipped the brown leather case and pulled out the laptop, switching it on. Time passed at half-speed as she waited for it to power up. She moved to sit by the window. That way, she could watch Monck Street below for any sign of Luka's casual gait approaching home.

Guilt caught up with her, and she moved her hand to close the laptop. Luka had been clear with her about his boundaries regarding his job. But then the password prompt appeared. She told herself that if he had changed it from 'Liverpool FC', she would take it as a sign to walk away. But the computer accepted the password, and she was in.

She navigated the built-in mouse across the home screen until she found the Tulsa case management system. Clicking it open, she began exploring the database to determine which area she needed.

She paused when she reached the birth information and tracing database, and scrolled until she found a tab labelled *Records held by Tusla*. Included in this was a list of homes and agencies, arranged in alphabetical order: Ard Mhuire Mother and Baby Home, Bessborough Mother and Baby Home and CLANN Adoption Services at the top. She continued scrolling until she reached the Dublin Health Authority, then clicked it open with trembling hands.

But before it could reveal any details, she heard the apartment's front door open.

'Dammit!' she cursed.

She had been so absorbed that she'd lost track of Luka's arrival. Panic fluttered in her chest as she scanned the room, her heart racing. Should she hide the laptop under the bed and return for it later? The indecision gnawed at her, but before she could settle on a plan, Luka stepped into the room. His gaze shot to the computer in her trembling hands, and with a rush of mortification, she dropped it onto the bed, her cheeks burning.

'Luka . . .' She jumped up and moved towards him, desperation lacing her voice.

'So that's why you wanted to come over,' he said, his tone icy and emotionless. The disappointment on his face pierced her heart, and she struggled to hold back her tears.

'I wanted to see you. I missed you so much,' she said desperately, each word a plea for understanding.

The look he threw at her was so scathing that it made her shiver. She needed to heal the rift that had suddenly appeared between them.

'I came in here to rest because I was utterly exhausted. I didn't sleep a wink last night, and then the laptop caught my eye, so I—'

Luka raised a hand, his gesture cutting through her words like a knife. 'Stop. Please don't insult me with a pathetic excuse when we both know what you're doing.'

Vega's stomach tightened painfully, her rising panic spilling out as she fumbled over her words. 'I spoke to Caoimhe again . . . She demanded proof before she'd even consider believing me. I was desperate! You have to understand how it feels for me,' she implored, her voice shaking with emotion.

'All I ever do is think about what it's like for you,' Luka replied. 'But it's not reciprocated, is it?'

'That's not true!' Vega protested. 'I think about you all the time.'

'That's why you returned my calls . . . not,' Luka replied sharply. 'I felt hurt when you didn't reach out on Monday. Even so, I made excuses for you, telling myself it wasn't your fault because you hadn't been in a relationship before. You were probably overwhelmed and didn't know how to respond to a situation where I'm the one who needs support.'

Vega tried to make sense of his words. What was she missing? She had ignored half a dozen calls from him. Had he left her voicemails? If he had, she had never listened to them.

'Then you finally got in touch today. I found your message strange. It felt cold, just mentioning you wanted to call over. But I convinced myself that you were coming to check on me in person. Better late than never, and all that.' He shook his head. 'I'm an idiot.'

He left the bedroom, and Vega followed him into the sitting room. His choice of words had surprised her, prompting her to look at him more closely. He was unshaven, sporting several days' worth of beard growth and dark circles under his eyes.

She felt her heart lurch and stepped closer. 'Luka, what's wrong?'

'You don't care about anyone but yourself, do you?' he replied, two spots of colour appearing on his cheeks. 'Did it even occur to you that I might need *you*? That I've been trying to get in touch with you because something is wrong with *me*?'

Vega felt heat wash over her, moving from her head down her body. 'I'm horrified at myself. I should have listened to your messages. I should have called you back. I honestly thought you were calling to chat.' His face was impassive, and Vega began to panic that she'd blown it with him. 'Please, Luka. I genuinely am so sorry. I didn't listen to your voice messages. After the awards, I spiralled. I've gone down so many rabbit holes trying to solve this mystery. I think I've lost my mind.' She paused, knowing that none of this truly mattered. 'Is it one of your cases? Has something happened to that girl you've been trying to rehome? Please tell me what's wrong.'

But nothing could have prepared her for his response. 'My mother had a heart attack two nights ago. She's in critical care at Wexford Hospital.'

They stared at each other in deathly silence for a moment before Luka sank onto the sofa, burying his head in his hands. Vega rushed to his side, trembling with shame. How could she have been so oblivious to someone she cared for deeply?

He turned to her, and the look on his face made her heart sink. His jaw was set, and his eyes were cold as he said, 'I've had a lot of time to think over the past forty-eight hours, sitting beside Mum's bed, holding her hand and praying for a miracle. And I've wondered if there will ever be room in your life for anything other than your all-consuming need to find Nova and your mum. I told myself it didn't matter, that I could live with only having seventy per cent of you, and that maybe one day you'll get those answers you desperately need and then I'll have all of you.'

Vega received the words like slaps to her face. She held back her protests, because there was no excuse for her behaviour. She had behaved despicably. Instead, she gently asked, 'How is your mother? What have the doctors said?'

Luka looked so stricken that she thought he might cry. 'She's had surgery today. They've inserted two stents to keep her blocked coronary arteries open.'

'Is she conscious?'

He nodded, his bottom lip trembling. 'She's scared. Doesn't like hospitals, but sure, who does?'

'You must have been so worried.'

'I've never been so scared in my life. When she called to say she was having chest pains, I called an ambulance and drove straight to her house. When I arrived, the paramedics were with her. She couldn't speak . . . she was terrified. I thought she was going to . . . I thought . . .' He began to sob. Vega moved in closer and wrapped her arms around him, comforting him. She vowed to herself that she would do everything possible to support him during the next few days. But before she could tell him this, he pushed her away, disentangled himself from her embrace and stood up, walking towards the front door and opening it.

'I'm tired, Vega. I want to fall into bed and sleep. You should go.'

'I'm not surprised you're exhausted. But please let me take care of you. I bet you haven't eaten properly. How about I make us some soup? Nothing heavy. Then you can go to sleep. You need to keep your strength up. I'll call Kieran and tell him I'll take a personal day tomorrow. I'll stay here with you.'

Luka's usually friendly face twisted into a grimace. 'You'd enjoy that, wouldn't you? Should I log onto the laptop for you and spare you the trouble of searching for passwords? Or did you get what you wanted before I came home and interrupted you?'

Another wave of shame washed over Vega, and she felt tears glisten in her eyes. 'Luka, please let me make this right. None of that matters; I want to be here to support you.'

'I wish I could believe that. Just go, Vega. I'm done.' Then he walked into his bedroom and closed the door behind him.

43

Vega drove home on autopilot. Her eyes were bloodshot from the tears she'd shed since leaving Luka's apartment.

As she turned into the driveway of her cottage, her heart jolted when she spotted a figure sitting on the front step. She squinted to get a better view, unable to believe her eyes.

She jumped out of the car and ran, shouting, 'Mama Lulu!'

Her grandmother extended her hand, allowing Vega to help her stand.

'What are you doing here?' Vega asked incredulously.

Mama Lulu's brow furrowed with concern. 'I thought you might need me, and judging by your appearance, I wasn't mistaken.'

Vega felt her shoulders sag in relief. She'd never been so glad to see someone in her entire life. 'Oh, Mama Lulu. I've messed up. So bad.'

'Hush now. Come here...' Mama Lulu opened her arms wide and pulled Vega into her embrace, patting her back comfortingly until she stopped sobbing. 'As much as I'm enjoying this cuddle, I was nearly frozen sitting on that step. A cup of coffee would be very welcome.'

'Of course!' Vega quickly opened the front door and stepped inside, grabbing Mama Lulu's case before inviting her grandmother into her home. 'How did you find me?'

'With difficulty! When you said you live in the country, you weren't lying. I decided to surprise you. I thought I'd return the favour since you'd done the same for me,' Mama Lulu added with a wink. Vega chuckled as she filled the kettle and flicked the switch. 'I took the bus from Dublin airport to Wexford. After that, I hailed a cab, and the driver brought me to Ballagh village. At the post office, I met a lovely woman named Mary, and she arranged for Sean Óg, the charming young man who owns the shop, to drive me here.'

Vega shook her head in amazement at her grandmother's remarkable gumption. She had known her for only a month and had been surprised several times already.

She prepared coffee for Mama Lulu and tea for herself, then brought a tray into the small sitting room, forgetting about her Post-it note marathon until they entered the room.

'Oh dear,' Mama Lulu said, absorbing the arrangement on the coffee table. She retrieved her reading glasses from her clutch handbag and started to read the notes. 'And here I was worrying that you'd let this search become all-consuming . . .'

'Very droll,' Vega replied. 'Look, this helps me; it keeps everything clear in my mind. And all these notes prompted me to speak to Martha and Mark again yesterday, which was extremely helpful. I discovered that a film crew had been in Connemara in 1991, making a documentary about communes! I've been following up on that with a contact I have because it's not available anywhere online.'

'That does sound hopeful. Do you think Cassie might be in the documentary?'

'I don't know, but Mark said she was in discussions with the film crew. And perhaps, if there is a record somewhere, it might provide a clue about what life was like for her back then.'

'Or her state of mind. Was she happy? Yes. I'd very much like to see that.'

'There's more,' Vega said. 'Erm . . . this is big, and it's not definite, but I might have found Nova.'

Mama Lulu's hand flew to her mouth. 'Oh Lord, girl, why didn't you start with that!'

'I'm sorry. I honestly planned to call you to provide an update. But you arrived before I had the chance. Do you recall that I attended the Journalism Awards a few days ago?' She told Mama Lulu about her encounter with Caoimhe at the awards and earlier today at the café.

'Do you have a photo of this girl?' Mama Lulu asked, her voice thick with emotion.

Vega opened her Instagram and accessed Caoimhe's profile. Her grandmother browsed the posts for a few minutes, her eyes widening with each photo.

'She's quite a looker,' she remarked. She frowned, and added, 'She doesn't exactly resemble you.'

'Ouch!' Vega exclaimed, rolling her eyes.

'Oh, calm down. You're beautiful too, you know. But you are as different as chalk and cheese. I can see that you resemble your mother. But this one ... I'm not sure. How can you be certain it's Nova?'

Vega sighed, biting her lip. 'I can't. I've asked myself that question constantly since I saw that birthmark. But the thing is, while my head says it's impossible, here in my heart, I feel it's her.' She held her hand to her chest.

'That's good enough for me,' Mama Lulu said, nodding in approval. 'So how do we prove it?'

Vega felt warmth flood her cheeks. 'I was trying to do that earlier ...'

'Something tells me that whatever you were crying about when you got home is connected to that look of shame on your face. You didn't break any laws, did you?'

'I've lost Luka,' Vega said, fresh tears welling up in her eyes. 'I wasn't sure that I loved him, you know? I knew I cared for him, but love ... what does that even feel like? But I know it now. The moment I lost him, I realised I loved him.'

'That man is in love with you, too! Infatuated. Flick and I talk about that often, saying you've found a good man who cares deeply for you. How on earth did you manage to lose him?'

'Take your pick. I ignored his calls over the past few days because I was so caught up in this.' She waved a hand towards the coffee table. 'And he needed me. His mother had a heart attack. I would have known if I had bothered to call him back.'

'Oh dear,' Mama Lulu tutted.

'And then I shattered his trust by doing something unforgivable. I'm mortified to even share this with you.'

'Spit it out. You've come this far.'

'Well, you know he's a social worker. A few weeks ago, I tried to log into his work files to find out where Nova was.'

'Oh, that's not good. How did he take it?'

'Remarkably well, but he made it clear that it would be a breach of his trust and ethics if I ever did it again. So I swore to him that I wouldn't, and I meant it. But I was so desperate...'

'You didn't!' Mama Lulu exclaimed. When Vega nodded miserably, she continued, 'You silly girl. You have messed up. It's a good thing I flew over here today! Goodness knows what trouble you'd get into without me.'

'I can't tell you how glad I am to see you,' Vega said. 'What am I going to do?'

'You need to make it right with Luka. Let him know you love him and that you're sorry. Make him feel your sincerity. It's about actions, girl, not just words. Demonstrate your remorse that way.'

'But how? I don't know what to say or do besides apologising again.'

'You'll figure it out.'

'And what about Caoimhe? She's adamant that she doesn't want to hear from me again without proof.'

'Let the girl catch her breath. You've just dropped an earth-shattering bombshell on her, and it seems she's also bearing the weight of a shattered heart. So let her heal. Allow her to process this whirlwind of emotion. Only then should you consider reaching out to her again.'

'Okay,' Vega replied, her voice laced with uncertainty. 'I'm not very good at being patient.'

'I've gathered that much!' Mama Lulu shook her head, and

Vega felt a spark of joy when she saw the despair on her face. Not because she was causing her grandmother upset, but because she saw love there, too. And the knowledge that someone cared enough to be annoyed with her, well, this was new territory for her.

'It'll be okay. I promise you that,' Mama Lulu said. 'But you look like you're barely holding it together right now.' She stifled a yawn. 'I'm completely exhausted from the flight. So this evening we'll do nothing but relax, enjoy something nice to eat, and then sleep. Our minds will be clearer tomorrow once we're refreshed. Then we can face the day and whatever it throws our way.'

'I like that plan,' Vega said, smiling her thanks. But then she frowned, her eyes moving towards the kitchen. 'I don't think I have much food in the cupboards,' she confessed. 'I wasn't expecting company.'

'Now why doesn't that surprise me? We'll return to that charming shop in the village to stock up on essentials, and I'll prepare something nourishing for us in no time.'

Neither of them could have foreseen that their much-needed quiet evening was a prelude to a storm that was about to shatter them all.

44

Vega sent Luka several messages throughout the evening, but received no response. He might have been sleeping. Or perhaps he was giving her a taste of her own medicine. It didn't feel good to be ignored. The lesson was a bitter pill to swallow.

By nine p.m., Mama Lulu insisted they both go to bed, and Vega didn't bother fighting the suggestion. She was bone tired, with every muscle in her neck and lower back feeling tight and achy. Once she had Mama Lulu settled in the spare room, she fell into a deep sleep almost as soon as she hit the pillow.

The following day, she awoke to the unusual sounds of someone in the kitchen, accompanied by the aroma of freshly brewed coffee. Mama Lulu had woken up an hour earlier and had been busy, cleaning the kitchen and whipping up a stack of fluffy pancakes.

'Keep this up, and I won't let you go back to America,' Vega said as she walked into the kitchen. She kissed her grandmother's cheek and accepted a mug of coffee.

'It warms my heart to make you breakfast. I owe you a lifetime of pancakes. As long as I can, I intend to make up for all those lost years and spoil you rotten.'

'It's me who should be taking care of you!' Vega protested. She felt her stomach growl in appreciation when Mama Lulu placed a plate of pancakes in front of her.

They chatted as they ate, Mama Lulu sharing updates on Red Maple Farm, telling her that Aunt Flick had remained at home to take care of the business.

'She wanted to come over too, but it's our busy season, preparing the products for the Christmas markets,' she explained.

'I'm still pinching myself that you're here,' Vega admitted. 'It means a great deal to me.'

'You've thanked me more than enough already. I never thought I'd see the day that I'd get to visit Cassie's children. So what are your plans today? Please don't change anything on my behalf. I'm happy to hang out here if you have work.'

'I work from home and have handed in all outstanding copy to Kieran, so for now, I'm good,' Vega replied. 'I'm going to Wexford shortly. You can come along if you'd like. I've been thinking about your comment about actions, not words. I thought I'd drop a care hamper off at Wexford Hospital for Luka's mother.'

'That's a nice idea,' Mama Lulu said.

'I could get some flowers, sweet treats and magazines. Anything else you think is appropriate?'

'Hand cream. Something that smells nice. While I was getting my knee treated, my skin became very dry. The scent of antiseptic is quite off-putting. Flick brought me this beautiful hand cream that smelled like a summer's day and was a lifesaver.'

'Perfect!' Vega exclaimed.

'Will you try Luka again and tell him about the hamper?'

Vega shrugged. She wasn't sure what to do. 'I don't want him to misconstrue my motives. Doing the hamper isn't to excuse my behaviour or to curry favour. I thought I'd leave it without a note.'

'I think that's a good idea. May I offer a suggestion?' Mama Lulu asked. When Vega nodded, she continued, 'Write him a letter expressing how sorry you are. Anyone can send a text, but a letter conveys so much more. Then step away and give him time to consider everything. I know it's a cliché, but time is a great healer.'

Vega contemplated her words for a moment. 'I love that idea. You'll have to keep an eye on me, though. That's two people I have to wait patiently for – Caoimhe and Luka! I might break!'

Mama Lulu smiled. 'There's no time like the present. Do it now, and I'll tidy up here.' She held up her hand to ward off objections, so Vega went into the sitting room to compose her letter, wondering what she should say. But once she picked up her notebook and began writing, the words flowed quickly and effortlessly.

> Luka,
>
> I will never forgive myself for hurting you. Please know that when I say I'm sorry, I mean it with every part of me.
>
> You've shown me such love and understanding since we've been together, but never more so than in the past few weeks since I shared with you about the Nowhere Girls. You accepted my past and supported my present, unwavering at every turn.
>
> If you cannot get past my actions yesterday — and I understand if you can't — I want you to know that I'll always be grateful for everything you've done for me.
>
> Seeing you so vulnerable and worried about your mother broke me. It shamed me because you've been dealing with this on your own unnecessarily. I should have been there, and I have no excuse other than that I got caught up in my search for Nova, which made me pick up your laptop again.
>
> I have an issue. I can't let things go, and my judgement becomes impaired when I'm desperate. I'm not sure that the impulsive part of me will change; it's who I am. But I am deeply ashamed that I overlooked your boundaries and code of ethics in my need for answers.
>
> I'm a work in progress, Luka.
>
> I've spent most of my life alone, and I am not offering this as an excuse, because my behaviour is inexcusable. Instead, it's a way of explaining myself. Letting my heart and head catch up with this relationship has taken me a while. If you can find a way to forgive me, I know that I can show you I can do better.
>
> I can't promise that I won't make mistakes again. I can't promise that I won't misread a situation. I can't promise you a perfect girlfriend. But if you can give me a chance, I promise I'll do everything in my power to make your happiness a priority, and I'll walk by your side in every part of your life — the good and the bad — if you'll have me.
>
> Vega x

45

Seeing Wexford through Mama Lulu's eyes took Vega's mind off Luka and Caoimhe. The sun made a rare November appearance, glistening on the bridge as they drove over it. Mama Lulu was charmed by the winding, cobbled Main Street, along with its historic buildings and shopfronts. Vega brought her to see Selskar Abbey, and she was amazed to learn that its roots dated back to 1169, when the first Anglo-Irish peace treaty was signed.

Afterwards, they sat outside Trimmer's Lane Café, enjoying a coffee with a scone, and watching the world go by.

'I can see why you've fallen in love with Wexford.' Mama Lulu said as she buttered her cherry scone.

'I don't do this often enough,' Vega admitted. 'I'm always on the go. I should do. It's nice.'

After their twenty-minute reprieve, they wandered down to Monck Street.

As Mama Lulu admired the overhead retractable canopy, open today to let the sunshine in, Vega's eyes scanned the street, hoping to see Luka. She dropped her letter into his mail box, glancing upstairs at the bedroom window, fingers crossed that he would see her and call out that she shouldn't worry – he understood, and now that he'd had a good night's sleep, they were back on track.

But there were no calls, and forgiveness was not hers. Vega didn't blame him. He shouldn't let her escape the consequences of what she had done.

An hour later, she had purchased all the items she needed for her care hamper. At Slaney Flowers, Mama Lulu proved invaluable once again, persuading the owner, Ingrid, to create a lovely hamper that included a bouquet of fragrant blooms and the items Vega had already acquired.

'Is it too much?' Vega worried, doubting herself as she walked into Wexford Hospital with Mama Lulu. The basket felt huge in her arms. 'I planned on giving a small gift. This looks like something a family member might bring.'

'Hush,' Mama Lulu said. She approached reception, and a few moments later, she began walking towards the wards.

'Can we not leave it here?' Vega enquired.

'The receptionist insisted that we take it in ourselves. Come on. It'll be good for us to stretch our legs. Sitting on that aeroplane for hours isn't good for my hips.'

'I'll take you to Curracloe Beach for a walk, then. I don't want to see Luka's mother, or for Luka to see me. I don't want to upset him,' Vega hissed at her grandmother's retreating form as she hurried down the corridor. It wasn't visiting time, so she could only hope they'd be shown the door.

When they arrived at the ward, Mama Lulu took control again and barrelled up to the nurses' station. She was a force of nature. Vega didn't know whether to be impressed or scared.

'This way!' she said, marching on with her head down, ignoring Vega's whispered pleas to slow down. After a glance to the left and right, she turned to Vega and said, 'That's her in the corner bed.'

Vega shot her grandmother a withering look, but it didn't faze her. The only saving grace was that Luka's mother was dozing.

'Stay here,' she instructed Mama Lulu, who smiled sweetly.

She tiptoed to the foot of the bed and set the hamper on the table. Luka's mother looked small and frail against the white bed linen, connected to monitors and drips. But there was no doubt as to her identity; she and Luka were very alike. Vega felt another lump form in her throat as she thought about how worried he must be. And she hated that he had to deal with it alone.

She turned to leave, but as she did, Luka's mother woke up, her eyes wide in surprise at the sight of the hamper. 'Is that for me?'

'Yes, a delivery for Mrs Wilczek,' Vega replied with a smile. 'I hope it cheers you up and you get better soon.' Then, with her cheeks flushed, she turned to leave.

'You're Vega,' Mrs Wilczek called out.

Vega stopped, astonished. 'Yes, I am.'

'I recognised you from your photo – the one in Luka's flat. It's lovely to meet you in person.'

'It's a pleasure to meet you, too. I'm so sorry you've been unwell.'

'You have nothing to apologise for. You didn't cause my heart attack. Bring that hamper over so that I can look at it properly.'

Vega did as asked, and Mrs Wilczek said, 'You shouldn't have gotten me all that. It's too much!'

'Just a few treats,' Vega said. 'The florist made it look fancier than it is, that's all.'

'You're not very good at accepting compliments, are you?' Mrs Wilczek said with a grin. 'Can you stay for a moment?'

'My grandmother is waiting for me,' Vega replied, looking behind her. But Mama Lulu had disappeared, no doubt enjoying a cup of tea at the nurses' station. 'I don't want to disturb you.'

'I'd appreciate the company. Please, have a seat and chat for a little bit.'

Vega moved to the chair beside the bed and sat. 'How are you feeling?'

'Like someone has opened my chest and ripped it in two,' Mrs Wilczek joked. 'I've felt better, I must admit. It's taken a lot out of me.'

'I'm sure. It must have been very frightening,' Vega said.

'How is Luka doing? Is he coping all right? Is he eating? Sleeping?' Mrs Wilczek asked anxiously.

Vega experienced that familiar wave of embarrassment once more. 'I only saw him briefly yesterday, and he was heading straight to bed, so I'm sure he'll be well rested today.' She thought she wouldn't add lying to her list of crimes.

'He hasn't left my side for the past few days. I worry about him because he's one of those people who always puts others first.'

Was that a jab at Vega? She narrowed her eyes and observed the woman, but Mrs Wilczek's face remained innocently impassive.

'Luka has been an incredible support to me, especially over the past few weeks,' Vega said. 'And I know how much he loves you, so I can only imagine how good he's been to you.'

'I'm lucky. He's a wonderful son and hasn't given me many grey hairs. A few during his teenage years, but he managed to turn things around.'

'Good thing I wasn't your daughter. You'd be snow white from me,' Vega quipped.

Mrs Wilczek giggled, then clutched her chest. 'Oh, don't make me laugh. It's too sore!'

'Luka is already mad at me. Don't tell him I made you feel worse!' Vega said, causing Mrs Wilczek to giggle again. Then her expression shifted, and she frowned.

'Aside from his concern for me, I knew something was wrong with him. Have you two had a falling-out?'

Vega nodded, trying to figure out what to say. Speaking the truth seemed like the best option. 'I've made a mess of things. It's a long story, but the bottom line is that I got so caught up in my own problems that I didn't notice Luka needed me.'

'Which of us can say we haven't been self-centred at times?' Mrs Wilczek said kindly.

'Oh, that's not the worst of it. If it were just that, we might be okay. But I also broke his trust.'

Her face clouded. 'You cheated on him?'

'Oh God, no!' Vega quickly exclaimed. 'I'd never do that. I have no interest in anyone else.'

'Then what did you do?'

'I crossed a line he told me was uncrossable.'

Mrs Wilczek's eyes flicked towards the hamper. 'Is that what this is about? You want me to butter him up and get him to forgive you?'

'No!' Vega exclaimed. 'There's no card in the hamper. I planned to leave it in reception anonymously. I felt so bad that you'd been so ill and that I didn't even know about it. Genuinely, there's no game plan here.'

Mrs Wilczek smiled. 'I believe you. I have the impression that you are a straightforward person, and that when you say something, you usually mean it.'

'I am,' Vega agreed. 'It gets me into trouble, though.'

Mrs Wilczek chuckled. 'I'm sure. I have a question for you and expect a truthful answer.'

'Go on,' Vega replied.

'Do you love Luka?'

She didn't need any time to consider this. 'I suspected that I might before, but when I lost him, I knew without a doubt that I did. So yes, I love Luka with every part of me.'

Mrs Wilczek patted her hand. 'Thank you for being honest. I like you, Vega. You've been good for Luka. I've noticed that myself over the past few months. And he returned from America with a spring in his step that I hadn't seen before. But . . .' she paused and locked eyes with Vega, 'if you broke his trust and he's finished with you, he didn't do that lightly. And I won't push him to forgive you.'

'I wouldn't want you to. This is my mess. I've written to him, and if he's willing to give me a chance, I'll be over the moon. But no matter what, I'd prefer you didn't mention I was here or that the gift was from me. It will cloud things. If he forgives me, it has to be his choice.'

Mrs Wilczek nodded her approval.

A nurse entered and frowned upon seeing Vega.

'I should go. I'm not supposed to be here,' Vega whispered quickly, standing up. 'But I'm happy I met you.'

'And you. For what it's worth, I'm rooting for you, Vega. I hope to see you again soon.'

Vega returned to reception, where she found Mama Lulu.

'Did you have a pleasant visit?' her grandmother asked, her face a picture of innocence.

'As it turns out, I did. You orchestrated all of this, didn't you?'

Before Mama Lulu could respond, Vega's phone rang. 'Sorry, I have to take this.' She pressed to answer. 'Hey, Kieran, how are you?'

'Good, kiddo. Look, I need to tell you something that's been bothering me since the awards. It probably means nothing, but it's best you know all the same.'

'Go on . . .'

'Well, I haven't thought about it for years, but when you met Caoimhe Delaney and were so sure she was Nova, it got me thinking.'

Vega felt every nerve in her body stand to attention.

'Now I want it to be acknowledged and noted that you were the ideal candidate, regardless of the circumstances—'

'Kieran, just get to the point!'

'Senan Delaney's wife, Caoimhe's mother, called me and asked for a personal favour. She requested that I offer you a job.'

Vega felt as though she had been sucker-punched. 'I don't understand.'

'She mentioned that one of her charities had sponsored your scholarship to college.'

'Foster Care for Life,' Vega replied, her mouth falling open.

'Yes, that's the one. She said that the trust had been following your career and would like to help you get started at a newspaper. She asked me not to mention it to Senan or you.'

'I cannot believe you're only telling me this now!' Vega exclaimed, trying to work out how to process this news and what it meant.

'Your body of work speaks for itself. Recommendation from Mrs Delaney or not, you had the chops for the job. I wouldn't have hired you otherwise. You've proved yourself every day since you started, so I haven't considered it. Until you met Caoimhe and thought she was Nova. It felt a little . . .'

'Too coincidental,' Vega concluded. 'Thanks, Kieran. I'm glad you told me. I need a moment to work this out.'

No sooner had she put the phone down than it rang for the second time. This time it was John O'Brien.

'Hi, John. How are you?'

'That documentary was never aired. Don't ask me why – probably scheduling or censorship issues. So it's a rough cut on tape, didn't get a proper edit. I've sent you a file via email. And don't call me again,' he added, cutting off Vega's thanks as he hung up.

46

'This just shows how important it is to listen to your heart,' Mama Lulu said after Vega updated her on the conversation with Kieran. 'You've felt so strongly that Caoimhe is Nova. It would truly be a miracle if you've found her!'

'Let's not discuss miracles just yet. She's not as enthusiastic about this as we are. I'm going to message her on Instagram and ask her to call me,' Vega said, frowning. 'Since I don't have her mobile number, I'll give her mine. I hope she agrees to reach out to me.'

'Okay. Don't go charging in, though. You'll startle her,' Mama Lulu warned.

Vega opened Instagram on her phone and navigated to the messages section. 'I can leave an audio note. Would that be better or worse than a typed message?' Vega drummed her fingers on the dashboard as she tried to solve that conundrum.

'Try the audio note. It might be more personal.' Mama Lulu reached across the gearstick. 'Gentle now . . .'

'I know. No charging bull from me.' Vega cleared her throat and hit record. 'Hi, Caoimhe, I hope you're doing okay. Could you call me back when you have a minute? I'll send you my number. I know you didn't want to discuss this further unless I had some evidence. There's something I think you need to be aware of.'

She glanced at Mama Lulu, who nodded her approval, and pressed send.

'Now what?' Mama Lulu asked.

'We go home and wait for her to call,' Vega said, quickly typing her mobile number into a message and sending it to Caoimhe.

'I need something sweet,' Mama Lulu declared. 'This is all very stressful. I can't handle stress without a slice of cake.'

'I'm on it,' Vega said as she started the car.

She stopped at St Aidan's Pettitt's and picked up a fresh cream and jam sponge, and a couple of almond croissants, which were Luka's favourite, just in case he dropped by. Once they were back in the car, her phone rang, startling both of them.

'It could be her,' Vega said, her voice quivering.

'Only one way to find out,' Mama Lulu replied.

Vega answered the call, cringing when she realised that her voice sounded too high and tight.

'Hi, Vega. It's Caoimhe.' She, on the other hand, sounded perfectly normal and sane.

'Thank you for calling.'

'I assumed you'd probably stalk me at the tennis club later if I didn't call you back,' Caoimhe said drily.

Vega laughed nervously. 'You play tennis? That's cool. I'm not very sporty. I've never played anything competitively before.'

'I don't like the gym; tennis is more fun and has a nice social scene,' Caoimhe replied. 'But let's cut to the chase... Go on, tell me what this evidence is.'

'Do you know Kieran, my boss at HLD Media?'

'Yes. We've met.'

'He called to tell me something that feels too coincidental not to mean anything.' Vega took a breath, looking at Mama Lulu nervously. 'I told you that I grew up in foster care.'

'Yes,' Caoimhe answered warily.

'Well, I received a college scholarship. It was awarded by Foster Care for Life, a charity that assists children with their educational needs.' Vega paused for a moment. 'I've just discovered that your mum is on the board of the charity.'

Silence followed, until Caoimhe said, 'Yes, she's their Chief Executive. And she works for several other charities too. It's her life's work.' She sighed. 'Honestly, Vega, this is hardly earth-shattering news, is it?'

'It was for me. That scholarship changed my life,' Vega replied honestly. 'But that's not everything.' She looked desperately at Mama Lulu, who nodded encouragingly for her to continue. 'Back in 2018, your mum called Kieran and asked him for a favour. She wanted him to give me a job at the newspaper, but she was adamant that he could not tell anyone she'd requested this. She said it would be a personal favour to her.'

'What?' Caoimhe exclaimed. 'You're making this up.'

'I'm not. I promise. And I was as shocked as you are when he told me.'

'And he chose *now* to tell you?' Caoimhe's voice brimmed with scepticism.

'I know that must seem suspicious, but when I met you at the awards and suspected you were Nova, I confided in him and my boyfriend, Luka. Kieran said it was only after that that he remembered your mother's phone call.'

'Jesus, Vega. Who else have you told? I don't want this story doing the rounds. My parents would be so distressed if they knew their personal lives were being discussed like this. My mother, in particular, is so private!'

Vega's heart raced, and she quickly reassured Caoimhe that it was only a small circle that knew about their possible connection.

'When's my birthday?' Caoimhe asked, catching Vega off guard with the unexpected change of subject.

Vega felt a flip in her stomach. 'I don't know.'

'Ha!' Caoimhe scoffed, as if this proved everything to her.

'I was too young to remember,' Vega quickly explained. 'You were three when I last saw you, so you were born in 1992. But

I don't know exactly when. The social workers guessed our ages when we were found.'

She heard Mama Lulu give a half-sob beside her.

'Look, I still believe this is all nonsense. But I can't stop thinking about it, all the same. After you ambushed me—'

'Hardly an ambush,' Vega countered.

'You were hovering outside the toilets! What is it with you and bathrooms, by the way?'

'Er, I was in the toilet before you at the awards—' She yelped when she felt a dig in her ribs from Mama Lulu, and quickly added, 'But of course I understand how upsetting this must be for you. I'm sorry, Caoimhe. I'm not trying to cause you any problems.'

'Thank you. And I suppose it must be equally upsetting for you.' Caoimhe sighed again. 'Look, I did listen to you and question myself. I even examined family photographs and pictures of my aunt, who I've been told my whole life I resemble. When she was younger, we look so similar we could be twins.'

Vega bit her lip, her heart sinking at the inevitable 'I'm sorry' that was about to come. However, Caoimhe surprised her by saying, 'But I agree that it's strange my mum has shown such a particular interest in you. And if I add the birthmark too, I think it's time I talk to her about this. I'm sure there's a logical explanation, but I'd like to find out what it is.'

'Thank you. Honestly, I'm very grateful. I want to know the truth. And if this turns out to be nothing but a series of coincidences, I promise to back off and leave you in peace.'

Caoimhe laughed. 'Can I have that in writing?'

Vega laughed too, then asked, 'Will you call me back after you've spoken to your mum?'

'Yes. Give me a couple of hours.' Caoimhe hung up.

Vega looked at Mama Lulu, whose eyes were glistening with emotion.

'You okay, Mama Lulu?'

'That's Nova. I feel it in every bone. Hearing you two chat

and laugh together brought me back to Cassie and Flick. They were the same.'

So much was out of Vega's hands now. She could only wait for Luka to read and respond to her letter. For Caoimhe to talk to her mother, and for the truth about what happened to Cassie to come out.

47

They returned to the cottage, and Vega prepared coffee while Mama Lulu sliced two thick cake wedges for them. Vega's eyes remained glued to her phone, willing Caoimhe to call her back, as she paced the kitchen, moving from one side to the other.

'You'll wear the tiles out if you keep going around in circles. You're making me dizzy!'

'Sorry, Mama Lulu. It's the waiting that's the hardest.'

'Let's go in and watch that documentary that John O'Brien sent you. It will help distract us.'

They moved into the living room and sat on the sofa, with the laptop on the coffee table in front of them.

'Are you nervous?' Mama Lulu asked, her face etched with concern as she observed Vega.

Vega shrugged. She reached out to hit the mouse pad, but paused, her hand hovering mid-air. 'A little. It's just . . .' Try as she might, she couldn't articulate her thoughts.

'It's just that your mother might appear on that screen. And you haven't seen her since you were four years old. You don't know how that will make you feel.' Mama Lulu's voice was quivering with emotion. 'Everything you are feeling, I am too. You've spent thirty years waiting for your mother to find you, and I've spent over fifty years waiting for my daughter to come home.'

Vega reached over and took her grandmother's hand. They sat for a moment in silence, each offering the other comfort.

'We're in this together,' Vega said.

'Together,' Mama Lulu agreed. 'We'll give each other strength.'

Vega nodded, then pressed play.

The opening shot featured an impressive view of the Connemara coastline, showcasing the rugged Atlantic coast and the green mountains. Then the camera shifted, and the presenter walked into view. He appeared to be in his thirties, with coiffed brown hair, and was dressed in a brown check suit jacket, a white shirt and a brown tie over brown slacks. Vega thought he looked vaguely familiar, but couldn't recall where she had seen him before. His name flashed on the screen: Kevin Keeney. He had been a regular on afternoon TV in Ireland in the nineties but had vanished over the past two decades.

He looked into the camera lens and said earnestly, 'Imagine a community where everyone lives on the same farm, sharing a communal house. Picture a place where your neighbour is just down the hall or across the field. You all share one goal: to live a peaceful life, free from anarchy and oppressive systems. That's what the residents of a commune in Connemara hope to achieve.'

The camera then panned over a green field where cows grazed, a small wooded area with tall leafy trees, and a yard featuring a swing set, slide and mismatched patio furniture around a large fire pit, in front of a farmhouse.

'That's Apollo's farm!' Vega said excitedly. 'I can't believe it. Those plastic seats are still there today!'

'Cassie has to be in this,' Mama Lulu said, her voice quivering with excitement.

They both leaned forward, watching as the camera followed the presenter towards the farmhouse.

A tractor rumbled slowly in the foreground, with a large round bale of hay held high on its front fork. The driver looked over and smiled for the camera as it zoomed in before moving on. The next shot was of a barn, where two men were milking cows and a third was stacking hay bales.

'Here at Cosmo Farm, everyone pitches in with a role in bringing food from the farm to the table,' Kevin said.

'It hasn't changed at all,' Vega said, barely believing her eyes.

The camera tracked him as he entered the farmhouse. It followed him down the dark hallway, where Vega had been just days earlier, and into the kitchen.

Four women stood at the kitchen table, working side by side to prepare food. One, who wore a baby sling, was kneading bread, while the others chopped vegetables and placed them into a pot.

'Cassie,' Mama Lulu whispered, clutching Vega's arm, at the same time as Vega said, 'Mum.'

She paused the screen, her eyes greedily absorbing every detail of her mother, who held a knife in one hand and a carrot in the other. Cassie's hair was as she remembered – long and loose, flowing down her back. She wore a T-shirt over her jeans and, from the looks of it, no bra. She appeared sexy, healthy and happy, laughing and joking with the women she worked with.

'Keep it going,' Mama Lulu said. 'Please, I need to see more.'

Kevin moved back into the frame and smiled at the camera. 'As you can see, here at Cosmo Farm, the women work together to prepare food for the men, who are busy outside on the farm. There are seventeen adults living here and two infants: six from Ireland, six from the UK, two from America, two from the Netherlands, and one from Germany. However, that number is fluid, as residents come and go. Some of the residents are happy to share their names; for the others, we shall respect their request for anonymity.'

The sound of a child crying made the four women pause in their chores. Then Cassie moved to a small wicker bassinet in the corner of the room, reaching down and picking up a baby.

'Oh, Vega,' Mama Lulu said, clasping Vega's arm so tightly it hurt. Vega couldn't breathe; she felt dizzy and sank back into the cushions behind her.

That was her in her mother's arms.

And Cassie cradled her with such love and gentle care that it took her breath away.

Vega heard her grandmother crying softly beside her. 'I always knew she'd be a natural mother.'

The Nowhere Girls

Suddenly a bell tinkled in the distance. And almost imperceptibly, Cassie's face changed. Her smile disappeared.

'Apollo,' Vega said. 'He had the same bell when I was there.'

Cassie handed baby Vega to one of the other women, all frivolity now ceased, and left the kitchen.

Kevin told the camera, 'It takes a village to raise a child, and here everyone takes care of the children, including baby Vega, who is six months old. Marion Collard, one of the residents here at Cosmo Farm has kindly agreed to chat with me.' He approached the woman holding Vega and asked, 'Do you mind helping out with this little one?'

The woman's name appeared on the screen as she replied in a Liverpudlian accent, 'Not at all. We love little Vega as if she were our own. And when I have a baby one day, I know Cassie will do the same for me.'

The camera shifted to another woman, with a German accent, who added, 'I'm pregnant. My husband and I know people here will support us and our child when they arrive.'

The presenter then approached the young red-haired woman with the baby sling, who scored a cross on the loaf she was making and looked down with adoration at the child nestled against her front.

'I'm Mary Reilly. My little man isn't sleeping well at the moment. Marion took him last night so I could sleep through. So yes, I'll do the same for her when her time comes.'

'She's from Cork by the sounds of it,' Vega said, scribbling in her notebook. 'That's two names for me to look up. They might know where Mum is.'

A couple walked into the kitchen: the man was tall, with a long, flowing beard, and the woman was young and pretty, sporting a wide smile.

'Several couples live at the farm, including Galway-born Brid and Fred O'Sullivan, originally from Yorkshire.' Kevin continued his narration.

Vega's mouth dropped open as she waved a finger at the

screen. 'That's Petra! That's bloody Petra!' She hit pause to examine it more closely. 'No doubt. One hundred per cent!'

'The woman who helped drug you?' Mama Lulu asked crossly.

'Yes! She must have changed her name at some point after this. Estelle told me her father abandoned them and went back to England.' Vega scribbled their names down. Where was Fred O'Sullivan now? Did it mean something that he'd disappeared and so had her mum? Was *he* Cassie's new boyfriend? She restarted the recording.

'How long have you lived here, and can you tell us how you became part of this community?' Kevin asked them.

Brid gazed at Fred with apparent devotion as he replied. 'Brid and I met in Galway. I was performing in a pub frequented by students, and she was there with her university friends.'

'I fell in love with his voice first of all,' Brid added.

'She sounds so different,' Vega said in wonder. 'So young and carefree here.'

'From the moment we met, we knew that traditional nuclear family life was not for us. We wanted to find a true community, with people of all ages, all social classes and all equal,' Brid said passionately.

'What about your families?' Kevin asked.

Fred shrugged. 'There's no one at home for me any more. I've been in Ireland for a few years; this is where my family is.'

'And you, Brid?' Kevin asked.

'I have parents and a brother in Galway,' she answered with a bright smile. 'I haven't seen them for a while. But I'll visit soon.'

'How did you end up here?'

'Fate!' Brid answered. 'Fred was busking in Galway. One day, Apollo stopped to listen, and they chatted for a while. Apollo then invited us to visit.'

'Best day of my life, the day Apollo walked down my street. We spent the day here on the farm and knew instantly that we'd found our tribe,' Fred went on. 'We might miss out on some creature comforts that others find necessities, but they don't seem to matter here.'

'We believe minor inconveniences are for the greater good and give us a more meaningful existence,' Brid agreed.

'Oh, she sounds like Petra there!' Vega said, rolling her eyes.

'And what are your roles here?' Kevin asked.

'Well, I take care of the house and am in charge of the kitchen. I churn our butter and make yoghurt. I also prepare chutney and jams, which are sold at the farmers' market every Thursday, along with vegetables from the garden,' Brid said.

'Where on earth is this Apollo then?' Mama Lulu asked crossly.

And as if the documentary had heard her, the camera shifted to a new room: Apollo's den.

He sat in his chair, wearing a long purple silk robe that was open to his waist, exposing his bare chest. Dark blue jeans clung to his lean torso. His hair and beard were nearly identical to when Vega had met him last week, except they were vibrant auburn.

'Aside from his hair colour, he's hardly changed,' she said.

Cassie stepped into the frame and handed him a tall glass of what looked like fruit juice.

Kevin sat down next to him and asked, 'Are you the leader of this commune?'

Apollo smiled. 'We have no leaders here. We live as a cooperative community, one with each other and nature. I am happy to welcome anyone who wishes to live here according to our rules and beliefs.'

'But it's you who owns the farm, so surely you get to decide who lives here?' Kevin persisted.

'This is a family home, and technically I do own it. However, everyone living on the farm is now my family, and thus we all own it.'

'We have seen the traditional nuclear family evolve over the past ten years, both globally and here in Ireland. I'd love to hear your thoughts on what the family means for you here at the farm.'

Apollo took a slow sip of his drink, his eyes downcast as he pondered this question. Then he looked up, his piercing gaze focused straight on the camera. 'Family has always been society's most stable unit, but as you said, it has faced change and unrest. Multigenerational families living under the same roof are a thing of the past, as people now desire their own houses, space and lives, with little thought for others. We've become a selfish world.' He paused and took another sip of his juice. 'But here at the farm, we want something different. We have evolved and defined our own family. We've moved forward with open minds and greater personal freedom.'

'That sounds idyllic, but what does it mean in practice?' Kevin asked.

'It means that we have stronger interpersonal relationships here.'

'And does that mean polyamorous relationships?' Kevin's tone was serious as the camera panned to Cassie's face, which flickered before turning impassive again.

Apollo laughed. 'We practise monogamy here. I'm sorry to disappoint. We believe in the union of man and woman. While the world continues to become isolated and disconnected, we strive to form connections and lasting relationships with each other. So we gather for work, sharing the labour of the land, and for food, sharing produce from the farm to our tables. And we gather for pleasure, sharing songs, stories and laughter.'

'He never gives a straight answer!' Mama Lulu exclaimed in annoyance.

Kevin turned to Cassie. 'And you are happy here?'

'Yes, of course.' She held his gaze, unwavering, her chin lifting a little, as if to dare him to question her response.

'I can't help but notice that the roles at the farm are defined by gender. Is that intentional?' he continued to probe.

'To achieve equality, we must have roles that allow us to play to our strengths.' Apollo answered before Cassie could get a word out.

'I believe the world's feminists would disagree,' Kevin said, chuckling.

'Too right! You tell him, Kevin!' Vega said.

Apollo sat up straight, pushing his shoulders back, jaw set. 'The age of equality is upon us. But at what cost to the family? For thousands of years, man has been the hunter-gatherer, and woman has been the mother, the carer. So yes, here at the farm, I appreciate women. Every home needs them. But men here are men, and women like that. They put their faith and trust in us, in each other. We live an integrated life, together with nature, with ourselves. You should try it, Kevin. It is rather idyllic.'

'He sounds so rehearsed,' Vega noted.

The camera then shifted back to the large oak kitchen table. Seventeen people were seated around it, Apollo at one end and Fred at the other. Large platters of food occupied the centre of the table and were passed from one person to another.

The documentary came to a close with the farm residents sitting around the fire pit outside, Fred playing his guitar and singing Leonard Cohen's 'Hallelujah'. Apollo, smiling broadly, had his arm around Cassie's shoulder.

Kevin's voice concluded, 'The age of equality is upon us. However, at Cosmo Farm, they ask, "What is the cost to the family?" While people's attitudes are changing, insisting that gender bias be challenged, the residents here reject this climate of discourse and instead choose a climate of harmony. Can they sustain these ideals? Only time will tell.'

'My girl doesn't look happy,' Mama Lulu said, her voice heavy with sadness. 'Look at everyone's faces; they are all smiling as they listen to Fred singing. But Cassie's eyes are downcast.'

Vega couldn't help but agree. 'I know. But aside from that, what have we learned?'

'We have names!' Mama Lulu exclaimed, pointing to Vega's notebook.

'I'm sure I can find them. And I would also like to know when Brid became Petra. It struck me that perhaps it's not a coincidence that Fred left and so did Mum. Is there any chance they're together?'

'Let's not get ahead of ourselves,' Mama Lulu advised.

Then the credits rolled and Vega's heart stopped. Mama Lulu grasped her arm again, noticing it simultaneously.

Listed as the documentary's executive producer was Senan Delaney.

48

Extract from an interview with Marion Collard

Marion: Wow, I haven't thought about that documentary in decades. We never got to watch it, as it was canned for some reason. I'd love to share it with my kids.

Vega: Of course, I'll email it to you. Seeing my mother, with me as a small baby was quite emotional. You were holding me in one scene, too.

Marion: Not a day went by without you being in my arms at least once – you were the happiest, sweetest child. Hearing from you has made my day. And to think that you're a journalist!

Vega: (Laughing) I'm not sure anyone would ever describe me as sweet now. But I'm happy to talk to you, too.

Marion: It's funny, I've rarely thought about that time in Connemara. But when you reached out, it felt like just yesterday. Memories came flooding back. Don and I have been chatting for hours, remembering things.

Vega: How long did you live on the farm? Please share a bit about life there.

Marion: Well, let me see. Don and I got there in 1986. We stayed for seven years.

Vega: So you left in 1993?

Marion: That's right.

Vega: Which means you must have known Nova, my little sister.

Marion: Absolutely. Another beautiful baby. We all doted on you both.

Vega: Did you live in the farmhouse?

Marion: No, we had a Volkswagen camper. We were only a few hundred feet from the house and the rest of the commune. There were a couple of caravans, a few campers and one tent. Although I wouldn't have fancied that, as the weather could be treacherous. One winter, we experienced a ferocious storm, and I thought the wind would pick up the camper and toss us away!

Vega: Did anyone live in the house with Apollo and Mum?

Marion: An American man. But he came and went. If I remember correctly, he only stayed for a few months.

Vega: Mark Perry?

Marion: Yes, that's the one. Funny chap. One minute he could be friendly, then the next, he might take your nose off.

Vega: That sounds about right. (Both laugh again) How did you come to be at Cosmo Farm?

Marion: In the early 1980s, the UK was in recession, and we had had enough. Don was made redundant, and I struggled to make ends meet working at a local supermarket. We lost our house when we fell into arrears on the mortgage. A friend of a friend told us about the farm. We reached out, and Apollo invited us to come. We purchased the camper second-hand and took the ferry over.

Vega: And were you happy there?

Marion: For a long time, yes. It was so different from the world we had just come from. There was no worry about meeting mortgage payments, paying for electricity or putting food on the table. We had everything we needed at the farm. We lived at zero cost as long as we were willing to work alongside the other members there.

Vega: Did you spend much time with my parents?

Marion: Initially, yes. We would light the fire pit every evening, and everyone would gather around it after dinner. We would play music, share stories and sing songs. I don't have a note, but Don is a lovely singer. And Fred O'Sullivan could make the hair stand on the back of your neck when he sang the ballads. Great voice.

Vega: Sounds idyllic.

Marion: It truly was. We all celebrated when Star told us she was pregnant with you. It felt hopeful – a new generation. It was the first time Don and I considered having children as well. We had always said we didn't want to bring a child into the world as it existed. At the farm, it felt different, safe.

Vega: Why did you leave?

Marion: (Sighing) It started to change during Star's pregnancy. She brought home a pregnancy book from the charity shop and read it cover to cover. She was determined to do right by her baby, which meant she wanted to live clean.

Vega: You mean she didn't want to take drugs?

Marion: Yes. (Lowers her voice) I wouldn't want my kids or grandkids to know about everything that Don and I did back then. There were a lot of drugs for a while, and we enjoyed smoking pot more than anything else. We grew our cannabis behind the derelict cottage. However, Apollo preferred psychedelics. If you ask me, they messed with his brain.

Vega: How so?

Marion: He believed that when he was high, he experienced direct contact with a messenger from the stars, who guided him on how everyone should live. Let's say that we didn't necessarily agree with his diktats!

Vega: Do you remember anything in particular?

Marion: Well, he made all sorts of claims. He became controlling, and it started to feel less like a community and more like a dictatorship. He was adamant that women should only speak when spoken to, which I found ridiculous. I've always been quite talkative. My Don laughed when he heard this, saying that if Apollo could shut me up, good luck to him. (Chuckling)

Vega: I've seen him discuss female and male roles in the documentary, and his chauvinism was startling. I'm curious, why did he agree to being filmed in the first place?

Marion: A producer called to the house one day, out of the blue. Apollo and Star spoke to him. Star thought it was a great idea. She said she wanted to show the world that the way of life we'd chosen wasn't sinister or depraved, but was one of love and acceptance.

Vega: And Apollo?

Marion: He wasn't keen at first. I can remember them arguing about it. Star told him that it might bring some new members to the commune. We were down half a dozen or so – people who'd left around the same time. And that was the game-changer for Apollo. He liked an audience. The following day he announced that his messenger had told him we should do the documentary.

Vega: Funny, that.

Marion: Yeah. (Laughing) His messenger was very obliging.

Vega: Did you meet any of the producers or crew?

Marion: No. Not directly. Apollo insisted that we shouldn't interact with them. We had all agreed to his terms that we would have no contact with the outside world through TV, radio or newspapers. We had to renounce all that to achieve our inner harmony.

Vega: And was my mother under the same directive?

Marion: Well, that was the strangest thing. We'd noticed a change in their dynamic ever since you came along. An imbalance in power. Apollo wanted to be top dog and they fought a lot. In fact, the morning the film crew arrived, he said he wanted us women to wear uniforms. He had bought matching shapeless grey dresses with white aprons to tie around our waists. We all laughed, because jeans and T-shirts were the only uniforms we wore.

Vega: You wore jeans in the documentary, so he didn't win that battle.

Marion: Your mother had a powerful presence. She stood her ground. They argued relentlessly for hours and were still in the midst of their disagreement when the producer arrived. However, Star ultimately won.

Vega: Was Fred O'Sullivan still there when you left?

Marion: Yes. Brid was pregnant.

Vega: So he left at some point after Estelle was born.

Marion: I assume so.

Vega: Were my mother and Fred close?

Marion: Yes. They were good friends.

Vega: Were you surprised when you heard Brid and Apollo were in a relationship?

Marion: No, not really. They were always a little flirty together. She was a pretty one, and Apollo liked pretty girls. I used to think he was deliberately flirting with Brid to wind Star up.

Vega: Did Brid change her name to Petra while you were there?

Marion: No. That must have been after we scarpered back to Liverpool. My mum died, and my dad was on his own. He asked us to move in with him, God rest his gentle soul. (Sniffing) We got out in the nick of time, by the sounds of it.

Vega: I reckon you did. Was Apollo ever violent with Star while you were there?

Marion: (Taking a deep breath) We saw her with bruises now and then. Once, when he was high, he shook her so violently that a couple of the men had to pull her away. I remember telling Don that night that if she didn't leave Apollo, he would kill her.

49

Seeing Senan Delaney's name on the documentary credits eliminated any doubt that Caoimhe was Nova in an instant. The coincidences stacked up to one monumental conclusion that Vega's sister had been adopted by the Delaneys. The sequence of events was not clear, but it was the only logical answer. Vega began searching online articles about Senan and his wife, Vivienne. Most of the images she found were of Vivienne at charity functions, a glamorous philanthropist. She wasn't sure what she was looking for. But information was power, and somehow with the Delaneys she felt she needed every advantage possible in order to get past them to Caoimhe.

Mama Lulu busied herself in the kitchen, insisting she needed to stay occupied while they waited for Caoimhe to call them back. Vega rang Luka, more in hope than expectation, and wasn't surprised when her message went straight to voicemail.

'Hi, Luka. I just wanted to check how your mum was doing and see how you are. Do you need anything? I'm happy to come over and cook for you, or if you'd prefer to come here, Mama Lulu would love to see you. Bye.'

'You didn't tell him about the documentary or the scholarship,' Mama Lulu said from the doorway. 'I wasn't listening, I walked in as you were speaking.'

'He's enough to worry about without me banging on about my stuff,' Vega said. 'He's done enough of that for a lifetime.'

Mama Lulu smiled. 'It's funny how we care more about those we love than about ourselves. Beautiful really.'

'I wish I could go back . . .' Vega began, pausing when her

phone beeped. She grabbed it, hoping it was Luka, but instead saw it was a message from Caoimhe.

She read it aloud to Mama Lulu.

'"I've spoken to Mum, and she thinks we should all meet. If that suits you, you can call to our house in the morning at eleven o'clock. I'll drop a pin with the address, assuming you can make it."'

'Say yes, of course!' Mama Lulu said, grinning. 'To think I'll finally get to meet Nova.'

'Do I tell her about the documentary credits or wait till tomorrow?'

'Tell her in person when you see her. But you better ask if it's okay for me to come. Mind you, if she says no, I'm still going to go!'

Vega texted back: *Thank you, that suits perfectly. My grandmother, Mama Lulu, is here visiting from America. I'd like her to come with me, if that's okay.*

Three dots appeared. 'That means she's typing,' Vega said.

'I know! I'm not that old,' Mama Lulu replied with one of her tuts.

In the end, it was nearly five minutes before the phone beeped again with a new message.

Mum said she'd like to see Mama Lulu too. Pinned location attached.

'We need to celebrate,' Mama Lulu declared. 'This is a win!'

'We've already had cake. And it's a little early for a drink!' Vega responded, giggling. And then Mama Lulu began to giggle too. Within a few moments, they were clinging to each other, laughing almost hysterically, a release from the tension. They only stopped when Vega's mobile began to ring.

'Oh, it's a Wexford number, but I don't recognise it.' She hit answer and said hello.

'Vega? It's Estelle. From the farm.'

This Vega had not been expecting. She switched the phone to speaker so that Mama Lulu could hear. 'Hey, Estelle, this is a surprise. Is everything okay?'

'You said to call if I needed you.'

'Yes, I did. How can I help?' Her heart began to accelerate.

'I'm in Wexford at the station with Altair. Erm . . . I'm sorry, but can we come to your house?'

'Of course! Stay where you are. I'm on my way to get you. I'll be about twenty minutes, okay?'

She hung up and grabbed her handbag and keys, her mind racing with this new turn of events.

'I'd better get some dinner sorted. They'll be hungry if they've been travelling all day,' Mama Lulu said. 'What age is the little fella?'

'Four or five, I'm not one hundred per cent sure.'

'I'll keep it simple, as we're not sure what everyone likes.' Mama Lulu wandered back into the kitchen. 'Go on, Vega. Don't leave them waiting.'

Fifteen minutes later, Vega pulled up in front of Wexford's O'Hanrahan station, where she found Estelle and Altair standing close together with a large rucksack on the ground.

She jumped out of the car, smiling brightly at both of them. Altair moved behind Estelle, his small face pale. Estelle's eyes darted around as if she expected someone to leap out from the shadows.

Vega hugged her as she asked, 'Are you okay?'

Estelle whispered back, 'Later. Not in front of Altair.'

Vega understood and turned to the little boy, saying, 'I'm so happy you've come to Wexford for a holiday. I'm Vega, a friend of your mum's.'

Altair nodded solemnly, then said shyly, 'I've never been on holiday before.'

'Well then, we better make sure this is the best!' Vega declared, opening the back door of the car.

'Will you sit with me?' Altair asked, tugging at his mother's sleeve. He looked so vulnerable, his blue eyes wide and round underneath his mop of long brown hair.

Once they were both settled in the car, with their seatbelts on,

Vega began the drive home. She put some music on, and other than pointing out one or two things that she thought Altair might like, the chit-chat was kept to a minimum. Back at the cottage, a garlicky aroma filled the air when she opened the front door. They found Mama Lulu in the kitchen, drying a large saucepan. The table was set with a water jug that Vega couldn't remember even owning.

'Pasta bake will be ready in five minutes. Perfect timing!' Mama Lulu said.

'You are a marvel!' Vega replied. 'I'd like to introduce you to Estelle and Altair.'

Mama Lulu walked over and shook hands with Estelle, then leaned down to lightly ruffle Altair's hair.

'Your home is very pretty,' Estelle said.

'It's small and cosy, but I love it. I'm not an open-plan, modern-home type of gal.'

'We're so grateful you came to get us. Would it be okay if we stayed here tonight?' she added.

'Of course!' Vega replied instantly. 'Where else would you go? You and Altair have my bedroom. I'll take the couch.'

'You can't do that!' Estelle said, looking shocked at the thought. 'We'll have the couch.'

'I've had some of my best sleeps on that couch. And the subject is not up for negotiation! I'll show you the bathroom if you want to freshen up. Then we'll eat.' Vega turned to Mama Lulu. 'I want to change the linen on my bed. I'll be down in a few minutes to help.'

'Nothing to do, love. I'm happy in the kitchen. You look after our guests and I'll make sure we don't go hungry.'

Vega brought Estelle and Altair upstairs and showed them where everything was. While they went into the bathroom, she grabbed some clean sheets from the hot press and quickly got her room ready for her impromptu guests. She pulled out her pyjamas and a change of clothes for the next day, then called out to Estelle that they should follow her down when they were ready.

Mama Lulu played a blinder during dinner. She was clearly a natural with kids and chatted happily with Altair until he began to relax. Estelle barely touched her food, playing with the pasta bake Mama Lulu had managed to create in such a short space of time. And Altair didn't do much better, yawning continuously. The excitement of the day had clearly caught up with him.

'I think it's straight to bed for Altair,' Estelle said, smiling indulgently at her son. 'Is it okay if I bring him up?'

Vega lightly touched the young woman's hand. 'You don't need to ask. You treat this home as your own while you are here, okay? Come find us when you're ready.'

'She looks terrified,' Mama Lulu whispered when they left. 'Do Apollo and Petra know where you live?'

'No. It's not on any public forum. And I didn't disclose it when I was there.'

'Good. We don't need him banging down the door in the middle of the night, frightening that poor little boy any more than he clearly is.'

They tidied up and washed the dinner plates. Then Mama Lulu opened the fridge, took out a bottle of Sauvignon Blanc and poured two glasses. She was at ease in Vega's kitchen, as if she'd been popping in for years, and it was a joy to watch.

'Do you know where Altair's father is?' she asked.

Vega took a sip of her wine and sighed with the pleasure that only the first sip of wine could give. 'I haven't a clue. I didn't ask her about him when I was there last week. But there was no sign of a likely candidate.'

The door opened and Estelle walked in. Her face was flushed, and Vega could have kicked herself. She'd heard them talking.

'Sorry, we weren't gossiping,' Vega explained.

'It's fine. It's an understandable question,' Estelle replied.

'Would you like a drink?'

She shook her head. 'Water is fine.'

Vega poured a glass and handed it to her. Estelle took a long sip, and then, after what felt like an impossibly long moment, she said, 'I don't know how to tell you about Altair's father.'

'You don't have to tell us anything!' Vega responded, feeling awful that she might feel compelled to confide in them. 'Altair's father is your business. Not ours.'

Estelle continued to avoid eye contact, fixing her stare on the flagstone tiles in the kitchen. 'I didn't know I was pregnant until I began to show.'

'That happens,' Mama Lulu said kindly.

'But Petra and Apollo were not surprised. They seemed to expect it. And then Apollo said it had been prophesied that I would have a baby boy. A son and heir for him.'

Vega felt her stomach plummet as she listened aghast to Estelle's damning words.

'Altair is Apollo's child.'

50

Vega looked at Estelle in horror. 'That means . . .' She paused, trying to frame her thoughts as they rushed at her. 'Wow. That must have been terrifying for you. To not know you were pregnant . . . I'm sorry . . .' She broke off, trying to grapple with this news. Then the realisation hit her. 'That means that Altair is my brother?'

Estelle looked up for the first time and nodded. 'You're disgusted. I knew you would be.'

Vega quickly tried to rearrange her face into a more neutral expression. But it wasn't easy. Thinking about Estelle and Apollo together made her feel ill. She took a large sip of her wine and closed her eyes momentarily.

'I know you'll want us to leave. But please don't kick us out tonight. Altair is asleep. Please.'

Vega pulled herself together at these words and moved closer to Estelle. She put her glass on the kitchen counter and placed her hands on Estelle's shoulders. 'You are welcome to stay here with Altair as long as you need. Don't even think about leaving. I won't hear of it.'

Estelle slumped, and she sobbed, 'I'm so sorry. I was so scared to tell you. But I knew I had to.'

Vega pulled her into her arms and hugged her, whispering, 'Shh . . .' as she rubbed her back gently, until Estelle's sobs subsided.

'Let's go into the sitting room,' Mama Lulu said. 'My old bones are tired. I need a comfy seat.'

They did as she suggested, and Vega sat cross-legged on the floor before her two guests on the couch.

'Did you tell Apollo and Petra that you were leaving?' Mama Lulu asked.

'No,' Estelle responded, shaking her head, her long ponytail moving side to side down her back. 'After you left, Vega, things changed at home. I don't know . . . it was as if your being there brought back memories for Petra and Apollo of when he was with your mother. They fought continuously. Petra accused him of still loving Star. He taunted her. Cruel jibes that she could never be half the woman that Star was. And Petra began unravelling in front of our eyes. Ranting and raving about how her life was ruined because of Apollo. It was scary for me, but terrifying for Altair. I knew we had to escape. I packed a bag, ready to leave, and waited for my chance.'

She took a deep breath. 'I got my chance this morning. Tommy, the farmer who leases land from us, called over to make a payment. Apollo and Petra were both asleep. They always sleep late after one of their ceremonies. So I asked Tommy if he'd help me. He didn't even think about it, told me he'd bring me anywhere I needed. He drove us to Galway and we took a train to Heuston in Dublin. Then we went to Connolly station on the Luas and got a bus to Wexford Station. I didn't have a plan other than finding you.'

Vega whistled. 'I'm impressed. You've been so brave.'

Estelle shrugged. 'Your words kept replaying in my mind. If I stayed, they'd do something to Altair. I had to get him to safety.'

'You did the right thing,' Mama Lulu said.

'Why didn't you call me from Galway?' Vega asked.

Estelle shifted in her seat, colour flaming her cheeks again. 'I was afraid you might tell me I couldn't come. And then I'd chicken out and go back to the farm. I just kept moving forward. That was all I could do.' She looked over to Vega. 'I should never have doubted you. Because you've been so kind.'

Vega smiled back and felt a glow of happiness that she was in a position to help. Then her mind went to Luka, as it seemed to do every few minutes now. She couldn't wait to tell him about Estelle and Altair. But then it hit her that of course she could do no such thing. She'd lost her right to tell him about her day when she broke his trust.

She pushed Luka from her mind and instead focused on Estelle again. 'Tomorrow morning, Mama Lulu and I have a meeting to go to. So you and Altair make yourselves at home. Help yourself to anything you fancy to eat. We'll be back in the afternoon.'

Estelle smiled her thanks. 'Are you going anywhere nice?'

Vega smiled back, shrugging her shoulders as she replied. 'I hope so. I might have found Nova. I'll tell you all about it tomorrow. I just need to find Mum now . . .'

And that was when she saw it. Estelle's face changed in an instant. Her smile disappeared, and in its place she looked terrified.

Mama Lulu saw it too and leaned in. 'What's wrong?'

Estelle looked from one to the other, her eyes glistening with tears. 'I don't know how to . . .'

'Just tell us,' Mama Lulu said, her voice sharp in a way Vega had never heard before.

'A few years ago, I overheard Petra and Apollo talking. Arguing, really, their voices were raised. So I stopped and listened in to see what it was about.' Estelle shivered visibly as she looked at Vega.

'Someone had offered to buy the top field. It's where we first lived when we came to the farm. Where the camper vans and caravans were.' Her voice trembled as she spoke. 'There's a derelict cottage there too, right at the back. It was the original farmhouse, where Apollo's grandfather was born. But Apollo's father built the farmhouse we live in in the sixties, and I guess the cottage just fell into ruin. Anyhow, a cousin of Apollo's wanted to buy the field. Said that they would apply for a grant to rebuild the cottage.'

'The vacant property refurbishment grant. We've done pieces

on it in the paper. It's getting a lot of attention in rural Ireland,' Vega said.

'Apollo was saying that it was easy money. That they needed it. But Petra said . . .' Estelle paused, and glanced at them both from veiled eyes, 'Petra said they couldn't sell because of the body.'

51

Mama Lulu gasped and placed a hand on her chest. Vega's eyes remained fixed on Estelle's while her body began to shake in protest at the inevitable blow that was about to fall.

'Apollo screamed at Petra that it was her fault; she was the one who'd said they should bury the body in the cottage.' Estelle sighed. 'I'm so sorry, but I think they killed Star, and she's been in the cottage all along.'

The room stilled, and Vega felt as if she were floating out of her body. She could almost see herself below, her face frozen in horror. Then she heard Mama Lulu cry out, and this shocking, horrific, profoundly sad sound galvanised her. Mama Lulu was so strong, always ready to hold them all up. But now she needed Vega.

Somehow Vega shuffled on her knees towards her grandmother. Not sure who was cradling whom, they embraced each other and cried for a mother and a daughter.

They remained in each other's arms until Vega's knees ached to the point where she had no choice but to move. She heard Estelle repeating the same thing she had said dozens of times since her arrival, over and over again: 'I'm so sorry. I'm so sorry.'

Once she found her voice, Vega replied, 'None of this is your fault. But you can help us now. I'm going to call Detective Gilmartin, and I was hoping you could make a statement. Tell him what you heard. Will you do that?'

'Yes,' Estelle said.

And it was only when she agreed that Vega unclenched her fists and realised her nails had bitten into her palms.

'I won't rest until they're both locked up,' she vowed, her voice laced with determination.

'And I'll throw away the key when they are,' Mama Lulu added, pulling a handkerchief from her pocket and blowing her nose.

Vega picked up her mobile and walked to the kitchen. Detective Gilmartin had told her to call any time if she needed him, and now certainly warranted it.

'Hello, Vega,' he said, his voice warm. 'Is everything okay?'

'No, I'm afraid it isn't. Estelle and her son have left Cosmo Farm and are now with me in Wexford. Estelle has told me that she overheard a conversation between Petra and Apollo regarding a body they buried at the derelict cottage behind the farmhouse.'

Detective Gilmartin inhaled sharply. 'Will she make an official statement?'

'Yes.'

'Okay. Keep her there. I'll send someone to your place to take a statement tomorrow. Then I'll secure a search warrant. I'll need to apply to the district court judge for it.'

'They can't get away with this,' Vega said, trembling.

'They won't. I give you my word; if there's a body in that cottage, I'll find it. I'll be in touch tomorrow.'

'Thank you.'

'For nothing. Is there anyone with you?'

'Mama Lulu is here as well.'

'Ah, that's good. You can lean on one another. Take care of yourself, all right?'

'You too,' Vega replied before she hung up.

When she returned to the sitting room, she updated Mama Lulu and Estelle about her conversation.

'I'll tell the Gardaí everything I know. You can count on me,' Estelle promised. Her face was ashen, and dark circles lurked under her eyes. 'Do you mind if I go up?'

'I told you, you can do what you want here. We'll see you in the morning.'

Once Estelle left, Vega turned to Mama Lulu, who appeared to have aged in the past hour. 'I'm worried about you. Can I make you some tea? Or would you prefer another glass of wine?'

'I'm going to bed, Vega. We'll need our strength, won't we? For whatever is coming our way.'

'We will.'

'Promise me you'll go to sleep now, too. You look exhausted.'

'Not yet. I think I'll get some fresh air. But you go on up. I'm fine, honestly.' They embraced and then went their separate ways.

Vega put on her coat, refilled her wine glass, grabbed a blanket and stepped outside. It was a dry night, but the wind had picked up, so she lit the gas fire pit. Taking a seat, she pulled the blanket over herself and looked up at the stars, searching for the sizeable W-shaped constellation of Cassiopeia. She could usually pick this out in any sky within moments of looking. But tonight, it was hidden. And try as she might, she could not see it.

'Where are you, Mum? Please, I need to see you tonight,' she whispered in desperation.

She found the two end stars in the bowl of the Plough and used them as her guide until finally she spotted the familiar outline of the W. Furiously wiping tears from her eyes, she kept them firmly locked upwards as she searched for her memories of her mother, which were more precious than anything else she owned, and lost herself in those fleeting moments of dancing, singing, loving.

'Hey,' a voice called out from behind her.

She jumped up and ran towards Luka, half expecting him to vanish when she reached him, certain that she'd conjured him up, so desperate was her need. But she felt the strength of his arms wrapping around her, holding her close as she sobbed into his chest.

'How did you know I needed you?' she whispered.

'Mama Lulu texted me this afternoon. She mentioned there might be news about Nova. Once Mum went to sleep, I decided to drive over. I thought you might be out here star-gazing.'

Vega was more grateful than she could express for her grandmother's interference. 'There's quite a bit of news. But first, how's your mum doing?'

'She's tired. The operation has taken a lot out of her, but she's allowing me to take care of her. It's nice to be able to do that. I'm working from home for a bit. No court dates in the diary either, thankfully.'

'I'm glad. That's really good news. Can I get you a drink? Tea or coffee?'

'Nah, I'm good. I'll sit with you for a bit, though. You can fill me in on Nova and everything else.'

'Well, Mama Lulu and I are invited to Delaney's house tomorrow to see Caoimhe and her mother.'

'So she believes you?'

'There have been several developments. Caoimhe discussed them with her mother, who requested the meeting.' Vega filled Luka in about Vivienne's involvement in her scholarship and her job, as well as Senan's role in the documentary at the farm.

'Wow,' Luka said. 'Honestly, that's wild. It has to be connected.'

'I know. I've been thinking about it non-stop, and the only logical answer I can come up with is that the Delaneys never intended to tell Caoimhe that she was adopted. However, when I came on the scene, they had no choice.'

'It looks that way,' Luka agreed. 'And it makes sense that they would feel some guilt about separating the two of you, leaving you behind. They were making amends with the scholarship and the job.'

'I think so.'

He watched her closely, taking in her downcast face. 'You must be excited?'

Vega nodded but felt her bottom lip quiver as she looked at the sky. 'Something else has happened.'

'Go on,' Luka said, his voice so gentle it felt almost like a caress.

'Estelle and her son are here. They ran away from the farm.'

'That's wonderful! I'm glad she found the strength to do that. It's courageous.'

'I told her that,' Vega replied, smiling. 'And it seems I might have found a little brother as well as a sister.'

Luka slumped back in his chair; the astonishment on his face would have been comical in any other situation.

'Altair is Apollo's son. It seems Apollo drugged Estelle, because she has no recollection of the conception, and Petra was in on it. It's so messed up.' Vega shivered again, just thinking about it.

'That's horrific.'

They sat in silence for a moment, each lost in their thoughts. Then Luka smiled. 'For someone who never liked inviting anyone to her home, it's got busy around here!'

They shared a chuckle. 'I've given them my bedroom. I'm couching it,' Vega said.

'Stay at mine,' Luka said, and for a moment, a joyful moment, Vega's heart jumped in elation. Until he added, 'I'm not there anyhow. I plan to stay at Mum's for another week. So the flat is all yours until then.'

The joy in her heart dissolved as quickly as it had arrived.

'You know, Estelle should file charges. It sounds like he forced himself on her,' Luka mused, seemingly oblivious to Vega's disappointment.

'I'll talk to her about that. The Gardaí will be here tomorrow anyway.' Vega's eyes filled with tears once more. She had cried so much today she didn't know where they came from. 'I've one more update for you. Estelle shared something this evening. I've saved the worst part of my news for last.'

Luka reached over and clasped her hand as she continued. 'Estelle overheard her mum and Apollo talking about hiding a body in a derelict cottage.' She couldn't stop the tears, no matter how hard she tried. 'So I think we might've found Mum too.'

Luka jumped up and pulled her to her feet, enveloping her in his embrace once more, whispering endearments as she sobbed. When her tears finally ceased, she looked up at him, unable to believe she had ever been foolish enough to let this man vanish from her life.

'Thank you,' she whispered.

'You never have to thank me. I'll always be here for you when you need me.'

Vega had never heard more welcome words, and she reached up to kiss him. But Luka pulled back, gently yet firmly pushing her away.

'Can you not forgive me?' she asked, her voice choked with emotion.

'I reacted poorly to you ignoring me because I was stressed about Mum. However, in hindsight, I understand why you became so overwhelmed by all of this. You have more on your plate this week than many people do in an entire lifetime. I copped on after I stopped feeling sorry for myself.'

Vega placed a hand on his chest and felt the thump, thump of his heart reverberating. 'That's incredibly generous of you. Thank you.' She wanted to leave it at that, but knew she had to confront the huge elephant in the room. 'What about the laptop?'

She held her breath while she waited for him to respond.

'I understand that as well, or at least I've attempted to see things from your perspective. So again, I get it.'

Vega half laughed and sobbed in response, the relief causing her knees to buckle.

'But . . .' That single word from Luka felt like a slap to her face. 'I can't trust you, Vega.'

'For now? Or ever?' she whispered.

He locked eyes with her and shook his head sadly. 'I want to trust you, but I can't be with someone if I have to change my laptop password every time they stay with me.'

This damning statement was one she couldn't deny. Of course he shouldn't have to live like that. Vega had done this to herself, fully aware that picking up his laptop would end their relationship, yet, like a moth to a flame, unable to stop.

It was over. He knew it, and finally she did too.

'I'm sorry that I did this to us,' she said.

'Me too.'

'So what now?'

'I'm still here to support you, Vega. I suspect this is going to be a rough few weeks. I told you I'll always be here for you.'

Vega sucked in a long, steadying breath and put on a brave smile. She patted his chest with a hand and then reached out to hug him. 'You get back to your mother. Thank you for offering your flat, but I'll hit my couch. We've got history, us two. It knows how to rock me to sleep! And I'll be in touch tomorrow. I'll let you know how things go with Caoimhe.'

Luka didn't move. He just stared at Vega with such intensity that she thought he was going to change his mind and tell her that everything would be okay.

But instead, he turned and walked away.

52

The entrance to Delaney's house was as palatial as Vega had envisioned. Two large granite pillars framed a tall black electric gate. She pressed the intercom, and a woman answered, saying, 'The Delaney residence.'

Mama Lulu and Vega exchanged wide-eyed glances before Vega responded. 'Hello, I have a meeting with Caoimhe Delaney. It's Vega Pearse and Lulu Kensington.'

'Follow the driveway to the front of the residence,' the woman replied.

'The residence. She likes that word,' Vega said.

'It sounds fancy,' Mama Lulu agreed, her gaze focused on the scenery outside the car window.

'I think we're about to enter a world very different from any I've ever known,' Vega replied as she moved forward. 'I kind of wish I had washed the car.'

'Could do with it,' Mama Lulu said bluntly.

'Hey! It's impossible to stay clean on our country roads,' Vega grumbled.

'Be honest! When was the last time you cleaned it?' Mama Lulu asked.

Vega began to giggle. 'Well, never. But . . . Oh look, here we are.' She parked beside a gleaming silver BMW saloon and two BMW jeeps.

'Don't say a word,' she warned, seeing how ridiculous her Kia looked in contrast to the Delaney cars. Mama Lulu pretended to zip her mouth, her eyes full of mischief.

'I guess they're a BMW family,' Vega said. 'All three are brand new, too.'

'Don't get out for a second. Let me fix my hair and sort out my lipstick.'

Vega looked at her grandmother indulgently as she puckered her lips to apply another layer of mauve-pink lipstick. 'You look great. I hope I look as good when I'm your age.'

'Want some?' Mama Lulu asked, handing her the lipstick.

'No. You're grand,' Vega said. 'This is me. They can take me or leave me.'

'You okay?' Her grandmother had caught the edge in her voice.

'I feel a bit . . . I don't know . . . somewhat judged by the Delaneys. And that puts my back up.'

'You've no reason to feel that way!' Mama Lulu stated. 'You're successful, beautiful, and have your own house and car, even if it is dirty. You walk in there with your head held high. I'm proud to call you my granddaughter.'

Vega swallowed a lump in her throat. 'Thanks, Mama Lulu. You're an amazing hype woman.'

'I only speak the truth. Now come on, someone is hovering at the front door waiting for us.'

'She's wearing a maid's uniform!' Vega hissed as they got out of the car, taking in the beige dress with a crisp white apron tied around the waist. 'I thought that only happened in movies!'

They approached the smiling woman, who greeted them warmly. 'Hello, welcome. I'm Mrs O'Connor, the housekeeper here. Mrs Delaney is waiting for you in the drawing room. Do you need the powder room to freshen up before we go in?'

'Er . . . no, thank you,' Vega answered, glancing at Mama Lulu, who also shook her head, appearing as bemused as Vega felt.

'This way, please,' Mrs O'Connor said.

They followed her through the entrance foyer, which was clad in caramel marble tiles, featuring a grand staircase in its centre that wound upwards to both left and right.

'This hallway is bigger than my cottage,' Vega said, her eyes round and wide as she took in the decor.

'I'd hate to be cleaning that floor,' Mama Lulu said.

'It's a devil, no word of a lie,' Mrs O'Connor replied, winking.

They passed a room with a piano at its centre, and Vega wondered if Caoimhe played. Then they walked by another spacious reception room decorated with chandeliers and a fireplace that must have been at least ten feet high.

Mrs O'Connor paused in front of a closed cream-coloured door and knocked twice.

'Come in,' a voice said.

She opened the door, and they stepped inside.

This room had a high ceiling and featured powder-blue wallpaper that extended to an ornate architrave and coving. Two cream sofas faced each other in front of a granite fireplace.

And standing in front of a window that overlooked the garden was the silhouette of Mrs Delaney, encased in a ray of sunlight.

Echoes of a parlour in The Woodstock Inn on the day Aunt Flick came to see her washed over Vega. She was about to step forward when she heard a gasp beside her. Mama Lulu grabbed her arm forcefully and gripped it so tightly that Vega almost yelped. She turned to her grandmother to see what was wrong.

Mama Lulu spoke in a strangled voice, her eyes fixed on Mrs Delaney. 'It's Cassie,' she said.

53

Mama Lulu stumbled into Vega's arms as Vega locked eyes with Caoimhe's mother in mutual horror. She placed her hands under her grandmother's arms and half carried her towards the sofa as Mrs Delaney moved away from the sunlight, her face creased with concern.

And then Mama Lulu's expression relaxed, and she shook her head with sadness. 'I'm sorry. I'm a foolish woman.'

'What's wrong, Mama Lulu?' Vega asked, her grandmother her only concern.

'I thought you were my Cassie,' Mama Lulu told Mrs Delaney, who was now hovering over them both. 'Something about how you stood and the sunlight played tricks on me.'

'It's quite all right,' Mrs Delaney replied. Her voice was cultured and didn't have a particular accent. You'd know it was Irish, but other than that, it could be from anywhere. She had a relatively unlined face that belied her age, which Vega surmised must be at least sixty.

'Mrs O'Connor, could you please bring Mrs Kensington a glass of brandy. Would either of you like tea or coffee?'

'No, thank you.' Vega said. 'Maybe later.'

Mrs O'Connor disappeared.

'I'm so pleased to meet you, Vega,' Mrs Delaney said.

Vega reached out to shake her hand and fought the urge to curtsey. What was it about this woman that made her feel like she was in the presence of royalty? 'Nice to meet you too.'

Mrs Delaney shook Mama Lulu's hand as well before sitting on the sofa opposite her.

Mrs O'Connor returned with a silver tray containing a brandy decanter and three glasses.

Vega declined one, but Mama Lulu accepted hers with gratitude. A few sips later, the colour returned to her face.

'Where is Caoimhe, Mrs Delaney?' Vega asked.

'She'll be here soon with Senan. Please call me Vivienne. I wanted to meet with both of you alone first, because while my husband has a big heart, he can sometimes be a little heavy-handed.'

Why would Senan Delaney be heavy-handed? Vega wondered. However, she set that aside, as there was only one thing she needed to know right now. 'Is Caoimhe Nova?'

Vivienne smiled. 'Straight to the point. I like that. Okay, let's get to the nitty-gritty.' She paused slightly too dramatically for Vega's liking, then said, 'Yes. Caoimhe is Nova.'

Vega slumped back onto the soft sofa and groaned, a long, deep, guttural sound emanating from the depths of her being.

'You found her,' Mama Lulu said tearfully, then took another sip of her brandy.

'I found her,' Vega repeated, feeling like she might burst into tears at any moment. 'Does Caoimhe know?'

'Yes,' Vivienne replied, her smile frozen. 'Senan and I had a long talk with her yesterday and explained everything.'

'Why the secrecy?' Vega asked. 'She's a grown woman; surely she had the right to know before all this?'

Vivienne raised her eyebrows delicately and shrugged. 'Well, the thing is, we thought it was best for her not to know about her mother's abandonment. That could have caused her great trauma with lasting damage.' Her eyes bored into Vega's as she spoke, judgement laced in her stare, as if to say: look at you, case in point.

'Her mother didn't abandon her,' Mama Lulu said. 'Her mother loved her.'

'I'm her mother,' Vivienne replied firmly, her jaw clenching momentarily as her smile vanished. 'Perhaps it's best to refer to your daughter as Cassie for now, or Star, whichever she preferred. This way, we can avoid confusing Caoimhe any further than necessary.'

Mama Lulu sat up straight, placed her drink on the coffee table before her and met Vivienne's eyes without flinching.

Game on, Vega thought, watching her grandmother with pride. She wouldn't let anyone speak ill of her daughter. The relief she felt that she had someone here with her with equal stakes, who was on her mother's side and hers, was staggering.

'Caoimhe is cherished by her family,' Vivienne said. 'She is our only child, and in fact, the sole granddaughter and niece, making her beloved by everyone. She's clever and funny, and we are very proud of her.' There was genuine warmth in her voice as she spoke.

'I thought she was all that when I met her,' Vega agreed, 'And beautiful too.'

'She changed all our lives when she came into this house. Before, it was just a grand house with no heart. Caoimhe made it a home.'

Mama Lulu picked up her drink again and settled back into the seat. 'That makes me happy to hear. It's all we want to know: that Caoimhe is loved.'

'I give you my word that she has received nothing but love from all of us,' Vivienne said, her sincerity shining from her eyes.

Mama Lulu cleared her throat and asked the question that had burned in Vega's heart and mind for decades. 'I guess that leads me to another question, and I'd like an honest answer. Why didn't you take Vega too?'

'Ah,' Vivienne said, shifting uneasily. 'That question has haunted me for years.' Turning to Vega, she continued, 'It was terribly upsetting for Senan and me to leave you behind. It tore us apart.'

Vega heard Mama Lulu snort beside her. 'I think it might have been a little more upsetting for the two sisters to lose not only their beloved mother but each other, too! It's not like you didn't have enough money to feed another mouth!'

Vivienne shot her a glance of annoyance. 'We had to do what was best for Caoimhe.'

'How was that best for her?' Vega asked. 'I loved her, and she loved me.'

The smile returned to Vivienne's face. 'I know. But she was so young. And we knew that in time she'd forget about her unfortunate start in life. She would put all that nastiness behind her and have a clean slate.' She sighed. 'You were older, Vega, and had such a strong personality. You wouldn't have let Cassie's memory fade, and that would have coloured Caoimhe's life.' She looked over to Mama Lulu. 'I do not apologise for doing what was in Caoimhe's best interest.'

Vega felt a shiver run down her spine at the stark realisation that Vivienne saw her as nasty and unfortunate.

The sound of a glass being placed sharply onto a table made her jump. Mama Lulu leaned in, her face tight as she locked eyes with Vivienne. 'If you had adopted Vega as well, and given her the same love you gave Caoimhe, she could have moved on from her trauma of being abandoned, too. Had that same clean slate. And while they might never have forgotten their mother, they would at least have been together.'

Vivienne shrugged delicately. 'Maybe. We'll never know. That's in the past, isn't it?'

Before they had a chance for further conversation, the door opened and Caoimhe and her father entered.

'Vega!' Caoimhe exclaimed, practically skipping towards her.

Vega jumped up, her face illuminating with joy at the sight of her sister.

'You were right!' Caoimhe said. 'Is your head completely blown apart by all of this?' She threw her arms around Vega, holding her tight. 'I thought you were crazy! I'm so sorry I doubted you. But honestly, I had no idea!'

'You have nothing to be sorry about!' Vega said, feeling laughter bubble up inside her at the speed with which Caoimhe spoke. She was so full of excitement and joy that it was infectious, taking the sting out of Vivienne's stark judgement from moments before. 'Are you okay? It must be a lot to take in.'

Caoimhe's smile dropped and her eyes glistened. 'I've cried more in the past twenty-four hours than I have in my entire life. It's hard to get my head round.'

'I'm sure. Especially as you didn't even know you were adopted,' Vega said kindly.

'My poor parents have been beside themselves. They did what they thought was best. And to be honest, I'm glad I didn't have to grow up thinking I'd been abandoned.' Caoimhe frowned and then put a hand to her mouth when she realised what she'd said. 'I'm sorry. That sounded awful.'

Before Vega could respond, Mama Lulu walked over and said warmly, 'I hate to interrupt you two, but I'd like to meet my granddaughter.'

'Mama Lulu, this is Caoimhe. Caoimhe, meet the most amazing person I've ever encountered. She's incredible! You are going to love her!'

They embraced for a moment, and Mama Lulu touched Caoimhe's cheek gently, just as she had with Vega when they met. Vega glanced over to the Delaneys and was taken aback to see Vivienne's obvious distress at the interaction as she watched the reunion.

'One of the happiest days of my life. To have my two granddaughters together. Your mother would be so proud.'

Caoimhe glanced at Vivienne in confusion and her mother quickly moved forward and took her hand. 'She means your birth mother, Cassie. I did stress that it would be confusing for you.' She shot Mama Lulu an annoyed look before saying to her daughter, 'Sit beside me.'

'Hello, Vega,' Senan said, speaking for the first time. He shook hands with Mama Lulu before joining his wife on the couch, Caoimhe between the two of them.

'You're tenacious, Vega,' he said. 'Guess that's part of why you're such a damn fine journalist. You keep chasing a story till you get it.'

'I've been searching for Nova and my mum my entire life,' Vega said. 'It's all I've ever wanted – to find them both.'

Caoimhe's eyes grew glassy as she shot Vega a sympathetic look. 'I'm so sorry, Vega. Was it terrible growing up in foster care? I feel so guilty that I was here, while you—'

'You mustn't feel guilty,' Vivienne quickly said, glancing at Vega reproachfully.

'No. You shouldn't. It wasn't so bad,' Vega lied, pushing aside the years of feeling not enough, unworthy and unloved.

'Wasn't Mum incredible, though? I'm blown away by how generous and thoughtful she was,' Caoimhe said, looking at Vivienne with adoration.

Vega felt puzzled, unsure what her sister was referring to.

'She told me that she joined the board of Foster Care for Life just so she could keep an eye on you . . . and then the job at the newspaper. I know it was awful that we didn't grow up together, but I'm so glad they could do that for you.'

All three of the Delaneys were looking at Vega with expectant gazes, and she realised they were waiting for a response from her. She felt Mama Lulu's hand, warm and comforting, resting on the small of her back.

'I'm very grateful,' she said, forcing a smile. The whole meeting felt surreal. It wasn't going as she had dreamed it would. She wanted to focus on her sister, not Vivienne's philanthropic work. 'What have you been told about your life before your adoption, Caoimhe? You must have questions for me.'

'I know we were found at Pearse station in 1995. I was three, you were four, and we were taken into foster care. I was adopted shortly after.'

'That's right. Well, I've learned quite a bit about our mother over the past couple of weeks, both from Mama Lulu and from those who knew her as a young woman.' Vega glanced at Senan, wondering when she should mention that she knew he'd met Cassie.

But before she could further ponder that, Caoimhe took the

wind from her sails by saying, 'I know about the commune. I'm finding that part the strangest to understand.'

'Of course you are, darling,' Vivienne said soothingly. 'Communes are far from how you were brought up. Thank goodness.'

Senan patted Caoimhe's knee reassuringly. 'I was able to tell Caoimhe about Cassie because I knew her too, for a while.' He put his arm around her shoulder as he continued. 'And there's something you should know too, Vega. Caoimhe's not your sister; she's your half-sister.'

Vega glanced between Senan and Caoimhe, her mind racing to grasp what he meant by this.

'I don't understand,' Mama Lulu said. 'How on earth could you know that?'

'Because I am Caoimhe's biological father.'

54

'I knew I was a Delaney. I look too much like my aunt,' Caoimhe said. 'I told you that.'

Vega nodded as her mind struggled to catch up with this turn of events. She looked at Senan. 'So you were in a relationship with my mother?'

'Not a relationship. But we had a brief dalliance.' He glanced sideways at Vivienne, who kept her eyes fixed on the arm of the sofa. 'We met when I was a producer on a documentary about communes in Ireland.'

'We saw it last night,' Vega said. It was as if he were a step ahead of them all the time.

'Ah. Of course you did,' Senan said, smiling. 'I should have known you'd uncover that! It's been a long time since I thought about it. It was never aired, axed by the station. Probably just as well.'

'Mum looks so young and beautiful in it,' Vega said. 'It was really emotional for Mama Lulu and me to see her. I can send you a copy, Caoimhe.'

Caoimhe bit her lip and looked at her father uncertainly.

'If you want to see it, I'll get you a copy. But there is no pressure for you to watch it. All in your own time, Caoimhe, as we told you last night.'

'Exactly,' Vivienne added. 'And if you don't want to see Vega or Lulu again, they'll understand.' She shot a look at them both, daring them to disagree.

'Thank you,' Caoimhe said, her voice wobbling.

Vega longed to swap places with the Delaneys to comfort her.

'It's a head-melt, isn't it?' she said, locking eyes with her sister, who smiled back weakly.

'I'm sure you must have questions for Senan,' Vivienne said.

Vega could think of at least half a dozen, but the most urgent one was: 'Did you know that Nova was your daughter when you adopted her?'

'I did,' Senan replied.

It all began to make sense now. Questions she hadn't even known she had were answered. 'So that's why you didn't want me. I wasn't your daughter,' she said.

'Not true. As my wife has undoubtedly shared with you, we were concerned that you might never forget your past. We didn't want that for Caoimhe. Our goal was to provide her with the best possible chances in life.'

Vega raised her hand. She didn't believe she could endure another rerun of why she hadn't been chosen for the Delaney home.

'How did you know that you were her father?' Mama Lulu asked sharply, her eyes narrowing as she watched Senan.

'Cassie told me. I was covering President Clinton's visit at College Green, and she found me there. It had been years since I'd seen her.'

'How did she know you'd be there?' Vega asked.

'I'm not sure. I'm guessing she called the station.'

'How long was your relationship with her?' Vega asked.

'Only a few weeks, during the time I was in Connemara shooting the documentary.'

'Did Apollo know?'

Senan shrugged. 'I'm not sure. I don't think so. We were discreet, and as I said, it was over as fast as it began.'

'Were you in love?'

'No. It was a fling. Nothing more for both of us. Cassie made it clear that she was only looking for a distraction from life at the farm.'

Mama Lulu looked at Vega sadly, and the room fell silent for a few moments.

'What did she want when she came to see you?' Mama Lulu asked.

'Money.'

Vivienne sighed, as if she expected nothing less from someone like Cassie.

'She said she wanted to go home to America. To you,' Senan said, and Mama Lulu groaned in response.

'Had she left Apollo?' Vega asked.

'Yes. She said he was unstable, and she was scared of him. She wanted a better life for both of you.'

'Poor Cassie,' Caoimhe said, wiping a tear from her eye.

Vega knew it was understandable that Caoimhe would call her Cassie, not Mum. Yet it hurt all the same, showing another difference between them.

'She wanted to come home to me,' Mama Lulu said, tears streaming down her cheeks. She pulled out her handkerchief to dab them, but as quickly as she did, fresh tears appeared.

'Did you give her money?' Vega asked Senan.

'Of course! Or at least I told her I'd get it for her. I asked her where you both were, and she said you were safe. She never mentioned at any stage that you were alone at a train station of all places!' he said adamantly.

Vivienne shivered. 'Anything could have happened to you. I can't bear to think about it.'

'It's okay, Mum. We were fine,' Caoimhe reassured her. Flanked by her parents, whose love was evident and undeniable, she had support enveloping her from both sides.

And in some ways, Vega felt comforted by that. It was all she'd ever wanted for her little sister.

'Did she tell you that you were my father straight away?' Caoimhe asked, turning to her dad.

Senan smiled. 'Pretty much. She said she'd always suspected it was me, but the older you got, the more certain she became, because you looked so much like me.'

'And were you upset by that?' Caoimhe asked.

'No,' Senan replied. 'Shocked, of course, but that was all. She mentioned she'd be in touch once she settled back in America, and if I wanted to meet you, she'd make that happen. I told her I did want to meet you, but it suited me to have a little time. I needed to tell Vivienne, who by that time I'd met and married.'

Caoimhe turned to her mother. 'You must have been shocked, too.'

Vivienne half smiled. 'Oh, your father has shocked me on more than one occasion, but this was a doozy! He told me about the meeting that night. He was worried because Cassie hadn't returned for her money. He assumed she'd gone back to the farm with the two of you. To Apollo.'

Senan took up the story again. 'I said to Vivienne, I can't let my daughter grow up there.' He sighed heavily. 'But then the news broke that two little girls had been found at a train station. And don't ask me how, but I knew it was Cassie's girls.'

'A father's instinct,' Vivienne concurred sagely.

'Perhaps.' He looked at his daughter. 'I was lucky that my father was a judge. And I'm not ashamed to admit that he used his position to ensure that we could adopt you. He pulled some strings and we were allowed to foster you until the adoption went through, once it was clear that nobody was going to come forward to claim you.'

Vega inhaled deeply. So many questions were finally answered.

Senan turned to Mama Lulu then. 'By the way, she always called herself Cassie when she was with me. I know she was referred to as Star with Apollo, but she said she'd grown tired of that nickname.'

'She had come to her senses!' Mama Lulu exclaimed. 'She was free from the spell of Apollo, I know it.'

'It was clear to me when we interviewed him that Apollo was delusional and paranoid. We filmed several hours, but most of the conversations were unusable because he was ranting.'

'So where did Mum go after you saw her at College Park?' Vega asked.

Senan exhaled and shook his head. 'I wish I could tell you. I told her to meet me at my apartment later that day, after I'd finished work, and I'd give her the money then. She never showed up.'

'From what we know about her, she wasn't the most reliable. She could have returned to Apollo, or met someone new,' Vivienne said. 'How she could do that to her children, though... it's unfathomable.'

'She didn't do anything to her children!' Mama Lulu said furiously, beating Vega to it.

'It wasn't her fault she couldn't come back for us!' Vega said.

'Well, I'm not sure it's anyone else's.' Vivienne looked at Senan, who nodded in approval.

'You're wrong!' Mama Lulu exclaimed, her voice high and tense.

Vega placed a calming hand on her grandmother's knee. 'There's something I need to tell you, Caoimhe, about Mum.' She spoke as gently as she could. 'I went to Cosmo Farm last week and met Apollo and his partner, a woman named Petra – plus Petra's daughter, Estelle, and her son, Altair, who've both come to stay with me in Wexford. It turns out Altair is my half-brother. I thought he was your brother, too, but since Apollo isn't your father...'

'Wait, I thought you said Petra was Estelle's mother?' Caoimhe said, her nose wrinkling in confusion.

'She is.'

Senan grimaced. 'This is like an episode of a ghastly soap opera!'

'And what is it with all the strange names?' Vivienne said, sniffing in derision.

'They're all named after stars,' Vega said. 'Like Nova and I were.'

Vivienne had the grace to blush.

Vega ignored her and continued to break the news to Caoimhe as sensitively as possible. 'Based on a conversation that Estelle overheard between Petra and Apollo, we believe that Mum might be dead.'

Silence filled the room. Senan blanched, and Vivienne's fixed smile vanished. But Vega kept her eyes on Caoimhe, her only thought being for her little sister.

'What did they say exactly?' Senan asked in a curt tone.

'Are you okay with me continuing?' Vega asked Caoimhe. 'I know this is a lot to absorb.'

Caoimhe gave a small smile of gratitude and nodded for her to continue.

'Estelle overheard them talking about a body hidden in a derelict cottage on the farm,' Vega said.

'That's horrific,' Caoimhe whispered, and she began to cry softly. Senan and Vivienne both rushed to wrap their arms around her once more.

After a moment, she brushed them off, assuring them she was okay. She looked at Vega. 'We need to find out if that's true. We can't leave her in a shallow grave . . . she deserves better.'

That's my sister, Vega thought with pride. 'No, we can't. I've reported it to Detective Gilmartin, who I'd already reported Mum missing to. He'll obtain a search warrant once Estelle has given her statement to the Gardaí.'

'Thank you for doing all of that. It's horrible to think she might have been there all this time,' Caoimhe said.

'We'll not rest till we get justice for her if it's true,' Mama Lulu added. 'I'll not believe it till the Gardaí confirm it, though.'

'How do you think she ended up back in Connemara, though? She told Dad that she'd left Apollo,' Caoimhe said.

Vega exhaled slowly. 'Mama Lulu and I have discussed various scenarios. The most plausible is that Apollo followed Mum to Dublin and took her back to the farm against her will. We think she didn't disclose our location to him because she believed we were safer with strangers than with our father.'

'She left you at the station to protect you. I know my girl. She was a good person. She did that out of love, I'm sure of it,' Mama Lulu stated firmly, throwing a scathing look at Vivienne.

Caoimhe had gone quite pale and was visibly trembling.

Vega desperately wanted to tell her that she understood how she felt better than anyone else. She knew this was overwhelming because she was living with it, too.

But she couldn't, because the Delaneys were like guards on duty.

'I think it's best if we leave it at that for now,' Vivienne said, standing up. 'It's been a stressful morning for everyone.'

'Quite right,' Senan agreed. 'Let's wrap this up.'

Wrap it up? He was acting as if they'd just had a business meeting!

'Do you want us to leave?' Vega asked her sister.

Before she could answer, Vivienne said, 'Let's not pressurise Caoimhe. That would be selfish, wouldn't it?'

Vega felt Mama Lulu stiffen beside her. She stood up and turned to help her grandmother to her feet.

The door opened and Mrs O'Connor entered, frowning. 'Mrs Delaney, there's a phone call for you.'

'Take a message,' Vivienne replied curtly.

'I tried. But they were insistent, saying it was urgent. They said to say it was about that matter with the charity regulator.'

Vivienne's lips twitched for a moment, then she fixed a smile on her face and turned to Vega and Mama Lulu. 'I need to take this call. Mrs O'Connor will show you to the door.'

Vega looked at Caoimhe, 'We have all the time in the world to catch up. You've got my number. Call me day or night, okay? I'm here for you.'

'You were looking out for me even before you knew who I was,' Caoimhe said, her voice quivering with emotion. 'Just like a big sister should.'

'Like I always will,' Vega said.

Mama Lulu clasped Caoimhe's hands between hers. 'I live on a maple farm in Vermont. And you have a family there who would love to meet you. Cassie's sister, Flick, will be so excited to hear that we've found you. You also have three cousins, a little younger than you. They're spitfires, too. I think you all could have a lot of fun together.'

'Thank you,' Caoimhe said politely. 'That's kind of you.'

'Could you please walk our guests to the door?' Vivienne repeated, this time with more urgency.

'Of course,' Mrs O'Connor replied. And before they had time to say another word, they were ushered out of the room.

Vega and Mama Lulu spoke only when they were back in the car and driving out of the grounds.

'I'm not sure the Delaneys approve of either of us,' Vega began.

'Fur coat and no knickers, that's what we always said about women like Vivienne Delaney back in my day!' Mama Lulu exploded. 'And I'm not sure I approve of either of *them*!'

'They love Caoimhe. That's something,' Vega said.

'Yes. That's something. But I'm not sure how close we'll get to her with them both gatekeeping.'

And as if to punctuate Mama Lulu's words, the tall black gates closed behind them, sending them on their way.

55

Two detectives from Wexford Garda station visited the cottage to take Estelle's statement that afternoon. She performed exceptionally well, concisely articulating and recounting the conversation she had overheard between Petra and Apollo. Vega informed Detective Gilmartin about her mother's connection to Senan Delaney and his meeting with her at College Green on 1 December 1995. He said he would follow up with Senan and take his statement.

Then Vega discovered herself in uncharted territory.

She was a plane in a holding pattern, waiting for its turn to take off.

She awaited news on the search warrant from Detective Gilmartin; she awaited further contact from Caoimhe, who had gone quiet except for a short, pleasant text message. And somehow, she knew that waiting for Luka to trust her again would be the longest wait.

She had spent her entire life searching for answers, and now that she was so close to finding them, she felt lost. It was Vega's little brother, Altair, who rescued her as she immersed herself in making his holiday to Wexford one he'd remember for a long time. Their first stop was a trip to Ballinesker Beach, Vega's favourite on the Wexford coastline – a hotspot for locals when Curracloe became crowded with tourists.

'I've never been to a beach before,' Altair said, his eyes shining with excitement.

This was unbelievable to Vega: to live so close to the beautiful Atlantic Way, with its stunning coastline, yet never visit the beaches. Sadly, Estelle and Altair had been reclusive, and rarely left the farm.

'This is my favourite time to go to the beach,' Vega told them as she parked in the empty parking lot. 'Nobody is here but us. It's our very own private place.'

'Do up that jacket,' Mama Lulu said, fussing over Altair and zipping up his fleece, a recent addition to his wardrobe. Vega had insisted on buying new clothes for both Estelle and Altair, and they'd had a fun morning shopping in Wexford Town.

'We're lucky. It's a mild day for November,' Vega said, looking up at the grey skies. A few dark clouds drifted overhead, hinting at a change in the weather soon. 'Let's have fun before it starts to give us the predicted drizzle.'

Watching Altair squeeze his toes into the sand for the first time and chase the waves back and forth as the water lapped at him, his voice squealing into the dark grey sky, was a balm for them all.

'He's missed so much,' Estelle said.

'You've missed so much, too,' Vega replied, putting her arm around her new friend. They had only known each other briefly, but she felt a connection that felt like family.

She recalled Apollo's words in the documentary, where he spoke about the family of choice that had gathered at the farm. If Vega had stayed and grown up in that home, she and Estelle would have been as close as sisters. And now, with Altair, they were family too.

'I'm glad you're here,' she said.

'Me too,' Estelle replied, laughing out loud as Altair screamed ecstatically.

Twenty minutes later, fearing he might catch his death, they had to coax him into coming home with the promise of hot chocolate.

'I'll even add marshmallows and cream on top!' Vega promised.

Altair looked at Estelle. 'Can I have some, Est . . .' he paused and corrected himself, 'Mama?'

'Yes, darling,' Estelle said, her voice choked with emotion at the poignancy the word could evoke. Altair was learning to refer to her by this new name. It was yet another adjustment for them, but one they welcomed with love.

Detective Gilmartin finally called while they were enjoying their promised hot chocolates at the cottage. 'We've obtained the search warrant. We're heading to the farm now.'

Vega's body began to tremble at this welcome news. The wait would soon be over.

'Will you call me?'

'I promise to get back to you as soon as I can. But if you don't hear from me for a few hours, please don't worry.'

The three women sat on the sofa, watching Altair build his first Lego toy.

'I need a distraction,' Estelle said. 'Can you put on the documentary about Cosmo Farm?'

'Are you sure?' Vega asked, her brow furrowing with concern. They'd offered to show it to her the previous day, but she'd refused. Hesitant to see her parents on the screen, fearing it would be too upsetting.

'Please, I want to see.'

So for the second time, Vega hit play on the documentary. This time, everyone else on the screen vanished and her eyes focused solely on her mother. She absorbed the curve and elegance of her neck, the warmth of her lightly bronzed skin, kissed by the sun, the row of freckles adorning the bridge of her nose, the way her hair was poker straight yet waved at the ends, and the Cupid's bow of her lips.

Mama Lulu pressed a handkerchief into her hands, and each tear they shed was a regret for the years they had missed. When Apollo appeared on the screen, his arrogance seemed magnified, and now Vega's distaste for him morphed into an intense ball of burning fury. This man had destroyed her mother's life, and her entire being wanted him to pay for every misdeed.

When the documentary ended, Vega turned to check in on

Estelle, whose expression was sorrowful. 'It's a lot, I know,' she said sympathetically.

'I don't remember my father. That was the first time I've seen his face.'

'A handsome man,' Mama Lulu said kindly.

'And my mother . . . she looked so young and carefree. She's unrecognisable compared to the woman I know.'

'Even her voice seems different,' Vega said.

'Yes. I thought that, too. But how she looked at Dad . . . She adored him, didn't she? At least, she did then. No wonder she hates him so much now. He broke her heart when he left us and returned to the UK.'

'He might not have had a choice,' Vega said. She told Estelle about Frankie Chalupka and how he had been banished from Island Pond.

'I'd never considered that,' Estelle said, biting her lower lip. 'Petra has always been so vitriolic about him, painted him as the baddy.'

'You should try to find him. Ask him for his side of the story,' Vega said.

Estelle shrugged. 'Even if he was forced to leave, he never returned for me, did he? So why would he want me now if he didn't want me then?' She looked down at Altair, who was balancing a stack of Lego pieces with such concentration that his tongue was sticking out. 'I don't want Altair ever to feel unwanted. I've had enough of that for both of us.'

'Yes, you have, and I understand that. We'll carry those scars with us for a lifetime,' Vega said, shaking her head, refusing to feel sorry for herself. 'But you're wanted here for as long as you need.'

'What would I do without you? But even you, our very own superhero, can't sleep on the sofa for ever,' Estelle said with a sad smile.

'When Mama Lulu goes home, you and Altair can move into the spare room. Problem solved,' Vega said. 'You're family, Estelle. Both of you.'

Mama Lulu beamed with approval at these words.

'I don't know how to thank you,' Estelle said.

'You have done. Several times. Not another word on it now,' Vega said firmly.

'Speaking of family . . . I wonder if my mother's family is still in Galway.'

Vega jumped up and seized her laptop. 'Let's see if we can find them!'

'But I don't know her maiden name.'

'I know. But your parents were married. Let's search for their wedding certificate. Her maiden name should be on that.'

Estelle shook her head in amazement. 'You always know what to do.'

Vega shrugged. 'No biggie. This is what I do for a living. Research is my middle name.'

'I'll leave you to it and get dinner sorted,' Mama Lulu said, standing up to retreat to her favourite place, the kitchen.

Then the phone rang, freezing them all like a game of statues.

'Put it on speaker,' Mama Lulu said, the first to rally, and somehow Vega pressed answer.

'Hi, Vega. It's Detective Gilmartin.'

'Hello,' she replied, her voice shaking.

'We've found the remains of a human body in the abandoned cottage, just as Estelle said.'

56

Body.
  State pathologist.
  Examination of remains.
  DNA analysis.
  Identification.
Thoughts spun around her mind like a tornado, throwing her from side to side, as Detective Gilmartin gave her the update.

'There's something else you need to know. The remains are not female.'

The room stilled.

How could they not be female?

It had to be her mum.

'We'll need confirmation from the pathologist, but we believe the pelvis and skull belong to a male,' Detective Gilmartin went on.

Vega felt as though she had been struck hard in the stomach. While she resisted accepting the idea that her mother was dead, she had been convinced that she had met a brutal end in 1995.

Did this mean she was alive?

And if it wasn't her mother, who was it?

'I'm sorry; I know you were hoping for some closure. We've brought in Brid O'Sullivan and Robert Shaw for questioning. Or Petra and Apollo, as they insist on being called. I'll get back to you once I know more.'

More tea.

Waiting.

Every nerve tensed.

Dinner, followed by a family movie with Altair snuggled

between Estelle and Vega. Mama Lulu nodded off five minutes into the story.

Bedtime stories for Altair.

More tea.

Then Detective Gilmartin finally called back, with the three of them huddled on the sofa – their new headquarters.

'Estelle and Mama Lulu are here with me, listening in,' Vega told him when she answered.

'Good.' Detective Gilmartin cleared his throat. 'We've questioned Petra and Apollo, and they crumbled pretty quickly, each confirming the body's identity. I'm sorry, Estelle, but it's your father, Fred O'Sullivan.'

Estelle shifted her gaze between Vega and Mama Lulu, trembling as she attempted to process the revelation. 'He never abandoned us,' she exclaimed, her eyes wide in disbelief. 'All this time, she claimed he'd left us. But he was with us the whole time.'

Vega felt a pang in her heart and reached to clasp Estelle's hand, attempting to provide strength to the woman. The parallels between their lives were striking; both had been abandoned by a parent, only to discover that that parent had been taken from them.

'Petra was the first to break,' Detective Gilmartin went on. 'She said that Apollo had hit Fred with a brick during a confrontation over a developing relationship between the two of them. She asserts it was an accident and that she assisted Apollo in burying Fred in the cottage, stating that he deserved that much.'

'He deserved so much more,' Estelle whispered.

'Apollo insists it was the other way around: Petra killed Fred and he helped her bury the body.'

'They're both guilty,' Estelle said, her jaw clenching. 'Have you arrested them?'

'Yes. We'll continue our investigations and interrogations to determine their exact roles in the murder, whether as perpetrator or accomplice.'

'Did you question them about Mum?' Vega enquired, desperately praying that there would be an answer.

'Yes. And I need to discuss that with you.' He paused for a moment. 'Apollo denies seeing Cassie on the first of December 1995. He claims he never followed her to Dublin. As far as he's concerned, she left him and took the girls with her, most likely returning to America. He swears that he first realised this wasn't the case when you arrived at the farm last week.'

'He would say that!' Mama Lulu exploded.

'When we questioned Petra about Cassie, she became tearful, insisting they were good friends. She had never considered a relationship with Apollo until after Cassie left. However, she believes that he had something to do with Cassie's disappearance. She told us that Apollo wanted to throw Fred's body into the farm incinerator used for burning cow carcasses.' He paused, leaving a stunned silence. 'Petra said she was upset by how casually he stated that the incinerator would burn the body, bones and all. He told her they could throw the ashes out with the household rubbish. She said that it sounded as if he knew from experience how to do this.' Detective Gilmartin gave them a moment to digest his words. 'She states that now, knowing Cassie is missing, she suspects that he killed her and burned her body.'

Vega looked at Mama Lulu and Estelle, whose faces mirrored her horrified feelings.

'He threw her away like a dead carcass,' Mama Lulu whispered.

Vega's body shook, and she rocked back and forth as Detective Gilmartin continued his update.

'We are continuing our search at the farm. But as yet we haven't found anything to support Petra's accusation, although we cannot rule it out. I'll continue pressing Apollo for a confession. I'm sorry, but I'll have to return to the interrogation room now. However, I'll call again tomorrow. In the meantime, try to get some sleep.'

Vega sank into the sofa, tucking her knees under her chin and hugging herself tightly.

No more waiting.

Her mother would never come to get her.

57

November came to a close, marked by several emotional partings.

Vega could not have endured the past couple of weeks, since Fred O'Sullivan's body was uncovered, without the steadfast, calming presence of her grandmother. However, it was time for her to return to Red Maple Farm.

While Vega's heart ached as she said her final goodbyes, her sorrow shifted when Mama Lulu walked through the departure gate at Dublin airport. She knew this was not a for-ever goodbye, just a farewell until her next visit to Vermont, which was already planned for Christmas.

She surveyed the airport departures area one last time, looking for Caoimhe.

'She's not here. I've had a good look,' Estelle said, holding on tightly to Altair, who was trying to escape to investigate a Santa Claus statue.

'It was only half a hope,' Vega said as they started their walk back to the car.

When Mama Lulu had booked her return flight, Vega had sent the details to her sister, hoping she would come to the airport to say goodbye. She knew that Mama Lulu was hurting due to the lack of contact with her. However, Caoimhe disappointed them both again by responding politely that she hoped Mama Lulu had a safe flight.

Vega had seen Caoimhe only once since that fateful meeting at Delaney's home.

She had driven up to Avoca in Kilmacanogue to inform her about the developments at the farm in Connemara. She had dreaded breaking the news, desperate to shield her younger sister from any further pain.

But Caoimhe had taken it in her stride. She was saddened; there was no doubt about that. However, there was no avalanche of emotion, as Vega had experienced when the news was broken to her.

She had explained herself to Vega gently. 'You've spent your entire life looking for me and our mother. But for me, it's different. I didn't know you existed until recently. I have a mother and father whom I adore and who adore me. Hearing about Apollo and Cassie and this Fred guy sounds so fantastical and unreal, like you're telling me a story you've written in the newspaper rather than one about people I'm supposed to connect to. I need a little time to catch up.'

That truly summed it up. Caoimhe felt as though she was meant to feel a connection rather than actually feeling one.

Vega had reassured her that she should feel no pressure, emphasising that she had all the time she needed to come to terms with her new family.

Two days later, Vega received a solicitor's letter, sent by courier, on behalf of the Delaneys. She was instructed that she could not reveal Caoimhe's identity at any point in the future, that her adoption was closed with the records sealed, and that Caoimhe had rights protected by the constitution, which upheld privacy and anonymity. If Vega breached this confidentiality and shared the information, they would sue.

The letter insulted every part of her. She would never share Caoimhe's details unless her sister gave her permission. She did not need a solicitor's letter to assert this. Although she declined to respond to the letter, she called Caoimhe to reassure her.

Since then, there had been no face-to-face contact.

She sent her sister a message every other day, and she always received a sweet response. However, there was no indication that Caoimhe wanted to see her or Mama Lulu again.

Vega knew this might be all she would ever get from her. That her little sister might never catch up, as she put it. And they might remain polite acquaintances.

She accepted that. It wasn't what she desired, but knowing that Nova was safe, happy and healthy was sufficient. It had to be.

Now they were on the second part of their planned journey. Vega, Estelle and Altair were driving to Connemara to collect important paperwork. They would meet Tommy, who leased land from Apollo, to talk about keeping an eye on the farm and the house for them.

Apollo had been charged with murder, and Petra with accessory after the fact. Both were remanded in custody, without parole, until the trial, which was expected to occur the following spring. The news had reached the media, as would be expected, making headlines on both television and in print.

Brid O'Sullivan's family in Galway had reached out through Detective Gilmartin, a pleasant outcome of the story breaking. Brid's younger brother had travelled to Wexford to meet Estelle and Altair, resulting in a happy reunion.

Vega's connection with Apollo and Petra, and her identity as one of the Nowhere Girls, had not yet been revealed. However, she understood how the media operated and knew it was only a matter of time before someone pieced it all together. Kieran had been a pillar of strength and wisdom, advising her on the next steps without ever making her feel that he prioritised the paper over her. And Senan agreed that it was better if HLD Media controlled the narrative, as long as the Delaney name was kept out of it.

Vega had completed the piece she had started a few weeks earlier, updating it with every twist and turn, except for Nova's identity. She'd also omitted her mother's involvement with Senan Delaney. She couldn't risk revealing that, as it might inadvertently expose Caoimhe. Nova's story would remain a mystery. Then, once she received the go-ahead from Mama Lulu, Estelle and Caoimhe, she gave the story to Kieran to publish.

Luka had visited the cottage several times to support her, for which she was very grateful. He had also assisted Estelle and

Altair, whose births had not been registered, in completing the necessary paperwork. He helped Estelle learn how to use her new mobile phone, another recent purchase, and something she had never owned.

When Vega's story had been published last Saturday, she'd spent the day at home with Mama Lulu, Estelle and Altair. Luka had arrived that afternoon, too, his face creased with emotion when she opened the front door.

'I've never been prouder of anyone in my entire life,' he said, holding out a bottle of champagne. 'Your story evoked so many emotions in me. You did it again. You moved me to tears. You'll go viral again when it's up online.'

'Kieran has already been asked to relay several interview requests. *The Late Late Show* wants me. Imagine that.'

'Will you do it?'

She shook her head. 'I don't think so. But it's nice to be asked all the same. I am, however, taking a meeting with a publisher. I've collated a lot of interviews over the past few weeks. I think there's a story there to share.' She pointed to the champagne. 'Is that for me?'

'Of course.'

'The good stuff,' she acknowledged, seeing the label.

'Thought if anyone deserved the good stuff, it was you.'

As she sipped a glass with him and her family, it felt as if things were as they had been before she'd messed everything up. However, when Luka noticed her struggling to suppress a yawn, he said his goodbyes and left.

Much like with Caoimhe, Vega understood that she had to let him go. She also realised that she didn't have the strength to be his friend. She loved him, but it hurt too much to pretend otherwise. She would talk to him soon and make him understand.

The drive west was pleasant, and time passed by with I Spy and the car registration game. Altair eventually tired himself out and fell asleep in his car seat, another new acquisition. Vega watched him in the car's rearview mirror, her heart lurching at his sweet innocence. The strength of her love for him, already evident after only a few weeks, took her breath away.

She had booked a room in a local hotel; they would stay the night and return to Wexford the next day. Once they'd checked in, they dropped their bags to their bedrooms. Vega's mobile rang as she was about to leave again.

'Hey, Kieran,' she said warmly when she saw his name on the screen.

'Hey, kiddo. Can you talk?' His voice was grave.

'Sure. What's wrong?'

'Remember I mentioned a few weeks back that I'd heard a rumour about the Delaneys?'

'Yes.'

'Well, the rumours have turned into something a little more serious. Vivienne Delaney has been accused of fraud.'

Vega gasped. This she had not expected.

'I know. It's pretty damning. She's the chief executive of Foster Care for Life, as you know, and has been accused of spending excessive and inappropriate amounts of money.'

'On what?' Vega asked, her heart racing faster as her mind ran through the repercussions this might have for Caoimhe.

'Travel, first-class tickets here there and everywhere. Five-star hotels. Michelin-starred restaurants. The watchdog has found that there was not adequate control of the management of expenditure by Vivienne and other members of the board.'

'Shit,' Vega said, exhaling slowly.

'Yep. Sure is.'

'And is the news out?'

'Will be on the front page of every newspaper, bar ours, tomorrow.'

'Should I call Caoimhe? She must be reeling,' Vega said, biting her lip.

'Don't know, kiddo. I'd say she's up to her neck in it right now. Maybe leave it a day or two. I'll keep you posted if I hear anything else.'

As they made their way to Cosmo Farm, Vega's mind was filled with worry for her sister. In the end, she decided to text her, let her know that she was available to listen if Caoimhe needed to talk. It began to rain as they drove, the afternoon grey and dismal. When Vega pulled up in the empty yard, Altair asked tremulously, 'Will *they* be here?'

Vega and Estelle shared a glance. There was no need for him to say who *they* were. She pushed the Delaneys and their issues to the back of her mind and concentrated on her little brother.

'No, my love. I told you, Petra and Apollo don't live here any more. The farm is empty.'

'What about Farmer Tommy?'

'He'll be around, as he always is. We might see him.'

'I like him,' Altair said.

'I do too,' Estelle agreed. 'Let's go inside; it's too wet to play out here right now.'

She ran her hand over a stone ledge above the front door, holding up a key. 'Got it!' She opened the door, and they walked in.

Vega shivered, once again feeling the shadow of her mother in every step she took. Her hand trailed along the walls as she moved, as if absorbing Cassie's touch somehow. When they entered the kitchen, she walked to the table, where her mother had chopped carrots. Then she looked to the corner where her crib had sat. In its place was a large wicker basket, with blankets spilling onto the floor.

'So much has happened in this home since our mothers were our age, sharing chores and cooking side by side,' Vega said.

'It feels different here today,' Estelle said, her eyes roaming the kitchen. 'Their absence . . . It's changed the energy.'

Vega understood what she meant. The air felt lighter, less oppressive somehow.

'My uncle has asked me to come to Galway to live with him,' Estelle blurted out.

Vega felt her stomach drop, but pushed her disappointment aside, saying brightly, 'That's wonderful. And will you accept?'

Estelle shrugged. 'I don't know. You've been so kind to let me stay with you, and I know I can stay as long as I want. But maybe I should go to Galway; it's close to here, and there's a comfort to that somehow.'

Altair approached them, holding a plastic spaceship, one of his favourite toys. He began to fly it around them, up and down, spinning it in circles while laughing with delight. 'Can we stay here tonight?' he asked.

'We're going to the hotel tonight, then back to Wexford, remember?' Estelle reminded him.

'Oh. Is our holiday still on? I thought it was over.'

'Well, we thought we might stay in Wexford a little longer.'

Altair scrunched his nose. 'But I want to come back here. I miss the cows. And my kite.'

Vega and Estelle exchanged a glance.

Altair continued his spaceship's flight, running out of the kitchen and down the hall.

'That was a surprise,' Estelle said. 'I didn't think he'd want to stay.'

'It's the only home he's known,' Vega said, looking around the kitchen again as an idea began to form. 'You could stay here, you know. Make this a home for you and Altair.'

'No, I can't,' Estelle protested, alarmed at the idea.

'Think about it for a minute. Apollo and Petra will be found guilty, no doubt about it. They've confessed, and at their age, they'll spend the rest of their days in prison – rightly so. This farm will be Altair's one day. Why wait until it's gone to rack and ruin, left empty and unloved?'

'It's yours too,' Estelle protested. 'You're Apollo's daughter.'

'I don't want it. I have a home. But you could make this a happy house again. Redecorate. Open those dreadful curtains and let the light in.'

Estelle's expression shifted, and her eyes widened as she paced the kitchen. 'It's such a beautiful house. I've always believed it would look wonderful if this room were painted a sunny yellow.'

'It would be stunning. Get a skip and fill it with anything that doesn't spark joy for you. Then, room by room, make it your own. And for the love of all that's good, throw out those plastic chairs in the yard. They give me the creeps!'

'Really?'

'Yes, really. I'll help you. And since you're so close to Galway, you can still stay in touch with your uncle.'

'What if Petra and Apollo get off?'

'It won't happen,' Vega said with certainty. 'But if it does, leave and come home to me, because you'll always have a room in my house.'

Estelle threw her arms around her. 'You're my guardian angel.'

'Not sure about that,' Vega said, feeling warmth in her cheeks, embarrassed and chuffed by the compliment.

Altair returned and landed his spaceship on the kitchen table, which had become a runway for him.

'What do you think about living here, just you and me?' Estelle asked.

'That would be cool!'

'We might make some changes, decorate every room.'

'Can I have a room like an astronaut's? With stars and the moon on the ceiling?' he asked.

'Of course!'

'Can I go to school?'

'Yes, you can go to school. We'll register you to start next September, when you turn five. And I'll look for a job locally.'

'Yes!' Altair exclaimed, then grabbed his spaceship again, shouting, 'Blast off . . .'

'Looks like it's been decided,' Vega said. 'Now, why don't you go with Altair and help him decide what colour to paint his bedroom?'

Once Vega was alone again, she opened the back door and looked outside. In the short time since they had arrived, darkness had fallen. She looked up at the sky and found the stars.

'I hope you're at peace now, Mum. It's time to for me to accept that you're gone. I want you to know that your girls are okay. Nova is happy, and I'm happy too. Mostly. Because I'm not alone any more. I have a new family: Mama Lulu, Flick, Estelle, Altair and maybe one day Caoimhe. I love you, Mum. I always have and I always will.'

Then she closed the door and followed the sounds of excited voices from Altair's bedroom.

It was time to begin planning for the future.

58

Vega strode to the centre of the bustling concourse. Streams of passengers flowed past her; some energetically wheeled suitcases while others trudged along with heavy rucksacks cinched tight on their backs, all singularly focused on reaching their respective platforms.

Amid this chaos, a mother and her two young daughters entered Vega's line of sight. The mother struggled slightly with a large, bulky suitcase in one hand while tightly gripping both girls' small hands with the other.

'Stay close to me,' she urged, her voice a mixture of authority and warmth. She paused briefly in front of the digital departures and arrivals sign, her eyes likely scanning for the crucial details of her destination.

The girls erupted in giggles at something playful their mother had said, their laughter bubbling up like a melody and filling the vast station. Every other noise faded into insignificance for Vega.

In another world untainted by loss, Nova and Vega basked in the warmth of their mother's love, much like these little girls. There, they had grown up together, inseparable and bound by the deep, unbreakable bond of sisterhood.

Vega shook her head and walked towards their bench. The station had evolved over the past thirty years, with many changes. Yet the bench remained the same, as if it were a monument to Vega and Nova and everything they had lost. She ran her fingers along a line of graffiti carved into the wooden back, then sat down, suppressing her emotions as her mind and heart wandered back to that fateful day in 1995. Exactly thirty years ago to the day.

She knew her mother was dead, and somewhere over the previous week she had come to terms with this reality. Her quest for the truth had finally unveiled what had happened to Cassie. Leaving Woodstock for Rochester and then Island Pond, then to Connemara, Dublin and back to Connemara again. Along the way, she'd discovered more about who her mother truly was. And while there were things that Cassie had done that Vega didn't like, she knew that she loved her mother and was proud of her. And would always regret the life they hadn't shared.

Until recently, Cassie had been little more than a pencil sketch in her mind, lacking definition and depth. Throughout her journey, Vega had coloured her in, one testimony at a time, until she was almost a complete painting.

But Apollo refused to admit what he'd done to her, and Vega recognised that the painting would never truly be finished until she uncovered what had happened to her mother on 1 December 1995.

Mama Lulu insisted that they had to let Cassie go. But Vega had held onto her mother so tightly for all these years. Could she accept that it was time for her to finally live her own life, out of the shadow of Cassie's legacy?

Letting go was hard, but holding on was harder.

'Hello,' a voice said softly, drawing her attention back to the platform. She looked up and gasped.

Caoimhe sat down beside her.

'How did you know I was here?' Vega asked, her voice trembling with disbelief.

Caoimhe glanced at Luka, who stood a few paces away. 'He slid into my DMs,' she giggled. 'But not with the kind of proposition I normally get. He told me about your trip here every year on the anniversary of Mum leaving us. He suggested that you might like some company, especially this year.'

Vega's heart ached with love for this man, who continued to think of her even though she no longer had the right to expect it from him.

'Is this the bench?' Caoimhe asked.

'Yes. But you were sitting on the other side of me, and we had a brown suitcase there.' Vega pointed in front of her.

Caoimhe jumped up and switched seats. 'Now that's better. I wish I could remember, but I honestly have no memory of that day.'

'I'm glad you don't,' Vega said. 'You shouldn't remember... We were so young, too young. Terrified. Confused. I wish I could forget.' She glanced at the tracks and observed a train arriving at the platform. Passengers moved forward, awaiting their turn to board, while others disembarked.

'She's never coming back,' she whispered, pain marking her features, her heart weighed down by sorrow.

'I know,' Caoimhe responded softly, sensing her anguish. Then, with a reassuring squeeze, she took Vega's hand. 'But I'm here now. You promised you would find me again, Vega. You kept your promise to me. I think our mother would be so proud of you.'

They sat in silence for a moment, the warmth of their hands intertwined giving Vega hope amidst the despair of their past.

'How are things at home? Are your parents okay?' she asked gently. She'd tried ringing Caoimhe a few times, but her calls had all gone to voicemail.

'Sorry for not taking your calls. I couldn't talk about it. But it meant a lot that you checked up on me. As you can imagine, Mum is furious. And scared, too. They're with their barrister now, trying to sort through it. It's the scandal that's the hardest for Mum to cope with. Her good name is everything for her. And now the watchdog is looking at all the charities she's worked on. Dad said there might be further charges coming.'

Vega tried to look sympathetic. But she found it hard to sympathise with Vivienne, who'd spent money donated by the public when she had a fortune at home. She'd keep her thoughts to herself, though.

'There's a chance she'll get a custodial sentence,' Caoimhe

said, shivering. 'You want to know the craziest thing? I've been thinking about everything that has happened over the past few weeks. And how my parents – and me too – were so desperate not to have our names tarnished by Apollo's arrest.' She looked down. 'I felt sorry for you, Vega. That you were related to someone like him. And I was relieved to have my parents, who I thought were so perfect.' She pulled a face. 'Serves me right, doesn't it?'

'You're human, so of course you didn't want to be part of Apollo and Petra's mess. Who would choose that voluntarily?' Vega sighed. 'I can't step away from it, though. He's my father. My mother loved him once. They had a life together. And even though the answers I've got are not the ones I wanted, I'm grateful that at least I have answers. If nothing else, I know where I came from.'

'Where I came from, too.' Caoimhe said. 'Let's not talk about Mum and the fraud case. That okay? I want to concentrate on us.' When Vega nodded, Caoimhe pointed to her left. 'Your ex is still standing there. He looks a bit awkward.'

Vega looked over to Luka, who gave her a small wave. Her stomach somersaulted as she asked, 'What should I do?'

'You should talk to him. I'll wait here,' Caoimhe said firmly, giving Vega a nudge.

Vega walked the twenty paces to Luka's side, smiling shyly, 'You remembered that I always come here on the anniversary.'

'I remember everything you told me.'

'I can't believe you got in touch with Caoimhe.'

'Well, I can't take all the credit for that. Mama Lulu texted me to tell me to do it. She said she'd clip my ear the next time she saw me if I didn't.'

Vega felt a bubble of laughter erupt. Thank God for Mama Lulu and her meddling. 'I was having a little pity party for myself until you both showed up.' She looked back at Caoimhe, who was admiring her nails. 'How's your mum doing?'

'She's back to full health,' Luka said, grinning. 'I'm home in my apartment, and as much as I love my mum, I'm glad to be back in my own space. She can be a lot!'

'Ah, we women often are,' Vega replied.

'She told me you visited her in the hospital and gave her the biggest hamper she'd ever received.'

Vega looked at him sharply, taken aback.

'She also told me that I was an idiot for allowing my issues with trust to cloud what was a poor judgement call on your part during a time of monumental stress.'

'Oh,' Vega said, unable to find any other words.

'And I couldn't deny that she was right. I'll let you get back to Caoimhe, but first of all, remember you allowed me three questions?' Vega nodded, her heart racing. 'Will you give me a fourth before I leave?'

'Sure.'

'I wondered if you would go on a date with me this Friday night?'

Vega felt a buzz in her head and a flip in her stomach. 'I'll need to check my diary,' she joked weakly.

'Well, if Friday doesn't suit, I'm pretty much free for the rest of my life.' Luka stepped closer and placed one hand behind her neck and the other in the small of her back in a gesture that was achingly familiar.

'I'd like that. Very much,' Vega replied breathlessly.

He leaned down and kissed her until whistles from Caoimhe pulled them apart. 'I'll see you on Friday,' he said, then walked away, turning back as he reached the turnstile and smiling at her so tenderly she almost wept.

She returned to the bench and sat down, exhaling a deep breath.

'I take it it's back on then,' Caoimhe said, grinning.

'Did that just happen?'

'Yep. And it was hot! So what do we do now? Just sit here and watch the trains?'

'Pretty much. I used to pray that you would show up one day. You took your time.'

'Better late than never,' Caoimhe replied. She nudged Vega's shoulder. 'I'm catching up, by the way.'

'Better late than never,' Vega repeated, and they grinned at each other.

Caoimhe swirled sideways so that she faced her. 'I'm a nightmare. Spoiled rotten. I grew up knowing I was the most important person in every room. Honestly, it was great. I've never worked a day in my life. Mum has always wanted me to help her with the charities, but I'd prefer to go to the salon and get my nails done.'

'You're not selling yourself very well,' Vega pointed out.

'You need to understand what you're getting into if we are to become best friends and sisters.'

'Well, in that case, I'm stubborn. I'm single-minded when I decide to do something and won't stop until I achieve it. I have a strong dislike of cats. I'm uncertain about pets in general. Please don't get me started on birds; they seem to be plotting to take over the world. Oh, and I snore.'

'You sound just as charming as I do!' Caoimhe exclaimed, resting her head on Vega's shoulder like she did thirty years ago. 'Look at us, the Nowhere Girls.'

'Not any more we're not,' Vega replied softly. 'Now we're the Somewhere Girls.'

'Okay. So where is this somewhere then?' Caoimhe enquired.

Vega smiled as she turned to wrap her two arms around her baby sister. 'Somewhere is *together*.'

Cassie

1 December 1995

Had Cassie known it would be the last time she saw her daughters, she would have turned to savour every beautiful detail of them.

She left them at the train station, convinced it would be a haven until her return. People were always in such a rush when commuting. They would barely give her girls a second glance. Cassie hated leaving them on their own. They had rarely been out of her sight since she held them in her arms. But she was desperate. And while her plan was not perfect, it might just work.

Cassie pointed to the clock and told Vega that she would be back by the time it changed to two p.m. Vega wore a solemn expression as she vowed to care for Nova, assuring Cassie they would stay put until she returned. Vega was a remarkable girl – strong and independent, even at four, the best part of Apollo and herself. And then there was her sweet Nova, barely three, who had a heart brimming with love for everyone.

Cassie knew how lucky she was to have them. And it was for them that she made her way to College Green, weaving through crowds of people. She continued to the front of the stage, ignoring the annoyed comments from passers-by as she manoeuvred past them. A phone call to the TV station, during which she'd pretended to be Mrs Delaney, had given her Senan's exact whereabouts.

Her eyes found him instantly. Tall, dark and with a commanding presence. He wore a press badge on a lanyard around his neck. And as if he could feel her eyes on him, he turned around until their gazes locked. Would he remember her? Or was she a distant memory that had faded over almost four years?

Shock registered, but he then spoke to a colleague, who moved to Cassie's side and guided her behind the railings.

'Cassie! This is a surprise,' Senan said. 'Did you come to see Clinton? If so, you've missed it all; he's left.'

'I'm here to see you,' Cassie replied. Her stomach flipped, but she would not allow nerves to derail her plan. She would do whatever was necessary to protect her girls.

Senan's hand rose to tousle his wavy hair as he grinned, preening at her words. 'I'm flattered, Cassie. But I'm married now.'

Cassie jutted her chin out as she thought of her two girls sitting at the station, waiting for her return. She didn't have time to flatter his ego. 'I know your marital status, but you are unaware of all *my* facts.'

'Enlighten me,' he replied, arching a brow.

'You have a daughter. Her name is Nova.'

This he had not expected. His jaw slackened and his eyes widened.

Cassie continued, 'You need to take responsibility for her.'

'I can't talk about this here,' Senan said as he scanned the area. 'Plus, how do I even know this is true?'

'She's your daughter. I've suspected it since the day she was born, but I could never know for sure. But the older she gets, the more she becomes like you.' She pulled a photograph from her pocket, a Polaroid taken that summer.

Cassie watched Senan's eyes as they scanned the image, recognising the truth staring back at him.

'She looks like my sister,' he said. He touched the photo gently. 'Just like she did when she was that age.' Then his expression hardened. 'What do you want from me?'

'I want to go home to my mama, bring the girls back to America, but I don't have documentation or money. I need you to help.'

'I'm not sure how I'm supposed to do that,' he replied.

'Your father is a judge. He must have contacts. You either find a way to help me, or . . .' She paused, inhaling deeply, before stating bluntly, 'or I'll tell your wife about Nova.'

'You wouldn't dare.'

'Try me.'

'I don't take kindly to blackmail, Cassie.'

'I don't like not being taken seriously. I have to think about my girls. We're not safe with Apollo. He's . . . he's become unhinged. I think he suspects that Nova isn't his. He's convinced I'm unfaithful with every man on the farm. He wants to change how I dress. To silence me. Most of the commune has left. It's become unbearable there.'

'Is he dangerous?'

Cassie's eyes filled with tears. 'I'm scared, Senan, not just for me, but for the girls too. When he takes his drugs, he's not in his right mind. He's likely to do anything! He said he would kill me before he'd let me leave. Look, I don't have much time. I need to sort this out with you today.' She looked at her watch, frowning when she saw that it was already a quarter to one.

Senan reached into his trouser pocket and pulled out a set of keys. 'I have an apartment in the city for when I work late. Go there; it's only a five-minute walk from here.' He scribbled down an address and the alarm code, rapping out directions. 'I'll follow you there in thirty minutes once I've finished here.'

The girls had been alone for almost an hour now. Plus they'd been up since dawn, catching the first bus to Dublin. But she reasoned with herself that she'd left food and water in a bag for them. Vega was a good girl. She'd take care of Nova and they'd be all right for another hour. 'If you're not there in thirty minutes, I'm calling your wife,' she warned.

She found the apartment quite easily, following Senan's directions. It featured an open-plan design, with floor-to-ceiling windows overlooking the River Liffey. She wandered through each room, running her hand along the smooth marbled surfaces and gleaming chrome fittings, picking up a framed photograph of Senan and his glamorous wife on their wedding day. The woman's face blurred and for a moment, she saw her image smiling back. Cassie shook the notion from her head.

They had never loved each other, and a life with Senan would have suffocated her. Now it was time to find out what kind of man he truly was. Despite his arrogance and self-importance, Cassie believed he had honour, and would want to do right by his flesh and blood.

A few minutes later, she heard the door open, relieved that Senan had managed to arrive sooner than he'd predicted.

'Who the hell are you?' a woman's voice asked, ice cold.

Cassie turned and came face to face with Senan's wife, who whipped off a pair of large sunglasses and stared at her.

'I'm a friend of Senan's,' she said, jutting her chin and pulling her shoulders back. She felt scruffy in her jeans and home-made knitted jumper, with loose, uncombed hair, compared to the woman in front of her, who wore a black trouser suit and a camel wool coat. 'He gave me the key. I didn't break in, Mrs Delaney,' she added quickly.

'Are you having an affair?' Mrs Delaney asked, her voice calm and collected.

'No!' Cassie denied. 'I knew your husband a few years ago. Before you were married.'

'Well, that's a relief. Call me Vivienne. And then you can tell me what you want with him.'

'I'd rather discuss that with Senan if you don't mind.' Cassie replied.

'My husband has no secrets from me. He'll tell me everything when he arrives, so you might as well say it.'

'I need to return to America. But I don't have passports for me or my daughters. My husband is controlling and keeps our documents locked up. And I have no money . . .'

'Ha! So you want money!' Vivienne said, her mouth forming a sneer. 'I should have realised the second I walked into the room!'

Cassie felt anger surge within her at being judged so unfairly. 'I only want what's owed to me.' She took a steadying breath and thought of her girls as she admitted, 'For Nova, Senan's daughter.'

Vivienne's face turned ashen, and she stared at Cassie in horror. 'What exactly are you claiming?'

'I'm sorry. I didn't mean to blurt it out like that. But I'm desperate. I need to get away from my husband. Senan knows people who can make things happen. When we were together, he told me about his father. About the things he witnessed as he grew up. The corners his father cut to get what he wanted.' Cassie's voice was desperate as she pleaded with this woman for her understanding and support.

'You could be making all of this up!'

'I promise you I'm not. Senan is my younger daughter's father. He's meeting me here to discuss it.'

Vivienne moved closer, her face now changing as anger sparked from her. 'You want to take him from me!'

'No, I don't! I don't love him. I promise you. It was just a fling that resulted in Nova. That's all.'

'You're telling me it's not a coincidence that a week after I find out I can't conceive, you show up here with a daughter! He told you, didn't he? You've been plotting this together.'

'I swear to you. I only told him about Nova today. I showed him a photograph. Look.' Cassie reached into her handbag to retrieve the snap and passed it over.

Vivienne snatched it, her eyes greedily taking it in, and then she groaned out loud as she saw the undeniable truth in the child's resemblance to the Delaney family.

Tears streamed down her face, and a low, guttural growl emitted from deep within her as she pushed the photograph back into Cassie's hand.

Cassie opened her bag to put the photograph back. 'I'm desperate and I don't want to have to—'

But her sentence was left hanging as she felt a blow to the side of her head. She stumbled and fell backwards, crashing down through a glass coffee table. Sharp fragments sliced into her body, yet she felt no pain. Not then, at least.

Vivienne's eyes met hers in horror as she realised what she'd done. She stepped back, raising her hands as if in surrender, sweat beading her forehead.

'Help me...' Cassie gasped, her breath ragged as finally the pain overwhelmed her. Shock registered when she felt warm liquid on her cheek and saw crimson blood pooling on the oak floor beside her. She knew she had to try to stem the bleeding, but found she couldn't move her arms.

She blacked out, and when she awoke moments later, Senan was there, his horror immobilising him for several moments as her breathing slowed. With her eyes, she silently pleaded with him to help her.

'What have you done?' he screamed at Vivienne.

'It was an accident. She came at me. She tried to hit me. I had to strike back, to protect myself.'

'Liar,' Cassie tried to say. She thought it might be all right when she saw Senan reaching for the telephone.

'Wait,' Vivienne said. 'I know about your daughter. She showed me the photograph. That little girl should be ours. Living with you and me. If Cassie dies...' She glanced at Cassie, then looked away.

'Let me think!' Senan said, running his hands through his hair and cursing under his breath. Then he started to dial.

An ambulance would come. They would save her, and Cassie would tell them where her girls were.

Help was on the way.

'Dad, we're in trouble. Vivienne has killed a woman in self-defence... We need your help, please,' Senan said into the receiver.

'Not... dead...' Cassie whispered, but her words faded as she felt the blood draining from her body.

She thought of Mama Lulu, baking pies in her kitchen, warmth and love radiating as her floured hands kneaded the dough, over and over.

She thought of her sister, Flick, laughing and happy alongside David, watching the children she imagined they had, swinging on the tyre at Red Maple Farm.

But her final thought, as Cassie drew her last breath, was of the greatest loves of her life: her shining stars, her daughters – Vega and Nova.

I'm sorry . . . I'm so very sorry . . .

Acknowledgements

Writing this book has been a joy. And that's in no small way due to the team that I'm lucky to be a part of.

Thank you to:

My agent and dear friend, Rowan Lawton, for always believing in me and taking care of business so effortlessly. Also to Eleanor Lawlor and the rest of the team at The Soho Agency, the rights team at ILA, and Tara Timinsky at Grandview LA, for all you do behind the scenes.

My editor and publisher, Jennifer Doyle at Headline Books, who continues to have me at 'bonjour', and champions me in a way that I'll never take for granted. The talented team at Headline, who have worked on *The Nowhere Girls*, includes Hannah Bowstead, Alara Delfosse, Alexia Thomaidis, Becky Bader, Tina Paul, Emma Rogers, Jane Selley, and Nikki Sinclair. I'm forever grateful.

The team at Hachette Ireland – Jim Binchy, Ciara Doorley, Elaine Egan, Siobhan Tierney, and Shauna O'Regan, who take care of my heartland publishing. And to the international team, Eleanor Wood and Ellie Walker.

To Hazel Gaynor, who sent me an article she read about three children abandoned at a train station, saying, 'I think there could be a Carmel Harrington novel in this.' And, of course, she was right. She always is!

And to Catherine Ryan Howard, another who is always right and continues to ensure that I'm never ignored. (A deliberate in-house joke, sorry!)

To the incredibly supportive writing community in Ireland and the UK, who inspire me every day. The book retailers, media, bloggers, podcasts, reviewers, libraries, book clubs, and

Acknowledgements

festivals whose passion for sharing books with readers helps authors like me each day.

To my friends, who have always supported me in this somewhat unconventional career I've chosen: Ann Murphy, Sarah Kearney, Davnet Murphy, Maeve Tumulty, Fiona Deering, Siobhan O'Brien, Gillian Jones, Sheila Keogh, Liz Bond, Siobhan Kirby, and Maria Murtagh.

To all the O'Grady and Harrington families, another book means we've had another spin around the sun with each other – my parents Tina and Michael O'Grady, my siblings and their families, Fiona, Michael, Amy and Louis Gainfort, Shelley and Anthony Mernagh, Sheryl O'Grady, John and Matilda O'Grady, my aunt and godmother Ann Payne, my stepdaughter Eva Corrigan, my mother-in-law Evelyn Harrington, and sisters-in-law and their families – Adrienne Harrington and George Whyte, Evelyn, Seamus and Paddy Moher, Leah Harrington. As I always say, *all that matters is family.*

Extra thanks to my niece, Sheryl O'Grady, a Senior Social Worker, whom I am so proud of. Luka inherits his passion for supporting the marginalised from her – and his love of ink! Thank you for answering my questions about Tusla and helping me choose Leenane in Connemara.

Good to note, though, that I sometimes need to take artistic licence, so any mistakes around my characters' careers are entirely mine and probably deliberate to make the story work!

Extra, extra thanks to my mother, Tina, my first reader. Every time I send her a new book, she tells me it's my best yet. Please don't ever stop saying that!

Thank you to my husband, Roger, and my children, Amelia and Nate, for being my greatest cheerleaders. I love how excited you all become when I finish a new book. This year, there has been lots of good news, and each time, the loudest cheers come from you three. And George Bailey, my little shadow and constant companion, you know you have my heart.

Acknowledgements

And last but never least, to you, my readers, for every time you've told friends and family about my books and spent your hard-earned cash on a new release. You have made this career possible for me.

Author Note

Dear reader,

Thank you so much for reading *The Nowhere Girls*! I hope you enjoyed your time between the pages with Vega and Luka. I always like to share with you all the inspiration behind my stories, and the origin of *The Nowhere Girls* came from an article that my bestie, Hazel Gaynor, sent me. It was about three young children who were abandoned at a train station in Barcelona in 1984. I was fascinated to read Elvira, Ricard and Ramón's story, with questions buzzing through my mind: Where were the children's parents? Why did nobody claim them? Surely there were family or friends who must have recognised them in the subsequent media campaign, and if not, why? And of course, how did this abandonment shape them in their adulthood?

As Hazel predicted, the article sent my imagination into overdrive. I began noodling ideas, and before I realised it, two young girls left at a train station in Dublin began to occupy my thoughts. They don't know their parents' surnames or where they are from, except that they lived in the middle of nowhere. This phrase became a recurring theme in the story and, in turn, inspired my title: *The Nowhere Girls*.

If you'd like to read that article, here is a link: https://www.theguardian.com/world/2023/mar/28/three-abandoned-children-two-missing-parents-40-year-mystery-elvira-moral-barcelona

I decided to tell my story entirely in the present day, through the point of view of Vega Pearse, who is on an all-consuming and at times dangerous quest to find out what happened to the so-called Nowhere Girls. It was important to me that my

Author Note

readers discover answers at the same time as Vega does. I hope that added to your enjoyment and helped keep you guessing!

Vega's quest led her into the dark, controlling and coercive world of cults and communes. Including this subject in the story was particularly interesting to me. I've always been fascinated by cults; I think many of us are. What draws people to live in a community cut off from the wider world? And what are the ramifications of choosing a life like this?

And, as always with my stories, hidden gems revealed themselves as characters came to life for me. The mistakes they made as they muddled their way through their circumstances. I loved asking them compelling questions about their culpability, and exploring their capacity for forgiveness.

Location-wise, I often include my beloved home county of Wexford in my stories; this time, it was personal because Vega lives in The Ballagh, a village a few miles from me, where my father was born. I loved taking Vega and Luka to some of my favourite places in Wexford. I chose Vermont because many young people migrated there in the sixties to set up communes when they dropped out of mainstream life in America, rejecting the violence of the Vietnam War. And many years ago, I fell in love with Vermont's charming small towns and stunning woodlands and mountains, which I'm always drawn to. And finally, I chose Leenane, Connemara, because its remote and wild beauty was the perfect setting for Orion Farm and its inhabitants.

I'm so proud of this novel. As I always say, as soon as it's published, it's no longer mine. Now it belongs to *you*, the reader.

Carmel

Book Group Questions

Which character did you relate to the most? What was it about them that you felt connected with?

Vega's traumatic childhood has shaped her as an adult, making her incredibly guarded. What or who shifts that mindset for her as she searches for the Nowhere Girls?

Vega sometimes makes questionable choices in her relentless quest to discover what happened to the Nowhere Girls and their mother. Did you understand her actions? Were they justifiable?

Did any of the events leading up to the reveal of what happened to Star catch you by surprise? Did you see each of the plot twists coming?

Location has always been a key element in Carmel's novels. How significant to the story were the landscapes in Vermont, Connemara and Wexford? Would you like to visit any of the places Carmel described?

Book Group Questions

The novel explores complex themes, including abandonment and coercive control. Were there any moments in the book that made you see things differently?

Vega and Nova's childhoods were worlds apart. Can a bond be built later in life after such differing experiences?

How did you feel about the ending for each of the characters? Were you surprised? Did you think the villains of the story received their just deserts?

Which three words would you choose to describe the novel?

Carmel's stories are always emotional reads. Which part moved you the most? And have any parts of the story stayed with you since you closed the final page?

RAISING READERS
Books Build Bright Futures

Dear Reader,

We'd love your attention for one more page to tell you about the crisis in children's reading, and what we can all do.

Studies have shown that reading for fun is the **single biggest predictor of a child's future life chances** – more than family circumstance, parents' educational background or income. It improves academic results, mental health, wealth, communication skills, ambition and happiness.[1]

The number of children reading for fun is in rapid decline. Young people have a lot of competition for their time. In 2024, 1 in 10 children and young people in the UK aged 5 to 18 did not own a single book at home.[2]

Hachette works extensively with schools, libraries and literacy charities, but here are some ways we can all raise more readers:

- Reading to children for just 10 minutes a day makes a difference
- Don't give up if children aren't regular readers – there will be books for them!
- Visit bookshops and libraries to get recommendations
- Encourage them to listen to audiobooks
- Support school libraries
- Give books as gifts

There's a lot more information about how to encourage children to read on our website: **www.RaisingReaders.co.uk**

Thank you for reading.

---

[1] OECD, '21st-Century Readers: Developing Literacy Skills in a Digital World', 2021, https://www.oecd.org/en/publications/21st-century-readers_a83d84cb-en.html

[2] National Literacy Trust, 'Book Ownership in 2024', November 2024, https://literacytrust.org.uk/research-services/research-reports/book-ownership-in-2024